a stories of faerth novel

FARZANA'S
SPITE

Felix Graves

FARZANA'S SPITE

ISBN: 9798987144916
eISBN: 9798987144923

Edited by Charlie Knight (cknightwrites.com)
Cover Illustration and Design by Fay Lane (faylane.com)
Interior Design by Adik Graves (makeshift-miscreants.com)
Interior Images by Karolina Grabowska (pexels.com)

content notice

Farzana's Spite is a dark fantasy and as such contains scenes and topics that may cause distress for certain readers. Please check the final page for a non-exhaustive list of content warnings.

This story is dedicated to all of the queer kids who were made to feel worthless and unlovable, and who are now traumatized adults who feel irreparably damaged. You are more than the sum of your trauma. You are worthy of love, and I hope you find it.

contents

PROLOGUE

THE MEAGER GLOW OF THE CRESCENT MOON did little to illuminate the group of imps skulking through the palace garden, a purple-winged pixie leading the way. Erasto of the House of Violets hefted the short sword in his hand, relishing in the unfamiliar and deadly weight, and worked to contain his glee. His scheme was finally nearing fruition, and he couldn't help the slight bounce in his step as they neared the palace, though it wouldn't do for his excitement to foil the execution of his plan.

A pair of elderly guards were the only opposition at the main palace doors; they were cut down where they stood without a chance to sound an alarm. Erasto's delight waxed as they proceeded further into the palace, slaying the guards and palace staff as they went. A trail of bodies wound through the palace not unlike abstract line art. And why not? This was his masterpiece, after all.

The hulking imps were lethal, wielding razor-sharp claws like knives. Despite their incredible size—nearly a foot taller than him and twice the weight—they were quite light-footed, and the group was able to make it all the way to the living quarters without allowing a single guard to call for help.

They found the nursery first. Without pause, Erasto leapt forward and slashed through the crown prince's delicate neck, decapitating him with one slice so as not to chance the infant's cry waking the monarchs. A gurgle of blood and the child was dead.

So much for their precious legacy.

One more corner to the royal bedroom. Four heavily armed guards stood outside; their moment of hesitation at the sight of him and his imp entourage was enough to give Erasto the upper hand. Adrenaline coursed through him as he ran up and stabbed his sword into the closest guard's stomach. A fount of blood spilled forth as he slid the sword out. He relished the sight without bothering to check his surroundings; he knew the imps could be trusted to keep him safe even in the fray. He paid them well enough.

Erasto shoved the door open. The king and queen huddled together, their crimson wings curled around each other in slumber. Erasto gestured for the imps to drag the royal couple out of their bed and wiped his bloody sword clean on a velvet armchair. He wanted the blade pristine for his performance.

Queen Tatiana—her dusky skin, so bleached with fear, was pale as the strip of white in her ebony hair—remained silent while King Oberon protested, his brash voice echoing in the quiet of the palace.

If only there was anyone alive left to hear his call.

Erasto straightened his shirt collar and ran a hand through his short hair, ensuring no strands were out of place. He needed to make a good first impression. Clicking his fingers, he pointed at the mirror, and an imp rushed to switch it on.

Erasto had already taken the necessary steps to make certain this mirror would be broadcast to every residence in the kingdom of Dradour. It had been easy to slip money to the station in charge of royal broadcasts with the promise an "extra special" announcement would be taking place. With the knowledge that potentially millions of viewers were now tuned in, he stepped into place before the mirror.

"Good citizens of Dradour, I want to apologize for the

late hour of this broadcast. I assure you, what you are about to witness is worth it."

Erasto turned and motioned for the royal couple to be dragged into the frame. He stood between them, a hand resting on the king's head while the sword hung at his side by the queen's wings.

"Too long has this kingdom been ruled by an obsolete monarchy. Too long have you been lorded over by pureblood pixies old enough to have seen other kingdoms turned to dust. Who do they think they are? Why should they be our rulers simply because they are pureblood?"

Erasto caressed Oberon's head, his hand hesitating at the white lock that indicated he was a pureblood. He wanted to rip the strip of hair out of the king's head.

"I am here to release you, dear faeries, from the yoke of these geriatric purebloods. I am here to save you from their antiquated ways."

With blinding swiftness, Erasto drew the edge of his sword against first Oberon's and then Tatiana's neck. Their vermilion blood gushed forward, spraying the floor and speckling the mirror. Erasto's wings quivered behind him, and he cursed them for betraying his emotions.

But it was so damned beautiful that the viewers would now be forced to peer through a sheen of blood in order to see him. He allowed himself one last look at the gaping wound in the queen's neck, strands of flesh barely holding her head in place, before turning his attention back to the mirror.

"Please do not be alarmed. Their time had come, and we will not mourn their end. Instead, we will rejoice as this nation moves forward into a new age. I will take charge of the kingdom, though I will not be ruling you from a gilded seat. I will become your High Manager and will take charge of all Centers throughout Dradour."

Erasto smiled, careful to show just the right amount of teeth so as not to appear frightening. He had practiced this smile many times, and he knew it would put his viewers at ease. It had so perfectly swayed the humans countless times on Earth; why shouldn't it work here on Faerth? A politician was a politician, no matter the planet.

"I am Erasto of the House of Violets, and I bid you good-night."

1

A STORM CAME IN THE NIGHT. IT STARTED AS A
docile drizzle before wreaking havoc as a torrential downpour.
The pounding of the rain on the roof woke Farzana in time
for the late-night broadcast from the palace.

I am the daughter of a murderer.

It didn't matter that Erasto had fled the planet before she
was born and likely didn't know of her existence; she knew of
his. She'd often fantasized about meeting him someday: they
would pass each other in the street and their identical purple
eyes would meet. He would see her purple wings—his wings—
and know she was his.

Those dreams were ruined now, twisted by the fact that
he was a killer who had managed to dismantle the monarchy
and take over the country. Everyone who saw Farzana and her
wings could easily guess she came from him, that she was born
of a monster. How was she supposed to get out of bed with
that hanging over her?

A hesitant tap at her bedroom door had her lurching from
her covers.

"Farzana…baby, do you know what time it is?"

Farzana yanked a hand through her wayward curls and

decided against wearing them down; today would be a scarf day. Winding her ebony hair tightly around her hands, she pulled it into a messy bun and wrapped a black scarf around her head, tucking the ends in. The black seemed fitting—the perfect mourning color for the father she thought she would one day have.

"Farzana? Are you even up?" Sitra's voice boomed as she rapped again on the door.

"Yes, Mother, I'm up," she grumped, loud enough to be heard through the closed door while grabbing a pencil skirt and button up shirt from her closet.

"Well, you're going to be late unless you hurry," Sitra said, disapproval apparent in her voice.

Farzana rolled her eyes. Of course the one day she was running late was the one day her mother was out of bed before noon. Had she even slept after the broadcast ended?

"I'm hurrying." Irritation edged her voice as she tugged on the zipper of her skirt. The flats at the end of the bed completed her outfit.

Farzana peeked at the mirror. Dark circles under her eyes punished her for a less than lovely night of sleep. The puffiness from her late-night crying was still evident as well, and combined with the all-black ensemble, she looked like she was heading to a funeral.

Would there even be a funeral for the royal family? Or was Erasto truly cold-hearted? She wasn't sure she would go if there were to be one; the thought of seeing that tiny corpse nestled in a box of satin made her stomach lurch.

After tucking a loose curl under her scarf, she was ready to go.

Sitra and Enzi were in the family room staring at the mirror when she went downstairs; Farzana gave her younger brother a warm smile when he noticed her.

"Another broadcast?" She peeked over the matching pair of amber wings to see a gray-winged common-fae talking in front of the palace.

"It's going over what happened last night. They keep replaying the clips of the actual deaths." Enzi shuddered. "I can't believe you watched that live."

"Yeah, it was a real treat."

Enzi snorted at her sarcasm and turned to her, one arm hanging over the back of the couch while the other stroked his short black beard. "What are you going to do today? People are going to ask questions. Are you sure you want to go to work?"

Farzana shrugged. "I don't know what else to do. I can't hide out here until this blows over. He's our new ruler."

Sitra pursed her lips. "I want you to be safe, baby. Wear a jacket to cover your wings. Maybe you won't get harassed."

A bang from the mirror had them all jumping; a crowd had gathered at the palace gates, and someone had thrown something at the mirror crew filming. Shouts erupted as the various faeries—mostly common-fae pixies—began shoving the news crew out of the way and attacking the gates.

"Not our ruler!"

"Imposter!"

"Murderer!"

Farzana flinched at the words; she knew who they were aimed at but being his daughter and an extension of him made her feel as though the attacks were personal. The mirror crew beat a hasty retreat to a safe distance as the crowd became a full-on riot. With a wrenching screech, the gates gave way to the flood of faeries as they poured onto the grounds, fists and voices raised.

"All they need are pitchforks," Enzi muttered.

The palace main doors opened, and the mirror crew zoomed in on Erasto's face as he stepped out to face the crowd. A smile graced his thin lips, and he raised his right hand to snap his fingers once. A swarm of imps slipped past him, heading for the rioters, swords and blitzes in hand.

"Oh gods, I can't watch," Sitra whimpered, standing and shuffling to her room.

With a roar, the two groups collided; precision gave the imps the upper hand while pure, unbridled anger had the rioters pushing back. Screams of pain lashed the air as one of the imps fired their blitz; the beam of energy it emitted left smoldering holes in the bodies nearby. Farzana stared at the mirror, numb, even after Enzi switched it off. Her own haunted reflection stared back at her.

"So this is what our kingdom has come to." Enzi shook his head.

"Country."

"What?"

"We aren't a kingdom without a king." And Erasto was no king.

~ ☼ ~

Araj called an hour later. Farzana passed the mirror in her pacing circuit of the room right as her best friend's avatar lit up the mirror screen, and she leapt to grab the controller to patch in the call.

Piercing blue eyes under a disheveled mop of brown hair appeared as his video call took over the mirror. "Farzana!" His voice was rough with what she could only assume was worry.

"I'm here," she said, settling onto the couch. She gave him a bright smile; after fifty years of steadfast friendship, he always greeted her every morning with a matching grin.

Instead, his face darkened before he asked, "Why aren't you here? At work?"

"If you haven't noticed, the country is in shambles. There are rioters outside! Someone threw something against our window ten minutes ago, and now there's a huge crack running through it."

Araj scowled. "I'm sorry about your window, Farzana, but the FRMDC is still operating. Or it would be, if all the resource manipulators and their managers were here. But we're missing one: you!"

She scowled back. Trust the Fae Resource Manipulation and Distribution Center to notice the one day she played hooky. "I'm not coming in today, Araj. I can't even open my front door without being assaulted by angry faeries."

"Well, I'm not covering for you," he said, pinching the bridge of his nose and sighing. "You can try to make up for lost work tomorrow by staying late."

"I'm not-"

Without so much as a goodbye, the call ended, leaving Farzana staring at her open-mouthed reflection.

~ ☼ ~

"You have to leave the house sometime," Enzi said, pulling on his coat.

Farzana sat on the couch and twisted the tasseled edge of the blanket around her shoulders. The storm from the previous night had abated but the storm of people could still be heard outside. Shouts of 'Murderer!' periodically echoed down the street, rattling in her head. How could she leave the safety of her home now? How could she go in public after the massacre Erasto, her *father*, had ordered?

"Enzi...I can't." Her voice broke on the last syllable, and she huddled deeper under the blanket.

Enzi placed a hand on her shoulder. "It's going to be okay," he said in a low, soothing voice. She looked up into his amber eyes and wished, not for the first time that day, she had been born with their mother's coloring, like him. His common-fae father hadn't left a single imprint on Enzi, looks-wise; he instead looked like a carbon copy of Sitra: black hair and dusky skin, with amber eyes and wings.

What a luxury.

"Want me to walk you to work?"

She perked up. "Would you?"

"Of course."

Well now she had no excuse. She let out a groan and reluctantly pushed herself up from the comfort of the couch. "I'll be right back."

In her room, she donned her usual skirt and shirt attire, flats, and pinned her hair up in a neat bun. She had spent an hour combing through it that morning while riddled with anxiety, so her tempestuous curls were more subdued than they had been in a long time.

Facing herself in the mirror, she didn't realize at first that it was her shaking and not the room. Chills wrapped her spine and squeezed her lungs as she thought of stepping out in public.

What if I get attacked?

Ragged breaths came from her throat, deafening in the silence.

Harvester protect me.

Having thrown a quick prayer to her god, she steeled her spine and marched downstairs. Enzi waited by the front door, leaning against the wall next to the oak coat rack upon which hung both her light spring jacket and heavy winter coat. Grabbing the latter and bundling herself up to the throat, she turned to Enzi with a half-hearted smile.

"Let's go!"

He chuckled at her sarcastic enthusiasm and opened the door for her.

Outside, a brisk late spring breeze swirled the coats and skirts of passersby. Farzana had braced herself for hordes of angry faeries but only a small group of protesters stood across the street, holding various signs touting their ire at Erasto.

"We don't want you!" they chanted, shoving their signs into the faces of passing faeries. Everyone else up and down the street hunched over as they walked, staring at the ground before them, not daring to make eye contact.

"See? We'll be okay."

Farzana nodded as Enzi locked up, and they made their way downtown, where the main FRMDC building stood. It was a short and easy five-minute walk, punctuated by efforts to skirt the puddles of muck on the cobblestones from the storm. A flock of dragons cooed in the middle of the sidewalk, vying for the attention of an elderly elf tossing out scraps of bread. Farzana glared at the dragons—noisy, annoying pests—and shooed them out of her way.

As they neared her work, they reached the throngs of faeries—some elves and sirens, though the majority were the gray-, brown-, and black-winged common-fae pixies—bustling through The City's downtown district. More chanting protesters stood in the streets, their cries for justice barely audible in the hubbub. Farzana relaxed as they walked, and soon, she spotted the line for the lifts for her building.

"Here I am," she said, stopping to give her brother a hug. "Thanks, Enz."

"Anytime, Zana."

He turned back, swallowed by the crowd, and Farzana shivered before heading toward the front of the line. Everyone knew that aristo-fae—the colorful-winged close descendants of pureblood pixies—got caste-specific privileges, so she was surprised by the scowls she received as she skipped those waiting.

"Back of the line!" someone barked as she passed.

"Excuse me?"

"You've got to wait like the rest of us," he huffed, crossing his arms. "Who do you think you are?"

"I'm an aristo-fae," she said, bristling.

He scoffed. "And I'm the queen's brother."

"Excuse me?"

"Prove it. Let's see your wings."

A not insignificant number of faeries had heard enough to take interest in the confrontation, and Farzana's pride—weak as it may be—wasn't about to back down. She started peeling back her coat before she realized what it would mean if anyone saw the color of her wings. All sense of bravado evaporated as she shrank back into it.

"I can't."

His sneer stung. "Like I said, back of the line." A few spectators chuckled before they all turned back toward the lifts, her existence so swiftly forgotten. Humiliation rooted her to the spot as the line slowly progressed past her. She struggled with the lump growing in her throat as she fought back tears.

It's just a line. I won't cry.

She'd thought her days of being shunned were over when she took the job at the Fae Resource Manipulation and Distribution Center five decades back. Before, she had been an outcast—a low-ranking, bastard foreigner. There was no purple-winged House native to Dradour, and everyone knew that. Her schoolmates had been ruthless in their ridicule.

That all changed once she had been promoted to a lower management position at the FRMDC. Araj, the Assistant Manager of the company, had taken a shine to her; even after learning about her sexuality, he had decided being a friend was more important than his crush. Because of his friendship, the other aristo-fae had accepted her into their world.

And here she was again, standing in the cold. An outsider. Obediently, she turned toward the back of the line.

"Farzana!"

She spun on her heel, coming face to face with Araj. His eyes twinkled as his face split into a grin, and he pulled her into an embrace, the tips of his sapphire wings tickling her nose.

"Araj!" she gasped, breathless.

"I wasn't sure I'd see you today," he said, holding her at arm's length.

"Well, I have a family to support," she said.

"Admirable of you. I was worried you would quit on us."

"After one day of missed work? Hardly."

He searched her face, and as always, seemed to see right past her emotional mask. "You aren't pitying yourself, are you? Because, despite what people are saying, nothing has changed about you for the worse."

Farzana sputtered. "What are people saying?"

"Well, that you're his daughter." His thumbs rubbed her arms. "But listen to me; that doesn't mean anything. You're a strong, smart, absolutely gorgeous fem-fae. Keep being you. So what if your father is a monster. That doesn't change who you are, Farzana."

Her lip quivered as she struggled not to cry. Her father was a monster. And she was pitying herself for it.

Pathetic.

"So I need you to stand up straight and be proud of who you are. Damn anyone who looks down on you for being related to him."

"Yeah," she said, sniffling and wiping her eyes. "You're right; I don't need anyone's approval."

But it doesn't hurt to have yours.

"Come on," he said, throwing an arm over her shoulder. "Let's go to work. We're late as it is." He shot her a look, a twinkle in his eye. "You and me, waltzing in late together. Now, what will everyone think?"

A laugh bubbled up in her throat, the first in days, and she gave his shoulder a gentle shove. Araj's crush wasn't a secret, but neither was her preference for fem-fae. She doubted anyone would think something had happened between the two of them.

Araj took her hand and strode up to the lifts, bypassing the queue of common-fae, elves, and sirens, and waited for the doors to open. Farzana stood next to him, hyper aware of the disgruntled stares aimed at her. She felt sheepish about jumping the line. The doors opened onto an empty lift, and Araj pulled her in with him. No one else had moved to enter the lift by the time Araj pressed a glowing rune for floor six, grimacing as the rune sapped some of his strength to propel the lift upward.

"Thanks," she murmured. It was common courtesy for the lowest ranking faerie to use their own strength, but Araj always used the runes for her.

He smiled down at her, his eyes crinkling. "I don't want you getting a headache this early in the day. Besides, you know the runes don't bother me like they do you."

"I know that. But I can still thank you," she said, rolling her eyes. "And hey, thanks for knocking some sense into me. I needed that."

He flashed his fangs at her in a grin. "Of course! I'm here for you, Farzana."

The lift doors opened, and he dropped her hand, heading left; she let out a pent-up breath and turned right, heading for her cubicle.

2

A FAMILIAR REDHEAD WITH A DELICATELY pointed spine sat in Farzana's chair in her cubicle, her booted feet kicked up on the corner of the desk and narrowly missing the lip of a potted pothos trailing off the edge.

"Tathi!" Farzana exclaimed, rushing in for a hug.

Tathi stood up, a broad smile lighting up her face, and embraced her.

"I'm so sorry!" Tathi said, pulling Farzana over to her seat. "Sit, sit. Oh gods, are you okay? I've heard the rumors. I mean, who hasn't? Talk to me, darling. What's going through your head?"

Being half-siren, Tathi didn't need to ask questions to get answers; she had inherited the vocal siren powers of manipulation from her mother. In a pinch, Tathi could enchant anyone into telling her everything. But while she did get liberal with her powers every now and then, she knew when to step back and ask instead.

Farzana opened her mouth to speak, paused, and hummed under her breath. "I...I'm not doing well. I found out my long-lost father is actually a murderer. Who kills the royal family? What a madman," she said, using an Earth term. It seemed fitting.

Tathi nodded, her green eyes wide with concern. "I can't even imagine how you feel right now, darling. Let it out. Tell me everything."

"He massacred all those people? In cold blood? He ordered his imps to do that! Like he was ordering food to-go."

"Yes. Yes."

"Oh gods, and the fact that there's no purple-winged House in Dradour? I can't even hide that we are related! Everyone knows!"

"Mhm. Mhm. Say it."

"I'm so damn angry! I'm angry at Erasto for coming back into my life like this. I'm angry at him for killing all those faeries. I'm angry at the gods for letting this happen!" Belatedly, Farzana realized she had stood up.

Tathi sucked in a breath. "Wow. That's a lot of feelings. Like, that's intense."

Farzana sank back into her chair, deflated from her outburst. Her thoughts spiraled in a slow whirlwind of muted anger, shame, and self-pity. How long would she feel this conflicted? How fast did one get over the knowledge of their father being a monster?

Tathi pulled Farzana into a tight embrace. "This won't last forever, okay? You will get through this. The anger, these feelings…they won't last. But that doesn't mean it's wrong to feel this, darling."

Farzana's chin quivered on Tathi's shoulder. "Thanks, Tathi," she whispered, pulling away and wiping at her eyes.

Tathi gave her shoulder a gentle squeeze. "Well, you know I'm right next door if you ever want to talk about this stuff. I'm all ears."

Farzana snorted. "I know you are."

Tathi grinned, fangs flashing in the light. "You know what I mean."

"I know. Thank you, Tathi."

Farzana stared out the window as Tathi padded out of her cubicle and over to her own. The gray sky cast a gloom over everything. Even the luscious gardens at the far end of the block looked sad and dismal.

With a sigh, she picked up her tablet mirror and switched it on; the screen showed her files of work completed by the resource manipulators assigned to her. Each file included columns listing energy users and distributors. The job of the resource manipulators was to match the numbers as effectively as possible, and Farzana's job was to approve the matches so the FRMDC could distribute energy to the consumers. The better the match, the more efficient the transaction, which meant more money for The Center and less waste. Even distracted, Farzana worked hard to ensure there was no wasted energy; that would mean a fine for The Center and a cut to her own paycheck.

The numbers became a blur as she worked, time ticking past as file after file was approved for distribution. She came across one file which had to be resubmitted for manipulation; otherwise, it was a steady stream of approvals.

After several hours of work, someone tapped on the doorway to the cubicle. Farzana turned, eager for a break.

Araj had a tray of food in his hands and a soft smile on his lips. "Lunch time. I brought your favorites."

She stood and stretched, her back popping as she straightened out of her hunch. She eyed the cup of berries and cream on the tray, and her stomach let out a growl. How long since she had eaten a real meal? She hadn't been able to keep anything down. Araj settled onto the floor and patted beside him; Farzana slid down and reached for the berries and cream.

"Mmm," she moaned around the first bite. "You know how to make me happy, Araj."

He chuckled. "I figured you could use something nice in your life right now." He picked at his sandwich, nibbling at the crust before setting it down.

Farzana swallowed and glanced at him. "What's wrong?"

"I have something to tell you. Something…you don't want to hear."

"Okay." She set the cup down, nervous.

Araj sighed. "Erasto made another broadcast and formally denied the rumors of you being his daughter. He said you were probably spreading the rumor for a few minutes of fame. He called you…" His eyes shifted away, and he cleared his throat. "He called you Farzana the farce."

A farce! What could she hope to gain by lying about him being her father? Her ear tips burned. After all the internal torment, he wasn't going to admit they were related. Part of her felt relief, but adding an insult to that?

How dare he!

"I don't understand," she croaked, her throat parched. "Why would he say that? Why would he call me that?"

"I mean, it's kind of a cute nickname," Araj said, with a hint of a smile quirking his lips.

"What? No, it's not. It's awful. I'm a farce now? What did I do to deserve that?" She couldn't stop the rising anger in her voice. Araj winced at the tone.

"Okay, you're right. I'm sorry. What if I go and fix this? I'll talk to him. Set everything right."

Farzana shook her head forcefully, curls threatening to explode from their pins. "He's a maniac. There's no point in talking to him. What he needs is to be punched in the throat."

Araj stared at her wide-eyed, and she knew why. She was not a violent person; this was a new and unfortunate facet of personality. Erasto brought out the worst in everyone, it seemed.

"I'll fix it, okay? It's going to be alright." He stood and hurried away, leaving Farzana sitting alone with her ugly thoughts and her cup of berries.

"Everything okay?" Tathi asked, popping her head around the corner.

Farzana shoved a spoonful of berries in her mouth, trying not to choke, and nodded, not making eye contact. The day was turning out worse than she thought possible.

~ ☼ ~

"Farzana!"

She continued staring at her tablet mirror screen, clicking "accept" on the latest file. "What?"

Tathi tapped her shoulder. "Come quick! It's Araj!"

Farzana was out of her seat in an instant, following Tathi to the break room. The mirror played loudly, and a small crowd of faeries mulled around, watching the show. Erasto had allowed a mirror crew inside the palace earlier that day to interview him but now, Araj was on the screen.

In the throne room, Araj yelled at Erasto, who sat on the late king's gilded seat. "You're not good enough for her anyway! You wrote her off without even getting to know her! She lived her whole life a bastard because of you!"

Farzana gaped at him, not believing her eyes or ears. How on Faerth had Araj managed to get into the throne room? And why was Erasto regarding Araj with a bored look rather than ordering his death?

With a howl, Araj leapt forward and pulled Erasto from the throne. Araj slammed his fist into Erasto's face; the crack of his nose breaking echoed and his eyes rolled back in his head. Holding him up by his shirt collar, Araj hit him again.

And again.

The imps stood frozen, uncertainty on their faces, before Erasto came to and managed to scream, "GET HIM OFF ME!"

It took three imps to pry Araj from Erasto's huddled form. Once he was freed, Erasto got to his feet, holding a hand to his bleeding nose. Araj made an unsuccessful lunge at him before the imps spun him around and began to march him toward the exit.

"Wait!" Erasto ran up behind Araj and kicked the back of his knee; with a cry of pain, Araj fell to the ground. Erasto kicked him, over and over again. Blows rained down on Araj's face, ribs, stomach, and Farzana heard a sickening crunch as something broke before someone reached over and turned off the mirror.

The reflection of Tathi and Farzana holding each other stared at them, tears streaming down their faces. Farzana struggled to breathe as she tried to block the image of Araj's bruised face peering up at Erasto. Tearing away from Tathi, she raced to the bathroom where she quietly and thoroughly emptied the meager contents of her stomach into the trash.

This is all my fault.

If she hadn't gotten so upset about the farce thing, would he have gone? Maybe he wouldn't have run headlong into a fight with the country's most dangerous pixie. Maybe he would be at work, safe and sound. Instead, his blood was a stain on the marble floors of the throne room.

What would become of Araj?

After work, Farzana took a waterhorse trolley out toward the outskirts of town, where the big aristo-fae Houses all resided. It took two transfers, but she ended up at the House of Sapphire, a stern looking red brick building. An enormous mosaic above the front door depicted a blue-winged pixie in flight—an oddity for this day and age when wing usage was considered barbaric. The art, usually a welcome sight, looked like it was judging her, and she averted her eyes while reaching for the door knocker.

Two taps and the door opened, held by the House butler. "Miss Farzana," he said, inclining his head toward her. "Come in."

"Thank you," she said, breathless. The parlor's focus was a golden vase nearly her height, covered in large sapphires and tiny moonstones. Skirting around it, the butler motioned for her to follow.

They took the curving staircase to the left and went down a hall toward a room Farzana had never been in. After a quick tap, the butler opened the door and ushered her inside.

"He's in the healing sleep, miss. I'm told it's possible he can sometimes hear what goes on around him. He'll be happy to know you're here."

Farzana took in the sight of her broken best friend. Purple and blue bruising marred his handsome face; there was a cut on his swollen lips. Even in sleep, he looked like he was in agony, eyebrows furrowed, and mouth set in a deep frown.

She wondered if he always looked like that while asleep or if it was the pain.

The room was bare but for the bed and a simple wooden chair in the corner; she dragged the chair to sit by his side. Grasping his cold hand in hers, she forced herself to smile.

"Hey, you," she whispered, before finding herself at a loss for words. What did one say to someone who was so incredibly reckless yet so selfless? He almost sacrificed everything for her.

Why did you do this?

She hung her head, trying and failing to hold back tears. He was alive; that was the important thing. Nothing else mattered. He was alive, and he was safe, and he was healing. A talk about what he had done, and why, could wait.

3

TATHI WAS WAITING IN FARZANA'S CUBICLE the next day, her red tresses wound up in a messy bun with a pen holding it together. Farzana gave her the best smile she could muster and set her bag on the desk.

"Morning, Tathi. How do you always get here so early? You beat me here every day."

Tathi fluttered her long lashes at her and stood, resting her hip against the desk. "It's called time management, darling. You should try it."

"I don't get paid enough for that."

A light laugh. "So…how are we today, darling?" she crooned, her voice deliciously silky.

If Farzana didn't know any better, she would have said Tathi's self-control was warring with her desire to use her siren abilities. Withstanding her siren charms was usually a simple matter of no eye contact; those green eyes always made it hard to focus, which of course made succumbing to her voice that much easier. Farzana slipped into her chair, not meeting Tathi's gaze.

"Oh, please. I'm not going to enchant you," Tathi huffed, twirling a loose lock of hair around a slender finger. "I just want to gossip."

Farzana snorted. "Your usual method of learning gossip is using your abilities, so pardon me for assuming."

Tathi's responding grin was feral. "Yes, but this time I'm sharing the gossip with you, not the other way around."

Ah.

Farzana rested her chin in her hands, waiting for the juicy tale.

"Okay, so, you remember that absolute hunk of an elf, Enka? The one I met at the club the other night before...before everything happened? Well...guess who slept with him last night?" Her alluring green eyes twinkled with glee as she gave Farzana a slow wink.

"I'm guessing you." Farzana celebrated and supported Tathi's sexual escapades, but the aftermath was rarely pleasant. Tathi got attached to masc-fae too quickly for their comfort, and her lovers tended to vanish after a day or two of her affections. Wallow fests always followed these ghostings as Tathi mourned not finding her perfect mate.

"It was me!" Tathi squealed, hopping onto the balls of her feet and bouncing in place. "Oh gods, he was such a good lay. Like, I'm not gonna give you the hairy details, but, wow, could he make my body sing!" She giggled, her mirth contagious to the point of drawing a laugh from Farzana.

"Well, I'm glad you had fun," Farzana said, leaning back in her chair. She was grateful Tathi hadn't mentioned Araj. Seeing his injuries had been too painful, and it wasn't a subject she could handle talking about.

"You know, Farzana, you really should get out more. There are plenty of attractive—and single!—fem-fae out there. And you're so cute! They would flock to you, if only you'd ever leave your bedroom."

"What's wrong with being an introvert?" Farzana's stomach bubbled with anxiety at the thought of going out to a crowded place like a bar or club.

Tathi shrugged, a delicate rise of her shoulders. "Nothing, but you're not an introvert, darling. You're scared of meeting new people. There's a difference."

"Doesn't seem like a significant difference."

"It's the difference between wanting to die alone or accidentally dying alone."

Farzana choked on unexpected laughter. "Thanks for the vote of confidence. Is it too much to ask for the love of my life to waltz in here someday and make it easy for me?"

"Life doesn't work like that." Tathi smirked, a single fang peeking from between her crimson stained lips. "Hey! I know! Come out with me tonight. Just me and you. We'll go out to a bar and have some drinks. Totally low key, and hey, maybe you'll see someone cute." Tathi had a frenzy in her eyes, and a wide grin showing all her pearly teeth.

Farzana's heart raced at the proposition. Being in public was not a comfortable feeling for her since Erasto murdered the royal family and massacred innocent civilians. She didn't even dare to leave her house without wearing a bulky coat to hide her wings. How would she be able to relax in a crowded bar of all places, where intoxicated faeries might pick a fight?

But this was Tathi asking. They rarely met outside of work, and it was a lovely gesture on her part to invite Farzana out for a night of fun. Gods knew she could use some fun.

Farzana took a deep breath and forced a smile. "Okay, let's do it."

Tathi left the cubicle with a skip in her step, and Farzana resigned herself to a day full of distractingly anxious thoughts of her newly made plans.

Farzana shut off her mirror tablet and pulled on her coat, ready to head home after a frustrating day of resource manipulation. One file had been corrupted, leaving her with no choice but to do all the hard number crunches on her own, on paper. The math wasn't difficult, but it had been decades since she had done manual math. The processors available to The Center were efficient at their job but couldn't do anything with a corrupted file.

The numbers had finally matched up in the end, right before her last break for the day, and she had spent those precious five minutes in the bathroom, covered in a cold sweat. Thoughts of what could go wrong during her night out raced through her head and tugged at the pit of her stomach, begging her to vomit and ease the physical pain of anxiety.

Nothing will go wrong.

If only she could believe that. Grabbing her bag and slinging it over her shoulder, she headed for the lifts. Most everyone else on the floor had already left or were staying late, so she stood alone at the lift, pressed the call rune, and waited for the doors to open. A runic headache bloomed in her skull, the pain threatening to split her head in two. Inside the lift, the familiar glow of the torturous runes cast a blue gloom over the interior. Without anyone pressing a rune, the lift reverted to its natural state by gliding to the ground floor.

Outside, dragons chattered to each other on eaves overhead as crowds of faeries swarmed the sidewalks. A small group of protestors stood at the garden at the end of the block, holding their signs and chanting "Leave Dradour! Murderer!" at anyone who dared to make eye contact.

As if a random citizen would be able to do anything about the new High Manager, as he called himself.

Farzana huddled behind her collar and began walking home. That morning, Enzi had offered to meet her at work and walk home with her, but she refused, saying she needed to get used to walking on her own eventually. Enzi had given her a hug and kiss on the cheek before leaving for his own job as a chef at a prestigious restaurant across town, leaving her to stand in the long line for the lift.

As she trudged home alone, she regretted turning down his offer. The moderate hum of conversation around her was enough noise to keep her anxiety spiked. She assumed everyone around her was talking about her or noticing her in some way. Were her wings completely hidden? She clenched her back muscles, tightening her folded wings until the tension brought tears to her eyes.

Someone stepped in front of her, and she narrowly avoided running into them.

Smile. Don't make eye contact.

What would the night bring? Would she meet a cute fem-fae and hit it off? Would she even have the courage to speak to anyone other than Tathi? Would she get drunk and vomit on someone? What if she got mugged on the way home?

Shouts interrupted her ruminations, and she looked up to see a swath of faeries running toward her. The faeries around her were panicking, twisting around each other like eels to try and get out of the path of the stampeding horde.

What's happening?

The shouts dissolved around her as a roaring in her ears and black spots in her vision overwhelmed her.

No! Not now!

Wrapped in the grips of a panic attack, Farzana dropped to the ground and curled into a ball, tears streaming down her face as she fought to breathe. The rioters streamed around her, over her, feet trodding and tripping over her fetal form as their angry voices rang in the street. A foot clipped her temple and left her reeling from the impact, stomach flipping over and over as she fought the urge to vomit.

Leave me alone!

The onslaught abated, leaving Farzana sobbing on the cobblestones. After an eternity, someone gripped her arm, pulled her to her feet, and wrapped her in an embrace.

"I'm here," came Enzi's soft voice in her ear. "I'm here. It's okay."

Farzana hiccupped, looking up into his amber eyes. "I—I can't...can't breathe."

"I know, it's okay. Slow down. Count with me. In, 2, 3, 4. Out, 2, 3, 4, 5."

Farzana obediently turned to the simple task of counting her breathing, and after a few moments, she let out a shuddering breath, shoulders relaxing. "Thanks, Enz."

The sadness of his smile tugged at her heart. "Let's go home, sis."

She nodded against his sternum, holding his hand in a death grip, and turned toward their house.

Enzi unlocked the door; Farzana was shaking still and unable to hold the key steady enough to get it into the lock. Once inside, Farzana took her first real deep breath since leaving work, calmness settling over her as she took in her surroundings.

Enzi dropped his keys onto the kitchen counter, walked over to the chill box, and grabbed a bottle of juice. "Drink this; you need some sugar."

Farzana twisted the lid, her mind wandering as she walked into the family room and plopped onto the couch. Her temple throbbed from the kick, and she touched it, wincing. Her hand came away clean, so at least there wasn't any blood to worry about. She often got headaches from the smell of it, though it probably couldn't be worse than how her head already felt.

"Try to relax, okay? I'll cook dinner tonight."

"Thanks," Farzana croaked, her throat still raw from crying. She took a sip of juice, before she remembered. "Oh! Tathi!"

"What about Tathi?" Enzi asked from the kitchen.

"She invited me out tonight. Oh gods, there's no way I can go. I can barely stand straight."

"Well, that makes sense. Because...you know."

"Know what?" Farzana turned and saw a sheepish grin on his face.

"Well, you aren't straight."

Farzana snorted and rolled her eyes. "You're so funny, Enzi."

"I know."

Settling back into her seat on the couch, Farzana glanced at her reflection in the mirror. She was starting to get some color back in her cheeks, though the haunted look in her eyes didn't sit well with her. A bruise was developing on her temple, and she pursed her lips, pouting. She wasn't what you would call vain, but she hated blemishes on her face. Farzana had been known to cry upon waking up to discover a pimple on her nose, let alone a dark bruise.

"Are you going to call Tathi?"

"I should. I hate to cancel on her, though."

"So you do want to go?"

"No!" Farzana jumped up, dizziness hitting her and making her sway. She grabbed the mirror controller to call Tathi's house mirror number.

A black background with a loading circle appeared on the mirror, and Farzana fidgeted as she waited, plucking at some fuzz on her coat sleeve. The mirror beeped rhythmically as it dialed in the call. She wrenched the coat off, feeling suffocated and overheated, and threw it onto the couch behind her.

Tathi's face appeared, and her welcoming smile dimmed as she took in the sight of Farzana's face. "Oh gods, you look like shit. What happened? Are you okay?"

Farzana gave her a weak laugh. "I got caught in a riot stampede. I'm okay, though. A bit dizzy."

"Do you want to cancel?" Tathi gave her a sympathy pout.

"Yeah, that's probably best."

"Totally understandable, darling. Take a hot bath and try to relax, okay?"

Farzana nodded.

"Love you, darling. Feel better," she said, blowing a kiss before ending the call.

With that out of the way, Farzana used the remote to switch the mirror to viewing mode and opened up the local dance competition channel. Watching competitive dancing always relaxed and delighted her.

Before she could even settle down in her seat, a royal broadcast began, the crimson background flashing onto the screen with the words 'News from the palace' scrolling past. Could it really be called a royal broadcast with the royal family dead? Farzana was tempted to switch off the mirror, but curiosity got the best of her, and she called Enzi over to watch.

The screen changed to show the late king's throne with Erasto perched on it, hands resting on the arms of the gilded chair. Though his smug face was set in a permanent half smile, his purple eyes looked lifeless. Farzana studied his features—

pale skin, light brown hair, hard jawline and flat cheekbones—
and felt grateful she hadn't inherited anything from him but for
the color of his eyes and wings. Every aspect of him revolted
her, and the less of him she saw in herself, the better.

"As your first ever High Manager, I will be in charge of the
Managers of the twelve Centers of Dradour. The Managers will
answer to me and I in turn will make decisions on important
business matters. This will usher us into a new age of what I
call capitalism."

Farzana couldn't understand what her mother might have
ever seen in him. He wasn't what she would call handsome,
though that might have been his violent history that had her
thinking he looked horrific.

"I will begin construction on twelve new buildings to house
the Centers in their entirety. For far too long, this country has
slumped on what our Centers actually need from us, and it's a
wonder none of them have failed. I will create new structures
and new policies that will propel us into a more productive
future."

"Look at you, getting a shiny new building," Enzi said, his
words dripping with sarcasm.

"I'm jumping for joy," Farzana deadpanned.

"In addition to the twelve new Centers, I will build a thir-
teenth building: the High Management Center. It will be right
in the exact center of The City, with the twelve new Centers
surrounding it like a clock face."

Farzana shuddered. Thirteen was an unlucky number. Had
he chosen that on purpose? What a risky decision to make as
his first official act as High Manager. Enzi took the remote
from her hand and switched off the mirror midword, leaving
them staring at their reflections.

"Well, that sounds like a wonderful plan," Farzana said.

Enzi turned to her with a frown, his thick, dark eyebrows
furrowed. "I don't like it." He ran a hand through his short
curls, making his unruly hair even wilder.

"What can you do?"

"Yeah…"

Farzana patted his shoulder and headed for the kitchen. After an announcement like that, it sounded like a glass of wine should accompany her long, long bath. A good book wouldn't hurt either.

4

FARZANA EXITED THE LIFT ONTO HER FLOOR, a runic headache blooming in her skull, only to run headfirst into the last person she expected to see at work: Araj.

"Farzana! Sorry, I didn't see you there. I'm a bit preoccupied." He gave her a wane smile.

"Araj!" She moved to crush him in a hug but hesitated as she took in what a beating looked like after only one day in a healing sleep: green and yellow bruises decorated his face and jaw, a scabbed-over cut on his lip, and if the arm hovering protectively over his ribs gave indication, a still fragile bone break. Her heart twinged at the thought of him lying there broken on the throne room floor, his blood pooling beneath him.

He's alive. He's safe.

She shrugged off the guilt weighing her down and gave him a wide smile, trying not to cry. "You look awful. Why aren't you still in a healing sleep?"

His expression darkened. "Erasto sent someone to wake me up and come here to settle things."

"Settle things? That sounds ominous."

"That's because it is. Apparently, I am no longer worthy of the title Assistant Manager, or any position at the FRMDC, and I'm being demoted to construction work at the new High Management Center."

Dread latched onto her limbs at the implication of the news. "This is because of me, isn't it? Because you stood up for me."

"Farzana…"

"Oh gods! I'm so sorry!" she gasped, choking on a sob.

He grabbed her shoulders, giving her a little shake. "Hey. This isn't your fault, okay? He was the one who insulted you. He was the one who retaliated against me. He was the one who ordered Megami to fire me."

Farzana sniffled. "I can't believe she would do that, though. You're her favorite employee here. What kind of Manager takes orders from someone else?"

He shrugged. "I don't blame her for complying."

"You worked so hard for Assistant Manager though! And it's all for nothing."

He rubbed her shoulders before releasing her, his right arm going back to its protective position over his ribs. "Well, I'll get over it. Anyway, I'm heading to Megami's office."

"I'll come with you."

"Farzana, there's nothing you can do to fix this."

"I'm coming with you," she repeated, raising her chin to meet his gaze. "I'm going to make sure she does everything in her power to keep you here."

He pursed his lips but said nothing, turning on his heel toward Megami's office. Farzana followed him down the hall of cubicles, around the corner, and down a short hall lined with frosted conference room doors. Megami's office waited for them at the end, door wide open. A white wood desk sat before a pale gray wall covered in various plaques and awards. A simple white couch faced the desk; Megami sat slumped on it, her silver wings folded behind her.

Araj gave a courtesy tap to the door frame before stepping in, while Farzana hung back in the doorway.

"There you are!" Megami's tinkling voice was harsh with worry as she stood and turned to him. Her bleach blond curls were pinned up in an elaborate updo, small tendrils framing her lovely face, and a deep green velvet dress hugged her slim frame. As the sole fem-fae Manager in the country, Megami worked hard to ensure she presented herself and her Center as professionally and elegantly as possible. Even for all of her efforts, there were many who still spoke with disdain about how unseemly it was for a fem-fae to have that much power.

"Sorry to keep you waiting," Araj said, leaning in to exchange the customary cheek kisses of an aristo-fae greeting.

"I cannot believe this is happening. Oh, Araj, why did you have to go do something so stupid for some low brow bastard?"

Farzana cleared her throat; Megami turned to notice her in the doorway.

"Oh. Hello, dear. No offense, of course." She bared her teeth in a feral smile, eyes scrunching nearly shut. "Except because of you, I'm now losing my most important employee. So I suppose some offense is meant after all."

"Some offense taken," Farzana shot back.

"Wonderful. So we are all on the same page then. Araj made an obtuse decision based on feelings he has for a bastard lowlife aristo-fae, and now I am the one who's going to suffer for it." Her smile didn't waver once as she moved to sit at her desk, hands smoothing nonexistent wrinkles from her perfectly pressed dress.

Farzana's ear tips burned at the insult and insinuation but, for once in her life, she managed to hold her tongue. There was no use goading Megami into possibly firing her as well.

Araj folded his wings and settled himself gingerly onto the couch. "Listen, Megami, you're going to be fine. You have a strong team of upper and lower management here, and you'll find a replacement for me in no time."

"Would that I didn't have to find a replacement at all! And what, exactly, are you doing in my office?" she snapped, turning her attention to Farzana.

"I'm here to make sure you do whatever it takes to keep Araj here," Farzana replied, folding her arms across her chest. Her pulse roared in her ears as she stared down her boss.

"Of course I'm doing everything I can, but pray tell, what

else is there for me to do? I'm being ordered by the High Manager himself to—wait a moment. This Erasto…he is your father, yes?"

Farzana nodded, unable to form words. If she opened her mouth, she might vomit.

"Oh, this is *beautiful*." Megami stood and walked toward Farzana, predatory in her approach. Her silver wings shimmered behind her, and Farzana caught a glimmer of excitement in her hazel eyes.

Farzana took an involuntary step back as Megami stepped into her personal space. "What is?"

"You, dear one, are going to have a little chat with your father for me," she crooned, her finger caressing Farzana's jaw. A nasty smile curled her lips. "Now won't that be fun?"

I can't believe she talked me into this.

Farzana walked the long halls of the royal estate, a sense of foreboding clinging to her limbs and weighing her down like lead. Every step took arduous effort, and her brow and the small of her back broke out in cold sweat. It was a straight shot from the front entrance to the throne room, but even as she walked toward it, the distance seemed to double.

Shafts of light from skylights in the vaulted ceiling pierced the hallway; the warm patches of sunlight were at odds with the cold and silent interior. Various doors lined her path, their gilded frames gleaming in the bright light. Up ahead, she could make out a segment of the throne room through the slight opening of the massive double doors.

A pair of imps stood guard, their pallor deathly pale with blue veins swimming beneath partially transparent skin. In their hands, they held gold-tipped spears, though why they needed weapons when their deadly, razor-sharp claws would do more damage, Farzana couldn't say. Maybe Erasto wanted an opulent show of strength.

She paused abreast of them and tilted her head to study

their faces; high cheekbones stretched skin tight with no amount of facial fat in sight and impassive gray eyes stared down at her. Both sported ivory tusks, their rounded tips protruding from their dark lips. One turned to look into the throne room for a moment before looking back at Farzana. When both imps then ignored her to resume their watch of the hall, she took that to mean she could pass. Breathing a small sigh of relief, Farzana entered and allowed herself to take in the full majesty of the room—in particular, the dais directly in front of her. Wide enough for both bejeweled golden thrones and so large as to take up most of the room, Farzana wondered where the adoring crowds were meant to stand when the monarchs held their royal assemblies.

She shook her head; those wouldn't be happening again. The gesture made the figure on the late king's throne look up at her.

Even seated, he was tall. His beautiful amethyst wings fluttered behind him, and the juxtaposition of his bold wings to his pale skin was startling. He looked like a beetle with his large, round eyes.

Why did Mother ever fall for him?

Farzana's eyes flickered to the table at his side. Erasto had redecorated since Araj's visit. On the table were three skulls, each with a strip of white hair falling from its crest. The smallest was a tiny, delicate thing, its white hair just a small bit of fuzz. It could have fit in the palm of her hand.

Her insides turned to ice, and her body wracked from the sudden chill. A harsh and repeated rasp in the stifling silence of the room made her realize how fast and uneven her breathing had become; she made a futile effort to calm down.

He had kept the single lock of white hair to prove to anyone curious or in doubt that these were indeed the skulls of the late purebloods. How diabolical must he have been to strip bare that infant skull and keep it by his side as a testament to the horrors he had inflicted? This was a source of pride. A trophy. Three grotesque trophies.

To keep herself from becoming sick right there, she tore

her gaze away only to find Erasto smirking down at her.

"Do you like my decor?" His voice came out as a soft purr.

The air rushed out of her lungs. She couldn't breathe. She was gasping for air and he sat there, his voice smug and his expression stoic, upon his throne of blood.

His eyebrow raised as if to repeat the question. When she still stood there, struck dumb by his decor, as he so lightly called it, he changed his question. "Why have you come to me, daughter?"

So he admits it.

Farzana swallowed her nerves. "I come as an ambassador," she said, her words starting out shaky and growing stronger with her conviction. "I am here on behalf of Megami of the House of Silver, Manager of the FRMDC, to plead a case for Araj of the House of Sapphire. Megami wishes to impress upon you the importance of Araj as her Assistant Manager and states that he is irreplaceable."

"Irreplaceable? Why, what an error on Megami's part to allow any one person to become so precious and important. Especially since there is nothing she, you, or anyone can do to change my mind. Araj will come work for me in my High Management Center." His voice neither rose nor fell, betraying no emotion, though the half smile never left his lips.

Farzana stood there for a moment longer, unsure if that was it. Turning to leave, she heard him speak one more time.

"Don't worry, daughter. You will join him once your rooms in my Center are finished."

A cry of fear tore her throat as she fled.

~ ☼ ~

"Wait, say that again?" Araj stared at Farzana in confusion.

"He kept their skulls as decoration! Oh gods, I'm going to be sick," she gasped, fanning herself as she perched on Megami's couch. The office had a clean, clinical smell to it, but all she could smell was the sweet stink of imagined decay.

The poor prince... He'll never find peace.

"What did he say in regards to Araj?" Megami asked, snapping her fingers in Farzana's face.

Farzana came back to reality and glared at her, shifting on the couch to get away from her hand. "He said no."

"What did he say, exactly?"

Farzana wanted to scream. "He said that nothing you or I or anyone said could change his mind. And that you were wrong for letting someone become irreplaceable."

"Well, that was pointless. I am still going to lose my Assistant Manager. You're useless." Megami sniffed, turning up her nose. She stood and began pacing along the back of the couch.

"He also said I would be joining him in his Center," Farzana mumbled, dropping face down into a prone position. The seat cushion scratched her face, but she remained there, cheek pressed into the rough fabric, intent on hiding her tears from them both.

Araj knelt beside her, his knees in her view through a veil of curly hair, and gave her a reassuring pat. "That's awful. I'm so sorry, Farzana."

"My life is so great," she said, voice muffled by the cushion.

"Why now, though? What does he have to gain from holding you hostage?"

Farzana shrugged and rolled onto her back. The ceiling was covered in small iridescent tiles, which together built a vague and warped reflection. She stared up at the spot which should have been her face; all she saw was a shapeless brown spot. "I have no clue what he is thinking."

Megami stopped her pacing. "This is all well and good, but I've got a real plan for keeping you here, Araj, rather than whatever it is you're doing, dear. She's on her way here now."

Araj shot up to his feet. "Don't tell me you called *her*."

"I know you hate her, but she is our best chance. So kindly remain civil."

Farzana bit her lip and wondered who they were talking about. She didn't know of anyone that Araj hated. He was the sort whose charm helped him connect with anyone and everyone.

A firm knock sounded on the door and Megami said, "Come in!"

The door opened and Araj scoffed and crossed his arms, turning his back on Megami's mystery guest.

"Thank you, Ettares, for meeting with me. I know your time is valuable."

Ettares? I thought this was a fem-fae. Why does she have a vowel at the start of her name?

"Always a pleasure to meet with a Manager. It's not every day one of you contacts me for my services." Her voice was husky, with a slight and lilting accent that Farzana couldn't place. Curiosity sufficiently piqued, Farzana stood up to look at the newcomer.

Blood red wings... She's a noble!

Farzana had never met a noble before. Bastard children of the late king, they shared his wing color and also a genetic quirk: every Dradourian noble had albinism.

She stood tall—as tall as Araj—her slight frame garbed in a tailored black suit with a crimson tie at her throat. Her white hair was a soft halo, curls falling in her eyes, which were the palest ice blue. Her fangs glinted in the light as she spoke, a slight and crooked smile perched on her full lips.

Farzana's breath caught in her throat as Ettares continued talking to Megami, the huskiness pulling heat into her cheeks. She was grateful her dusky complexion couldn't show a blush. The way one corner of Ettares's mouth was perpetually raised as she spoke was hypnotizing. Farzana couldn't have torn her eyes away if her life depended on it.

A raised voice startled Farzana out of her daydream-like ruminations of Ettares's lips.

"Are you kidding me? Why on Faerth would I do that?" Ettares's tone was incredulous.

"It is in your job description," Megami pointed out.

"First off, I don't do everything that anyone asks of me."

"Oh, we know," Araj muttered, rolling his eyes.

Ettares shot a glare at Araj. "Second, if you think I'm going to help you blackmail the most dangerous pixie in the country simply so your precious Araj, whom I hate, will stay with you, you're out of your damn mind."

"Name your price."

Ettares scoffed, looking Megami up and down. "You wouldn't be able to afford it."

"Blackmail Erasto?" Farzana asked, unsure of what she had heard. Who would blackmail the person who had a small army of imps at his disposal, someone who had made it very clear he had no qualms with murdering innocent people?

Ettares turned to face Farzana for the first time, eyes widening in recognition. "Ah, you must be the infamous not-daughter," she said, stepping up to her. Grasping Farzana's hand, she brought it to her lips. Without breaking eye contact, she murmured, "Merry meet."

Farzana's head spun, and the last thing she saw before the world turned black was concern in those ice blue eyes.

5

FARZANA OPENED HER EYES AND WINCED AT the harsh light. A lump on her head throbbed with blinding pain. Dimly, she realized she had been laid onto Megami's couch.

"That's going to leave a mark," came a husky voice beside her.

She jerked her head to the side, wrenching her neck, to see Ettares sitting cross legged on the floor, watching her.

Ettares gave her a warm, albeit crooked, smile. "I would have caught you, but your masc-friend stopped me."

Masc-friend? I don't have a romantic partner…

Farzana gaped at her as realization dawned. "Oh, no, no, no. No. Araj and I are not dating."

Ettares raised a delicate eyebrow. "With the way he reacted to me touching you, I assumed there was more than friendship there."

"He wishes. I'm not even attracted to masc-fae, and certainly not him."

She grinned, a fang winking in the light. "Well, now it seems like you don't even like the guy."

A strangled sound came from the doorway, and Farzana popped her head up, regretting the sudden movement, to see

Araj standing there in shock. His face rapidly turned purple, and he sucked in a breath before turning on his heels.

"Shit," Farzana said, dropping her aching head in her hands. "I think I upset him."

"I agree with that assessment. Go. Mend your friendship. I'll be here, waiting for Megami to come to her senses."

With one last look at her, this time noticing the long, pale lashes that framed her large eyes, Farzana stood and rushed after Araj. She caught him standing at the lift, his right arm cradling his side. "Araj! Wait." She stopped, out of breath.

"There's nothing to say," he spat, not looking at her.

"I wanted to say I'm sorry. It was rude of me. I know how you…feel about me."

He glanced at her out of the corner of his eye before sighing. The lift doors opened, but he stood still, pursing his lips. "It hurts, knowing that no matter how much I care for you, no matter what I do for you, you won't reciprocate those feelings."

Farzana shuffled her wings, uncomfortable. "I know."

"It would be nice, you know, to be given a chance."

She stayed silent. There was no right thing to say when he got like this.

He sighed again. "You know what, let's forget this. We haven't hung out in a while, and we are missing each other; we need some quality time together. What about a dance-off? Tonight?"

Farzana beamed at him. "You're on."

"One thing, though? I can't stand being here with Ettares around. I'm going to head home. Cover for me?"

"Of course."

"Okay. I'll see you tonight." The lift had long since closed, so he pressed the call rune again.

"Bye," Farzana whispered as he stepped into the lift, disappearing behind the closing doors. With Araj gone, someone would have to go through his management files and finish any tasks for the day. Someone would have to keep Megami busy, so she didn't notice his empty office. And with all the work Farzana already had to catch up on, this would be an arduous task.

Thankfully she knew someone who might be willing to help. She rushed toward her cubicle, calling out, "Oh, Tathi!"

Farzana sent Enzi a message using the tablet mirror before heading home. Her personal mirror had cracked when she had been trampled by rioters and she hadn't had a chance to replace it. Not that she could even afford to. When she arrived home to see Enzi limbering up in the family room, she wasn't surprised; he took dance-off nights very seriously.

"Hurry up!" he yelled as she shut the front door.

"Calm down," she said, grinning as she ran up the stairs. Safe inside her room and behind closed doors, she stripped out of her restricting skirt and blouse and pulled on an old t-shirt and a pair of flowy lavender pants. She ran her palms down her legs, luxuriating in the softness of the fabric, before heading back downstairs barefoot.

Enzi was stretching his calves when she entered the room. He waggled his eyebrows at her and she smiled. That smile faded as she remembered the threat Erasto had made. Should she tell him?

A resounding knock echoed in the house and the front door opened, Araj popping his head in. "I'm here!" he called, stepping in and hanging up his coat in the corner.

"Well, come on! Help me move the couch," Farzana said, grabbing an end.

Together, they pulled and prodded the couch until it was against the back wall. Sitra's door was partially blocked by one end of it, but she always slept through dance-off night anyway; she preferred to hide if anyone was over.

Farzana did a small spin in the newly empty space before the mirror.

"Are we ready?" Enzi asked, clapping his hands.

"Ready as I ever am," Araj said, stretching his arms above his head.

"Let's do this!" Farzana grabbed the controller and switched the mirror on to the local dance competition channel.

A pair of elves finished up a dance routine and the music faded away to the sound of applause. Farzana loved watching the elven dancers most; their lithe bodies were so graceful as to look like they were floating, though they had no wings.

A new couple stepped onto the stage, one water nymph and one pixie. The glow of the stage lights on the water nymph's blue skin gave the illusion of her being underwater, sunlight drifting through the ripples. The pixie had copious amounts of blue glitter on her gray wings, making them shimmer like stars.

The first beat of the drums hit, and Enzi, Araj, and Farzana stamped their feet.

Boom. Boom. Boom.

Other instruments wove around the drum beat, and they all whirled into action.

Enzi rocked back on his heels and began undulating his arms at his sides, shoulders shimmying.

Careful of her balance, Farzana dropped her hip and snapped her fingers to the beat, then did a slow twirl on her toes, arms flung out. The lump on her head pulsed with the pounding drumbeat, and she struggled with a bout of nausea.

Araj took a couple sassy steps forward, his right arm curled around his side, then bent at the waist, bowing to Farzana. He straightened and held out a hand to her; she grasped it and allowed herself to be pulled into his arms. He grabbed her waist, lifting her a bit into the air, his face straining, and dropped her back down, hands shaping themselves to her body as he led her into a square step around Enzi.

Enzi stood rooted to the spot, his dance becoming more and more elaborate, his arms writhing like snakes.

Araj danced with Farzana, holding her tight, their bodies meeting and parting, moving to the beat. Always to the beat.

Sweat beaded on her shoulders and neck, and despite her headache, she found herself laughing, spirits high. Araj and Enzi joined in and as the last drum beat hit, they joined hands in the middle of the room and collapsed to the floor.

"I think Enzi won that round," Farzana said in between heavy breaths.

"No, it was Araj. That was some graceful stuff."

"I have to disagree. Farzana was enchantingly beautiful."

Enzi rolled his eyes. "For the last time, she's a lesbian! Your flattery won't work on her."

"As if I care! I still love her," Araj said, smiling.

Farzana flashed him her widest smile. It was good to be loved.

~ ☼ ~

The muted sounds of the mirror lent a comfortable layer to the gentle hush as Araj and Farzana lounged on the couch. Dusk had come and gone, the shining blanket of stars visible through the floor length windows. Farzana twisted a curl around a finger as she stared at the night sky.

"How are you feeling, with everything going on?" Araj asked, his voice low.

"Honestly? I'm trying not to think about that. Everything is a bit overwhelming."

"I can't imagine your shock when you saw Erasto on the mirror stream that first night."

Farzana let out a deep breath. "It was…something. Mother doesn't even have pictures of him, so I never knew what he looked like. I knew his name. I thought he would look different. Kind, or charming. Lovable."

Araj chuckled, leaning against her arm. "We are both about to be reassigned to his new Center, and you're worried about his looks?"

"Shut up." She shoved his shoulder with hers, careful of his ribs. It did seem silly when he put it like that. "Thinking about the reality of our situation would probably crush me and I'm not ready for that. I don't want to shut down. I'm going to be in denial for a little while." She rested her head on his shoulder, snuggling up to him.

He nodded, his stubble tugging her curls. "I don't blame

you. You haven't told your mother yet, have you?"

"I don't even know if he was being serious. I'm not going to get her upset over possibly nothing."

"Did you tell Enzi?"

Farzana bit her lip. She told Enzi everything but this...this wasn't something she could share. Describing everything that had happened would make it real and would make it that much easier for her to have a meltdown. "I didn't have time."

Araj didn't say anything for a long moment. His hand rested on her other shoulder, his thumb stroking her shirt. "Well, if it does actually happen, at least we will be together."

"That's an optimistic view, considering we would be living with a murderer."

"That does put a damper on things." He stretched his arms above his head, letting out a yawn.

"It's late. You should get home," Farzana said, standing up.

"Can I stay here tonight?"

"Of course!" She walked over to the linen closet and grabbed a couple blankets. "Do you need a pillow, or do you want to use the couch pillows?" she asked, walking back and handing him the blankets.

He accepted them with one hand, looking sheepish as he said, "I was thinking we could share your bed instead. I know you like cuddling."

She laughed and stood on tiptoe to brush his cheek with a gentle kiss. "Very funny. Sleep well, Araj."

"Good night, Farzana."

6

FARZANA SAT IN HER CHAIR, A MUG OF COFFEE
in hand, as she chatted with Tathi during their morning break.
Break times were only five minutes long; there was no sense
in going anywhere when a friend was in the next-door cubicle.
A gentle knock on the doorway alerted her to a second visitor;
Ettares poked her head into the cubicle, a sly smile on her full
lips.

Farzana's eyes bulged from their sockets as she took in
Ettares's attire. A severely tailored pale pink suit hugged her
lithe frame, a glittering black tie at her throat. A tiny black bow
peeked out of her frosty curls, the volume of her hair all but
consuming it.

"I hope I'm not interrupting," she said in a voice that sent
shivers down Farzana's spine.

"O-of course not! What's up?" Farzana tried and failed to
cross her feet at the ankles, almost upending herself from her
seat. Tathi shot her a look, obviously fighting a smile from
quirking her lips.

"I wanted to check and make sure you're recovering from
your tumble yesterday," Ettares said, reaching up to rumple
her hair even more.

"How kind of you. I'm doing great, though." Farzana leaned back in her chair, feinting nonchalance.

Tathi hid a smirk behind her hand and turned to face the window. Her fiery hair parted behind her, revealing the top of her pointed spine.

"Your back!" Ettares gasped. "You're a siren!"

Tathi whirled around, glaring daggers at her. "What of it?"

"Sorry, I've never had the pleasure of meeting one before."

Tathi fluffed her hair with a small smile of pride. "Well, only half, actually. And, darling, you must be very sheltered not to have met a siren before."

Ettares shrugged, leaning against the wall. "The siren population in Dradour has been dwindling for centuries. Plus, in my line of work, I don't ever meet sirens."

"Your line of work? What exactly do you do?" Tathi arched an eyebrow.

"I'm a bounty hunter and purveyor of knowledge."

"A what and a what?" Farzana asked, incredulous. Those sounded like dangerous careers.

"Just how it sounds. I find people, and I find information. For a price, of course. And due to their spectacular abilities, sirens never need to ask me for help."

Well, that explains the blackmailing Megami asked for.

"Maybe sirens who don't have a conscience," Tathi said with a grimace. "I don't mind some harmless influencing, but I don't full on enchant people without their consent."

Ettares tipped her head in Tathi's direction. "And I admire you for it. Siren abilities are a hot topic lately."

"A few bad sirens spoil it for the lot of us. This is why most of my family has left Dradour. Other countries aren't so anti-siren," Tathi grumped.

Farzana stared at Tathi, concerned. She had never realized her friend faced persecution or racism, let alone that those problems had cause her family to leave her. Was Tathi all alone in Dradour?

"Anyway, if you ever get bored being lower management here at the FRMDC, you should give me a call. I've got a job opening for an assistant and a half-siren would be perfect."

Tathi laughed. "I doubt I'd be much help. I just influence people to gossip with me; I've never tried to get specific information."

"Well, the offer is there."

"Actually...do you know an elf named Enka? I've been seeing him but he's so secretive. I know nothing about him."

Ettares grinned. "Oh, I would be happy to get you that information! For a price."

Tathi and Farzana exchanged glances before bursting into laughter. "Yeah, well, I'm not hiring you or anything," Tathi wheezed, tears in her eyes. "I work at the FRMDC for crying out loud; I don't make enough dradens a week to budget for some special, secret services."

A crimson stain splotched Ettares's face. "Ah, see, I don't actually know how much you make working here. I've never looked into it."

Tathi snorted. "Well, you should probably know that if you're going to solicit yourself here."

Ettares nodded, her cheeks still rosy. "You're right. Um, you both have a wonderful day," she said, backing out of the cubicle.

"See ya!" Tathi waved, waited a moment, and then pounced on Farzana. "What was that?! You were so awkward!"

Farzana's cheeks heated, and she dropped her head into her hands, hiding her face. "She's so pretty! I keep acting like a fool around her," she moaned.

Tathi chortled. "I'll say! That was the best gossip I could ever hope for and I didn't have to influence you at all!"

"Shut up!" Farzana turned her full attention to her window, ignoring Tathi's giggles.

"I'll leave you to your thoughts then. Buh-bye!"

Outside, Farzana could make out the beginning work on the High Management Center a couple blocks away. She was apprehensive about how fast it was being built. Apparently, the imp army wasn't only for terrorizing citizens—the vast majority of construction workers were imps as well. Farzana had never seen so many imps at once; the imp population in Dradour was by far the smallest minority, until Erasto arrived.

The High Management Center already had two floors intact, and she wondered how tall it would be when completed. Would she really have to live there with Erasto? The thought made her head swim, and she gulped down some cold coffee.

"Okay, I lied," Tathi said, scurrying back into the cubicle and hovering over Farzana. "I need more gossip. What was this tumble she mentioned? Also, um, how do you even know a noble of all faeries?"

Farzana grinned up at her. "Alright, settle in for a story so ridiculous, you might not believe it."

Enzi and Sitra were cuddled up together on the couch watching the mirror when Farzana got home. "Hey, Zana," Enzi called as she shut the door.

"What's up?" she asked, dropping her bag beside the coat rack.

"The cooking channel was interrupted for a broadcast from the palace. Get in here."

Farzana rushed over. "Is it Erasto?"

He was indeed front and center in the frame, sitting tall in the gilded throne of the late king. That annoying half smile was perched on his thin lips as he spoke.

"I want to apologize for a misunderstanding. It has come to my attention that I do indeed have a daughter. Her name is Farzana, and she is a purple-winged pixie who works at the FRMDC."

Dread latched onto her as she realized he was announcing to everyone where she could be found. It was already suspicious enough that she wore a coat to and from work, what with the summer weather coming in hot and fast. Faeries gave her side eye looks when she passed, bundled up as though for winter.

"How mature of him to apologize," Enzi spat.

"Well, he apologized for a misunderstanding, not for calling me farce."

"Again, I deeply apologize for the misunderstanding, and of course to my daughter, Farzana. I look forward to building a relationship with you, daughter." His eyes pierced into hers, and she shivered, wings shaking violently, as she wondered whether he could actually see her standing there in her family room.

"Farzana? Why is he making this announcement?" Sitra asked, concern on her face.

"Why would she know why he does anything?"

"Well, maybe something happened. Is everything okay, baby?"

Farzana stood still, chewing on her lip. "I, uh…met him. I had to go see him. Yesterday, actually."

Sitra stared at her, dark eyes impenetrable, and Farzana feared she would have one of her depression spirals, locking herself away in her room for days. This wasn't how Farzana wanted to spend what might possibly be her last few weeks with her mother.

"Say something," Farzana whispered.

"I never wanted you to meet him," Sitra said after a moment of silence. She wrung her hands together, fingers twisting hard enough to bruise. "He's cruel, cunning. He knows how to get what he wants. Always. Though back when I knew him, that meant manipulating people, not murdering them. Earth really changed him, I suppose."

"Why did he leave Faerth anyway?" Enzi asked.

"He couldn't get me to agree to terminate my pregnancy. He thought his life would be ruined if he had to take care of a child, though I assured him I would take care of Farzana all on my own. I guess running away to Earth was preferable."

"But for 160 years? I thought the Earth visa program only allowed you to stay for a decade?" Farzana settled onto the couch between Enzi and her mother.

"That's true, but the House of Violets has always been very wealthy. And in his home country, they were able to bribe the visa program Manager. His travel ticket was one way." She sighed, looking exhausted.

Farzana was more confused than ever. "But why would

someone from a super-rich family be interested in someone from a low ranking aristo-fae family in the first place?"

Sitra's eyes flashed with what might have been anger before she looked away. "I'm tired," she said, standing and heading for her bedroom.

"Real nice," Enzi said under his breath. "Let's hope she doesn't lock herself up in there for the next week."

"Sorry," Farzana snapped.

"Why would you refer to us as low ranking anyway? You know she's sensitive about that."

Farzana threw her hands into the air in exasperation. "It's what we are, Enzi! Plus aren't you the least bit curious why they got together in the first place?"

"Why do you care though?"

Farzana didn't have an answer for that. Why did it matter? She sighed. "I should apologize."

"Try in the morning. Give her some space first," he said, slouching down into the couch and watching the cooking channel again.

"You're right. Night, Enz," she said, standing and trudging to the stairs. Outside, it began to rain.

"Night, sis."

7

ARAJ MET FARZANA OUTSIDE OF THE FRMDC AS she carefully traversed puddles left by the night's showers. A light mist settled over the world as she looked up and smiled at him.

"Good morning," he said, walking her to the lift doors; once inside, he pressed the rune for floor six.

"Thank you."

"Don't mention it."

She studied his face, wondering whether it was the bruises or the stress that made him look like he had aged a century in the last few days. When the doors opened on their floor, she expected him to head for his office; instead, he turned right with her.

"You don't have to walk me to my cubicle," she said as he fell in step with her.

"I'm trying to be as lazy as possible during my last few days here." He jammed his hands into the pockets of his rumpled suit. He hadn't even bothered to wear a tie. Since the news of his transfer, it was apparent that Araj had stopped putting any care or thought into his attire for the day.

"Well, thank you, I guess?" She shrugged out of her bulky coat, hanging it over her arm. They rounded the last corner and entered the cubicle to find Tathi and Ettares already there, deep in conversation.

"Ettares!" Farzana squeaked, waving at her.

Ettares beamed at her before noticing Araj; her smile turned into a scowl.

Farzana turned to Araj to see his pale complexion transform into puce as his anger threatened to boil out of him.

"What on Faerth are you doing, Farzana?"

"Me? What?" she sputtered, not understanding why she was the target of his ire, rather than his supposed enemy.

"Why are you hanging out with this...this...this—"

"...noble?" Ettares offered.

Araj growled low in his throat, fangs bared. "I can't believe you, Farzana." He turned on his heel.

Farzana stood still, in shock. What had just happened?

Ettares gave her a wane smile before turning back to her conversation with Tathi, who had watched the exchange with wide eyes.

"Wait!" Farzana yelled, dropping her things and running after Araj. He was at the lifts when she caught up to him. She had no doubt he was going to leave and go home for the day, despite it being morning.

"Talk to me," she panted, leaning against the wall.

He shot her a glare. "She's dangerous, Farzana. I don't know how to get that across to you, but she is. And I don't want to see you hurt by her."

"I didn't invite her. I don't know why she's here."

"Avoid her, okay?" The lift doors opened, and he grabbed her by the arm, dragging her inside with him.

"What?" She stumbled against the wall.

The lift doors shut and Araj came up to her, a hand on the wall on either side of her head. His face was close, so close.

"I worry about you," he breathed. "I want to protect you."

Without any runes pushed, the lift began to revert to its ground state.

"Farzana," he whispered, leaning in to stroke her cheek, a creeping, feathery touch.

Farzana couldn't breathe.

He leaned in even closer and all she could see was blue: his wings, his eyes, boring into hers.

She froze.

It hit her then. His lips, cold velvet and unrelenting, moving in unfamiliar patterns. His hands wandered over her, tugging at her shirt, his chest against hers, hips pinning her back.

Help me!

But she couldn't speak, couldn't breathe, couldn't move.

The lift brightened as the door opened; she braced herself against the wall and pushed Araj with a strength she didn't know she possessed.

In slow motion, she watched him fall, his back in a graceful arc, his arms flailing out to find nothing. Falling against a group of fem-fae, his hands grabbed their shirts, their skirts, anything to save himself. He landed flat on his back in a muddy puddle, splattering filth against the group of fem-fae, and like a soufflé, they collapsed in on him.

Farzana jabbed the rune for floor six and huddled in the corner of the lift; the doors slid shut, hiding her from the world, and she no longer had to see that face, that expression of enraged indignation.

She pulled her shirt back together and sobbed.

Ettares was waiting in the empty cubicle when Farzana made her way back; Tathi must have returned to work. The impeccably-dressed noble sat in Farzana's chair, leaning back onto its two back legs, and gazed out the window, no doubt watching the bustling City. She didn't seem dangerous, like Araj said, though since he was the only one of the two who had attacked her, she wasn't quite willing to trust his judgment.

She watched Ettares for a moment longer, emotions rushing through her. She wanted to run, to go home to the safety of her bedroom, to hide for a day or two until the unclean feeling left her lips. Instead, she leaned against the doorway, crossing her arms, and blurted out, "Why are you here?"

Ettares jumped, tilting the chair back too far, and tumbled to the floor.

So much for dangerous.

Farzana stifled a laugh at the sight of her crumpled on the floor, a blush creeping up her pale neck.

"Well, if you must know, I have a message for you and Megami. But I wasn't interested in waiting in Megami's office, so I came to your cubicle instead."

"What's the message?"

Ettares righted herself, brushing off her black silk jacket and pinstripe pants before shrugging her shoulders. "I haven't opened it yet." She stopped then, peering down at Farzana with concern. "Are you okay? You look like you've been crying."

Farzana gave her the biggest smile she could muster. "I'm fine."

Ettares didn't seem convinced. "Okay...well, I'm here if you want to talk. I know we don't know each other that well, but I'd like to get to know you better."

"Why?"

Her expression faltered. "What do you mean?"

"I mean, why would a noble want to get to know a bastard, low-level aristo-fae?" She worked hard to keep a whine from her voice. The self-deprecating language was enough.

Ettares leaned her hip against the desk. "I don't care about caste. You seem like a thoughtful, positive, caring person, and I could always use more people like that in my life."

Farzana raised an eyebrow and burst out laughing. "You like me for my positivity? I'm the most sarcastic person I know."

"That doesn't mean you're a negative person. And I happen to like that blend of sour and sweet." She winked. Farzana blushed.

"I'm not much of a people person. I've been told I'll die alone because I'm always locking myself away in my room."

"I'll change that for you," she said with a grin.

"Ettares! There you are," Megami said, popping her head into the cubicle without so much as glancing at Farzana.

"Here I am indeed."

"I hear you have a message for me? Let's talk privately in my office."

Ettares straightened. "I do have a message for you and Farzana. But yes, let's go to your office." She brushed past Megami.

Ettares led the way, Megami and Farzana trailing after her, and Farzana marveled at how well she navigated the floor. Built like a maze, it took someone with excellent spatial memory to be able to get from Farzana's cubicle to Megami's office with no help.

Once inside, Ettares plopped down onto the couch, crossing her long legs. She looked up at Farzana and smiled, patting the seat cushion beside her.

"Let's get this over with," Megami said as Farzana settled onto the couch.

Ettares retrieved an ivory envelope from her breast pocket and broke the aubergine seal; pulling out a single sheet of paper, she read in a formal voice:

"To Miss Megami of the House of Silver, and to Miss Farzana of the House of Violets, regarding Miss Farzana. This message should be noted as being a direct order from the High Manager, Erasto of the House of Violets. The High Manager requires Miss Megami to terminate Miss Farzana's employment upon the completion of the High Management Center. Miss Farzana is to be relocated from her current housing once it is declared finished and will remain there until such a time that the High Manager relinquishes his Parental Rights. Under the order of law Number 8, parents have certain inalienable rights, one of which is to claim compensation time for extended periods away from their child. The High Manager has also adjusted the law to include Miss Farzana though she is no longer under the legal age limit. The High Manager wishes you both a pleasant day and awaits the arrival of Miss Farzana."

Ettares turned to Farzana, horror dawning on her face. "Oh, gods. I'm so sorry."

The blood all but drained from Farzana's face as she sat there, a numb statue.

I'm going to live with a monster...and with Araj.

~ ☼ ~

Megami allowed Farzana to leave during lunch. Pulling on her coat, Farzana stepped through the rush of faeries heading to grab food and hopped into the lift with a group of other lower management staff. Out on the street, a waterhorse trolley pulled up beside her and she leapt on, almost losing her balance without being able to use her wings to steady herself.

She held onto the pole and watched the beautiful team of waterhorses as they pulled the trolley. Their velvet black hides had a shiny sheen as they walked, muscles rippling, and their flowing manes always moved as though they were still underwater. Glowing red eyes took in all the passersby on the streets, and Farzana wondered how often they were tempted to enchant the passing faeries.

Thank the gods for the water nymphs who ran the trolleys; they did a superb job at taming the waterhorses. She hadn't heard of any enchanting accidents in several decades.

A flock of dragons flew overhead before landing on the eaves of a house across the way; judging from the splotches of dragon poop scattered on the walkway below, it looked like a favorite perch of theirs.

Farzana hated dragons. Noisy, disgusting beasts who, without fail, chirped at dawn, no matter the day, and again at dusk. There was no such thing as a peaceful sleep with dragons singing outside your window.

As the trolley neared her house, she prepared to jump off. The trolley jolted forward just as she let go of the pole, and she tripped forward, catching her balance at the last second to keep from falling on her face.

That's exactly what she needed: another head injury on top of the two from earlier that week.

She trudged the last few steps up to her house and opened the door. Despite how many times she chastised her mother about it, Sitra never locked the door.

"Mother, I'm home," she called, peeling off the jacket and hanging it up. The lights were off throughout the house, and though it was broad daylight outside, the sunlight from the floor length windows in the family room didn't lend much visibility in the foyer and kitchen area.

She headed for the family room. Enzi would still be at work, so it was the perfect time to snuggle up on the couch and watch endless dance competition videos. Maybe even enjoy a glass of wine. Backtracking to the kitchen, she checked the chill box for her bottle of wine only to notice the empty bottle on the counter.

She sighed. "Thanks, Mother, for drinking all the wine that I bought for myself." Slamming the chill box door shut, she went to her room to change into something more comfortable. She begrudged Megami for insisting all the fem-fae staff had to wear skirt suits to work; if it were up to her, she would wear light, flowy skirts or loose pants every day. Apparently, that was too casual for Megami's tastes.

As she walked back down the stairs, the front door opened and shut.

"Enzi?" she called, settling on the couch.

"Farzana? What are you doing home?" He came into the family room holding a dirty chef's apron in his hands.

"Megami let me go home early. I've had a shit day." She patted the couch beside her.

He sat down, tossing the apron onto the coffee table. "What happened?"

"So, Araj kissed me today."

"You let him kiss you?"

"Well, no. He, uh, forcibly kissed me."

"What!" Enzi shouted, jumping onto his feet. "What on Faerth? What was he thinking? Are you okay?"

Farzana held up her hands, placating him. "I'm okay! I'm fine. It wasn't like that. He said he was worried about me and then...he kissed me."

"That's not okay. It doesn't matter how he was feeling. He assaulted you."

Tears sprang to her eyes as she tried to shut out the feel of his lips on hers. Shame bloomed in her chest. "Yeah, I guess he did."

"You guess? Don't tell me you're going to stay friends with him after this." Enzi sounded incredulous as he paced back and forth in front of the couch.

"What choice do I have? I have to go live near him soon!"

He stopped in his tracks, turning to stare at her. "Excuse me?"

Sniffing, she told him about the news Ettares had delivered. "And Araj is being relocated there as well, though now that I think about it, I'm not sure if he'll be living there or only working there," she mused.

"No wonder you went home early. Wow," he said, sinking down onto the couch and rubbing his beard. "Wow. I don't know what to say."

"Tell me it's not the end of the world. Tell me it's going to be okay," she pleaded, trying to inject a joking tone.

He continued looking at her, sadness in his dark eyes. "Zana, I'm so sorry."

"Yeah." The tears overwhelmed her then. The room felt overheated, and she tried to steady her breathing. She didn't want an anxiety attack.

The door opened behind her, and Sitra came into the room. "Children! Why are you both home so early?" She rested a hand on each of their heads in a loving, maternal caress.

Farzana debated telling her but knew if she did, she would fall into a depressive episode where she never left her bed and refused to eat for weeks. If these were the last few days—who knew how long it would take to complete the new Center—she had with her mother, she wanted Sitra to be her usual self.

"Megami gave us all a half day," she said, turning to Sitra with a smile.

"And my boss accidentally double booked the chefs, so I decided to leave early," Enzi chimed in, still looking at Farzana with concern.

"My babies, spending time with me," mother said in a sing-song voice. "I'm so happy."

And that's all that mattered. Farzana wanted her mother to be happy for the rest of the time they had together.

8

FARZANA STOPPED AT TATHI'S CUBICLE ON HER way to her own, intending to tell her the news. She had left the previous day without saying goodbye and she knew Tathi would welcome some gossip.

Tathi was busy at work, intent on the task on her mirror tablet, long red hair streaming down her back. Farzana tapped her shoulder and she turned, a grin already on her face.

"Hello, darling," she crooned, hooking an ankle behind a chair leg and leaning back. "Someone left work early yesterday."

"Megami let me go during lunch."

She raised an arched eyebrow. "Megami isn't known for being nice. Something dreadful must have happened. Tell me everything!" She propped her chin in her hands, staring up at Farzana with wide, green eyes and drank in the news. "Wait, so you're going to be in the same Center as Araj? That's nice, right?"

Farzana rubbed the back of neck, uncomfortable at the mere mention of his name. "Ah, about that. Yesterday, Araj kissed me. Nonconsensually." She swallowed the bile that came up with the last word.

"What an ass! I know he's your friend, but that shit is unacceptable. Oh gods, are you okay? What a loser."

"I'm f-fine. I wish I had known what on Faerth he was thinking, doing th-that."

"He has had the hots for you for decades. I'm surprised it took this long for him to show his nasty side and force himself on you." Disgust riddled Tathi's face like she'd smelled something foul.

Farzana tried for a light-hearted laugh and ended up crying.

"Oh, darling." Tathi scooped her into a hug, rubbing her back. "I'm so, so sorry this happened to you. You didn't deserve it. And he deserves a knife in the ribs."

"Yeah," Farzana sniffed, pulling back.

"Anyway, the real question is: why are you still coming to work?"

"What do you mean?"

"You're losing your job, right? And you're going to move into the new Center. So what are you doing wasting your time here?" She fluffed her hair, waiting for a response.

Farzana didn't have one. What was she doing? Megami clearly didn't like, want, or need her. And as per the law, Erasto would have to compensate her mother for any income she would be missing due to her child no longer living with her. Why not do whatever she wanted?

If she left, though, Ettares might not know where to find her. Her insides turned warm at the thought of seeing that gorgeous face again. Was it too wild to think that Ettares would be back?

"I don't know," she said finally.

"Well, think about it. I will obviously miss you terribly but there's no reason for you to keep dragging your butt here every day. Go out and enjoy what little time and freedom you have left without your father breathing down your neck."

"Yeah," Farzana said in a daze. She hadn't thought of what sort of restrictions Erasto would place on her once she moved to The Center. Would she even be allowed to leave the building?

"I gotta get back to work. You gonna be okay?"

"I'll be fine," Farzana said, giving her a quick hug and walking to her own cubicle. She dropped her bag on the desk and stared out the window.

The High Management Center was five floors high and growing fast. It was taller than half the buildings in the downtown area; The City of Dradour wasn't known for its skyscrapers, though it was the capital. There were many large cities in the country with dazzling skylines showcasing buildings made entirely of windows, but this was not one of them. As it was, the six-floor tall FRMDC was the tallest building for several blocks.

Farzana could see hordes of imps swarming the construction site, carrying beams of steel and panes of glass, ferrying supplies here and there. She had never seen so many imps in her life and wondered why Erasto had hired imps in particular for all of his grunt work. Construction, guard duty, massacres... was there anything they wouldn't do for him?

Sighing, she sat down and turned on her tablet.

After several hours of mind-numbing work, Farzana powered off her tablet to go grab some lunch. The cafeteria downstairs was serving their weekly special: flatbread and fried dragon wings. Farzana took every opportunity to eat wings; she took satisfaction in knowing she was helping to rid the world of another pesky dragon. Her mother had told her when she was a child that fried dragon wings actually came from dragon farms where they raised fat dragons specifically for eating, but she liked to pretend that every dragon she ate was one less dragon to poop on the sidewalks.

She turned right as Ettares walked up, a fangy grin on her full lips.

"Hey! Care to join me for lunch? My treat."

Farzana thought about what Tathi had said. "Why not?" She was flattered that someone as beautiful as Ettares was interested in spending time with her. Plus, free food was never something Farzana turned down. Ettares was rich enough that she no doubt knew all the best restaurants in The City. Farzana wasn't about to pass up an educational opportunity in culinary appreciation.

"Come on," Ettares said, heading for the lifts. Once they reached the closed doors, Ettares pressed the glowing call rune before Farzana could reach for it.

Farzana's eyes widened. Why would a noble press runes for herself when someone lower ranking was right there? Society rules dictated that the lower caste should always use their own energy in a situation like this, but there Ettares was, using her own energy and saving Farzana's. Farzana studied her profile as they waited for the lift to arrive, unsure of what to make of her.

Ettares caught her staring and smiled down at her. "You ready for a new experience?"

The lift doors opened and Farzana shivered violently, remembering the last time she had been in a lift with someone. Her stomach lurched, and she pressed a hand to her abdomen.

"I, um, forgot my coat," she said, not looking Ettares in the eye. "I should go back for it."

"You're cold? Here, take this," Ettares said, pulling off her suit jacket.

Farzana blushed as she took in the sight of Ettares's muscular biceps in the fitted white button-up shirt. She hadn't expected Ettares to have muscles since she looked so deceptively slim in her suit, but she supposed that's what good tailoring did. Unable to refuse, Farzana stepped into the lift.

Ettares wore crimson suspenders that perfectly matched the hue of both her bow tie and her wings, and never before had Farzana so wanted to undress someone.

Farzana accepted the jacket with a murmur of thanks, her hands brushing Ettares's, and glanced up at her eyes. Blue but ice rather than sapphire. Soft and kind rather than piercing and demanding. Farzana let out a shuddering, pent-up breath as the lift descended. The jacket was too big, the sleeves covering her hands, but it covered her wings too and that was all that mattered.

Ettares hooked her thumbs behind her suspenders. "Looks good on you," she said with a blush.

The lift doors opened on the ground floor, and she held out a hand, gesturing for Farzana to exit. "After you."

Farzana stepped out into the sunshine. A brisk breeze whipped at the edge of the jacket, and she was grateful for the extra layer. She glanced over at Ettares's shirt and wondered if she regretted handing it over.

"This way!"

They walked for a couple minutes in comfortable silence, Farzana noticing how the crowds parted before them. Everyone knew better than to stand in a noble's way; they were the original heirs to the throne until the crown prince had been born. After centuries of miscarriages, Queen Tatiana's live birth had been celebrated across the kingdom with parties and parades for weeks. The bastard nobles had all graciously relinquished their inheritance to the pureblood son.

They stopped in front of a tiny cafe tucked between two large, fancy restaurants. A faded sign reading 'Twy's Cafe' graced the space above the glass door.

"I hope you weren't expecting something flashy," Ettares said, grabbing the door. "But this place has the best bread you will ever try."

"Bread?" As the door opened, a warm rush of air hit Farzana, bringing with it the scent of fresh baking, wood fires, and a hint of fresh herbs, though she couldn't tell which ones. Her mouth began to water as she stepped inside and took in the sight of the giant brick ovens along the back wall, the checkered tile floors, and the vinyl booths. It smelled like home when Enzi baked his favorite pie on his birthday, only one hundred times better. She wouldn't tell him that though.

"It smells amazing," she sighed.

Ettares's eyes twinkled. "Just wait till you taste it. I'm telling you. Best. Bread. Ever."

Farzana giggled at her enthusiasm as she led them to a corner booth. Sliding in, Farzana asked, "Do you come here often?"

She nodded. "I try to support small, local businesses. This place has been owned by the same family for 14 decades. I like to think I've helped with that."

"Wow." Small businesses tended not to last long in The City; they were better suited for smaller towns. In the past century, more and more corporations were buying up all the lots in The City, turning huge profits to feed their expansions. This business had been around for almost as long as Farzana had been alive, which was impressive.

"My favorites are the thyme and rosemary flatbread, the blackberry bread, and the spiced apple bread. You have to try them."

"Okay!" Ettares's excitement was intoxicating. Farzana felt her spirit bubbling with happiness, and for a moment, she forgot she was in public with a near stranger.

"So what do you do for fun?" Ettares asked after placing their order with the pixie who came by.

"Oh, I dance."

"You dance? On competitions?"

Farzana laughed. "No, I wish. I dance for fun. My brother and I, we have dance-offs."

"That's great! We should go dancing sometime. I know some fun clubs."

"Oh, no, I…I don't go out in public. I mean, I don't dance in public."

"That's fine," she said, reaching up to ruffle her wild curls. "I forgot you said you were an introvert. Private dancing it is, then. Tell me about your brother."

"Enzi? Well, he's like you, actually." Farzana stopped, mortified at what she had said. What if she was wrong about Ettares being transgender?

"Like me?" She cocked her head.

"I mean, you changed your gender presentation, right? I guessed because you have a masc-fae name. Enzi changed his name when he transitioned." Changing one's gender was easy and common; you could go to any healer in The City and get a face and body change. But Farzana had never met anyone who had changed their gender and kept their old name.

Ettares winked. "Yes, I did. I love having a masc-fae name, honestly. But your brother transitioned as well? Good for him."

"Why did you keep your name?" Farzana asked, leaning forward against the table separating them.

Ettares leaned back, propping her hands behind her head. "Well, it was the name I was born with; I've loved it for centuries."

Centuries? How old is she?

"I thought about shortening it to Ares, but again, vowel first is still a masc-fae name. So I kept it as is. Plus"—she pointed a finger in the air—"people treat you differently if they're expecting a masc-fae. My correspondences are startlingly more polite when they don't know I'm a fem-fae. Maybe someday fem-fae will be treated equally, but I'm not sure when that will be. It's partly why I respect Megami so much; she's the only fem-fae Manager in The City."

If only she didn't promote outdated and sexist work attire.

Farzana nodded, smoothing down her pencil skirt.

The server came back laden with a tray topped with slices of fresh baked bread. Farzana's stomach gave a small grumble as the server placed the bread down along with a dish of butter and another dish of what looked like oil and vinegar.

"Oh, wow," Farzana said as the smell of bread slammed into her. How long had it been since she ate? She was ravenous.

Ettares spread her hands wide over the array. "Let's eat!"

9

DRAGONSONG WOKE FARZANA AT DAWN; SHE
laid in bed as the sun crept over the horizon. Beams cast against
the mirror shot threads of light all over the room in a dazzling
display. Worship Day, or Rest Day for the undevout, was her
one day off, and she intended to enjoy it. Her one goal for the
day: de-stress from the rough work week.

After sending a quick prayer to The Harvester, the faerie
god of death, journeys, and the unknown, Farzana dragged
herself out of bed and snuck down to the family room. Enzi
slept in on Worship Day, preferring to get as much rest as possible, and while Farzana usually did the same, that day she felt
like reading a book. Fiction was her escape from the mundane,
and in this case, the all too real stressors in her life.

Snagging a book from the shelf by the mirror, she made her
way back to bed, snuggling under the covers and propping an
extra pillow beneath her head. As the day passed, she read of
daring adventures on a desolate island, following pirates as they
plundered and fought their way to control their own destiny.

What she would give to be in control of her life…

By the time Farzana realized she hadn't eaten all day, she
found Enzi busy in the kitchen, cooking up an extravagant

dinner of fried dragon wings, baked cheese, and flatbread. The aroma of fresh bread lingered in the room, bringing to mind the delightful lunch Farzana had shared with Ettares the day before.

Full from dinner, Farzana sank into a piping hot bubble bath, lathering her curls with her best shampoo and allowing them to soak in the bath water. Pruny fingers flipped the last pages of her book, and after she closed the back cover, she collapsed into bed for a dreamless sleep.

Chirps woke her the next morning and she stretched, greeting the day with a smile. Her curls were soft as silk after her soak, and she used a hefty amount of curl lotion on them, pulling the moisturizer from root to end and scrunching up each curl to help define it.

She shook her head, enjoying the feeling of her tumultuous ringlets cascading down her back and hugging her head. Though they meant a lot of upkeep, she was forever grateful for her full head of curls for vanity's sake; they were absolutely gorgeous when she treated them well. And they were another trait she had inherited from her mother. She couldn't imagine having the limp, straight hair of her father.

She pulled on one of many identical shirt and skirt combinations, found her flats, and headed downstairs for breakfast.

Enzi stood at the counter mixing up some sweet cream. "Morning," he said, his voice still rough from sleep.

"Morning!" Farzana sat on a stool at the counter, watching him finish his task.

He spooned a dollop of cream into a bowl of fresh berries and slid the bowl over to her.

"You know how to make me happy," she said with a grin, grabbing a spoon and digging in. The sweet and sour taste of the berries mixed with the decadence of the cream lifted her spirits even more; she savored every bite before rinsing her bowl, giving Enzi a one-armed hug, and heading to work.

A waterhorse trolley passed as she shut the door, and she took a running leap to catch it. Her usual five-minute walk became a two-minute ride with a hop off at the end of the street.

After receiving several gawks and stares from the various

conglomeration of faeries by her building, she realized she had forgotten her coat, her purple wings on full display. A sense of panic gripped her limbs, and a violent shudder passed through her.

I'm okay. I'm safe. I'm okay. I'm safe.

The mantra worked to slowly drain the anxiety from her until she could breathe easier. No one was acting hostile. She could deal with some curious looks. Lifting her chin, she strode to the lifts with fake confidence. The doors were already opened, waiting for her, and a couple common-fae pixies and one elf got into the lift with her. Someone asked for her floor; with a shaky smile of gratitude, she told him floor six.

Ettares and Tathi were laughing together in her cubicle when she arrived; Farzana dropped her bag on the desk and perched on her chair.

"What's so funny?"

"Ettares had a little fall yesterday getting out of the bath. She has a bruise the shape of a soap bar on her ass now!" Tathi chortled as Ettares blushed.

"I had a bath last night too, though I didn't have any mishaps."

"Must have been nice," Ettares mumbled, her high cheekbones bright red.

"Farzana, when are you going to come out with me and Enka? I wish I had pictures of him. I always seem to forget to take any," Tathi mused, opening her pocket mirror and swiping the screen.

Ettares tapped her chin with chagrin. "About that…you probably shouldn't be seeing him anymore."

"Why…?" Tathi asked, drawing the word into several syllables.

"Turns out he has a wife and kid in another kingdom."

"What kingdom?"

"Ostrana."

"What's his wife's name?"

"Lhara."

Tathi sighed. "Damn. I really thought he was a good one."

"A good lay, you mean," Farzana pointed out, "and you were right about that."

Tathi had a dreamy smile. "Yeah, I was. I'll always have that memory. Too bad I can't experience it again. I'm not a home wrecker."

"And that'll be one thousand and fifty dradens," Ettares said.

Tathi and Farzana exchanged a look before bursting into laughter.

"One thousand! Ah! And fifty! Dradens!" Tathi had tears in her eyes. "Oh gods, Ettares, you are one funny pixie."

Farzana was laughing so hard she couldn't breathe. 1050 dradens? They didn't make that much in a week.

Ettares's face was a deep red, darker than any blush Farzana had ever seen. "I know, right? I'm so glad I could bring you all some merriment."

"This is why we keep you around." Tathi gave her shoulder a playful punch. "Who knew nobles were fun-loving folk like us lowbrow faeries?"

"Knock, knock," came a quiet voice from the doorway. Araj stood there, hands in his pockets and a forlorn look on his face.

The atmosphere in the cubicle turned icy as all three fem-fae grew quiet. After a long moment, Tathi squeezed Farzana's shoulder.

"I'm fine," Farzana said, and Tathi and Ettares left.

"Hey, Farzana," Araj said in a soft voice.

She turned her back on him, facing the window, and stared out at the new Center. It was seven floors tall, and she could stare straight across at the new construction, large enough now that she no longer had to look down to spot it.

"I just want to talk," he said, stepping into the cubicle, closer to her.

She shifted in her seat, discomfort cramping her back. She imagined his breath touching her neck and shivered.

"I'm worried for you."

I'm worried about you.

Farzana looked down at the street level construction, noticing several imps carrying what was probably a support beam. One of the imps tripped and fell, and the rest of them continued toward the building, stepping over and around the fallen one.

"I saw in the logs that you went home early one day? And then one day you took a two-hour lunch."

The fallen imp got to their feet and ran after the others, catching up right as they entered the building. The pixie guarding the door shoved the lone imp and pointed for them to go back to the end of the construction site.

"You're not going to get paid if you aren't working, Farzana. I know how much your family relies on your income."

The imp turned dejectedly and headed away, shoulders hunched over.

"Please talk to me."

Farzana whirled around in her seat, glaring daggers at him, fangs bared. "What should we talk about, hm? Should we chat about how you assaulted me? Or how I'm going to be stuck living in Erasto's new Center? What about me losing my job?"

He cringed, face growing paler with every word she spat at him. "I didn't know."

"You didn't know that you assaulted me?"

He frowned. "No, that's not what I meant. I know what I did."

"Great," she said, spinning back to the window.

"I'm not proud of it," he continued, not taking the hint.

"Good! Finally some sense."

"Farzana, please. I'm trying to apologize here. Look at me."

She shook her head, curls tumbling and wings quivering in anger. "Apologize then."

He stepped up beside the desk, looking down at her. "I messed up. I messed up bad and I know you don't need to forgive me, but I will do anything to make it up to you." He ran his hands through his hair, making it stand on end.

He sounded so sincere; his words tugged at her heart. She wanted to believe him. She wanted to forgive him. She wanted to embrace him and tell him everything was okay and then leave work together early to spend the day together, as friends. As best friends.

But what he did was unforgivable, wasn't it? What kind of pushover would she be to just say everything was okay?

She stared at him, emotions warring. "I don't know what to say. Please leave me alone."

"I'm not leaving. I need to know our relationship will be okay. Don't throw away five decades of friendship, Farzana. I was there when no one else was, and I'll always be there for you. You know that."

"I don't know what to say," she repeated, fingers tangling in her curls in frustration. "I can't think!"

Tathi knocked on the doorway. "Everything okay in here, darling?"

"Go away, Tathi. This is private," Araj growled.

"Go sit on a stick," she said in a prim voice. "I asked Farzana, not you."

"I don't know!" Farzana wailed.

"You need to leave," Tathi said to Araj, hands on her hips.

"I'm not leaving until Farzana says everything is okay," he repeated, crossing his arms over his chest. "Farzana?"

This was too much; Farzana's head felt fuzzy, and she desperately needed to scream, to let out her pent-up frustration. The walls were closing in on her and her own organs suffocated her.

Araj was an arrogant prick who didn't deserve her forgiveness or friendship. He had made that clear. He deserved to be thrown to the wind.

But he had apologized, right? He had said sorry, though not for hurting her. He actually hadn't even acknowledged her feelings at all.

Everyone made mistakes. Were some mistakes unforgivable? Didn't she have any self-respect? And what about the bond of a 50-year friendship? He had been with her through thick and thin, through everything. He was her rock, her foundation, her steadfast companion.

But trust, the very foundation of any relationship, had been broken.

Through a haze, she realized Tathi and Araj were arguing,

yelling in each other's faces. It was a testament to Tathi's self-control that she hadn't enchanted him into hitting himself or something worse.

"Shut up!" Farzana screeched, covering her eyes and letting out a sob. Silence descended, and she peeked out from between her fingers to see them both looking at her with concern.

"I can't take this," she said, grabbing her bag and brushing past them both.

Another shit day, another excuse to leave early. It wasn't like the company needed her anyway.

10

ETTARES, GARBED IN A TAILORED BLACK VEL-
vet suit, sat on the ground in Farzana's cubicle the next day, her
long legs sprawled out in front of her and her hands behind
her head. She waved at Farzana as she entered, a smile gracing
her full lips.

"You know, it's almost like you're stalking me," Farzana
joked, sitting in her chair.

Ettares laughed. "I like you, that's all. But if you would prefer to be alone, I can respect that. Tathi told me what happened
yesterday. Maybe I shouldn't have come," she finished in a rush.

"No! No, I'm happy you're here." Farzana's face heated at
the confession.

Ettares brightened. "How are you feeling? Is everything
going to be okay between you and Araj?"

Farzana wrinkled her nose at the question, trying not to
cry. "He's being difficult right now. He's usually a great friend,
but right now, it's hard to be around him."

Ettares nodded. "I know the feeling."

"Why does he hate you?" Farzana blurted out.

Ettares pursed her lips and stared straight ahead at the wall.
"I'm not sure that's something we should talk about. Let's just

say we had polarizing opinions on something."

Farzana snorted. "He can be very opinionated, so I get it. We once had a fight over which pasta base is best: tomato or cream. He didn't talk to me for a week."

Ettares eyes sparkled with humor. "Which one did you say?"

"Cream, obviously!"

"It's the only correct answer," Ettares agreed.

"See, you get it." Farzana laughed, light-hearted. Spending time with Ettares felt so carefree, so easy. So right.

"Question," Ettares said, sitting up and leaning toward her; Farzana could see her reflection in those crystal clear blue eyes.

"What?"

"Do you want to watch a movie together tonight?"

Farzana was speechless. Was this a date? Was Ettares really asking her to go to a movie with her? Her heartbeat thundered through her body, all the way down to her fingertips.

"I would love to," Farzana said in a hurry, before anxiety changed her answer. "What movie?"

"Well, I know you don't like being out in public, so I figured we could watch something at one of our houses."

Ah, so it wasn't a date. Or maybe it was?

"You can come over to my place. I mean, it's probably tiny compared to your house, but Enzi is a great cook, and he can probably whip up some yummy snacks for us."

Her face lit up. "Sounds great! I would be honored to try your brother's cooking."

"I guess this means I need to tell him about you," Farzana said, realizing she had yet to tell him that she not only knew but semi-regularly hung out with a noble.

Ettares raised a delicate eyebrow. "He doesn't know about me?"

Farzana blushed as she shook her head. "In all the excitement, I forgot to mention you."

"That's understandable. You've had some pretty intense stuff happen over the last week. I was just the bearer of bad news."

"The gorgeous messenger," Farzana said, then bit her tongue in embarrassment.

Had she really said that out loud?

A wicked grin crossed Ettares's mouth. "I'm gorgeous? I'll take it. You're pretty gorgeous yourself, Farzana." Winking one large eye, she stood, brushing off her suit.

"I should get to work," Farzana mumbled.

"And I should leave to help facilitate that," Ettares said.

"Oh! My address." Farzana rattled off her house number and street name, not daring to look Ettares in the eye.

"See you tonight," Ettares said, giving her a jaunty salute and exiting the cubicle.

"Tonight," Farzana whispered to the empty air.

~ ☼ ~

"Wait, you know a noble?" Enzi sputtered, leaning against the kitchen counter.

"Yeah. She's…oh gods, she's so pretty. And nice, and funny, and charming, and—"

"And perfect, I get it," Enzi laughed. "Why haven't you been gushing about her before now?"

Farzana shrugged. "With all the shit that's been going on, I guess I forgot about the one good thing."

"Well, I am happy to make you some delicious appetizers to snack on during the movie," he said, grabbing his apron and flinging the strap over his head.

"Thanks, Enz."

"Now get out of here so I can cook!"

Humming to herself, she went up to her room to change. What to wear! She still wasn't sure if this was a date or not. Did Ettares see her as a friend or something more? For that matter, did Farzana see Ettares as more than a friend?

Ettares was absolutely stunning, that was for sure. And like Enzi said, she was kind of perfect. But Farzana had never been in a relationship before. Were the sprites fluttering in her stomach supposed to mean that she liked her? Ettares's smile lit up her world and her laughter always made her happy. What did that mean?

Farzana grabbed her one good dress and pulled it on, zipping up the side. She turned to study her reflection in the mirror.

It was a deep plum color, just a shade off from her wings. The top was embroidered with golden thread in the shape of flowers and leaves; the skirt, which fell to her ankles, grew sheer past her thighs. It was loose and flowy and gorgeous, and she had never had a reason to wear it before.

It was perfect for her first maybe date.

Ettares arrived at exactly seven o'clock, right as the sun began to set.

"Come in!" Farzana said, breathless from excitement.

Ettares stepped inside, and Farzana looked around as if for the first time, taking in the oak coat rack in the corner, the kitchen with the bar counter—currently covered in various dishes of food—and stools, the door to the linen closet, the entrance to the family room, and the staircase just out of sight.

"You've got a nice place," Ettares said. "I expected Enzi to be hard at work in the kitchen, but it looks like he's already done?"

"He finished a bit ago and said he'll be tucked away in his room all night. And he hopes we have a lovely evening and enjoy the appetizers."

"What a sweet brother," she said, removing her velvet suit jacket. "I wish I had a sibling."

"I mean, don't you? Aren't all nobles your siblings?"

Ettares ran a hand through her curls and laughed. "I suppose technically they are my siblings, since the king was our father. But we all had different mothers, and the king gave each of his lovers their own house, so none of us grew up together. It was incredibly lonely."

Farzana was aghast. "I had no clue. I always assumed being a noble was the life. You're rich, you're the king's child, you want for nothing. As a bastard low-level aristo-fae, I envied you all."

"All nobles are bastards in the king's eyes," Ettares pointed out.

"I never thought of it like that." How wild for Farzana to think that, aside from the money, they had probably had similar experiences growing up.

"So, movie time? This is all getting very deep," Ettares said with a sheepish grin.

"Of course! I'm sorry. Let's just grab the food first," Farzana said, heading for the counter. She picked up a dish of bacon wrapped figs and the cheese and crackers platter. "Grab the baby quiche and the fiery dragon wings?"

Ettares obliged and followed Farzana into the family room, where Enzi had also placed a tablecloth over the coffee table, along with wine glasses and a bottle of sweet white wine.

"How fancy," Ettares said, placing her plates down and sitting on the couch. She looked up at Farzana with a smile.

"Um, so what do you want to watch?" Farzana asked, grabbing the remote and sitting beside Ettares. She wasn't sure how close to sit, so she opted for far enough for their legs not to touch. Switching the mirror on, she looked over at Ettares expectantly.

"Do you like scary movies?" Ettares asked, her bright red wings wiggling in excitement.

Farzana gulped. Scary movies were…well, terrifying. And she didn't much like being scared, even willingly. But she wanted to be pushed out of her comfort zone; she wanted to be the type of person who embraced newness and spontaneity. First lunch in public with Ettares, and now a maybe date with a scary movie.

Farzana clicked through the menu to the horror section. "Sure! Are there any you particularly like and want to watch again?"

Ettares watched as she scrolled through the list before letting out a gasp. "*Dragon's Breath*! Oh, gods, that's such a good movie. You have to see it."

Farzana felt a twinge in her stomach, partly from Ettares's contagious excitement and partly from the idea of watching a movie about giant, fire-breathing dragons, but she gave Ettares her best 'I'm game' face and selected the movie.

Ettares reached over to grab a bacon wrapped fig and popped it into her mouth. Letting out a low moan, which gave Farzana the shivers, she said, "Oh, gods, this is so good! Enzi is a wonderful chef."

"I'll be sure to tell him," Farzana said, nibbling on a cracker and settling back into the couch as the opening credits began to roll.

The movie was absolutely horrifying, and yet, mesmerizing in its own way. The graphics for the giant dragons did make them look real, and Farzana shuddered to think what life would be like if dragons were as big as buildings rather than the annoying little beasts who defecated on sidewalks.

She winced, she gasped, she hid behind her hands at the horror and gore. The body count grew and grew as the movie went on; at one point, a dragon tore an elf in half with its claws before trampling the corpse. Memories of being beneath the horde of rioters slammed into her, and her vision swam, dark spots floating in her field of view.

Ettares let out a giggle as the blood spurted from the two halves of the elf, and Farzana turned to stare at her, mortified.

"What? The rendering is so bad, you can see where he's still breathing; it's hilarious."

Wide-eyed with disbelief, Farzana turned back to the movie only to squeak as the dragon breathed fire at the main character; without thinking, she buried her face in Ettares's arm. In one smooth move, Ettares lifted her arm, placed it around Farzana's shoulders, and pulled her close to her side.

Farzana's pulse roared in her ears as she snuggled closer, hiding her eyes behind her hand and breathing in the sweet and calming scent of freesia. The dragon reared and screeched at the night sky, and she shut her eyes tight. All that did, though, was allow the memories of the riot to flow through her, and her body grew rigid as fear took over.

I'm safe. I'm safe.

The chanting of the rioters swelled in her ears, overlaying

the roar of the dragon. The anger of the crowd coursed through her, paralyzing her. She lay still, silent, locked in the prison of her mind.

I'm safe. I'm safe.

She repeated the mantra, blocking out the sounds of death and terror coming from the screen, and before long, she lost her hold of consciousness. The next thing she knew, she was being held in a gentle embrace, carried in strong arms. A whispered question and then Ettares took her upstairs and into her bedroom. Ettares placed Farzana on her bed and drew the covers up to her chin.

Farzana couldn't keep her eyes open, firmly in exhaustion's grasp. She must have imagined the tender kiss on her forehead and the husky voice whispering goodnight; she must have imagined it, because it was a dream come true.

11

FARZANA DIDN'T SEE ETTARES FOR A WEEK.
Each day since the maybe date was a monotonous cycle: get up, go to work, gossip with Tathi, eat lunch, watch the construction site, go home, hide in her room, read a book, go to sleep.

Rinse and repeat.

Araj had permanently left the Fae Resource Manipulation and Distribution Center for his new job on the construction of the High Management Center. Farzana mourned the loss of her friend but not so much him as a person, moreso the friend she once had: the supportive best friend who would never hurt her, never abandon her. The faerie she had met 50 years back, who had latched onto her like a lifeline though it was her who had been drowning. But every time she stepped into the lift, she couldn't help staring at the spot where their trust had been broken, where their friendship shattered.

She was grateful Araj was gone.

The High Management Center stood over 15 floors tall and every day, she wondered if it would ever stop growing. In a mere two and a half weeks, this behemoth had sprouted. It already overshadowed every building in The City, casting a gloom over the downtown area. Casting darkness on her future.

What would it be like, locked away in that tower?

She missed Ettares. Even though she had only been in Farzana's life for a short while, remembering that week of time together never failed to lift Farzana's spirits. Those luxurious outfits were inspirationally beautiful, and Ettares's gorgeous smile banished negativity.

And she hated it, but she did miss Araj. He had been horrible but mingled with the memory of the assault were the countless good memories. That time he brought her favorite snack to her when she was sick in bed. That time he spent all day with her, painting her room lavender, laughing when she got paint on her nose. That time he taught her how to use the teleportation pad at the FRMDC and they ended up in some random faerie's house. He truly had been a best friend for those five decades; she couldn't fathom why he would throw that away for one kiss.

She hoped it had been worth it for him.

At least Farzana still had Tathi, despite the impending termination of employment. Would Tathi come visit her in the new Center? They rarely spent time together outside of work; though they were close enough that Farzana felt she could tell her anything, she was what most faeries would affectionately call a work friend.

Which brought her back to her fount of self-pity: with her friendship with Araj lying in ruins, who would be by her side at the new Center? She knew Enzi would visit her, but that was another uncomfortable thing to think about; she had never lived apart from Enzi and her mother. What would it be like to live alone? Well, as alone as she could be, considering she would be living with Erasto.

The thought sent a chill down her spine. She would really have to live with that monster.

Soon.

~ ☼ ~

Farzana walked to work in dappled sunlight, dragons chirping overhead. She had just missed the latest waterhorse trolley and so had to make the trek on foot. She didn't lament it; it was a beautiful day. The crisp air was just short of being chilly, and she enjoyed the breeze. Her winter coat meant most days, she was stifling. The riots had died out as faeries resigned themselves to their new leader, so she no longer needed to fear an attack, but nevertheless, the coat stayed. For once, she was grateful to be outdoors and breathing in the fresh air.

Tathi was in Farzana's cubicle when she got there, resting her hip on the desk.

"Hey, Tathi," Farzana said, rubbing her temple as a runic headache began to bloom.

"We need to talk."

"Okay…" Farzana looked at her, wary.

"This can't keep going on," she said, gesturing around the cubicle.

"What are you talking about?"

"This! You! Every day, you come here, and you sit and stare out the window, Farzana. You aren't doing any of the work that's assigned to you. I know because it keeps getting rerouted to me. And that's okay! I don't mind! But, darling, why are you even here?"

Farzana's lower lip trembled. It was true; she had done barely any work since the news about her future had been delivered. At first, the excuse had been Ettares; she was always hovering in her cubicle, chatting away and distracting her. But Ettares hadn't been there in days.

"Tomorrow is Rest Day. Now is your chance to go up to Megami, tell her how you really feel, and then never come back. What's keeping you here?"

"I guess…I've been hoping Ettares would visit me. And I don't know, I thought… It's stupid."

"You thought you two would date," Tathi finished for her.

Farzana nodded. "But she's drop-dead gorgeous and rich and funny and charming, and I'm…I'm just me. So I don't know why I thought that would happen."

Tathi patted her back. "Darling, what happens, happens. I

mean, I hooked up with a married elf. You're not doing worse than me. And, plus, Ettares would be lucky to date you. You're adorable and caring. And I for one find you hilarious."

Farzana smiled in gratitude. "I thought, after the movie, that something would happen. She kissed my forehead. I know she did."

"Well maybe it was a goodbye kiss. Like, a permanent one."

"Yeah, I guess so," she mumbled, her chest heavy.

"Anyway, my point is that there is nothing keeping you here. You have to go! Be free! Enjoy life before you're locked away! Which could be, like, any day now, because that damn thing has to be near finished at this point." She turned to look at it and whistled. "It's so damn tall."

Farzana sent a quick prayer to The Harvester for guidance. A feeling of peace flooded her, and she knew what she had to do.

"Okay. I'm going to do it."

"Do what?"

"I'm going to tell off Megami."

A wicked grin spread across Tathi's face. "That's my darling," she said, clapping her hands before pulling Farzana into a hug. She smacked her lips against her cheek and pulled away.

"I'll miss you," Farzana said in a quiet voice.

Tathi waved her hand. "Nah, you'll be fine. You'll make new friends. None as cool as me, but pretty close." She winked.

"Bye, Tathi."

"Bye, darling."

Farzana left her cubicle for the last time and headed for Megami's office. A fire had been lit under her feet, and she strode there with a purpose, with confidence. She walloped on the office door before yanking it open.

Megami sat at her desk, talking into her pocket mirror. A look of annoyance crossed her face and she hissed, "I'll call you back," before shutting the mirror.

"I have something to say," Farzana said, breathing heavily.

Megami arched a thin brow and waited, folding her hands on the desk.

"You are awful," Farzana said with fervor. "Yes, you are the first ever fem-fae Manager and that should warrant some respect on my part, but you don't deserve it."

Megami pressed her lips together in a hard line.

"You've never given lower management a raise. I have worked 50 hours every single week for the last 50 years with no damn raise. You enforce outdated, gender specific dress codes. Dress suits? Seriously? What is this, the archaic age? Fem-fae aren't here to look pretty. We are here to work."

Megami rolled her eyes.

"You think you're so much better than me because you're from the House of Silver, but guess what? My father is your boss." The words felt rotten in her mouth, but she was committed to her rant. "You are not above me, Megami. You have always treated me like shit because I was a bastard. Well, I'm not now! You can sit on a stick for all I care."

Megami's eyes bulged, her face turning puce.

"Oh, and I quit. Have a great day."

With that, Farzana left the office, slamming the door behind her, and headed for the lift.

Farzana woke to the sound of rain drumming on the rooftop; the arrhythmic pitter-patter traipsed through her dreamscape, reminding her of the night Erasto came back into her life, and she jolted awake, her breathing erratic. After some breathing exercises to calm herself, she stretched out on her bed and contemplated what she would do with her life.

She was free. Freed from the shackles of her job, freed from a toxic relationship with Araj, and for the moment, free of her father's influence. And it was Worship Day. A day to reflect and be grateful for her life.

Lying on her back, she shut her eyes and meditated on The Harvester. Being the god of journeys and change, they had always fascinated her. She had often fantasized about the androgynous god taking hold of her life and altering its course, steering her toward something good, something better. She liked to think her decision to quit her job early was due to their influence, and she thanked them for it.

Hopping out of bed, she hummed to herself and fluffed her curls in the mirror. She smiled, showing off her tiny fangs. *I'm adorable.*

Still humming, she flounced out of her room and down the stairs. Enzi stood in the kitchen making pancakes, and she plopped down onto a stool to watch him.

He gave her side eye as he flipped a pancake. "Morning, sis. What's up?"

"Morning! Nothing is up. Why do you ask?"

"You're up early, and you're cheerful. Something must have happened." He gasped. "Did Ettares ask you out again?"

Her smile faded, and she grumped, "No, actually."

"Oh. Sorry. Well, what is it?"

"You're up early too; I don't see why you're making a big deal out of me being up already. And I was happy until I remembered that Ettares has disappeared from my life. I really thought something would happen between us."

"Why don't you call her?" he asked, flipping a pancake onto the stack on a nearby plate.

"I didn't program her into my pocket mirror, which is still cracked. Anyway, we never discussed it."

"Maybe these will cheer you up," he said, sliding a plate over to her.

The pancakes were dressed with slices of fresh fruit, a drizzle of berry compote, and a dollop of sweet cream. Her stomach growled. "Enzi, you are such a good cook," she said, digging in.

"You're lucky to have me," he teased, making up another plate. "Morning, Mother!"

Farzana twisted around to see Sitra walk into the kitchen, clutching her robe around her waist and blinking sleepy eyes.

"Morning, baby. Farzana, you're up early."

"Oh gods, fine, the rain woke me! That's why I'm up early," Farzana huffed.

Enzi smirked as he slid a plate over to Sitra, but she shook her head at the offering.

"I knew it was something silly like that," he said, taking it back and grabbing a fork for himself.

After Enzi and Farzana ate—and Sitra took two sips of coffee—they all moved to the family room, piling onto the couch. Enzi turned on the mirror, and they all jumped as Erasto's face appeared on the screen.

"—High Management Center is near completion, I wanted to address the public usage of the space in the building. The bottom half of the building will be what humans call a 'mall,' a collection of shops all enclosed in one common building. Faeries can come to one central location to do all of their shopping." He paused to smile. "I'm confident this will catch on here on Faerth, and I am excited Dradour will be home to the first Faerthian mall."

Enzi and Farzana exchanged a look before turning their attention back to the screen.

"This mall will need stores. Therefore, I am opening up for applications from businesses who wish to be in the first mall on Faerth. Submit applications to the royal palace for consideration. Thank you, and have a wonderful Rest and Worship Day."

The broadcast ended and the cooking channel resumed, a chef looking flustered as he stirred a pot which had boiled over.

Sitra stroked her curls, looking deep in thought. "That's certainly an interesting idea. What do you think of me opening a gallery there? It would be nice to have a place to showcase and sell my art finally." She turned to Farzana with a bright smile.

Farzana tried not to grimace at the thought of her mother bringing business to Erasto's new Center, but having her mother there, being able to see her every day, would be fantastic.

Enzi nudged Farzana and gave her a panicked look, clearing his throat. "Tell her," he mouthed.

Farzana sighed. It was time.

Turning to her mother, she took Sitra's hands into her own and looked into those beautiful and eternally sad amber eyes.

"Mother, I need to tell you something. And I don't want you to get upset."

Sitra blinked once and nodded. "Okay," she said in a shaky voice.

"Promise me?"

She gave a weak smile. "Of course, baby."

"Erasto is forcing me to move into his Center. He's claiming parental time with law 18. You'll be compensated, of course, but I won't be living here anymore. If you want to open up a gallery, I think that would be wonderful, because then I can visit you every day without leaving The Center."

Sitra's eyes welled up with tears, and she pulled her hands away. "You what? You have to go live-live-live with that-that... monster?! Oh, gods," she choked, standing and holding herself.

Farzana reached for her, but Sitra pulled away.

"I'm sorry," she whispered and fled to her room, slamming the door shut. A moment later, Farzana heard a thud and a muffled sob as Sitra slid down the other side of the door.

"Damn it," Farzana said, her voice rough as she fought back tears. Seeing her mother spiral was always hard on her emotionally. There was nothing she could do to make it better; she could only watch and wait as Sitra tortured herself, growing more gaunt day by day from starvation. Her mother was not well, but on her bad days, she was more ghost than faerie.

"It was the right thing to do," Enzi said, rubbing her shoulder. "She had to know."

"She's never going to come out."

"She'll come out eventually."

"Yeah, after I leave," Farzana said, low enough so their mother wouldn't hear.

"Rude," he said, turning up the volume to drown out Sitra's cries and give her the illusion of privacy.

Numb, Farzana turned her attention to the mirror and tried to engross herself in the technique of blanching vegetables. After a couple minutes of staring at the screen without absorbing any of it, she sighed and stood to leave.

"Where are you going? Do you want to watch something else?"

"No. I'm going to go lie down. Maybe meditate. I'm not feeling social right now."

He gave her a look of sympathy and moved his long legs so she could move past.

Hopefully a nap would help clear her melancholy misery. She didn't want the first day of the rest of her freedom to be tainted by this awful feeling in her chest.

12

FARZANA FOUND HERSELF HIDING AWAY IN her room despite her new freedom. Enzi came and went, to and from work and occasionally leaving to socialize with friends, all while Farzana and Sitra hid in their respective rooms, hardly daring to move.

The sound of her breathing was too loud in the silence of the house, a raucous noise rattling around in the pit of her depression. She tried to take shallow breaths, tried to hold it for as long as possible, but time and time again, she failed.

A resounding knock on the front door made her gasp, releasing her pent-up breath. She dragged herself out from under the covers, glancing at the mirror to check that she still looked as horrific as she had last time she got out of bed, and trudged downstairs. She opened the door after a second knock and immediately regretted leaving her room. The most beautiful pixie in the world was standing on her doorstep in a vermillion floor length sundress, her perfectly coiffed curls resting atop her head and her ice blue eyes looking Farzana up and down.

"Someone has been having a bit of a nap, I see," Ettares said in that husky voice of hers.

Farzana nodded, not daring to speak.

"May I come in?"

Why would she want to come in? Had she not noticed the state of Farzana's hair and attire? She was wearing a shabby bathrobe, a hole in the sleeve. Her hair was its own entity at that point, not unlike some chaotic horror out of a movie. How had she not scared her off?

Farzana opened the door wider, stepping to the side. "Of course," she said, her voice hoarse from disuse.

"Can I tempt you with a trip out?" Ettares asked as Farzana shut the door.

"Out?"

"There's a lovely open-air market that you must experience, and I figure I owe you a meal at a nice restaurant since the last time I took you out was to a hole-in-the-wall cafe."

Farzana couldn't believe her ears. Ettares wanted to take her out? Again? "I haven't seen you in over a week," Farzana blurted out.

Ettares grimaced. "I'm sorry about that. I had to travel out of the country unexpectedly for a job."

"Oh." Farzana rubbed her nose and blinked up at her. "Um, yes! I would love to go out. Let me change," she said in a hurry as Ettares continued to look at her.

"Wear that pretty dress from our movie night," Ettares called out as Farzana ran out of the room and up the stairs.

This is really happening! Be still my heart.

Thankfully she had laundered the dress after that night, removing the smear of sauce from the dragon wing she had dropped in her lap; it was freshly pressed, waiting to be worn. She pulled it on and did a little twirl, enjoying the sensation of soft silk against her bare legs. She slipped on her flats and turned to face herself in the mirror, only to be reminded of the abominable state of her hair.

She could have cried; it was so awful. Her hair had never been so mistreated! Coils sprung in every direction, and a large portion of it matted down. Gritting her teeth, she grabbed her comb and began beating her hair into submission. When it was orderly enough to fit beneath a scarf, she picked out a light green one, deciding she liked the combination of green and purple. It reminded her of spring, her favorite season.

Satisfied with her appearance, she skipped down the stairs and rejoined Ettares in the foyer. Farzana bubbled with excitement.

"I'm ready!"

Ettares beamed at her. "You're gorgeous."

Farzana's face heated to an inferno, and she looked away.

"Oh, please. I'm barely passable," she said, getting the door.

"You're gorgeous. And you shouldn't argue when someone compliments you."

"I'll remember that for next time," Farzana said with a light laugh. The laughter came to her naturally in Ettares's presence though merriment had been absent for days.

Ettares held out her hand. "Would I be remiss in thinking you would like to hold my hand?"

Trying to contain her glee, Farzana took it into her own; she had a hard time keeping her breathing even at the sensual contact.

"Let's be off!" Ettares said, swinging their arms between them as they walked.

At the open-air market, Ettares had her try so many things, she couldn't keep track of all the new experiences. Tiny thimbles of strong, dark coffee. Slices of fresh baked bread, butter running down their chins. A berry so sour, Farzana howled in pain and laughter. Mint jelly that made her lips go numb. Shortbread that melted in her mouth.

Through it all, Ettares held her hand, their fingers intertwined. Every now and then, Ettares would rub her thumb with hers, and each time it sent a shiver down Farzana's spine and brought a smile to her lips.

They reached the restaurant, The Red Door, and were seated immediately; the server led them out on the floor and to a table set directly below a crystal chandelier, which shot beams of colored light in every direction. Ettares pulled out a chair for her, guiding her with a hand at the small of her back. Her hand caressed the top of Farzana's head before she crossed to her own seat.

"How have you been?" she asked, cupping her chin in her hands.

Farzana cleared her throat, feeling self-conscious. "Not great."

"Did something happen? I mean, other than all the stuff you've already had to deal with, of course."

"I told my mother the news, finally, and she didn't take it well."

"Understandable."

"Yeah, but when my mother gets depressed, she goes into this spiral where she doesn't leave her room or even get out of bed for days, weeks. She just starves, wastes away. And this time, it's because of me." Farzana choked on a silent sob of guilt. "I'm...I'm not doing well." She swiped at a tear and tried to laugh. She couldn't believe she was crying at this romantic restaurant, in front of Ettares of all faeries.

I'm pathetic.

Though there was concern on Ettares's face, there wasn't a hint of disappointment or disgust. "I'm so sorry. I wish I could help," she murmured.

Farzana gave her a watery smile. "You are helping! I'm having a wonderful time. And I'm out of my house! It's a miracle."

She leaned forward, tone earnest. "I'm here for you, Farzana. Anytime you need me, whenever you want to talk, I'm only a mirror call away."

"I don't have your mirror connection," Farzana said, dabbing her eyes with her napkin.

"Oh! Silly me," she said with a self-deprecating smile. She held out her pocket mirror and Farzana reached for it, fingers brushing hers, before she remembered her own mirror was broken.

"I'll program my connection into your home mirror then," Ettares said when she told her. "Now that that's settled, let's order!" She flashed Farzana a fanged grin and signaled to the server to come over.

Farzana rested her head in her palm as Ettares talked to the pixie, who fawned over her and informed her that the chef would be making them a special four course meal to honor her presence. Marveling at how different their lives were, Farzana wondered what it was like to be not only recognized but adored wherever she went. With her wings on full display, she had received several glares during their jaunt through the market. But Ettares took it all in stride, never coming across as arrogant or conceited. She was so down-to-Faerth. What had Farzana done to deserve her attention?

"Hey," Ettares said, catching her wandering attention, "would you like to come to my place tomorrow? Get out of the house again for a bit?"

Farzana nodded with as much enthusiasm as she could muster. "Would I? Yes, please."

"Great! It's a date."

Another date? I could get used to this.

13

ETTARES SHOWED UP THE NEXT DAY RIGHT AS
Farzana finished her breakfast. She looked marvelous in a pale
lavender suit. A pair of sparkling crystals adorned her earlobes.

"Ready to go?" she asked after stepping inside.

"Almost! I need to brush my teeth."

"I'll wait here," she said, glancing over at Enzi, who stood
in the kitchen staring at her. She gave him a little wave, and he
plastered a frantic smile on his face before turning and scrubbing furiously at a dish in the sink.

Farzana stifled a giggle at his expense and headed for her
bedroom, a bounce in her step. She still couldn't believe she
was going over to Ettares's house. A real noble house! Was everything gold plated? Did she have a heated indoor swimming
pool? An exotic, domesticated dragon? All of those things
sounded ridiculously ludicrous, but she had seen these things
in movies and often wondered if rich faeries actually spent
their money on such luxuries.

Farzana took her time brushing her teeth and fangs and
admired her smile in the mirror. Her front teeth were slightly
crooked, but she had always found the imperfection endearing.
And with her confidence levels soaring, she almost thought she

looked cute. Was this what infatuation did? Paint everything with rose gold hues and make you feel alive? If so, she was hooked; she never wanted the feeling to leave.

Blowing herself a cheeky kiss in the mirror, she flounced down the stairs. Enzi and Ettares were deep in a conversation about properly cooked steak when she reached them, and she waited for them to finish.

"I hope I look okay," she said when she had Ettares's attention, doing a twirl for her. She wore a black handkerchief skirt with a loose azure blouse, the gauzy sleeves billowing out at the shoulders and ending in tight cuffs at her wrists.

"You look lovely," Ettares said, reaching for her hand and pressing her lips to her knuckles.

Farzana's cheeks blazed with heat as she caught Enzi staring, open-mouthed.

"Why is it so hot in here?" Farzana panted, fanning herself.

Enzi chuckled. "Have fun, you two," he called as they left.

Once outside, Farzana took a deep breath to steady her overexcited nerves; the smoldering summer air did little to calm her, instead making her gasp for breath. Summer was her least favorite season, but even the excessive heat couldn't faze her with Ettares's fingers wound around hers.

"Where are we heading?" she asked, looking up at Ettares.

"We are going to catch a trolley that way," she said, pointing in the opposite direction of the FRMDC.

Farzana nodded. It made sense; all the noble houses were on the edge of The City, near the royal palace. A realization dawned on her and she stopped in her tracks, dragging Ettares to a halt beside her.

"Wait, do you live by the palace?"

"What if I said yes?"

Farzana shivered despite the heat. The mere thought of seeing Erasto paralyzed her with fear.

"He won't be there," Ettares said, reading the look on her face.

"How do you know?"

"He's out of the country."

Farzana mulled that over before resuming their walk. Why would Erasto leave?

An approaching waterhorse trolley caught her attention, and they jumped onboard as it passed. They rode in silence, watching the bustling faeries all along the street. The trolley passed a park, and Farzana pointed it out to Ettares. It looked beautiful. Strolling lanes, an engraved bench, a pond surrounded by flowers. She suddenly wished they were going to a park; she would have enjoyed the fresh air and scenery.

"Just you wait," Ettares whispered in her ear.

They hopped off the trolley and onto another one going in another direction, and Farzana watched in awe as the houses grew taller, longer, more extravagant. She hadn't been able to enjoy the trip when she had taken this exact route to visit Erasto.

"Wow," she breathed, pointing out one house that had a beautiful set of amethyst front doors with statues of dragons on either side. Even from afar, she could tell the details on the sculptures were exquisite. They almost made her find dragons beautiful.

Farzana and Ettares leapt from the trolley a few blocks down, once they could see the towering wrought iron gates of the royal palace.

"Here we are," Ettares said, gesturing to an ivory three-story house. Ivy vines grew up the sides, nearly covering the face of the building. The front door was a deep crimson; two stone planters overflowing with ferns and bright colored flowers stood on each side. A large bronze knocker in the shape of a rose was set in the center of the door.

"First impressions?" she asked, facing Farzana and holding both of her hands in her own.

"It's beautiful. Like you."

Ettares gave her hands a gentle squeeze. "Thank you! Let's get inside. I want to show you something."

Curiosity piqued, Farzana followed and gasped when they entered the house. The ceiling stretched all the way to the top of the third floor, and a double spiral staircase took up the far end of the massive foyer. She felt small, standing at the edge of a massive and intricate mosaic pattern built into the floor. Wondering what it depicted, she sidestepped, trying to take it all in.

"It looks better from up above," Ettares said, watching her. "Here, I'll show you a trick." Leaping into the air, Ettares spread her wings and hovered above Farzana.

Farzana stared at her in shock; she had never seen anyone use their wings to fly. How archaic! And yet there Ettares was, flitting around the room, and all Farzana wanted was to join her.

She spread her own wings and flapped them; they gave a weak buzz, but she couldn't get off the floor.

"It takes practice," Ettares said, landing beside her.

Farzana gave her an exasperated look, and Ettares laughed.

"Here, try jumping as high as you can. I'll catch you if you fall."

Farzana counted to three and flung herself into the air, straining her back muscles; she wobbled, but she stayed aloft.

I'm flying!

She looked down at Ettares and let out a peal of laughter. "I'm doing it!" She noticed the full design of the mosaic then: an intricate arrangement of various flowers. She recognised a rose, a peony, and a sheaf of lavender.

Ettares clapped, drawing her attention back. "You are! It's easier to hover than to fly up. Even now, I still give myself a jumping start."

"This is amazing! I can't believe I'm actually flying," Farzana squealed. She hadn't felt such a rush of adrenaline in years; her happiness could have floated her even without the use of her wings.

Her back began to tire, and she landed on uneven footing, stumbling and clutching Ettares for support.

"You did so well! You've never flown before?"

Farzana shook her head. "Not that I can remember. Maybe as a baby, before I was taught to know better."

Ettares made a face. "Dradour society is so stuck up. Flying is fun, and in other kingdoms, pixies do it all the time."

Farzana pondered that. She had never been out of Dradour, never even left The City. How odd that what was deemed acceptable in one country would be seen as bad in another.

"Hey, I have something to show you," Ettares said, holding out her hand.

Farzana took it, relishing in the intimate contact, and followed her down a hallway and into a large family room. A plush rug covered most of the dark hardwood floor, and several couches and loveseats were arranged around a fireplace with a gilded mirror above it. The entire back wall of the room was constructed of floor to ceiling windows looking out onto what looked like a large, gated garden, with hedges creating a labyrinthine effect.

"What is that?" Farzana asked, marveling in the beauty of it.

"Those are the royal gardens," Ettares said, beaming and leading her to a sliding glass door.

"Oh, gods," Farzana breathed as they stepped outside. Ettares unlatched the gate for her, and Farzana stepped onto the springy path of fragrant wood chips surrounded by flowers and greenery. So many plants—plants she knew by name, plants she had never seen before, and plants she recognized from picture books from her youth. Giant variegated leaves of foliage, small flamboyant blooms, and tiny hardy succulents clinging to the soil.

"Come with me." Ettares tugged her hand, leading her around a bend which revealed a fountain nestled in a bed of—

"Violets!" Farzana rushed over and sank to her knees. "I love violets!" The sweet, heady scent floating in the air and the softness of the petite petals both delighted her senses. She took a deep breath and let out a sigh of contentment.

"I wasn't sure if you liked them, since they're the flower of your House but it's your father's House."

Farzana trailed a finger across the delicate blossoms, inhaling the fragrance. "They've been my favorite flower since I learned the name of my House. I'm not sure knowing my father will change that."

She glanced up at the fountain towering over her. A sculpture of a merfae raised half out of the water, holding a shell to their mouth; water spouted from the other end of the shell, cascading down into the basin and covering their tail. Farzana had always wanted to meet a merfae, to learn their hand language, but Dradour wasn't a coastal country. Maybe someday she would leave and travel to other countries, meet a merfae in the flesh. Until then, the sight of the carved merfae and the sound of burbling water was enough.

"I love that the aristo-fae of your father's country are named after flowers rather than gems and metals. The House of Violets sounds so romantic."

Farzana laughed. "You have no idea how many times other kids asked me if I was from a House of 'Amethyst' growing up. Despite the fact that no such House exists, it never occurred to them that my House might be foreign. As we grew up, though…"

"Was it hard, being labeled a foreigner?"

"I'm lucky I have the same skin as the purebloods here. The purebloods in Seletian are pale. Since I got my mother's coloring, the foreigner bit wasn't really what people used against me."

Ettares nodded. "And she's from the House of Amber?"

"Yes. The lowest of the aristo-fae Houses."

They stared down at the flowers for several more moments, allowing the conversation to die off. Farzana hated reminding faeries of her low rank, but for some reason, it was always the first thing she said after introducing her mother's House. Perhaps because she had been reminded so much in her youth that her standing in aristo-fae society was so tenuous, she had a hard time not clarifying to everyone that she did, in fact, know where she stood.

"Can I show you some other flowers?" Ettares asked, giving her a hand up.

"Of course."

They backtracked to go down a different branch of the path, ending up at a giant clay planter filled with freesias.

"Freesias! Your favorite flower!" Farzana looked up to find Ettares staring at her with confusion.

"How did you know they're my favorite?" she asked in a perplexed tone.

Farzana shrugged one shoulder, feeling self-conscious. "You smell like freesias. I assumed your choice of perfume was because they're your favorite."

A smile spread across her lips though her eyes held sadness. "You're so observant."

Farzana watched as Ettares looked away, studying the pot of flowers, and wondered where the sadness came from. Was it something she had said?

They wandered through the gardens for hours, each pointing out plants that they recognized, holding hands the whole time. When Farzana mentioned that her feet were starting to hurt, Ettares led her back through the maze to her house and asked if she wanted to go home. The sad look hadn't left Ettares's eyes yet, but Farzana said yes.

Farzana rested her head on Ettares's shoulder as they rode the trolleys in silence. As they stepped up to Farzana's front door, a light mist began to rain down on them. Farzana gazed out at the many delighted faces of passing faeries as they held out their hands for the midsummer rain. She held her own hands out and felt the prickle of precipitation, looking up at the sky in wonder. A team of waterhorses tossed their manes as they passed, no doubt enjoying the sensation of water descending onto them, and a laugh of delight bubbled out of Farzana's throat.

She turned to notice Ettares staring at her, her blue eyes soft around the edges and a slight smile on her full lips. Ettares reached out to touch the tip of Farzana's nose, her finger coming away wet with rain.

"Beautiful," she said, her face close enough for them to share breath.

"What is?" Farzana whispered.

"You."

Farzana blushed harder than she ever had in her life. Face aflame, she wondered if, for the first time, the flush was visible, tinting the apples of her cheeks. Her breath caught in her throat, and she felt lightheaded.

"May I kiss you?" Ettares asked, her voice husky, her lips tantalizingly close.

Farzana shivered and nodded, shutting her eyes tight and bracing herself. A moment later, a softness caressed her lips. A warmth bloomed in her chest and spread throughout her body; her ear tips tingled, and her hands shook, and she was floating, floating away. Ettares's mouth moved against hers with an unmatched gentleness, as though they had practiced for this moment, as though their lips had been made for each other.

And Farzana knew, in her heart, that this was truly her first kiss.

Farzana sighed as Ettares pulled away, noticing the tiny drops of rain clinging to her long lashes, the laugh lines around her eyes, and the sadness still lurking within them. She wanted to banish that sadness, but she was at a loss as to how.

"Have a good night," Ettares said, turning and heading down the street.

Farzana watched those crimson wings as she faded into the distance, just a flash of red among the crowd, and wondered what was so wrong that after such a wonderful first kiss, Ettares was still sad.

14

THE SCENT OF SMOKE PERVADED FARZANA'S
dreams, chasing her, choking her. The assault had her lungs
desperate for air; she gasped, searching for a way out.

Save me!

The screams woke her.

She jolted upright and stared, bleary eyed, at her surroundings.

Smoke. Smoke everywhere.

And the incessant screaming.

"Enzi?" she yelled, choking and crawling from her bed.

The screams paused and a faint, tearful reply of, "Help me!"
came from the next room.

Out in the hallway, a line of fire trapped Enzi in his room,
though Farzana could just make out his terrified face through
the thick smoke.

What on Faerth? Is this a dream?

The flames licked the walls, consuming the wood paneling
and growing taller.

Enzi resumed screaming.

A thought flashed in her mind, and Farzana called out, "Use
your wings! Fly out!"

"What? I can't fly!" He sounded incredulous.

"You need to jump as high into the air as possible and flap your wings, hard! Put your whole back into it!"

He sobbed. "I can't fly!"

"You can! I know you can! I promise, it'll be okay!" She ran her fingers through her curls as she watched him take a step back from the fire.

Please be okay.

A roar as a window shattered below had Farzana whirling around and running to the stairs. More flames. The whole house was on fire.

New screams came from below as Sitra stumbled into the family room. "Enzi! Farzana!"

"Get out of the house, Mother!" Farzana waved wildly for her to leave. Looking crestfallen, Sitra ran through the doorway toward the front door.

"You can do this!" Farzana yelled at Enzi, giving him a thumbs up.

He looked at her with panic in his eyes before determination took over. Taking a deep breath and a running start, he leapt into the air, eyes screwed tight and hands balled into fists. And he flew.

"Yes!" Farzana cried, clapping once before wiping her stinging eyes.

Enzi stared down at her in astonishment. "I'm flying!"

"I know!"

His excited cries turned to screams as the stairs and landing began to collapse, pulling Farzana down with them. She spread her wings and hovered above the wreckage, flames leaping around her.

"Let's go!" She coughed, grabbing Enzi's hand and flying with him down to the ground floor. "Mother!"

Sitra wrapped her arms around Farzana, pulling her toward the front door. "My babies!"

Hand in hand, the three of them ran from the building and into a swarm of faeries standing outside in the night air. A water trolley arrived, and the water nymphs onboard crowded around them, carrying water wands. Pointing the wands at the inferno, the water nymphs began to mutter their spell work, and fountains spurred from the ends. Steam began to mingle with the smoke in the air, making it even more difficult for Farzana to breathe.

"Give them some room!" someone shouted, and a path cleared.

"Healers!" another faerie yelled, and a couple healers in their maroon robes came rushing over to Farzana, Enzi, and Sitra.

"Come with me," one said to Farzana in a gentle voice, separating her from her family. "You've got some burns. We'll apply some aloe and get you into a quick healing sleep. You should be fine by tomorrow."

Farzana nodded, exhaustion and pain setting in as the adrenaline faded. Keeping her eyes open was a monumental task as the healer droned on about the precautions of the healing sleep and the properties of the aloe poultice. Before she knew it, a blanket had been draped over her shoulders and she was laid down on a cot where she surrendered to sleep.

She woke with a start, disoriented. Blinking, she looked around the room, feeling lost.

Pale lavender walls and amethyst drapes on the windows. A nightstand beside her had an ornate crystal lamp which shone light on the room in a soft glow, illuminating a painting of a pond with water lilies and fronds on the left wall, set above a desk. The right wall had two doors; one was partially open and revealed an immense bathroom with a sunken tub, and the other door was shut.

A giant, gilded mirror was directly opposite her, and she could see her entire reflection staring back at her, confusion evident on her face.

Where am I?

She got to her feet—belatedly realizing someone had changed her out of her smoke infested and burnt pajamas and into a pair of comfortable sweats—and padded over to the closed door. She heard the susurrus of a conversation on the other side. Careful not to make a sound, she turned the knob and pushed the door open the tiniest bit.

It was a sitting room of some sort, with a couch and a loveseat arranged around a fireplace. Two figures stood at the end of the room, talking in hushed tones. She cracked the door open wider to see their faces and stifled a gasp when she recognized both Ettares and Erasto.

What is happening?

Was Ettares working for Erasto? Had she kidnapped Farzana? Had it all been a lie?

It all made sense, finally. Of course someone like Ettares wouldn't be interested in someone like her. Of course it was all too good to be true. Farzana was just another job, another fount of information for the bounty hunter.

Traitor!

Unable to help herself, she burst into the room, startling Ettares. "What on Faerth is going on?" Farzana yelled, stomping up to the two.

Ettares had a panicked look on her face, but Erasto smirked down at her, unbothered—and maybe pleased?—by the interruption.

"Are you working for him?" Farzana asked, working to keep her voice steady through a haze of tears. The room spun and she spread her legs wider, unwilling to reach out for help.

"It's not what you think," Ettares gasped, her blue eyes wide.

"You are. Oh gods, you're working for him. It was all a lie."

"Erasto originally hired me to get close to you, but I—"

"I knew it. I knew it was too good to be true. Why on Faerth would a noble ever be interested in someone like me?"

"That's not—"

"This was all a game to you! Play a trick on the bastard!" Farzana spat her words, using them as a weapon. She was pleased when Ettares winced.

"Farzana, please, let me explain," she pleaded with a pained expression.

Farzana cut her off with a wave of her hand. "We are done. I never want to see you again."

Crestfallen, Ettares nodded, tears falling from her eyes and dripping onto the floor. "I'm sorry," she whispered.

"Get out!"

She turned and walked out the door without another word.

Unwilling to lose her composure in front of Erasto, Farzana ran back into the bedroom, throwing herself onto the bed and screaming into the covers. Why had she allowed herself to become so enamored with someone so unattainable?

I'm so fucking gullible.

A gentle rap on the door had Farzana looking up; Erasto walked in, hands in his pockets and a smug grin on his thin lips.

"How unfortunate for you to find out this way," he said in his slimy, silky voice. "But look at it this way: you didn't lose much if it was all fake."

A red haze spread through her vision, and she glared at him, baring her fangs. "This is all your fault!" She grabbed the crystal lamp and hurled it at his head; it clipped the edge of his jaw, and he crumpled, nearly falling.

Howling obscenities, he straightened and descended on her, grabbing her by the hair and dragging her off the bed. "How dare you?" His scream lanced her mind as he released her curls to grab her by the throat.

"Screw you," she choked, clawing at his fingers in an attempt to loosen his hold. He squeezed tighter, and she saw stars at the edge of her vision before he abruptly released her; she fell to the floor in a heap. For a brief moment, she allowed herself to believe that was the end of it, until his foot connected with her side. A sharp pain blossomed on her rib cage, unfurling and spreading over her body like the fire she had only just narrowly escaped.

This is worse than the fire.

He kicked again. And again. And again, until the pain from each new assault was indistinguishable from the previous one.

"How. Dare. You!" he screamed, accentuating each word with a kick.

Farzana choked on the pain, curling into a ball to try and shield herself from his attacks. Everything hurt, and she belatedly remembered that this was the most dangerous faerie in the country. How could she have forgotten his ire, his temper? He *murdered* dozens of faeries. She must be the most thoughtless faerie on Faerth.

The attacks abated and she hiccupped, recoiling from the spasms through her ribs, and lay on the floor, stunned. She watched as he left the room, heard him speak to someone, and then three pairs of legs walked into her line of sight.

"Take her to the other room," he said, and two strong pairs of arms grasped her and hauled her to her feet.

She glanced at the faces of her captors; they were imps, pale faces betraying no emotion as they dragged her broken body out of the suite and down the hall. They tossed her into a tiny room where a bare bulb swung from the ceiling, revealing a bed, toilet, and a sink. Stumbling, her head hit the frame of the bed, and she tumbled to the floor, a bright flash of light blinding her before everything went dark.

15

FARZANA SETTLED INTO A NEW ROUTINE: SHE would wake to the sound of the lock clicking open on the door; a tray of bread and water would slide in, and then the door would shut and lock again. She would take the tray into bed with her, contemplate eating, end up throwing the tray against the wall, and go back to sleep. At some point, someone would open the door to collect the tray and discarded food, then leave her again to her solitude.

The room was windowless, giving her no way to tell whether it was day or night. This mattered little to Farzana, who slept all day, every day. There was nothing else to do; there were no books to read, no shows to watch, no mirror at all. She didn't even know what she looked like anymore, though she could guess by touching her filthy hair that she was in an awful state. Her sweats, which had appeared to be brand new upon arriving at what she assumed was the High Management Center, quickly became rank, the material thinning through constant use.

Every now and then, Farzana would receive bread, water, and also butter, and for those meals, she would force herself to eat. The stale bread stuck in her throat as she tried to swallow around a lump of despair.

She had nothing and no one to live for. The faerie of her infatuation was a fake, working for her murderous father and pretending to have feelings for her. Her best friend had assaulted her and left her for good; though he worked somewhere in The Center, he had not come to visit even once, and her captivity made it impossible to search for him should she even want to. Her house had burned down, leaving her family homeless.

She often wondered where Enzi and Sitra had gone. She hoped they were with her grandparents in the House of Amber; the house was big enough for all of them to live comfortably together.

She wondered if she would ever see them again.

Depressed beyond belief, she lay in darkness, contemplating death. What would it be like to die? She was ready to feast in the halls of the gods with her ancestors. The pain of total isolation was too much for her—ironic considering how often she used to lock herself away in her room to escape the world.

In her dreams, she found happiness. Everything was normal: she worked at the Fae Resource Manipulation and Distribution Center; Araj was her best friend; and Ettares was her lover. She dreamt of gardens, strolling through the parks, sipping dark coffee, and eating chocolates. And always, Ettares would foil Erasto's plans to kidnap Farzana. They would embrace, they would kiss…but then she blinked, and she was back in the darkness of her prison.

She wept.

After who knew how long—several days? A week? Two?—the imps unlocked the door, dragged her limp body out, and deposited her back in the suite of rooms where she had first found herself. The outer door of the sitting room remained locked from the outside, and she was once again alone, though this time with a luxurious bed, a shiny mirror, and a bathtub she could float in.

The drapes on the windows had been replaced by bars.

Her leg muscles had atrophied from disuse to the point she shook when she walked to and from the bathroom and when she fetched her tray of food from the sitting room. Her food choices had been upgraded, and she routinely received leafy salads, warm loaves of bread with sweetened honey butter, and fresh fruit. Every now and then, she would actually eat some of the food, but more often than not, she preferred the company of her growling stomach as a reminder of the pain of living.

She took a bath every day, floating on her back in the scalding water, and pretended she was flying. Flying away from the tower, away from Erasto and Ettares and Araj, away from all those who had hurt her. She scrubbed at her skin, sloughing off all the detritus from her incarceration, until her skin was pink and raw. She scrubbed away her feelings, her heartbreak, her fear. She was a blank canvas, an empty and damaged vessel ready to be discarded.

Her bruises healed, her skin unblemished by the beating she took. She found herself longing for the bruises again; pressing them to feel pain had become a morbid pastime for her, one which she missed. If everyone else was intent on torturing her, she might as well join in on it. It hurt less when she hurt herself, dragging sharp nails across thin skin, than when the ones she loved stabbed her in the back.

She could have spent her time watching shows on the mirror. She might have even been able to call someone and chat. But she worried what would happen if Erasto found out. Instead, she spent her time carving symbols into her skin with a razor-sharp thumb nail, studying the drops of blood that trickled from her shallow cuts. She held onto her anger and her disillusionment.

She woke from a dream about the house fire and realized she was ready to die, to move on; she just needed to figure out how. She certainly couldn't set fire to the place, and her nails weren't long enough to slit her wrists. Plus, she wanted something dramatic, a grand gesture. A last performance before she left this world and journeyed to the next.

After several weeks of being locked in her suite, the imp guard outside her sitting room door informed her that she would be allowed to walk around and explore The Center. Bundled up in a thick robe to hide her disfigurements, Farzana walked on shaky legs down the hallway and beheld the massive, open staircase that spiraled through the entire 20 floors of The Center. It was breathtakingly beautiful, and as she walked up to the railing and peered down at the dizzying drop, she realized how she would meet her end.

Erasto would regret giving her such an opportunity.

She returned to her room and went to bed filled with glee at her plan. She pictured the blur as she fell to her death, imagining the sound of the air whistling past as she plummeted down. She could almost taste it.

She woke with renewed vigor and dressed herself in a sumptuous, floor-length, periwinkle dress with an elegant, high neckline cradling her chin. Her arms were bare, and she brandished her scars and wounds with pride as she made her way back to the staircase. Grasping the railing, she hauled herself over to the other side, and when faced with the reality of the situation, she felt more alive than she had in months. Adrenaline coursed through her as she shut her eyes, let go of the railing, and tipped forward.

The rush of air past her had her gasping for breath, and she dared open her eyes, ready to watch her end. Instead, her eyes picked out the shocking sapphire color of a pixie standing at the railing, staring at her in shock.

Araj.

She reflexively stretched a hand out to him, heard him scream her name...and realized she hadn't said goodbye. She hadn't said goodbye to anyone.

The ground approached her with blinding speed, and the faeries below were scrambling in a panic as she hurtled toward them. She twisted in the air to see Araj one last time and watching him leap over the railing, slowing his descent with his wings, holding his hand out to her.

She reached for him, her fingers brushing his...

Farzana hit the ground with a sickening crunch. Lying there, a heap of broken flesh in a pool of blood, she realized she couldn't feel her wings. She couldn't feel her hands.

She couldn't feel anything.

16

SHE FLOATED, LOST IN A DREAM STATE.

Where am I?

Sometimes she heard voices, tense and hurried. Sometimes she swore she heard her name.

Other times, it was just silence and darkness. She couldn't feel her body. That was nice though; no body meant no pain.

Is this death?

Was she lost, forever fated to float in an eternity of infinite darkness?

She woke with a start, pain searing through her sides as she struggled to breathe.

"She's awake!" someone shouted, and then several pairs of feet thundered in her direction.

She couldn't move her head. She couldn't move her body. Was she paralyzed?

Why wasn't she dead?

"Farzana!"

A familiar voice. Through the haze of pain clouding her

vision, she saw his face slide into view.

Araj. He's here! Where is here?

"By the gods, Farzana, you scared me! Oh gods, I thought I lost you!" His head bowed, and then he was gone.

A blanket of red covered the world as the pain hit her again in a wave. She gasped, overwhelmed.

"Out! She needs to go back into the healing sleep!"

Darkness, again. She floated in cold darkness.

Her hearing returned first. She could hear the blood coursing through her veins and her heartbeat pounding in her chest, though it wasn't entirely rhythmic.

Next came her sense of smell. She sniffed; her surroundings had a sterile, clean sort of smell with an underlying note of citrus.

Touch was next. She flexed her hands and felt the soft fabric beneath her fingertips. She wiggled her toes and felt a blanket weighing them down.

Her eyes opened and slowly focused on a single object: a small mirror hanging on the wall opposite her, placed at the exact level of her face. Her head was wrapped in white cloth; she touched it and felt hard plaster. For a moment, she feared her hair was gone before she felt the back of her neck, touched curls, and sighed in relief.

She looked down at herself; a white sheet covered her body where she lay on a long, wide bed, propped up by several pillows into a reclined position. She was surprised to realize she was comfortable.

A door opened to her right, and she turned to look; a tall pixie wearing the maroon robes of a healer walked in, holding a tray of food. He smiled at her as he placed the tray over her lap, little legs folding out to keep it elevated and balanced.

"How are we feeling?" he asked in a deep, soothing voice.

Farzana stared at the contents of the tray: a bowl of berries topped with sweet cream, a fluffy slice of bread covered in melted butter, and a steaming mug of coffee with a hefty dose of cream.

She couldn't have asked for a better meal.

"What?" she asked, realizing he had spoken.

"I asked how you're feeling."

"Oh. I'm...comfortable."

His eyes creased as he smiled. "That's great, Farzana. Would you be up for seeing a visitor?"

"I think so," she said slowly, wondering who it could be. *Please don't let it be Erasto.*

"I'll send him in," he said, exiting the room and leaving her alone with her tray of tasty treats.

She licked her lips and grabbed a spoon, intent on devouring the bowl of berries and cream. One oversized bite later, she made a small noise of pleasure, closing her eyes and relishing the comforting sweet and sour taste.

Someone cleared their throat, and her eyes flew open; Araj stood in the doorway.

"Araj!" she gasped, mouth still full of food.

"Don't choke," he said in a wry voice, pulling a chair over to her bedside.

She swallowed and marveled at the sight of him. He looked exhausted, and she wondered when he had last slept. Lines of worry circled his eyes, and his mouth was set in a hard line. She had expected to feel rage at seeing him or at least shame, but she was so happy to see a familiar face after so long in isolation.

"Are you okay?" she asked.

His eyebrows flew up. "Am I okay? Farzana, I should be asking you that. No...I should be apologizing."

She blinked and stared at him.

He let out a heavy sigh. "Farzana, I've been a terrible friend. First, I kissed you without your consent. That was awful, and I'll never forgive myself for it. And second, after I found out you had been moved to The Center, I never came to visit you. You were here for over a month! I have no excuse; I was too upset with our last exchange to come see you, and that was petty."

Farzana pursed her lips. Part of her flared with anger when

he mentioned the kiss. But a different part, a lonely part, wanted to forget all the nonsense and move on.

She missed her best friend.

"And I don't expect your forgiveness," he continued before she could speak. "I just hope we can manage to be friends again, real friends. I missed you, Farzana."

She gave him a small smile. "I missed you, too."

"And I can't believe I almost lost you," he said, choking on the last few words.

Guilt swelled in her chest, and it felt like a rock crushing her. "I can't believe I really did that," she whispered.

"What were you thinking?" he asked, incredulous. His dark blue eyes were wide with anger.

"I don't know."

"You didn't even say goodbye."

She covered her face with her hands as hot tears spilled over her cheeks. "I was so lonely. I didn't have anything to live for," she sobbed.

"And that's my fault. I should have visited. I should have told you the news."

She peeked out at him. "What news?"

A crooked smile spread across his lips. "Your mother opened up her own art gallery, here in The Center. And Enzi is head chef in the kitchens."

Her heart soared, and she couldn't stop the smile from her face. "Are they happy?"

"Once we found out you would survive, yes."

So it had been a question. She hadn't thought the healers would be able to save her, not from that far of a fall. Nineteen floors was a massive drop.

She sighed, biting her lip. "I'm still upset about the kiss. I'm not going to lie to you. But I do want us to be friends. So...I forgive you."

He beamed at her, eyes sparkling with happiness. "Thank you."

"And it's not your fault I jumped; I was more preoccupied with someone else," she admitted.

"Oh?"

"You were right…about Ettares. She was working for Erasto the whole time. I thought…I thought maybe she and I would be… Well, I really liked her. But it was all fake. I was a job."

He nodded, sympathy in his face. "I wish I had been wrong."

"Yeah…"

I wish that too.

17

AFTER A FULL WEEK IN THE HEALING SLEEP
and another two days of bed rest, the healers cleared Farzana
to go back to her suite. For an unknown reason, her left leg
had not fully healed, so they put a flexible exoskeleton cast
on her calf to hold everything in place. They allowed her to
choose the color, and she asked for purple, same as her wings.
In addition, she was given a cane to help her walk and prevent
her leg from taking her full weight.

As soon as Araj came to her room and saw the cane, he
disappeared and showed back up with purple paint, the exact
same shade as her cast and wings, and helped her decorate it.
They painted tiny purple flowers over the mahogany finish
and laughed whenever one of them accidentally smeared paint
across their face.

"I helped build this room, you know," he said, sprawled out
on the floor with her as they waited for the paint to dry.

"Really? I can't imagine you getting your hands dirty."

He held out his purple hands. "Oh?"

Laughing, Farzana held her matching hands up to his.
"What all did you do?"

"Erasto put me in charge of construction management

when I transferred here. I helped design your rooms, picked the colors and the decor. I even helped paint the walls."

"So this isn't the first time your hands have been purple in this room."

He laughed. "Not at all."

"I want to visit Enzi tomorrow," she said, shifting so she was lying on her stomach.

"I think that can be arranged. You've got a guard who will follow you everywhere, but when I talked to them, they said you were free to leave."

"Is Enzi the one I should thank for that delicious first meal in the clinic?"

He nodded. "He's been choosing your meals for you since he was hired. He was livid when he heard what they were feeding you in that other room."

Farzana grimaced. "You knew about that?"

"I can't believe he locked you in there! When I built that room, I thought it was supposed to be for a servant."

"You think that's a fitting room for a servant? It's barely bigger than a closet."

"I'm just glad you're out of there."

She traced a design in the carpeted flooring. "Yeah. It wasn't a good time."

"I should go. Erasto doesn't seem to mind my extensive breaks, but I don't want to try his patience. We're working on a huge project right now so I should make sure my workers are on task." He stood and stretched.

"I'll see you later, then."

"Tomorrow," he promised.

"Tomorrow."

He left her alone with her thoughts. It was hard to believe the faerie who had beat her and imprisoned her was fine with Araj slacking off. She closed her eyes and saw the hatred on Erasto's face when he screamed and assaulted her. Shivering uncontrollably, she opened her eyes and reached for her cane. Checking to see if the paint was dry first, she used it to stand and hobble to the bathroom, intent on cleaning her hands. She washed her face too, enjoying the sting of the hot water and the steam kissing her skin. After drying herself, she stared at her reflection in the mirror.

Haunted eyes stared back at her. Her cheekbones stood out in stark contrast to the gauntness of her face. The cast was gone from her head and her curls hung lank. She remembered being proud of her hair, caring for it religiously. Filled with a sudden need to pamper herself, she drew a bath and soaked her curls, using a wide toothed comb to pull curl lotion through the long strands. When her hair was finally soft and luscious, she looked in the mirror again. She wasn't her old self, but a hint of a smile teased her lips at the sight of her magnificent mane. The improvement was remarkable, and she whistled a little tune to herself as she walked back to her bedroom.

Resting on the bed for a moment had ugly thoughts pouring into her again: Erasto's contempt and hatred, Ettares's betrayal, Araj's assault. Unable to focus on anything else, she made her way through the sitting room, intent on leaving her suites even for a moment. The residual sorrow in the rooms made her queasy.

An imp guard stood outside her door and glanced at her when she stepped out. She realized she had no clue where she would go. She didn't know how to find her mother's gallery or the kitchens, and she didn't want to ask the guard, who stared at her with impassivity. She decided to take a walk back to her old prison room. When she turned to head further into the hallway, the imp stayed at the door. The hallway must not have any way out on this end, she mused.

When she reached the door, still within sight of the imp, she paused. Would anyone be using the room now that she was gone? Just in case, she gave a quick knock before pushing the door open.

The lightbulb was off but the light from the hallway illuminated the room enough for her to see a small imp child crouched on the bed, gray eyes wide in shock. She bared her fangs in a silent snarl.

Farzana took an involuntary step back, wary.

Dressed in a tattered, long-sleeved, white shift dress, her black hair was a tangled mess and hung down limp over her pale, dirty face. She looked like she was starving, all large eyes and sunken cheeks. Her lips were chapped and cracked, and as Farzana stood observing her, she licked them. She looked no more than 30 years old–hardly older than a toddler–and Farzana wondered where her parents were.

"Are you okay?" Farzana asked in a soft voice.

No answer.

"What's your name? I'm Farzana."

The child growled, low in her throat, and shifted as if to pounce.

"It's okay; I won't hurt you. I'm already hurt," Farzana said, showing her the cane.

The child stopped growling and stared at the cane before meeting Farzana's eyes.

"Are you hungry?"

A moment of hesitation, and then a slight nod.

"I'll be right back," Farzana said, pulling the door shut and hobbling back to her room. She hadn't finished her lunch and hoped no one had come to take the tray of food away. She found it on her bed, right where she had left it, and she grabbed a piece of bread and slathered it with butter before making her way back to the room, ignoring the guard's curious looks.

Knocking again, she slowly pushed the door open. The child was still there, sitting on the bed, her eyes wild with fear. Farzana held out the bread, and she snatched it, shoving the whole piece into her mouth. Barely swallowing, she licked her fingers, her eyes never leaving Farzana.

Her stomach let out a growl.

"I have more, but I can't carry it all here," Farzana said. "Do you want to come with me?"

She shook her head. "I'm waiting for my mother," she said in a tiny, hoarse voice.

"How long have you been waiting?"

The child shrugged, looking away. "I think it's been a couple days."

Farzana felt a pang in her heart. Who would abandon their child? "You can wait for her in my room," she suggested.

The temptation of food must have won the child over, because she nodded, getting to her feet. At her full height, she came to Farzana's chest.

So young to be alone...

Her eyes full of suspicion and hunger, she followed Farzana back to the suite. The child's eyes grew wide as she took in her new surroundings: the velvet couches, the painting of the lily pond, the giant mirror. She reached out to run a hand down the furs on the bed.

"You live here?"

"I do now. I used to live in the room where you were hiding."

The child made a face. "I wasn't hiding. I was waiting. I'm good at hiding."

"We'll leave a note for your mother in the other room, okay? So she knows you're here."

She nodded, eyeing the tray of food with ravenous eyes.

"Go ahead. Eat whatever you want."

The child lunged forward and grabbed the half-eaten sliced roast sandwich, polishing it off in a few bites. She grabbed the apple next, juice dribbling down her chin as she devoured it. Last was the glass of water; she brought it to her mouth with two hands and carefully drank it all in one quaff.

Looking sated, she stepped back, holding her hands to her belly. A small smile graced her lips, and she looked up at Farzana with a softness in her large gray eyes. "Thank you," she whispered.

"You're very welcome. Now, let's write that note." Farzana crossed to the desk and found paper and a pen in the drawers, along with a seal and wax beads. Taking a sheet of paper, she poised the pen over it and realized she didn't know the child's name.

"What's your name, sweetie?"

"Laraf."

"That's a beautiful name." Scribbling down her suite number and her name, she addressed the note to 'Laraf's mother' and folded it in half.

Together, they walked back to the room, passing the bored looking guard, before heading back to Farzana's bedroom.

"Can I use your bathroom?" Laraf asked once they were back.

"Of course. You should probably take a bath too," Farzana said.

Laraf paled. "I'm okay," she said, hugging herself.

Farzana wondered what lay hidden under that oversized, long sleeve dress. "Okay. No bath."

Laraf closed the bathroom behind her, and Farzana heard the sound of retching coming through the door. Alarmed, she knocked on the door.

"Laraf? Are you okay?"

"I'm fine," came a weak voice.

"Do you need help?"

Water ran in the sink and then shut off. Laraf opened the door, her face looking green. "It was a lot of food," she whispered. "I think I ate too much."

Farzana's mind spun. She couldn't imagine that little amount of food being too much, even for a child her size. How long had she been starving?

"I'm tired," Laraf said, rubbing her eyes.

"Do you want to sleep on the bed?"

Laraf eyed the bed before shaking her head. "Can I sleep in there?" She pointed into the sitting room.

"Of course." Farzana limped to the closet in her bathroom and grabbed a spare blanket and pillow. Holding them awkwardly in her arms while still holding onto her cane, she carried them into the sitting room. Laraf was lying huddled on a couch, staring vacantly at the fireplace.

Her heart aching for the unknown trauma Laraf had endured in her short life, Farzana shook out the blanket and tucked it around her tiny frame.

The child was asleep in moments, her lips parted as she

breathed. Watching her for a moment, Farzana sent a quick prayer to The Harvester to give Laraf sweet dreams before deciding she could do with a nap herself.

18

WHEN FARZANA WOKE THE NEXT MORNING,
her mirror glowed with a notification from Araj. She clicked
the remote to open it.

"The kitchens are on floor eleven. Say hi to Enzi for me."

Turning off the mirror, she snuggled deeper under the
fur covers, enjoying the comforting weight on her body for a
moment longer.

Laraf!

Jolting upright, she stared through the open door to the
sitting room and saw Laraf sitting on the couch, hugging her
knees to her chest, and staring at the fireplace. Breathing a sigh
of relief, Farzana grabbed her cane and got out of bed.

"Good morning!"

Laraf jumped, snapping her head to the side to see Farzana
standing in the doorway. Her small body trembled for a moment before she relaxed and gave Farzana a tiny smile. "Good
morning," she murmured.

"Are you up for a trip to the kitchens?"

Laraf eyed her suspiciously. "What about my mother?"

"I'll leave a note on the door saying we will be right back."

"Will we get food?"

"Of course."

Laraf nodded and got to her feet, stretching her arms out, always keeping an eye on Farzana.

"I'll just change and we can go, okay?" Careful not to make any sudden movements, Farzana turned back toward the bathroom. She dressed in a plain, floor-length, blush-pink sundress, pulling her hair up into a loose bun, and limped back out to find Laraf standing by the door, her posture rigid and upright.

"Ready?" Farzana asked.

Laraf nodded, and Farzana opened the door. Outside, a different imp stood guard, his dark eyes watching her.

"I would like to go to the kitchens," she said, unsure of whether he would allow her to leave.

He grunted, which she took as acquiescence, and she turned toward the end of the hall, Laraf close by her side. The three of them made their way to the lifts, passing the staircase on the way. The massive open spiral had been closed off at the 18th floor, and Farzana had no doubt it had been similarly reconstructed all the way down.

This must be the big project Araj is working on.

Without prompting, Laraf reached out and touched the call rune when they reached the lift.

"You don't have to do that," Farzana said, surprised.

Laraf gave her an odd look, as though she didn't understand.

"I can do that myself," Farzana continued, and when the lift arrived, Farzana made sure to touch the rune for floor eleven before Laraf could. She swayed on her feet as the rune sapped her strength, and she felt sick at the thought of the rune affecting Laraf, draining her of what precious little energy she had.

What kind of parent makes their child operate the runes?

The lift doors opened onto the eleventh floor, and the group stepped out. A sign on the wall read 'Kitchens' and 'Laundry' with arrows pointing in opposite directions. Farzana headed left and soon heard the familiar clatter and hubbub of the kitchens ahead.

She pushed on the door labeled 'Kitchen' and was greeted by chaos. Faeries scurried this way and that in an orchestrated dance. Spotting Enzi at the far end of the kitchen, she skirted the choreography, careful not to step in anyone's way. Laraf and the guard shadowed her as she made her way to Enzi's side.

"Enzi!" Farzana shouted to get his attention.

A crash and a howl echoed as someone dropped something, no doubt distracted by the interruption, and then Enzi turned with a big smile on his face.

"Zana!" he cried, running the few steps between them and embracing her. "Oh gods, I was horrified when I heard what happened!"

"Yeah, not my proudest moment," Farzana said, feeling self-conscious.

"I mean, falling like that? I guess it was too much for your wings to handle. I'm just glad the healers were able to heal you."

Farzana stared at him as he continued.

"And now they're sectioning off the staircase. They don't want another accident like yours. About time. Something like this was bound to happen with a staircase like that."

Does he not know the fall was intentional?

"I know, right?" Farzana faked a lighthearted laugh. "It was a wild experience."

"I'm so glad you're okay," Enzi said, leading them over to his workstation. Papers were scattered over the stainless-steel countertops, and Farzana spied a pen tucked behind Enzi's ear. "I heard you have a cast?"

Farzana lifted her skirt a bit to show off her purple cast. "You heard correct."

"How archaic," Enzi said, hands on his hips as he studied it.

"I shouldn't have it for too much longer."

"Oh! Who is this lovely lady?" Enzi asked, spying Laraf behind Farzana. He kneeled down to her eye level, smiling wide.

She gave him a fleeting smile. "I'm Laraf."

"Merry meet, Laraf. Any friend of Farzana's is a friend of mine too. I'm Enzi, Farzana's younger brother." He held out his hand, and, looking stunned, Laraf shook it.

"Merry meet," she replied quickly.

"Now, what can I get you two today?" Enzi asked, straightening up.

Farzana gave him a cheeky smile. "So you're head chef, yeah? That means you must have access to sweets."

Enzi rolled his eyes. "I don't know why I even asked. Candied nuts and chocolate cake, then?"

Remembering how Laraf had vomited the previous day, Farzana hesitated. Would she be able to handle sweets?

"Actually, maybe just something filling," she said, though she was indeed craving chocolate.

Enzi raised an eyebrow but said nothing. Grabbing the pen from behind his ear, he scribbled something onto a piece of paper before saying, "I've got a wonderful stew simmering. I'll send up a couple bowls and a loaf of dark bread."

"Sounds perfect." She stopped to bite her lip before asking in a rush, "Is Mother okay?"

Enzi gave her a soft smile. "You know, she actually is? When we lost you…the night of the fire. We didn't know where you were. We didn't know until your accident was reported on the news. She refused to visit, saying it was bad luck, and to just let the healing sleep do its job. She went to the temple of Majakim every day and prayed."

Farzana's got misty-eyed as she listened. Erasto hadn't even let them know where she was?

"She poured herself into her work. She's been painting non-stop, I swear. I think between the praying, you surviving, and her artwork, she really is okay. But you should go see her."

"Is she here?"

Enzi nodded. "She opened up an art gallery. Think about it, okay? I know she would love to see you."

Wiping at her tear-filled eyes, Farzana nodded. "Of course. I'll go tomorrow."

"Good. Now get on out of here. I'll bring the food to you," he said, a twinkle in his eye as he shooed them.

Laraf scurried away from him, darting toward the door ahead of Farzana.

Feeling unsteady, both mentally and physically, Farzana

focused on her feet for every step. "What do you think of Enzi?" Farzana asked Laraf when she caught up.

"I like his wings. But they aren't as pretty as yours."

Farzana blushed at the compliment. "Thank you!"

Outside the kitchen, they ran into Araj, who held a bouquet of flowers in his hands.

"Araj! Bringing Enzi flowers?" She attempted a bright smile.

He grinned back. "They're for you, actually. I saw your note and came to find you."

Farzana wasn't sure how to feel about him giving her flowers as a gift, but she accepted them and introduced him to Laraf. "She's staying with me until her mother comes back," she said, hoping he didn't ask any probing questions. Instead, his eyes tightened, and his smile vanished.

"I see," he said, clearing his throat.

"Will you come back up with us?"

"I'm actually working long hours today. I just have a quick break and then I need to get back to work."

Farzana gave him a sympathetic smile. "And you thought of me? Thanks, Araj."

"Anytime! I'll try to visit later tonight."

"Deal."

By the time they got back to the Farzana's suite, a runic headache had taken over her mind. Pain lanced her temples as she struggled through brain fog to open the door. Inside, she shuffled over to the couch and sank down onto it, letting out a huge sigh. She rubbed her forehead and looked over to see Laraf watching her with what looked like concern.

"Are you okay?" she asked.

Farzana tried to give her a reassuring smile but ended up grimacing. "I'll be fine. The runes give me a headache."

"Me too."

"I'm sorry you've had to deal with that. The adults around you should be the ones using their energy for the runes, not you." The statement reminded Farzana of the times Ettares had operated the runes for her, defying societal rules. Her chest tightened at the thought of the noble, and she shook her head, banishing Ettares from her mind and focusing on Laraf.

Laraf shrugged. "I guess so."

"How old are you?" Farzana switched topics, seeing the discomfort in the way Laraf held her body.

"I'm 67."

Farzana's eyes widened. She was so tiny! How severely and chronically malnourished did one have to be to have their growth stunted so much?

"You're so big!" she said instead.

Laraf gave her a tiny smile.

A knock sounded on the door before it opened, Enzi pushing his way in with an overloaded tray of food.

"I brought some other snacks for you two to enjoy," he said, placing the tray down on the coffee table. He leaned down to brush cheeks with Farzana before leaving with a cheery wave.

Laraf stared at the tray, her eyes huge. "All of that is for us?"

Two enormous bowls of stew sat in the center, surrounded by an entire loaf of fresh baked bread, a dish of butter, a pot of honey, sliced fruit, roasted vegetables, and a slice of chocolate cake. Two forks and two spoons laid on the small pile of napkins to the side.

"Well, we do know the head chef," Farzana pointed out.

"You eat this much every day?"

She shook her head. "I think this is a special occasion."

Laraf wrinkled her nose. "What's special?"

"Well, I met you. And Enzi likes celebrating even the little things."

A blush spread over Laraf's gaunt cheeks. "I'm special?"

"Of course you are! Now, eat." Farzana handed her a spoon and fork before tearing off a piece of bread.

After a moment of hesitation, Laraf settled herself on the floor beside the coffee table and took a bite of stew. A small gasp came as she tasted it, mulling it over in her mouth before swallowing. A look of ecstasy crossed her face.

"I want to eat this every day," she said, humming to herself as she loaded up her spoon with more stew.

"We can certainly ask for that."

"I think I like it here," Laraf whispered, not meeting Farzana's eyes.

A warmth grew in Farzana's chest as she watched the child eat. It had barely been a day since they met, and Farzana already knew she would fight anyone who tried to harm Laraf. And gods help her mother, wherever she was. Farzana didn't know or care whether the starving was intentional or unavoidable; the flicker of fear hiding behind Laraf's eyes anytime someone moved near her told her enough about the child's past. If Farzana ever met the mother, she knew the conversation would be anything but civil.

If she was lucky, Laraf wouldn't see her mother ever again. And if Farzana had to sneak out to destroy the note from the other room to make that happen, she would gladly do so. If she really cared, the mother would go to all lengths to find her daughter. And if not... Well, Laraf would be well cared for. Farzana would see to that.

19

FARZANA MANAGED TO CONVINCE LARAF TO take a bath the next day; Laraf conceded to the fact that she smelled but only agreed after Farzana promised not to open the bathroom door while she was in there. Farzana laid out a shirt and pair of pants for her on the counter and obediently left the room.

She could hear the occasional splash as Laraf bathed herself; she could have sworn she even heard a soft voice singing, which brought a smile to her face. When Laraf appeared, dressed in the ridiculously oversized clothes, Farzana stifled a laugh and very seriously said, "I think we need to get you some new clothes."

"Are you sure?" Laraf hugged herself and rocked back and forth. Farzana noticed a beautiful spread of freckles over her face, which must have been hidden before by the dirt and grime.

"After lunch, we'll go visit my mother and then go shopping for some clothes, okay?" Farzana didn't have access to her money anymore since she no longer had a pocket mirror, but she was sure Sitra would be able to give her some.

Laraf nodded before reaching up to touch her tangled hair.

She looked up at Farzana with a question in her eyes before hanging her head and heading for the couch.

"Do you want me to comb your hair?"

Laraf turned back, eyes lit up. "Can you?"

"Of course. It might hurt a bit to get the knots out."

Laraf stood up straight as a rod. "I'm tough. I won't cry."

"I believe you," Farzana said, getting up to grab her comb and curl lotion.

She beckoned for Laraf to join her on the bed, which she did after hesitating; Farzana massaged some curl lotion onto her scalp to soften the hair and picked through the tangles and knots, combing the lotion through her hair. It took a lot of effort, but when she was done, Laraf's hair shone like black silk.

"All done."

Laraf ran a hand through her hair, a shy smile on her face as it rippled around her. "Thank you," she whispered.

Farzana put the comb aside and asked, "May I give you a hug?"

Laraf stiffened, that fear flickering in her eyes again.

"You can say no."

A long moment of silence passed, during which a tear trickled down her cheek. "I would like a hug," she said in a small voice.

Farzana opened her arms, and the child fell into them. Wrapping her in an embrace, Farzana rested her chin on Laraf's head, breathing in the clean citrus scent of her curl lotion, and wondered when Laraf had last had a hug.

"You're going to love my mother," Farzana said as they walked on the seventh floor. The bottom half of The Center was filled with stores in what Erasto had called a mall, and if the crowds were any indication, it was wildly popular. Farzana had to work at maintaining her balance as she used her cane to maneuver between people. Laraf clutched her skirt to keep from being separated from her, and their imp guard followed closely behind them.

"Is she nice?" Laraf asked, her voice shaking.

"The nicest person I know. She cares about everything, sometimes too much. And I know she's going to love you."

Laraf blushed and hid a small smile by ducking her head. Her shiny onyx hair slid shut like a curtain in front of her face, only her pointed ear tips showing on the sides of her head.

They made their way over to a store front with a sign that read 'Sitra's Space' above the door. Inside, they were greeted by rows and rows of paintings. Paintings on the walls, on easels, on shelves out on the floor. Paintings of pixies and imps, sirens and elves, sprites and water horses. Landscape paintings with exquisite detail and portraits that captured raw emotion.

Sitra stood when they entered and came around her desk; tears shone in her eyes as she embraced Farzana. "Hello, baby. Oh, I've missed you!"

Farzana grinned. "Like a hole in the head, yeah?"

Sitra swatted at her hand, and Laraf flinched.

"I heard about your accident. I'm sorry I didn't visit. I...I couldn't see you like that."

Farzana nodded, her throat too thick to speak. Would she ever be able to tell them it wasn't an accident?

"But you're okay! You're here now; that's all that matters. And, oh! Who is this precious little one?" Sitra bent to peer at Laraf, who eyed her warily through lowered lashes.

"This is Laraf. She's staying with me for a little while."

"Merry meet, Laraf. Well, aren't you just the most darling little lass?"

Laraf's face flamed crimson, and she looked at the floor. "Merry meet," she mumbled.

"Farzana, why is she wearing your clothes? Those are way too big for her."

"I actually wanted to talk to you about that. I don't have access to my account. Can we borrow your pocket mirror to go shopping?"

Sitra reached into her pocket, pulling it out and handing it over. "Of course. There's a nice clothing store right next door. Why don't you check that out?"

"Thanks, Mother."

"You might want to get yourself a new pocket mirror too, baby."

"I should, but do we have the funds?"

Sitra laughed. "Are you kidding? Now that we're living with your grandparents and no longer paying rent, we have plenty of money. Plus, my paintings are selling so fast! I've been working all night just to keep the gallery stocked. We can afford a necessity like a pocket mirror."

Farzana smiled at the joy on her mother's face. Nothing made her happier than her paintings and earning money from her art must have been such a wonderful feeling. "I'm happy for you," she said, grabbing Sitra's hand and squeezing it.

"Thank you. Now go. Get that child some nice clothes!"

"Yes, ma'am!"

Farzana turned to leave, Laraf still holding her skirt, and stepped around the imp guard to open the door. She was glad her mother hadn't brought up the guard; it would have been tough trying to explain why she wasn't allowed to go anywhere unsupervised.

"What did you think of my mother?" Farzana asked once they stepped out of the gallery.

Laraf bristled. "She hit you."

"What?" Bewildered, Farzana tried to recall the entire interaction.

"You made a joke, and she hit you for it. I don't like her."

Farzana nearly laughed in relief as she realized what she meant. "Oh! No, sweetie, that was her joke. My mother would never hit me to hurt me. She was playing around."

Laraf looked skeptical. "You weren't hurt by it?"

"Not at all."

She visibly relaxed. "Okay. That's good."

They walked into the clothing store, and both stopped abruptly in the doorway. Every single color in the rainbow was represented everywhere that the eye could see. Silks, cottons, satins, patterns of every kind. Rows and rows of hanging clothes in every conceivable shape and size adorned the walls, and tables piled high with shiny clothes dotted the vast floor space.

"Wow," Farzana breathed.

"Yeah," Laraf said, looking dazed.

"Well? What color do you want?" Farzana asked, spreading her arms wide to take it all in.

"Blue?"

"Blue it is."

They traipsed through the store, checking every nook and cranny, and ended up with a bundle of new clothes for Laraf including five new shirts, a couple pairs of pants, a floor length skirt, and a collared long sleeve dress.

"It's so beautiful," Laraf said, twirling in the dress in front of the fitting room mirror. "I love it." Farzana heard a note of sadness in her voice and wondered why seeing herself in a beautiful dress would upset Laraf. Maybe she was worried about money?

"Well then we have to get it."

"Really?"

"Really."

Laraf gave Farzana a brilliant, albeit watery, smile. "Thank you, Farzana."

"Do you want to wear that out of the store?"

Laraf wrinkled her nose at the shirt and pants she had borrowed from Farzana, prompting Farzana to laugh.

"I'll take that as a yes."

Laraf twirled in front of the mirror again, admiring herself. "Okay. I'm ready to go."

"Let's pay for these and go find me a new pocket mirror then," Farzana said, grabbing the pile of clothes Laraf had picked for herself. On their way to the register, they saw a pair of imps, one fat and one thin, arguing with an employee.

"It's outrageous! No section for imps? You've got tons of clothing that accommodate wings, for crying out loud, but no clothing large enough for us? This is discrimination."

No imp clothing?

Farzana had been impressed by the extensive collection of clothing, but she had failed to notice the lack of imp clothing. Not that the clothing was labeled by species—each section just had winged and wingless clothing selections from which to choose. But she realized now that in all her searching, she hadn't seen any clothing made for the average build of a towering, hefty imp.

"Please calm down," the employee said, holding up her hands. "Have you tried the plus size section?"

The thin imp grabbed a skirt from the nearest plus size rack and held it up to her waist; it barely covered her hips. "I'm big and tall. How is this supposed to hide my ass?"

Her companion said, "None of these clothes fit. They're too short on both of us, no matter how wide they get."

The employee shrugged. "Look, I just work here, okay? I don't know what to tell you."

"Oh, you just work here. Okay. Well, maybe we will tell all our friends about the rotten customer service here! Not to mention the poor selection. I can't just wear an extra extra extra large and call it good. I'm fat and have a body shape!" The fat imp indeed had a gorgeous, voluptuous figure, which Farzana admired.

"No one said you were fat," mumbled the employee.

The fat imp laughed. "Oh honey, we all know I'm fat. The problem isn't me; the problem is your lack of imp clothing. This is the biggest store in the mall, and it doesn't cater to imps?"

Pinching the bridge of her nose, the employee huffed, "Look, I can't help you. We don't carry imp clothing! Please leave!"

"Well, I guess we will," yelled the thin imp.

"Thank you!" The employee took a shuddering deep breath as they left the store before plastering a desperate smile on her face and turning to Farzana. "How may I assist you?"

Laraf tugged on Farzana's skirt from where she stood behind her and said, "Am I allowed to wear these clothes?"

Farzana patted her shoulder. "Of course, sweetie. These clothes fit you."

"All ready to ring out?"

"Yes," Farzana said, handing the clothes to the employee and following her to the counter.

The employee stared at Laraf for a long moment before asking for the price on the tag of the dress. Tallying up the total on a mirror tablet, the employee said, "That will be 80 dradens."

Laraf sucked in a breath as Farzana opened the pocket mirror, clicked to her account, and then held it up to the mirror tablet; a green light flashed on both mirrors, concluding the translation.

"Thank you for your business!" the employee said with strained cheer, handing over the clothing in a cloth bag.

Farzana declined to answer, still miffed on behalf of the imps who had walked out without any clothing, and simply nodded as she grabbed the bag.

"I'll carry it," Laraf said, and held the bag with a look of pride on her face. Farzana's heart swelled.

Turning toward the exit, Farzana spotted a flash of red in the crowd outside the store. A jolt of recognition hit her; it was the exact same shade as Ettares's wings. Without thinking, she tore away from Laraf and hustled to the door as fast as her cane and bum leg would allow. She scanned the crowd but the red was nowhere to be found.

"Farzana? What's wrong?" Laraf asked.

"I thought I recognized someone… I'm sorry, sweetie. I didn't mean to leave you like that."

She shrugged. "Are we going to get you a pocket mirror now?"

"Yes, let's go do that."

"And then I can say thank you to your mother for the pretty dress."

"Absolutely! Mother will love it," Farzana said with a smile.

An uncertain look crossed Laraf's face before she held out her hand, hesitantly. "Can we hold hands?"

"Of course." Farzana took the tiny, cold hand in hers and

gave it a reassuring squeeze. A smile quirked Laraf's lips, and they set off to find a pocket mirror retailer. There was no use dwelling on the color red. There was no use in thinking of that faerie at all.

20

A WEEK LATER, FARZANA AND LARAF WENT IN search of the laundry rooms. For some reason, a guard was no longer posted at her door, nor did one shadow her. The likelihood of this being a choice of kindness and respect had to be about zero; most likely he had forgotten to schedule it. Why else would she be given this kind of freedom? She refused to believe that Erasto had found a well of love for his daughter. Regardless, Farzana relished the newfound chance to get out and do her own chores rather than ringing for laundry service. They dropped off their soiled clothes and went to eat lunch with Enzi in the kitchens before heading back to collect their clean clothes. As they rounded a corner, they came face to face with the last faerie Farzana expected to see: Ettares.

The bag of laundry fell from numb fingers as Farzana stared at her. No wonder the guard was gone; Erasto had found someone else to plague her. Trust him to add insult to injury. It wasn't enough that Ettares had humiliated her, had tricked her and seduced her and made her feel…things. Things that Farzana never wanted to think of again. Of course Erasto would choose now to spring this on her, right when she was finally healing, finally feeling mentally and emotionally stable enough to feel *happy* again.

And the nerve of Ettares! Farzana should have known that the half-assed apology—explanation, whatever—that Ettares tried to make before had been nothing but a load of shit. And yet…if Farzana didn't know any better, she could almost believe that Ettares was just as surprised as her. Ettares's beauty was unchanged and unmatched in a black pinstripe suit, a purple tie at her throat. Her frosty curls were arranged in a haphazard halo, and vermillion wings fluttered at her back. Her ice blue eyes pierced Farzana's purple ones. Though her expression largely remained neutral, save for the unnatural widening of her eyes, Ettares's hands clenched into trembling fists.

Blood pounded in Farzana's head as she felt her heart skip a beat. Laraf said something but she could hear, couldn't concentrate… All she could focus on were those full lips forming her name.

"Farzana?"

The floor rushed up to meet her, and before she could save herself, she found herself cradled in a strong set of arms, held against a warm body.

"Whoa! Steady, now."

Farzana tried to take a deep breath. She shuddered as a shiver traced her spine, and then the shudder became a tremor that wracked her body uncontrollably. Why was it so cold all of a sudden?

"Where are you two going?"

Away from here. Anywhere but here.

"To Farzana's room," Laraf said in a small, uncertain voice.

"Okay. You grab the bag and follow me."

The arms holding Farzana shifted, and then she was in the air, floating.

Where am I going? Oh, yes: anywhere but here.

"Is she okay?"

"Farzana is going to be fine."

"Okay."

She floated and floated, her vision swimming with red. Bright wings blocked her view. How long she floated, she couldn't be sure, before she heard, "Excuse me?"

That voice...

With the last of her fading strength, she twisted around enough to see Araj standing in the hallway, hands on his hips and anger in his eyes

"Araj," Farzana whispered.

"Farzana fell, and I was—"

A brief scuffle and some jostling, and then Farzana was in a different set of arms, blue wings hovering in the corner of her eye.

"I'll take her from here. Your presence isn't wanted," Araj growled.

Laraf whimpered.

"I was just—"

"Save it," he spat, whirling around.

Farzana's head spun. She looked over his shoulder to see Ettares standing in the hallway, her shoulders and wings slumped in defeat.

"Thank you," Farzana said in a weak voice.

"I've got you. Do you need a healer?" Araj held her tight against his broad chest.

"No," she said, shivering. "I'm just cold and tired."

"Laraf, get the door."

Araj placed Farzana on the bed and proceeded to cover her with blankets and furs. "You have a fever," he said, cupping her cheek.

"I'll be fine. I need sleep."

"Okay." Doubt colored his voice. "Get better."

"I will," she mumbled, rolling over and succumbing to sleep.

"Farzana."

She woke with a start and sat up in bed, squinting into the darkness. Laraf stood at her side, an envelope in her hand.

Farzana reached for the lamp beside the bed and switched it on, blinking rapidly at the bright light.

"Where did you get this?" she asked, taking the envelope and flipping it over. It had been sealed with blood red wax, a cursive E imprinted in it.

"The pixie from earlier today… She knocked and gave it to me."

Farzana broke the seal and pulled out a single sheet of paper.

Dear Farzana,

Erasto has secrets that could hurt us all. I can help you find them if you meet me in the hall after dark.

It was definitely after dark. Farzana's fever had broken sometime during her nap; her bed clothes were soaked in sweat and sticking to her skin, but she still felt surprisingly refreshed and well.

"Go back to bed," she told Laraf, who obediently headed for the sitting room. Farzana washed her face, sponged down her body, and changed into clean clothes. Walking past Laraf's still form on the couch, she opened the door to peek out into the hall.

Ettares sat on the floor across the hall, her legs folded under her. She gave Farzana a wry smile as she stepped into the hall and shut the door behind her.

"Nice cane," Ettares said, eyeing the artwork.

"I decorated it myself."

"I'm impressed, though knowing your mother, not surprised. You're talented in so many ways." Her voice was low and husky, and Farzana's heart remembered what it felt like when she used that same voice to ask to kiss her.

She wanted to melt into the floorboards and disappear. Standing in front of her, knowing it was all a lie… She hated being reminded of her gullibility.

"What do you want?"

"I want to show you something," Ettares said, getting to her feet.

"Then show me."

"This way," she said, turning and heading for the lift, hands in her trouser pockets. Farzana followed after a brief moment of hesitation, hobbling behind her. She still hadn't gotten used to walking well with a cane; each time that she misstepped prompted a glance from Ettares.

They made their way to the lift where Ettares pressed the call rune. She hummed as they waited, and once inside, she pressed the tune for floor twenty.

One whole floor... I can't even make it up one flight of stairs. I'm pathetic.

Ettares spent her own energy to propel the lift up a single floor solely because Farzana couldn't climb stairs; she felt like a veritable invalid.

I hate this.

They exited the lift and headed into a darkened hallway; at the end of the hall stood a door. Roughly speaking, the door was above Farzana's suite. She shuddered, knowing she was sharing a ceiling with her father. It felt like he could drop in at any time, though she knew that was true no matter where she went. He hadn't paid her a visit once since she had arrived, though, and she hoped to keep it that way. If that meant groveling and keeping her head down, then that's what she would do.

So why am I out here right now with Ettares?

Nevermind that. The door in front of her was a very intimidating door, surrounded by physical keypads and scanning devices. She assumed all the gadgets around it were for security purposes, and she wondered what on Faerth was so important to warrant the extra precautions.

"Inside are secrets that could kill us all," Ettares said in a hushed voice.

Let's keep the door closed then.

"Why would he want to kill us all?" Farzana asked aloud. Then again, the fact that he had no qualms about slaughtering people in cold blood meant he most likely had no love for any of his subjects, not even his own daughter. Especially not for his daughter. But no love lost didn't explain a desire to kill everyone.

"I'm not sure. I've been trying to piece things together, but I can't know anything for sure without getting in. You can get in, though."

"Me? And why on Faerth would I risk myself?"

Ettares gave her a sharp look. "Because this could save your family. Save that child you're living with. Save you. And you're the only one who can because you're related to him."

Okay, great.

Ettares tapped the edge of a keypad. "This is a five letter password. I don't know what it is. This is your standard iris scanner that most upper Aristo-fae Houses use so the family can enter without keys; it just needs a match on your eye color. And this one pricks your finger to check for a blood type match."

The mention of blood had Farzana swaying on her feet.

"I've checked your medical records; you have the same blood type as Erasto. And we all know you two are the only ones in Dradour right now with purple eyes; I'm assuming it's the same shade. You just need to figure out the five letter word."

"Oh is that all?" Farzana rolled her eyes. "That's impossible. What are the chances I'll accurately guess his secret password?"

Ettares gave her a look that she couldn't quite decipher. "Let's hope for all our sake that you can."

Farzana turned her attention back to the door and sighed. This was a monumental task, one she hadn't signed up for. Why did it have to be her? Why couldn't someone hack the security, somehow? She wasn't a hero, and she didn't want to be one either. She wanted to be asleep in her bed. She wanted to feel safe.

She wanted to never give Erasto another excuse to visit her.

"I'm tired," she said, not looking Ettares in the eye.

"I'll take you back, then." Ettares's voice held a distinct note of disappointment as she held her hand out, gesturing for Farzana to head back to the lifts. They walked in silence back down the long hall.

As the lifts came into view, so too did a green-winged pixie guard. The guard looked up and barked, "Who's there?"

Farzana stopped in her tracks. Were they even allowed to be there?

"Whoa, Farzana? Is that you?"

Recognition dawned on her as Farzana studied the guard's angular face. "Melara?" she gasped.

Melara looked her up and down, wearing a friendly grin. "Wow, what has it been—like 60 years now?"

"Since tertiary school! Wow, you look good," Farzana said, hoping the compliment would negate any need to ask what they were doing on Erasto's floor so late at night.

"I mean, same to you, love. Look at us, both adults now. How have you been?"

"Well, I can't say I've been wonderful. Times have been… stressful, lately." A self-deprecating chuckle escaped Farzana before she could catch it.

Melara gave her a sympathetic grimace. "Oof, yeah, I heard about your accident. I'm glad they closed off that open-air column so the stairs are safe now."

Farzana glanced up at Ettares to her standing stock still, a desperate smile plastered on her face. A vestigial impulse had Farzana reaching to give her hand a quick, reassuring squeeze before turning back to Melara. "Listen, it was great chatting with you, but I'm exhausted. These little walks tire me out. I'm actually heading back to my rooms now."

"Oh, good. Erasto doesn't really like faeries wandering around at night. But hey, as a favor from one school pal to another, I won't say anything," she said with a wink. "Have a good night, you two!" With a little wave, she left, turning a corner and out of sight.

"Thank gods you knew her. We almost got reported," Ettares whispered, pulling Farzana by the hand toward the lift and slamming her thumb against the call rune.

"For being out of bed?"

"You haven't seen what he's done to the faeries who step out of line. It's not pretty." She shuddered.

You haven't seen what he's done to me.

A thought came to Farzana as they stepped into the lift.

"Hypothetically speaking, when would I even have the chance to get in there without Erasto finding out immediately? He lives in there, doesn't he?"

"Hypothetically speaking…you'd have to wait until he's not on Faerth."

Farzana's mind whirled in confusion. He was a ruler here; what ruler would just up and leave the planet? And why wasn't that major news? "What? But that's… How? Why would he leave?"

Ettares shrugged then gestured for her to exit the lift first. "He has an illegal teleportation device he brought here from Earth. Every now and then, he uses it to go back without using an interplanetary travel visa. If he keeps to his schedule, he'll be leaving again in a couple days. I'll let you know when he's gone."

They stopped in front of Farzana's door, and Farzana looked up to see that strange, indecipherable look in Ettares's eyes again.

"Get in, find his secrets, and get out. That's all you need to do."

Without so much as a goodbye, Ettares turned on her heel and left. Farzana was left with an unsettling feeling in the pit of her stomach as she watched her tall form disappear around the corner, and she wondered…

What secret was so terrifying that Ettares was full of so much fear? And what would it cost Farzana to find out?

21

ANOTHER MORNING, ANOTHER TRIP TO SEE
Enzi and beg for special favors. The daily excursions to the
kitchens seemed to be rebuilding Farzana's strength; at the very
least, the dose of happiness from good food and good company
left her feeling more stable than she had in...too long. And
since Laraf's stomach had finally regulated to her new diet—
she was even starting to get some fat in her cheeks—Farzana
wanted to introduce her to the wonder of chocolate. Of course
this meant Enzi right away began mixing up pancake batter and
sprinkling in chocolate morsels.

As she watched Enzi pouring batter onto the piping hot
griddle, Farzana reminisced on her nighttime adventure with
Ettares. As he flipped a pancake, she asked, "Enzi, if you were
Erasto, what is a five letter word you would use as a password?"

He snorted, flipping another pancake. "I don't get paid
enough to read his mind. Why?"

She shrugged, nibbling on the edge of a finished pancake
from the ever growing stack at his side. "No reason."

"Money!" Laraf said after counting the letters on her fingers.

"Wealth?" Enzi suggested, wiping sweat from his forehead
with the back of his sleeve.

"That's six," Farzana pointed out.

Enzi glared at her as Laraf let out a quiet giggle. Farzana hid a smile behind her hand; it was marvelous to hear Laraf laugh.

"I don't think it has anything to do with riches. I mean, this guy is all about control, right?" Farzana tapped her nails on the counter as she thought some more. The aroma of the kitchens could at times be overwhelming from the numerous scents of food being prepared, but today, with her stomach growling, all the breakfast smells made for a wonderful amalgamation.

"If you say so. I just do my job," Enzi said.

"What's up?" Araj asked, sauntering over to them.

"Araj!" Farzana held her arms out for a hug, and he stepped into them.

"Hello, little one," he said, bending down to tweak Laraf's nose and eliciting another giggle. "What are you up to?"

"We're guessing a password," Laraf said in a whisper.

"A password? Whose password?"

"Erasto's," Enzi said, sliding a fresh pancake onto the stack and dropping a dollop of butter onto the sizzling griddle. The smell had Farzana closing her eyes in ecstasy.

When she opened her eyes, Araj was giving her a sharp look. "Why do you care about Erasto's password?"

She shrugged, unwilling to divulge her secret mission to him. "No reason. For fun? Want to guess with us? It's five letters."

Araj let out a laugh. "What about farce?"

Farzana glared at him. "Why on Faerth would he have that horrible nickname as his password?"

He laughed harder. "Oh, come on. Wouldn't it be funny, though?"

Laraf looked between Araj and Farzana in confusion. "Is Farce your nickname?"

"No!" Farzana blurted out, the steam from the pancake stinging her eyes. "No, it's not. It's a hurtful word that Erasto used to make fun of me."

Her eyes grew wide. "Oh…"

"Whatever. It's probably something stupid, like Earth or human," Araj said with a dismissive wave of his hand. "For a faerie, he is weirdly obsessed with all that."

Earth!

A lightbulb went off in her head, but Farzana stifled a triumphant grin and nodded her head. "Whatever. This isn't fun anymore. Just forget it," she said, fluffing her hair. A ringlet nestled itself around her finger, mirroring the shape of her thoughts. If Ettares was right about Erasto leaving... If Earth really was the password... If she was lucky enough to get in and out without a guard catching her... If she could even get past the idea of letting a needle stab her finger to test her blood...

Finger pain is a special level of torture. Do I want to chance ALL of this?

"What do you want to do instead?" Laraf's tentative voice interrupted the spiral of Farzana's mind, drawing her back into the kitchen and surrounded by steam and the aroma of decadence.

"Hey, remember that time you spilled coffee in the hallway at the FRMDC, and Megami slipped in it and fell?" Araj sapphire eyes held hers with a spark. "I'll never forget the look on her face! Oh, she was furious. I can't believe you kept your job after that."

Farzana blushed at the reminder. It hadn't even been her coffee; she had run to grab it for him. Megami had screamed at her after work that day, something Farzana never admitted to Araj. And, if Farzana was being honest with herself, the only reason Megami had shown mercy was because she broke down sobbing and groveling, begging to keep her job. "What about the time you left work early and forgot about the quarterly Manager Board meeting, and I had to pretend you had fallen down the stairs and gone to the healer's clinic?"

"Ha! And Megami was like 'Why were you using the stairs? Blah blah blah.' And I said, 'Um, have you heard of exercise, Megami?'" Araj howled with laughter; the sound scraped up Farzana's arms, leaving bumps.

"You were always forgetting important stuff."

"And you were always covering for me. What a great friend," he said, wiping away tears.

Enzi rolled his eyes and muttered, "Maybe if you hadn't put her in so many situations where she could almost lose her job covering for you, you would have been a great friend too."

Araj stiffened. "Excuse me?"

"You heard me," Enzi said, plating two pancakes with a heaping dollop of whipped cream and handing it to Laraf.

Araj narrowed his eyes, his lips set in a hard line. "I hope you aren't insinuating that I've been a bad friend to Farzana."

"Why would I need to insinuate it?"

"Wow, okay, let's all calm down," Farzana said, putting a hand on Araj's shoulder. He shook her off, stepping closer to Enzi.

"No, no. I want to hear how I've been a bad friend," Araj said in a haughty voice.

"Oh, don't get me started."

"Please don't do this," Farzana said, a desperate whine creeping in.

They both ignored her.

Araj closed the admittedly small gap left between himself and Enzi, accentuating their height difference and forcing Enzi to look up at him. "Go ahead, tell me."

Enzi glowered from beneath lowered eyelids. "First off, you were always making Farzana cover for you even though *you* were a big shot Assistant Manager and she was *lower* management. You got her into trouble countless times for not doing her work because she was trying to do yours for you."

"If Farzana felt like she couldn't cover for me, she always had the option of saying so. I would have respected it," Araj said through gritted teeth.

"Oh, really? So you would have stayed at work if Farzana had said no?"

Laraf grabbed Farzana's arm and squeezed it, her body trembling. "Why are they fighting?"

"They both love me in different ways, but they don't agree

on what love looks like," Farzana said, her voice low. Laraf stepped closer and held onto her torso. Farzana put an arm around Laraf's small frame to lend her some strength, and hoped she wouldn't take off running; if Laraf bolted, nothing would be able to convince Farzana to not follow her.

"No, I would have left still, because I had legitimate reasons for leaving."

"So Farzana still would have felt the need to cover for you. How is that respecting her?" Enzi slapped a pancake down onto a new plate.

"Farzana was never coerced into covering for me. That was on her." Araj stabbed a finger in her direction; Laraf winced and Enzi sputtered.

"Next." Araj folded his arms over his chest.

"Next?" Enzi let out a dark chuckle. "Okay, big guy, how about this one? You assaulted her!"

Farzana clapped her hands over Laraf's ears, dropping her cane, and gaped at Enzi.

Araj spun around to stare at her. "You told him that?"

Something in her spine refused to cower under his glare. "Was it supposed to be a secret? Of course I told him. I told Tathi, too."

"Well, it's a good thing I was already losing my job. Thanks, Erasto! Because if you had reported me, I would have been fired for sure!"

"How is that my fault?" Farzana demanded, her hands shaking on Laraf's head. Her weak leg barely held her up. "You attacked me. I forgave you. Why is this an issue?"

"Oh, wow, you're so generous for forgiving me!" he spat. "What about making me watch you try to kill yourself?"

The silence that stretched through the kitchen, winding around the sizzling griddles and bubbling pots, crushed Farzana's lungs and left her struggling for air. Araj's indignation held her down, weighted her to the floor until she felt like the smallest thing in the room.

"What?"

Araj turned back to Enzi with a cynical laugh. "Oh, you

didn't know? Your sister tried to kill herself. That fall wasn't an accident."

Enzi faced her, eyes shimmering with sorrow and fatigue. "Zana...I don't know what to say."

Shame burned her cheeks and she averted her eyes. "Don't say anything. I don't want to hear it," she mumbled.

"So, yeah, I think as far as shit we've put each other through, we're pretty even, wouldn't you say, Farzana?"

She nodded through tears that fell unhindered, her hands continuing to shield Laraf's ears from the conversation.

"See? And we still love each other, and we're still friends. Because neither of us is perfect or better than the other. So shut up, Enzi." If the threatening buzz of Araj's wings weren't enough of a warning, his fists at his sides added to his hostility.

Enzi's shoulders slumped in defeat. "I have nothing to say."

"Good." Araj turned on his heel and left.

Farzana watched his back until he disappeared out the kitchen doors. All around her, the kitchen came back to life, as the other workers seemed to realize the drama was over. Forcing herself to lift her expression, Farzana lowered her hands and pulled Laraf in for a quick kiss on the forehead. "Can you pick up my cane, sweetie?"

Laraf obliged, her body no longer shaking in fear. "Are you okay?"

"I'll be okay. Let's just go home," she replied, her voice rough as she tried not to choke.

"Okay. Bye, Enzi," Laraf said, grabbing Farzana's free hand. Enzi didn't react, instead staring down at the bare, smoking griddle.

"Let's go." Farzana turned carefully and began to shuffle away. She wasn't in a hurry to come back anytime soon.

"It infuriates me that he thinks I'm a bad friend!" Araj huffed, his arms crossed as he paced back and forth, in and out of the frame of the mirror.

Farzana had barely walked into her room when the mirror rang, Araj's face popping up so he could rant to her about Enzi's 'audacity.' As if that's what she really needed, instead of a week's worth of sleep. Or the ability to change the past, which seemed to be locked behind the same amount of impossibility.

"He doesn't even know about all the times you vented to me about the stupid stunts he has pulled. Remember that time he came home drunk and knocked over your mother's brand new painting? Talk about being a bad son."

Farzana snapped a hand up, fury ballooning in her chest. "That is uncalled for."

"But calling me a bad friend is okay? Do you hear yourself right now?"

Farzana deflated with a sigh. "Neither is okay. What he said was also uncalled for too, but he was saying it from a place of love. He was concerned. Enzi is a wonderful son and an amazing sibling."

Araj rolled his eyes. "Fine, I won't rag on him. But just know I was thinking of that the whole time he was insulting me."

"Noted."

"Anyway, what are you doing tonight?" And just like that, his stormy expression dispersed, and he had an easy smile on his face.

Farzana shrugged one shoulder, which was difficult considering it was attached to the arm holding her cane. She ended up listing and barely caught herself on the edge of her bed. "Nothing, why?"

Araj snickered before saying, "Well, we should have a dance-off. Laraf can take Enzi's spot. It'll be fun for her."

Farzana felt her lips turn up. It might be good to let loose. "Okay, sounds good. But you are going to get our dinner tray from Enzi and apologize personally, and you are going to make up."

Araj recrossed his arms. "Or what?"

"Or you're not allowed to visit," she said, enunciating every word.

He stared at her hard for a long moment, maybe waiting

for her to reconsider, before sighing. "Fine, I'll do it. But he better be civil."

"Thank you!" Farzana drawled the last syllable, drawing a half smile from him.

"Yeah, whatever. See you tonight, okay?"

"Okay." The mirror shut off, leaving her face to face with her reflection.

She looked sick. Her sunken eyes were sinking in dark circles; her cheekbones jutted out, probably because she hadn't yet regained all the weight she had lost during her hunger strike. Hard to believe she used to have a soft, round face. She stepped closer to the mirror and gingerly touched her cheek; it felt hotter than normal, like she still had a low-grade fever.

She really needed a nap. Turning to hop into bed, taking care to not trip on her cane, she stopped when she heard a knock at the outer door. Laraf was in the bathroom, so Farzana trudged through the sitting room and opened the door.

No one was there.

Something caught her eye, and she looked down to see an envelope sealed with bright red wax. She stooped to pick it up, knees cracking, and glanced down the hall, wondering where Ettares was.

Why didn't she say hello?

That was a ridiculous thought that she banished with an angry shake of her head. Ettares didn't like her; she was only back in touch because she needed Farzana for something. A dysfunctionally functional relationship and nothing more.

Farzana slammed the door and turned back to her bedroom. A splash of purple on the couch drew her attention. Moving closer, she saw what must have been a mockery of a faerie; a long pillow had been shoved into her favorite shirt and pair of pants, both the same delicate shade of lavender.

Laraf stepped into the room and stopped when she saw Farzana examining the pillow faerie.

"Laraf? What is this?"

"It's you," she mumbled, a blush splotched across her pale cheeks.

Farzana looked at it again. "Me?"

Laraf stared at the ground. "Sometimes...I have bad dreams. And I get lonely and scared. So I made a pillow Farzana to keep me company...and I hug her when the bad dreams come."

Farzana's heart constricted even as she held out her arm for a hug. Laraf rushed over and into the embrace, and Farzana steadied herself against the couch to keep from falling.

"Sweetie, you don't have to be lonely. I have a huge bed; why don't you sleep with me from now on?"

In a tiny voice, "Can we cuddle?"

The chest pain was as blinding as her burning tears. "Of course we can."

Laraf's eyes lit up as she looked up at Farzana. "Really?"

"Really."

Laraf bounced up and down in her arms, rocking them both. "When are we going to sleep?"

"Well, I'm actually tired right now. Want to take a nap?"

"Yes!"

As Laraf bounded off, Farzana realized she had dropped the envelope. She picked it up and broke the seal; inside was a single sheet of paper with one line written in elegant cursive: *He's leaving tonight.*

Erasto was leaving. Tonight was her chance...but was she willing to take it?

~ ☼ ~

Araj arrived later, waking them from their nap by tapping on the outer door and letting himself in. "Wake up, sleepyheads! Dinner is served." He brandished a tray full of food.

Laraf cautiously crept from under the covers and stared at Araj with wide eyes. Farzana couldn't help noticing her usual cheery demeanor toward him had changed after the fight in the kitchens and wondered if that would be a permanent change. But that meant thinking about what Araj and Enzi's future interactions would be like, which also meant that, if everyone didn't settle back down, all of her relationships would feel the strain.

At least it was a distraction from the shittiness named Erasto.

"How did the talk go?" Farzana asked, sitting up and pulling her hair away from her face.

Araj avoided her gaze. "It's good. We're all good."

Farzana stared at him, but he just set the tray down on the end of the bed with a flourish and went back to the sitting room, returning with an armchair. He placed it beside the food and went back for the other.

Laraf grabbed the bowl of berries from the tray and sat on the floor, popping one into her mouth.

"Why are you here, Araj?" Laraf asked between bites.

Araj looked over at Farzana. "Did Farzana not tell you?"

"Tell me what?"

"We are going to have a dance-off."

"What's that?"

"It's when we turn on the mirror to the local dance competitions, and we have our own dance competition right here. We dance and have a great time."

Laraf's eyes were wide. "You dance?"

"You bet I do! I'm probably the best dancer you know," he said with a smug look.

"But what about Farzana?" Laraf asked, looking over as Farzana got out of bed and made her way over.

"What about her?"

"How can she dance with a cane?"

Araj and Farzana stared at each other as the realization hit. Pressing her lips together as tight as possible kept her grounded as she grappled with that thought that...

I can't dance...

At least, not while her leg was still healing.

"Um, well, Farzana is actually going to be the judge tonight," Araj said in a soft voice.

"That makes sense. The judge is the most important part."

Farzana mustered a watery smile. "You can be the judge next time, sweetie."

She bounced a little and flashed a stunning smile in response. "Okay!"

Farzana watched as Laraf and Araj ate, waving away any attempts Araj made at offering food. Her appetite had vanished. She couldn't believe it had taken her this long to realize she couldn't dance.

Well, no one had told her that she couldn't try to dance. And until she tried, she wouldn't know for sure. So, as long as she held onto hope, it would all be fine. Her mind set, she grabbed a piece of buttered bread and took a generous bite. It wouldn't be that night, but soon, she would definitely try to dance.

"Tell me about your day," Farzana said, leaning back in her chair.

"Mine?" Araj asked, rubbing the back of his neck. He cleared his throat and a blush appeared on his cheeks. "Well, I was working with someone. Someone I happen to like."

"Oh?" Farzana gave him a wicked grin.

Araj hadn't had many crushes since their friendship started. He had, in fact, only dated one faerie in all that time—a pixie named Jela who had been a temp at the FRMDC for about a year. That relationship had not ended well, and Farzana was pretty sure the smoldering ruins of it had been the reason that Jela had ended up not applying for a permanent position.

Araj nodded, looking self-conscious. "She's a guard here. She's from the House of Emerald, and she's—"

Farzana spat out her food, nearly hitting him in the eye.

"Hey!" he yelled, jumping up and wiping his shirt.

Her hand flew to her mouth. "Oh gods, that's so gross. I'm sorry!"

"What was that for?" he asked, sitting back down and glaring at her.

"I can't believe you're interested in Melara."

He gaped at her. "You know Melara?"

Farzana laughed. "We went to tertiary school together! I literally just saw her last—yesterday," she said, remembering at the last second what Ettares had said about being out of bed after dark.

He raised his eyebrows and whistled. "Small world, huh?"

"You bet," she said, cramming more bread in her mouth.

22

FARZANA LAY IN BED, TOSSING AND TURNING
while Laraf slept like a rock beside her. The tiny imp breathed
steadily, her arms curled around one of the numerous pillows
covering the bed. Farzana's mind drifted from Laraf to the
shadows around them, every creak in the building causing her
to hold her breath in anticipation. Was that Ettares out in the
hall? Was there a guard out there, waiting to see if she broke
the unspoken curfew? She tried to time her breaths instead, to
even them out and relax into sleep, but she just ended up feeling
dizzy whenever she lost track of her inhale and exhale ratio.

Should I break in? Will I even be able to?

After what felt like hours of staring at the gray shapes
playing in the shadows on the walls, she gave up on sleep,
deciding to go to the door and take a look. Maybe her plan
would work! Maybe it wouldn't. But if Ettares was right about
the danger—and about Farzana being the only one able to do
anything about it—then she had to try.

Dressing as quietly as possible, she left the room with Laraf
softly snoring in bed. Down the hall, to the lifts, one rune to
call the lift and another to select the top floor… A monstrous
runic headache bloomed in her skull, threatening to crack it

wide open, but she stuck to her plan, shuffling down the hall to the door. It was still as intimidating as when she first saw it. The keypad and scanners glowed menacingly in the dim hallway.

Without any conscious thought, she reached out and brushed the keypad, felt the ridges of the buttons on the pads of her fingers, before punching in *E A R T H*. A beep and a flash of green; her breathing at once felt monstrously loud. Did that mean the password worked? The absence of any kind of wailing alarm emboldened her.

Steeling herself, she pressed the tip of her finger into the depression of the blood scanner. A needle shot out; an overwhelming sting spread from the fresh, miniscule wound. That maybe wasn't the correct way to place her finger but really, was there any correct way to be stabbed? Blood testing locks were diabolical, so it shouldn't have been a surprise that Erasto utilized one. The mechanism sucked up the drop of spilled blood; before a second drop could fall, Farzana sucked on the end of her finger, the taste of metal coating her throat. The scanner beeped once and flashed green.

This is working!

The last scanner, placed just above her eye level, called to her. Using her cane to prop herself up a bit higher, she stepped up to it and held still as a bright light swept over her eye. A beep, a flash of green, and then the latch let out a resounding and hollow click; the door opened ever so slightly, gliding on silent hinges.

Staring at it in awe, she almost didn't hear the scuff of a footfall behind her. She whirled around, finding herself face to face with a guard: Melara.

"Oh! Hi!" she said, trying not to fall over as her cane got entwined with her legs.

"Wow, we don't see each other for sixty years and now twice in one week? How are you?" Melara grinned.

Farzana plastered an answering smile on her face. "I mean, I'm stuck here against my will, so there is that."

"Oof. Yeah, that must be tough. What with your father being…you know, himself."

"Exactly," Farzana said, her voice as weak as her legs. "But hey, what can you do?"

"Break into his personal office, I suppose."

Farzana sucked in her breath and expelled it all in one gust. "Ha! Whaaat?"

Melara pointed at the door with a lazy finger. "I saw you unlock everything. But you know what? Knock yourself out. What do I care?"

If Farzana opened her mouth any wider, her jaw would hit the floor. "Excuse me? Aren't you a guard? Or is the uniform just for show?"

Okay but why did I say that? Do I want her to arrest me?

Melara shrugged. "Listen, he doesn't pay me enough to rough up his daughter. Just promise me you won't steal anything? Because that would make the break in, like, super obvious."

"I promise I won't steal anything," Farzana said with a mock salute.

Seriously, what am I doing?

"Great! Have fun!" Melara turned and sauntered away, whistling a low tune that bounced along the walls.

Farzana waited until Melara rounded the corner and silence reclaimed the hall before turning back to the door. It was still open a crack. Breathing a sigh of relief, and attempting to calm her racing heart, she pushed it open and stepped inside. Ahead of her was a short corridor lined with doors on either side. It opened up at the far end into an atrium; the center of the space was dominated by a giant machine that looked like some kind of teleportation device, though it was different from any other she'd seen before.

For one, the landing pad was large enough for probably over a hundred faeries rather than the standard individual pad. As she stepped closer, she could see five destination screens attached to it rather than just one. She wasn't sure why it would need four extra screens, but she also had never been interested in teleportation technology. No point in being interested in something you were too poor to have access to.

The door at the very end of the corridor, right before the teleportation chamber, was ajar; a glowing light emanated from it. Her curiosity piqued, she decided to start her search there. Pushing the door open and striding in, she gasped and muffled a scream with her hand. Chained to the wall was a figure that shone so bright that pain seared through her head, pain unlike anything she had ever experienced.

"Don't look directly at me, child," it rasped. "It can kill you."

Good to know.

Shielding her eyes, she glanced around the room and saw a wooden chair in the center, a table on the far end with what looked like torture tools, and a pair of tinted glasses hanging on a hook by the door. Grabbing them and shoving them on, she turned back to the figure.

The light was muted through the glasses, but she could see clearly that whatever had spoken was the most beautiful thing she had ever seen.

Gold skin, unlike any faerie she had heard of. Immense, white feathered wings, like illustrations she had seen of Earth birds. Its long, slender fingers were tipped with ivory claws. Full, blood red lips revealed rows of pointed teeth. And its eyes… Its eyes were pure white and and glowed softly like candlelight. It looked at her with an expression akin to kindness, though she had no idea why.

Sinking down onto the chair, she whispered, "What are you?"

The hoarse voice that answered was the most melodious sound she had ever heard. "I am a bright," it said with an inclination of the head.

Aptly named, then.

As she looked more closely, she saw other signs of its mistreatment: missing feathers from its wings, needle and burn marks on its golden skin, dried blood around its wrist and neck shackles.

"You must be the stubborn daughter," it said.

Stubborn? Erasto apparently has never met himself.

Pressing her lips together to keep herself from hissing in

indignation, she looked the figure up and down again. It was difficult to focus on anything else whilst gazing at such beauty. "Are you a faerie?" she asked, finding her words.

It shook its head, chains rattling. "I am not from this world."

"You're from Earth?" Farzana's voice was incredulous. She had never heard of such a being in any of the required Earth studies classes at school.

"There are more than two worlds, despite what you faeries like to believe. There are five: the world of humans, Earth; the world of fae, Faerth; the world of brights, Venus; and the world of wights, Mars. Us brights have watched Earth and Faerth and documented their histories, though we have never journeyed to either."

"Until now," she pointed out.

It threw back its head and laughed; thunder and lightning cracked in Farzana's head, and she clapped her hands to her ears, dropping her cane.

"Child, do you not see the burns, the wounds? I did not leave my world willingly; I was captured. Perhaps you know the one who ensnared me? I'm told she's famous."

Dread wound its way around Farzana's neck as she bent to retrieve her cane.

Could it be?

"Her name is Ettares."

Farzana fled, the glasses slipping from her face and dashing on the floor.

When morning came, Farzana told Laraf she felt sick and needed some alone time. Laraf gave her a hug before leaving to spend the day in the kitchens with Enzi, giving Farzana the solitude she so desperately needed.

It hadn't been a lie; the knowledge that there was an innocent creature trapped upstairs had her stomach in knots. It also made her head spin. How could entire other populated worlds exist? Worlds she had never heard of, with creatures, sentient beings? In school, they were taught about how the planet had split into two—Earth and Faerth—long ago, trapping the faeries on one and humans on the other. The split had been studied and no one as yet had come up with a reason for it.

Of course, interplanetary travel had been made possible over a millennium ago, though off-world teleportation had only existed for the last few centuries. Faeries frequently visited Earth for vacation, but just because they knew how to travel between the two didn't make the mystery of the split any easier to approach.

But to learn that there were multiple inhabited planets aside from those two? There could be millions and billions of other beings out there, living their mundane lives, and faeries were none the wiser. How had Erasto found out? Was it common knowledge on Earth that there were other worlds?

And Ettares! Ready and willing to capture that bright and dragging it from its home planet, handing it over to Erasto to be used for his twisted ends. What kind of faerie did it take to not only ignore the harm there but instigate more? Working with Erasto to manipulate Farzana seemed like nothing compared to this. Araj had warned her about Ettares but obviously she had failed to fully grasp the actual magnitude of peril that followed Ettares. Weren't bounty hunters just supposed to stalk faeries, not hurt them?

The fact that it had been so easy for Farzana to fall for Ettares's charms should have spoken to the level of expertise and depravity that the noble wielded, and yet... After Ettares was exposed, after the sting of betrayal colored their brief friendship, it had been hard to reconcile the gentle, caring, passionate noble with whoever had been paid by Erasto. To be revisited by her, to be told that something was wrong, that Erasto was wrong and that Ettares needed help against him... She had looked so scared and earnest. That speech about Farzana being the only faerie who could save everyone—to save *her*—that had to mean something. If it was fake, if it was just a load of shit, then what was Farzana risking herself for? What was worth the possibility of reigniting Erasto's wrath?

None of it made sense.

The air muddied around her as she twisted her fingers between each other, her nails scraping across her palms. The painful vibrations of it should have helped her focus, but the sheer number of unknowable variables overwhelmed everything else. Her eyes bounced around the room, seeking an anchor. They landed on the desk. Before she knew what she meant to do, she sat down and reached for the fountain pen and pad of paper.

A letter. That's what she needed to do: she needed to write to Ettares, explaining how she felt and that she never wanted to see her again. To pour out the hurt that she had shoved down somewhere deep. To speak the truth about how she couldn't forget what had happened. Again and again, she set pen to paper. Again and again, she crumpled the page, tossing it onto the floor. Words that couldn't properly express her emotional turmoil littered the floor, a cemetery of anguish and inadequate boundaries. What were you supposed to say when every fiber of your being wanted to hate someone, but you just ended up missing them instead? Farzana was too scared to ask herself whether that said more about Ettares or herself.

Ettares's actions were terrifying and loathsome. So why had she helped Farzana uncover her secret? What sane faerie would knowingly reveal that they had done terrible things, unless to gloat? What was her reason for helping Farzana find the bright? What did any of it mean?

Farzana dropped the pen and sighed. Her temples were being squeezed by a vice of stress. None of this had helped her made heads or tails of anything—honestly she was pretty sure she was more confused now than when she had started this train of thought—and she was exhausted from her late night adventure.

Begging Enzi for coffee couldn't hurt.

~ ☼ ~

Late that night, long after the sun had set and Laraf had succumbed to sleep at her side, Farzana lay still, once again contemplating the bright. She needed to go back; she had questions only it could answer. It had mentioned five worlds but only named four. What was the fifth? How and why had it been captured in the first place? What was a wight?

And, most importantly, she needed to know what Erasto's plan was for Dradour. There had to be a reason why he returned, why he had murdered the royal family.

Mustering her courage, Farzana slipped out of bed and began making her way upstairs. The midnight hush frightened her, as if the tower held its breath while it waited for her to make a mistake. Every tap of her cane and scuff of her shoes on the floor made her heart race; what if someone was listening? The finger prick didn't hurt nearly as bad as the idea of what Erasto would do to her if she didn't hurry up and get inside without getting caught. When the door opened, she threw a quick glance back to check if anyone was watching and then made her way in.

The glasses were on the ground right where she had dropped them; Farzana shielded her eyes until she could place them on her face. A small crack ran down one lens. The light from the bright splintered off in weird shapes as she turned to look at it. It was aptly named and, again, she marveled at its ethereal beauty, her gaze lingering on the patches of unblemished skin.

"Why are you here?" she blurted out. The sound of her own voice jarred her, and she sank to sit on the chair in an effort to steady herself.

The bright raised its head to look at her, its crystal white eyes looking dull compared to the previous night. "I am here because Erasto wants answers," it sighed, its voice full of exhaustion.

She pondered that. She too wanted answers, though she wasn't willing to torture anyone to get them. "Would you mind answering some questions? I won't torture you if you don't."

It smiled, showing off rows of pointed teeth. "Ask your questions, child."

"What is Erasto planning?"

It tilted its head to the side and blinked several times before answering. "Erasto is a politician in a powerful country on Earth with a remarkably high position of authority. He has promised his Earth men that he will bring peace and prosperity to them. Why he is on Faerth and how any of this will accomplish that...I am unsure."

Erasto was a leader on Earth. That finally explained why he had stayed on Earth for so long. But why would humans be okay with an immortal ruling them? He had been there for over five generations of human life. How much of that time had he been a ruler?

"So you don't know what he's doing here? What he wants?" Her pulse grew loud, thundering in her ears. She needed to calm down; having a panic attack in Erasto's quarters was a terrible idea.

"I know nothing for certain, child. My best guess is he might be planning an invasion of some kind."

An invasion? Will we go to war?

"What makes you say that?" Farzana asked around a shuddering breath.

It looked pointedly at the adjacent wall, where another set of shackles hung above a dried pool of what might have been black blood. "There used to be a wight there. It died from torture a month ago."

She shivered, looking at the massive stain of gore. The blackness was eerie; faerie blood was red, or in the case of amphibians like merfae or water nymphs, blue. Even humans had red blood, though maybe that similarity was due to them coming from the same history as faeries, albeit several millennia ago. How alien was a wight that the essence of its life was entirely devoid of color?

"What exactly is a wight?"

"A wight is a being of pure despair. It can read your thoughts and poison them, causing you to react violently toward others and yourself, even to the point of killing yourself." It lowered its head, resting its chin on its chest. "My kind have waged a war against the wights for an eternity. Even so, the things Erasto did to it…"

She stared at the floor as the bright's voice trailed off. She couldn't help mentally mapping out where she was in comparison to the 19th floor, and realizing she was, in all likelihood, directly above the tiny room where Erasto had kept her imprisoned. Could this wight have caused her suicidal ideation? It's not like she had never experienced depression before, but she had never harmed herself or even thought of it.

She shook her head, clearing those thoughts. There was no point in wondering 'what if' because what was done was done; she couldn't take any of it back.

Focus…

"Why would Erasto want a wight?" She shifted in the uncomfortable chair, her legs beginning to go numb from loss of circulation.

"Erasto asked it many questions, though the ones I was privy to were always about how to control a wight army. I can only assume he wants that knowledge because he himself wants to control a wight army. Since it makes little sense for him to wield such an army against Earth, the next logical conclusion would be he intends to bring one here."

Farzana's throat constricted; she rubbed at her neck, tugging at her collar in a desperate attempt to ease the phantom strangulation. What could Erasto do to Dradour, to Faerth itself, with an army of despair? And what would that do for him? None of it made sense. Faerth wasn't in a war against Earth. The two planets had always shared peace. An Earth leader attacking Faerth wouldn't help Earth; it would only ignite a conflict that would end in horrors for both planets.

This visit was making her feel worse rather than better. If she wasn't able to find some semblance of control and hope soon…

"Why were you captured? What is Erasto asking you?"

"Erasto wants to know about the history of Faerth, specifically about an intellectual convention from back in the year immediately following the split between Faerth and Earth. The convention sought to understand why the original planet split in two and what this meant for each planet."

"Did he learn what he was looking for?" The words were a mere whisper. Her grip on her cane tightened until her knuckles were white.

"No."

Our saving grace.

She released the chokehold on her cane. Whatever the answer was, it was important to Erasto's plan. And if he didn't know it, that bought them all some time. Maybe it would be enough time to find the answer before he could.

The bright cocked its head to the side as though listening to something Farzana couldn't hear. "You should leave now. Erasto will be here soon."

Her vision darkened momentarily. "What? But he was supposed to be gone for several days," she gasped.

"His interplanetary teleportation device has started up. He is coming."

Farzana limped to the door, slid the glasses off, and hung them on their hook. As she made to leave, she remembered one of her questions.

"What's the fifth world?" she asked, keeping her back to the bright.

It sighed, a lyrical breath. "My future world: Death."

Farzana's brows knit together as she struggled to wrap her head around its words. That's what she needed: one more thing that made absolutely no sense. She shoved that cryptic thought into the back of her mind. A flash of light drew her eye toward the atrium; one of the screens attached to the teleportation device was lit up, the word 'Wight' flashing on the screen. She leapt forward into the chamber to read the screen better, panic trickling through her. Numbers popped up below the text, steadily increasing. When the numbers hit the hundreds, her breathing started hitching.

A whole horde of wights! In Dradour!

She couldn't allow the wights to come. She had to do something, anything. Shadowy figures began materializing on the landing pad, and she stifled a shriek as she realized they were about to come through.

Harvester, help me!

A giant red button off to the side of the machine pulled her focus. The placard read 'Emergency Shut Off.' Farzana rushed to it, ignoring the sharp pain in her leg, and clawed at the protective cover. When it finally popped off, she slammed a hand on the button.

Nothing happened.

A guttural scream ripped her throat as she spun around. The incoming wights were quickly growing opaque; there was no telling what they would do to her when they arrived. She sank to her knees, ready to accept defeat. She wasn't a savior. Ettares had backed the wrong faerie; she would have had better luck handling it herself.

The whine of the machine grew with a frenzy, the sound deafening in her left ear...but not in her right. Turning, she saw a glowing tank of fluid and wires beneath the table that held the teleportation control board. Farzana had never quite grasped the science behind teleportation, but she knew one thing: if that's where the sound was coming from, that's what she needed to break.

Scrambling up, she reached down past the edge of the table and yanked at the cable connecting the control board and the tank. Not even a budge. She let out a scream of frustration, her cane shaking in her hand. Her cane...

As if of its own accord, the cane smashed down on the controls, again and again and again. A squeal and a pop and then the board emitted some smoke, but the whir of the machine was uninterrupted. With a strength she didn't know she had, Farzana shoved the entire table to the side, exposing the glowing tank. Taking her cane in both hands, she slammed it against the glass. A crack appeared, so small as to be inconsequential. Heaving, Farzana raised her cane; before she could hit the tank again, the crack splintered out, threading across the entire top of the tank like lattice work. With a roar, the glass shattered and the fluid surged out, swamping the floor and clinging to her clothes.

Immediately, the teleportation device quit humming. When she turned to the screen, it had shut off. The shadowy figures were gone as well. A sob spilled from her lips as she stared at the mess; she didn't dare wipe the tears from her eyes with her hands soiled by the mysterious liquid so they fell freely down her cheeks. Careful of the slick floor, she made her way out of the room, her footsteps squelching softly beneath her. Standing before the exit, she leaned her forehead against the door and took a deep breath. The cold of the metal was a welcome sensation after the heat of panic. Collecting herself, she stepped out, shut the door behind her, and made her way back to the lifts.

23

FARZANA'S BREATHING SOUNDED HARSH IN
the stillness of The Center as she made her way back to her
rooms, a runic headache throbbing in her temples. She jerked
to a stop in the hallway when she noticed Ettares slumped
against the wall opposite her door, face relaxed in sleep.
Seeing her should have rekindled Farzana's ire; instead, she
couldn't help noticing the little details. Like the dark circles
beneath Ettares's eyes, and the way her fingernails were
bitten to the bed. Even asleep, the stress radiating from her
was undeniable.

Maybe she hadn't been lying about needing help.

Farzana contemplated whether to wake her or ignore her.
On the one hand, waking her would mean they'd have to talk
through some tough stuff. Walking past her and going to bed
instead seemed like the easier choice. Then again, Farzana
hadn't finished that letter. This might be her best chance to
tell Ettares how she really felt…if she could figure that out
for herself. Sighing, she nudged Ettares's leg with her cane.

With a harsh gasp, Ettares startled awake, already pushing up from the floor. Her eyes met Farzana's and the shock
melted into what might have been fondness. Shaking her

head and settling back down, eyes trained on the floor, she said, "Oh, it's you."

"I'll try not to take that as an insult."

"No, I mean I'm glad it's you and not a guard. Or Erasto."

Farzana fumed. "So you knew he was coming back tonight and what? Didn't want to warn me?"

"What do you mean? He's back?"

The hint of fear in Ettares's voice coupled with the perplexion twisting her features was convincing. Farzana leashed her anger. "I mean, the bright warned me he was coming, and it was actually an army of wights, so I shut the machine off before they could teleport in. I don't know what that means for Erasto or if he was actually with them or not."

"Oh shit." Ettares scrambled to her feet. "Can I come in your suite so we can talk? Safely?"

Farzana gazed at Ettares for a moment, taking in the sight of her disheveled hair and sleepy eyes. She was so damn beautiful, and after everything she had done, it was so hard to keep that in mind and stay angry.

I hate it.

"Fine," Farzana said, turning and opening the door. "But only because I don't want us getting caught by a guard." She flipped on the sitting room light and went to shut the adjoining door to the bedroom, so as not to wake Laraf.

"Thank you," murmured Ettares, following her in and standing awkwardly in the center of the room. Seeing her in this room, looking like she wanted nothing more than to disappear… this is what she looked like last time. With fresh anger in her heart, it had been easy for Farzana to ignore the hurt in Ettares's eyes, the pleas on her lips. Screaming at her had felt cathartic at the time even though nothing had actually been solved by it. Farzana didn't magically feel whole after Ettares walked out the door. She wasn't sure what it would take to heal and move on from the betrayal, but maybe sitting down and speaking candidly would be a good start.

Farzana sat on the couch and gestured to one of the velvet chairs; Ettares perched on the edge of the seat, giving her a soft smile. Farzana steeled herself, unwilling to allow the smile to disarm her. Memories of her first night in The Center were pulling her apart. She needed to take control. She needed answers.

"Why did you capture it? And why did you torture it?" Farzana's voice shook with thinly veiled hostility.

Ettares held up her hands. "Whoa, I never tortured the bright! And I didn't even know it was a sapient being until after I gave it to Erasto. Look…" She reached up and brushed the curls back from her eyes, rocking slightly in her seat. "Erasto promised me a ton of money and an adventure. He told me to go to this, this *planet*, okay, and capture this beast. Another planet? Hello! I jumped at the chance to see another world, okay?" A telltale spark of excitement shone in Ettares's eyes, completely at odds with the unhappy set of her mouth and the tension in her shoulders.

Farzana nodded, pursing her lips. "So you'll really do anything for money, won't you?"

Ettares raked her nails through her curls, causing her hair to stand on end. "I won't do anything for money. I have standards! I just didn't—" Farzana hissed, pointing toward the closed bedroom door. Ettares let out a low growl before continuing at a lower volume. "I didn't know who Erasto was at the time. I didn't realize how dangerous he was, or I never would have helped him. This was all before he killed the royal family."

Disbelief lumped in Farzana's throat and she struggled to speak around it. "But that was months ago. He's been torturing the bright this entire time?" Her stomach roiled; she fought to keep its contents down.

"I didn't know!" she wailed, apparently abandoning the attempt to keep quiet. Her arms waved in the air as punctuation. "I was naive, okay? And I was wrong to take the assignment to get closer to you too. He wanted me to find out about you, get to know you, but as I got closer to you, I started falling for you."

Something shifted in Farzana's chest. Ignoring it, she snorted and rolled her eyes. "Yeah, okay. You don't have to pretend; he isn't here right now."

"No, you don't understand. Those few days when I didn't visit you? You were worried I didn't want to hang out anymore, but that's the furthest from the truth you can get. I was away working in another country because I gave all the money back to Erasto, and I had to make it all back, somehow. So I took a couple jobs in Ostrana."

The gears in Farzana's mind clicked and whirred as she processed the new information. "So the date...visiting your house...that was all genuine? He wasn't paying you?"

"No! He didn't hire me to date you; that was something I wanted to do. I liked being your friend. I wanted to be something more." Ettares stopped, her lip quivering as she sucked in a breath. Her watery eyes avoided Farzana's as she cleared her throat. "But I realized I couldn't date you with a clear conscience unless I gave back the money and canceled the job. When Erasto came back and heard...that was the night he started the fire."

Farzana sat there, mollified. The whole time, she'd thought... But what did it really change? Ettares had still accepted a job to spy on her. She had worked with Erasto, several times.

"Farzana, I am so, so deeply sorry. I know this is too late to fix anything, but I need you to know that I know I fucked up. I will always regret causing you pain." This time when Ettares made eye contact, tears spilled over onto her cheeks. "Just please, if there's anything I can do to try and make it right, let me know."

Ettares liked her. Farzana's heart tapped out a funky rhythm in her chest. It wasn't fake, none of it was fake. Ettares liked her, and she liked Ettares. That's all it took, right? Mutual attraction?

Her heart said 'jump' but her brain, for once, begged her to stop and think. The messages tangled up in her mouth until she heard herself say, "Maybe...we can try again...to be friends."

Ettares gazed at her with an overwhelming sense of relief. "Do you mean it? You're not just saying that to be nice? I swear, I won't betray your trust."

"You better not," Farzana growled. She didn't have the energy nor the intention necessary to put any real anger behind the sound. "And yes, I mean it. And…you can sleep here to-night, on the couch, if you want. I don't want anything bad to happen to you out there."

Ettares brought a hand up to her mouth in a rather awful attempt at hiding the smile growing there. "I'd like that," she said, a blush creeping across her nose.

"I'll grab some blankets," Farzana said quickly, heaving to her feet and rushing away so she didn't stop and stare at Ettares all night. The linen closet in her bathroom contained a small arsenal of blankets and pillows; she grabbed a couple of each, making sure to take her time returning to the sitting room.

In the bedroom, still swaddled by darkness, Laraf sat up in bed. "What's going on?" she asked, fear in her eyes.

"I have a friend who is going to sleep on the couch. Go back to sleep. I'll be back soon," Farzana said in a quiet voice.

"Okay," Laraf mumbled, lying back down and rolling over.

Farzana watched her for a moment, noticing the steady rise and fall of her chest as she breathed. Laraf had become so precious to her in such a short time. If the wights had gotten through… She shuddered at the idea of poor Laraf being tormented. She'd obviously had enough despair in her life already; Farzana would do whatever it took to keep her from accruing any more. She would do anything for her.

Maybe that's how Ettares had felt. Maybe, somehow, she really had fallen for Farzana in such a brief amount of time. Hopefully not in the sisterly way that Farzana felt for Laraf. Hopefully not in a familial way at all.

Maybe her feelings for Laraf were a horrible choice of comparison for her and Ettares. Regardless, Farzana wasn't ready to face those feelings yet. Not after the hurt and betrayal, and the harrowing events in Erasto's quarters. What she needed was rest.

Farzana entered the sitting room and plopped the bundle onto the couch. "Sleep well," she said, turning back around.

"Wait, please."

She stopped, not quite willing to look back but too anxious to miss whatever Ettares wanted to say.

Ettares stood and took a step closer to her. Somehow, with

the vast majority of the room still separating them, she felt farther away.

"I'm sorry."

"You did say that."

"And I'm saying it again. What I did was wrong. It was invasive. I am so incredibly sorry for doing that to you. I would take it back if I could." Farzana chanced a look back and met Ettares's ice blue eyes.

"Yeah, well. Don't do it again," Farzana said, clearing her throat and giving her a weak laugh. "That hurt. A lot."

"I can't imagine," Ettares whispered.

"Well, goodnight."

"Goodnight, Farzana." Ettares called after her.

Farzana couldn't help the smile that teased her lips. She and Ettares had made up. They were going to be friends, real friends this time, without a horrible, devastating secret hanging over them. And maybe, just maybe…

She snuggled under the covers, the smile pinching her cheeks. Unbidden, the thought of Erasto, the wights, and the bright pushed to the forefront of her mind. Her smile faded. What would morning bring?

~ ☼ ~

Laraf woke Farzana by jumping onto the bed, causing it to bounce. Farzana groaned, exhaustion weighing her down. Late night visits with an otherworldly being were seriously ruining her sleep schedule.

"Erasto is back," Laraf whispered in her ear, her breath tickling Farzana's cheek.

Farzana sat up, rubbing her eyes. "What makes you say that?"

"I went to the kitchens because I was hungry. His imps are beating up random faeries in the halls," she said in a solemn voice.

Farzana glanced at her sharply. That naked fear was back in Laraf's eyes, and Farzana wondered if it was in her own eyes as well. Did Erasto suspect her? Logically, if he was beating up random faeries, then he didn't have a suspect…right?

Farzana rolled out of bed and crumpled to the floor, wincing and muttering curses under her breath. Flailing her arms, she managed to snag her cane and use it to stand. She walked into the sitting room and yelled at Ettares to wake up; Ettares jumped up and fell to the floor, tangled in blankets.

How alike we are.

Farzana stifled the urge to laugh at the bewilderment on her face.

"What? What is it?" Ettares asked, kicking off the blankets and getting into a fighting stance.

"Calm down, no one is here. But Laraf said that Erasto is siccing his guards on everyone. Faeries are getting hurt."

"He's angry. He knows someone sabotaged his plans," Ettares said.

"But does he know it's me? Or does he think someone hacked into his rooms?" Farzana paced the length of the room. "He hasn't sent anyone here. That's good. No one knows it was me but you."

Realization dawned on her as she stopped and smacked her forehead. "Melara!"

"What?"

"That guard from the other night! She saw me go into his rooms."

"What?! Farzana, this is really bad."

"She said she wouldn't say anything!" Farzana wailed, tugging at her hair. "Oh gods." The room grew stifling, and she couldn't see straight. What would happen when Melara told him?

"I'm going to go check out the situation. You two stay here," Ettares said, straightening her suit jacket.

"No. I'm coming with you."

Ettares looked at her for a moment then sighed. "Fine. Come on, I'll protect you."

Farzana felt a warmth in her chest at the words but shook her head. Where was her mind? This was serious.

I'm a mess.

Ettares led the way to the stairway landing where they found utter chaos. Servants scrambled in every direction, some bloody, many of them crying or screaming. One of them bumped into Farzana; as she righted herself, she saw an ivory claw in his hands, golden blood dripping from the knuckle.

"A monster! A real monster!" he screamed, shoving her away from him.

Farzana knew that claw. Ettares caught her before she fell, but all she could see was the bright. Was it dead? Farzana grabbed Ettares's sleeve, pulling her close.

"He has part of the bright!" she yelled, pointing.

Ettares leapt into action, sprinting after him; Farzana attempted to follow before realizing she would never be able to catch up. Her only option was returning to her room to wait. Several faeries bumped into her as she made her way back to her hallway; she nearly fell several times, only managing to stay on her feet by some miracle, or maybe stubbornness. The hallway was quiet. Compared to the general mayhem of the rest of the floor, the silence was eerie. As she rounded the bend and her room came into view, she stopped in her tracks.

Erasto stood in the doorway, his hand on Laraf's shoulder in a controlling grasp. Fresh abuse decorated her face, and Farzana's stomach flipped as she took in the sight of Laraf's split lip, black eye, and the blood dripping down her chin. Despite her injuries, her chin was held high, her face set with a grim determination.

"What have you done?" Farzana gasped in anger, taking a step forward before remembering to whom she spoke.

"Ah, ah," Erasto said, shaking a bloody finger at her. "Manners."

Farzana shut her mouth, lips trembling. How dare he hurt Laraf? Tiny, innocent Laraf. Precious Laraf.

When Erasto spoke, his voice came out low and silky. "There was a recent break-in upstairs. Now, normally I would have my security force handle the investigation but—call it a parent's intuition—I decided to go through your room and see what I could find. And lo and behold, I found this little one hiding in your bed." He patted Laraf on the head. Farzana flinched, though Laraf remained steady.

"Leave her alone," Farzana said through gritted teeth.

"You should have left *my* things alone," he snarled, the sound echoing in the hall. "This is what happens when you mess with my things, Farzana: I mess with yours."

She couldn't afford to lose her calm. Erasto's volatility was one thing when it was her own skin in the line, but she wasn't going to risk it with Laraf there. "Fine, I learned my lesson. Now let her go."

Erasto lifted a brow, his eyes scrutinizing her as if waiting for her to remember her manners. She took a slow, shuddering breath.

"Please."

He released his hold on Laraf, and she ran into Farzana's arms, rocking her back on her heels. Silent tears streamed down Laraf's face.

"Don't think I'll forgive you this easily," he said, strolling past them. His hand glided over Farzana's shoulder in a deadly caress. "I'll be back."

Farzana's throat constricted; she ushered Laraf into the room while fighting the urge to be sick. Sitting Laraf on the bed, Farzana cupped her cheek. "I'm so sorry," she whispered, kissing her bruised forehead.

"It's going to be okay," Laraf said in a tiny voice.

Farzana broke down in sobs. How could Laraf be so strong through all of this? This was the limit; Farzana had been broken once again.

A shoe scuffed the floor in the doorway, and Farzana looked back to see Erasto flanked by a pair of fem-fae imps. One of them looked like a perfect adult replica of Laraf, down to the smattering of freckles on her broad cheeks. Beside her, Farzana felt Laraf's breathing hitch.

"Hurt them, but don't kill them." Erasto's bored tone made the sentence sound like a breakfast order rather than the sanctioned beating of his daughter and a child. After giving her one last look, he turned and left.

Farzana stared at the imps in horror as they cracked their knuckles and advanced. Leaping forward, she slammed the bedroom door shut and locked it, hoping and praying to the Harvester that it would hold and knowing it wouldn't. No god could save them.

A fist smashed through the door, shredding the wood as if it were paper. The imp grabbed the knob, twisting the lock. Laraf screamed and fell to the floor, crawling under the bed as the raven-haired imp slammed the splintered door out of the way and stepped into the room.

Farzana backed away from her, mind moving too slow. A fist flashed out and slammed into her head; she spun around from the force of it and fell against the bed. She held up a hand to fend off the imp, but she was hit again; with a searing pain, her lip split. Farzana gasped and spat blood onto her blanket, the bright red swatch swimming in her vision. The next hit landed on her back, narrowly avoiding her wings, and her muscles spasmed.

The fourth hit was against her cast. The snap of bone was loud enough to trigger her gag reflex, and she vomited onto the bed, onto the floor. Unable to breathe, unable to think. She reached up to wipe her face with a shaky hand and couldn't tell if she was wiping away bile or blood. She realized it didn't matter.

A slam on the crown of her head had her sliding to the floor, desperation the only thing keeping her conscious. Laraf's blurry face came into view. So much pain, so much regret. Nothing to do but wait.

Couldn't move, couldn't see, couldn't breathe. Everything red, blood red. Carried? Cradled against someone's chest. Doors. Public teleportation symbol. Screams.

Is this how I reach Death?

Pain, like a wave, like a riptide. The undertow swept her away, and she was floating, floating away into the darkness.

24

THE DARKNESS HELD FARZANA IN A COCOON, rocking her to sleep. A haunting far off song soothed her nerves, smothered the pain.

Who was singing? Can darkness sing?

It was a song she knew...or maybe not. She'd heard it once in a dream.

She floated, safe and warm, happy to be free of the pain. Happy to be free from Erasto.

Or was she? Would he barge in at any moment, pry her away from the embrace of the darkness to teach her another lesson?

Her heart began to race, but then the singing resumed. As long as the singing continued, she knew she would be safe. Erasto couldn't breach the song. She knew this. She didn't know how she knew this. Maybe it didn't matter.

The darkness held her close, crooning in her ear, as she drifted through the nothingness.

25

A FAMILIAR AND HAUNTING VOICE TUGGED AT
her, begging Farzana to wake up. The siren song didn't have
the power to shut off the warning screaming in her mind, the
one saying that waking meant being in agony. The darkness was
safe, warm, and painless. The relief of floating away, nothing
to pin her down and strangle her... She wasn't ready yet; she
wasn't ready for the pain.

Something touched her cheek, the barest of touches. She
flinched. It took her a second to realize that it didn't hurt.
Why didn't it hurt? The voice started singing a lullaby, one
she hadn't heard in a century and yet was such an integral
part of her that she could never forget it. Curiosity piqued,
she opened her eyes.

Soft light diffused through a strange room. A single window framed the yellowing leaves of a mature maple. Her eyes
flitted around the room before seeing the faerie sitting at her
bedside: Sitra.

Her mother gave her a wide smile, tears in her eyes as she
finished singing. "You're awake," she whispered.

"Where am I?" Farzana croaked, her voice hoarse from
disuse...or maybe screaming. Both? She couldn't be sure.

"You're safe, baby. You're in the House of Amber."

The House of Amber. Farzana and Enzi visited their grand-parents' home only once a year in autumn, always without their mother. After having not one but two children out of wedlock, the tension between Sitra and her parents had escalated to the point of shouts and tears any time she stayed in her childhood home for too long.

And yet here she was, holding Farzana's hand without any indication that she felt anything but happy being there. How long had it been since... The last thing Farzana could remember was the imp attack. She should have died, and yet...

Shocked laughter bubbled up out of her throat, echoing in the stillness of the room, before turning into ugly sobs of relief. She was free! Tears flowed hot and fast from her eyes as she looked around the room again, relishing in the knowledge that Erasto couldn't hurt her.

"Shh, baby, it's okay," Sitra said as she gathered Farzana into her arms. "It's going to be okay."

It's going to be okay.

Farzana held onto her mother like a lifeline, unwilling to believe anything else. "I love you," she cried.

Sitra pressed a kiss to Farzana's temple. "I love you too."

Farzana nuzzled her mother before jolting upright. Sitra's expression morphed into one of hurt and confusion for a moment before Farzana yelled, "Laraf!"

Sitra smiled and gave Farzana's hand a reassuring squeeze. "The child is fine. She's all healed up and has the run of the place."

Farzana allowed herself to relax back against the pillows, though questions burned inside her. Who had saved them from the imps? How had they escaped The Center? Were they truly safe?

Someone knocked on the door and entered; Farzana wiped her eyes, releasing Sitra to look at the newcomer. An elf in maroon healer robes stood at the end of the bed, holding a tablet and wearing a smile.

"Hello, Farzana. I'm Healer Demsi. I work for House Amber.

Now that you're awake, I'd like to talk about your injuries and healing progress."

"Okay." Farzana sat up straighter.

Healer Demsi poked at her tablet for a moment before meeting Farzana's eyes. "You were wearing a cast before you came here, presumably because a previous healing sleep was insufficient in correctly healing your broken bone. That same bone was damaged again."

Farzana pulled the blankets aside to find a new cast on her leg. Instead of purple, it was black. Not the color she would have picked but she didn't hate it. It was weird that her leg hadn't healed yet, but maybe she hadn't been in the healing sleep for very long. She flexed and was relieved to not feel any pain.

"I had to put a new cast on you because the healing sleep still did not correctly heal your bone. I don't have a definitive reason for why, but I can run some tests to see if I can figure that out. My guess is there might be a genetic condition slowing the healing process. Realistically the only thing we can do is be patient and give your leg the time it needs to heal on its own."

Farzana pondered that. "If the tests can't help me heal faster, then I don't see why we need to do them."

The healer nodded, typing something on her tablet. "The tests would not be able to heal you faster, only tell us why you aren't healing. It might be worth it to know what associated risks you need to be aware of, but I can't make that decision for you. In the meantime, keep using your cane. No strenuous exercise. Taking a walk every day will help you build up those leg muscles. I noticed significant muscle atrophy on both legs."

Farzana rubbed the back of her neck, trying not to outwardly cringe. "I haven't exactly been keeping up with a daily workout schedule."

"I recommend you start, but again, nothing strenuous. It's not too late to strengthen those muscles. The healing sleep can't do that for you, unfortunately."

"I understand," Farzana said with chagrin.

Healer Demsi gave her a knowing smile. "Aside from that,

you've healed quite nicely. You're cleared to resume normal eating and all other activities."

"Thank you. I do have a question..." Farzana hesitated a moment before asking in a rush, "Will I ever be able to dance again?"

Healer Demsi narrowed her eyes and looked down at her tablet. "I don't see why not. Bone breaks are rarely permanent. It will take a couple months to fully heal, but at that point, you'll be good as new."

Farzana let out a pent-up breath of relief. "Oh, good. Thank you, Healer Demsi."

"Of course. Have a great day," she said, giving Farzana and Sitra a little wave before exiting the room.

Farzana looked over at Sitra. "I still can't believe I'm here. What happened? I don't remember how I got here."

"Well, Ettares said she came into your room to find you and saw that you were being attacked. She said she 'incapacitated' the imps, whatever that means." Sitra grimaced but shook it off. "She grabbed you and Laraf and took you to the teleportation room and teleported to her house. Then she called me and teleported you both here."

"Ettares...saved me?" Farzana's mind was racing. How on Faerth had Ettares incapacitated two guards? Did she have help? Those imps had been terrifyingly huge; the fist that came through the door had been almost as big as Farzana's head. The fact that Ettares had fought them off to save Farzana though... A fuzzy feeling filled her chest at the same time that her lips curved involuntarily into a smile.

"She's certainly a wonderful friend to have," Sitra gushed.

"She is," Farzana murmured, warmth heating her cheeks.

"Thanks to her, you and dear Laraf are safe and free of Erasto's control."

"So he doesn't...he doesn't know that we're here?" Terror struck her as she imagined him showing up at any minute and dragging her back.

"No! No, baby, we were very careful. He was able to track where his teleportation pad was used for travel, of course, and he ransacked everyone's houses who used it that day, including Ettares's. You could be anywhere as far as he knows."

The explanation did little to assuage Farzana's fear. "Won't he search here too? He has to know you live here, right? And it makes sense you would be hiding me."

"He did! He came here a day after searching Etares' place, but thankfully your grandparents have a hidden panic room. I always said they were being paranoid, but it was perfect for hiding you and Laraf while he searched."

"Okay. Okay, that's good," Farzana said, holding a hand to her chest and feeling her heart rate slow.

Sitra patted Farzana's cheek. "Now, focus on resting and healing."

Farzana laid back down and snuggled into the pillows. Resting and healing... She could definitely do that. Sending a quick prayer of thanks to the Harvester for sending her a savior, she closed her eyes. Her intentions of sleep were beaten back by an image of Ettares fighting off the imps single-handedly. So much blood... She shivered and opened her eyes, hoping to banish those thoughts. She was safe. She was free. And Ettares... wherever she was, she was probably safe too.

Sitra reached over to touch her shoulder. "You okay, baby? Are you cold?"

Farzana shook her head and offered her mother a smile. "I'm just fine."

Farzana lounged in bed the next day, enjoying the relaxation. Her mother brought her meals and fawned over her, which was unusual, but it was something Farzana could get used to. During one visit, Sitra lamented over Farzana's disappearance after the fire.

"We didn't know where you were that night. The healers only told us that you were somewhere safe."

Farzana snorted. "If by safe you mean locked in a tiny closet and starved, then yeah. Totally safe."

Sitra looked miserable. "I wish I had known. I wish—"

Farzana waved away her words. "I survived. That's what matters. And he can't hurt me anymore."

Sitra gave her a watery smile. "I'm so happy you're here, baby. You don't know what it means to me to have all my children back with me. And Laraf! She is such a delight. I think she has your grandparents wrapped around her little finger."

Farzana couldn't help grinning at that. Shy, timid, and terrified Laraf had truly blossomed into herself since Farzana had found her. Gods only knew what would have happened if someone else had found her. She likely would have been sent to The City's Orphan Center, lost and anonymous among the many children who had no parents. Would she ever have eaten chocolate cake? Would she have been able to buy pretty dresses? Would she have had someone to cuddle at night?

"Where is she sleeping now?" Farzana wondered out loud.

"She's been sleeping with me. Poor darling has nightmares almost every night and crawled into my bed during her first night here. She wanted to know where you were, but I told her you needed to heal first."

"This bed is a bit small for two faeries, anyway," Farzana said, looking down at the narrow mattress.

"Don't worry; we have a room set up for you once you're feeling up to walking. And if you and Laraf want to share it, you can. This is just the healing room."

"Why do Grandmother and Grandfather have a healing room?"

Sitra clicked her tongue and pointed at the plate of untouched food; Farzana rolled her eyes but took a bite. After waiting for her to finish chewing and grab more, Sitra said, "Grandpa is getting up there in years, and his condition is getting worse. Sometimes he goes into a healing sleep to try and combat it."

Farzana wasn't sure what condition she meant, but Sitra looked distressed, so she didn't ask. "I'm glad you're here, Mother," she said instead.

"Of course I'm here, silly."

"No, I mean, spending time with me. We haven't spent quality time together in…well, a long time."

"And that's my fault. But healer Demsi has been helping me with medication to combat my depression. It's been wonderful having energy and motivation again. I have always loved spending time with you, baby. I just wasn't always able to do that mentally."

Farzana felt a weight lift from her chest. Her mother was getting help, finally. She was happy and healthy. A bit ironic that all of this was only possible after Sitra came back to live with her parents, which of course meant that the fire that destroyed their home was actually a blessing. Farzana couldn't figure out where she should laugh or cry at how it all worked out. Instead, she sniffed and cleared her throat before saying, "The medication suits you. I'm glad it's helping."

"Me too, baby. Me too." Sitra brushed Farzana's curls back from her face and planted a kiss on her forehead. "I have to go worship now. I've been going to the temple for Majakim every week. I'm loving the community so far, and the temple is so beautiful! Someday, I'll show you."

"I'd like that."

Sitra blew a kiss as she left, leaving the door cracked. Farzana smiled to herself. Majakim was the queen of the pixie gods: the goddess of love, nurturing, home, and health. It made sense that, in her healing, Sitra had turned to her.

Farzana tried napping, but after staring at the blank wall for nearly an hour, she gave up and decided to go explore. It had been decades since she'd seen any part of the house other than the dining room, kitchen, and bathroom. When she and Enzi visited in the past, they came over for the Harvester Festival meal and that was it. Enzi cooked the feast while Farzana kept him company in the kitchen, not wanting to sit around alone with her grandparents. Then, they all ate together in relative silence before Enzi and Farzana went home to finish celebrating with their mother.

But Enzi and Sitra had been living in the house for months. Had the strained relationships in the family had been mended in that time or was the tension still ubiquitous? Either way, Farzana was bored of the healing room and ready to move on.

The healer had left a cane in the corner of the room for Farzana to use, since her painted one had been left behind in the chaos. She didn't mind the loss; the fact that Ettares had been able to save both her and Laraf was more than enough to be thankful for.

Farzana wandered down the hall, stopping every now and then to rest and admire the various paintings on the walls: majestic portraits of her family members, ornate depictions of holy temples, and wondrous landscapes of floral fields. Each was a masterpiece, and if Farzana hadn't been so breathless from merely getting out of bed, the art would have done that job on its own.

She reached the arched opening to a large family room and poked her head in to see if anyone was there; her grandmother sat in a chair with a book while Enzi and Laraf had their heads bowed together over a puzzle.

"So here's where you've all been hiding," Farzana said, stepping into the room.

Laraf whirled around at the sound of Farzana's voice, a wide grin spreading across her unblemished face. She looked like she might have even gained some weight since their escape. "Farzana!" she cried, running over to her.

"Careful!" Enzi yelled, and Laraf slowed her approach, embracing Farzana with care rather than flinging into her.

"I'm so glad you're okay!" Laraf's eyes shone with tears that spilled over onto her cheeks.

"Aw, sweetie, don't cry. I'm fine," Farzana said, though she had to wipe tears from her own cheeks as well.

"I was so scared," she mumbled, looking down at the floor.

Farzana bent to give her a kiss on her forehead. "I know, but we made it. We're going to be okay now."

Laraf threw her arms around Farzana again, giving her one more squeeze, before running back to the puzzle-laden table.

When Farzana straightened, she saw Grandmother Lanis watching the exchange from over the top of her book. Closing the book and placing it in her lap, Lanis made a 'come here' gesture.

Farzana hobbled over, a tad more unsteady on her feet than usual, and stood in front of her grandmother, a wry smile on her lips. "Thank you for your hospitality, Grandmother. I don't know what Laraf and I would have done if you hadn't opened your House to us," Farzana said in a low voice.

Lanis rolled her eyes and made a face. "Well of course you're welcome here! You are family, and family is always welcome, no matter what your foolishly stubborn mother likes to say. We are happy to have you here."

Farzana blushed and ducked her head. Sitra had indeed told her children many times over the years that she wasn't welcome at home because she had birthed two bastard children. Farzana wondered why she had felt the need to say such a thing if the opposite were true. Perhaps Sitra had imposed judgment on herself, feeling unworthy of the House of Amber aristo-fae status after having children out of wedlock and assumed her parents agreed?

In all the times Farzana and Enzi had attended the Harvester Festival at their grandparents' House, Sitra had never joined in the festivities. She had made sure they knew the importance of having a relationship with their elders, of course, and never pried about their time at the House of Amber, but also never gave an answer to why she herself wouldn't visit. Farzana hadn't thought to bring up the matter to her grandparents, and yet here her grandmother was, dismissing what she had always assumed was fact as mere fiction.

"Well, thank you anyway. And thank you for the use of your healer. I didn't realize you had one for the House."

Lanis steepled her fingers in her lap, pursing her lips. "Yes, well, with your grandfather's blood sugar disorder, we felt it prudent to have a healer on staff in case of any complications. He can fall sick remarkably quickly."

Farzana didn't want to admit she had forgotten about the disorder. "And how is Grandfather?"

"He's resting. It is Rest Day, after all."

"So it is," Farzana said with a laugh. "And here I am, hauling myself out of bed because I thought I should be active today."

Her grandmother chuckled. "I applaud you for attempting some form of exercise, however small it may be."

Farzana grinned, puffing out her chest. "Thanks! It'll be the last time you see me force myself to walk this far, though; your hall is much too long."

"It better not be the last time! Stay in bed all you want, but Harvester Festival is in two days, and you will be up and about for that," Lanis said, shaking her finger.

"The Harvester Festival already?" Farzana mused.

The yearly celebration of the end of autumn and beginning of winter was so named for the pixie god of death and endings—and Farzana's chosen god—the Harvester. Even if Harvester Festival wasn't dedicated to her god, it would still be Farzana's favorite holiday, mostly because of the glorious feast Enzi never failed to prepare. It also celebrated the start of a new year and was a time for pixies to set new goals for their lives. Farzana loved coming up with goals for herself, though she rarely stuck with them for more than a couple weeks.

Last Harvester Festival, she had vowed not to eat as many sweets, but she blamed Enzi's cooking for her devouring an entire bowl of candied nuts only a few days later. And though that felt like years ago, it also didn't seem possible that she had been living at The Center for all of autumn.

"Time flies when you're locked in a tower, I assume," Lanis said, her dark, flinty eyes looking at Farzana with a glimmer of sympathy.

"I suppose," she sighed in answer, unwilling to share any details.

Lanis waited a moment longer before picking up her book and leafing through the pages. "I must get back to my reading. Go, spend time with your brother and enjoy your Rest Day. You deserve it after everything."

Farzana ducked her head in some semblance of a bow and trudged over to Enzi and Laraf, settling into a seat between them.

"Here's the box," Enzi said, handing over the lid with the picture of the completed puzzle. It was a watercolor landscape of a serene pond with a multitude of water lilies overlapping on its still waters; a weeping willow stood tall over it, boughs draping down and nearly touching the surface. A waterhorse rested on the bank. Farzana looked closely at the waterhorse, noticing the delicate feathering strokes of its mane, the softness of its glowing eyes, and the subtle sheen to its velvet hide.

"You going to help or not?" Enzi asked, pushing a pile of pieces over to her.

Farzana diligently bent over the pile, studying the pieces and their partial designs to find their place in the bigger picture. The tangle of pieces was a mess, and she sighed, wondering how best to handle it. It reminded her of her life, full of edges that bumped against each other, never quite fitting together. Clashing pictures and an incomplete view. Ever since Erasto had come into her life, nothing went right, and every step further made everything worse.

And yet.

After some careful studying, Farzana managed to find two edge pieces that fit together, and she placed them on the table with pride. It wasn't a whole picture, not yet, but it was a tiny start to building something new.

"Good job," Laraf said, patting her hand in praise.

Farzana smiled at her. It was a special day, the start of the rest of her life, free of Erasto's tyranny. There was nothing she would rather do than spend time with Laraf and her little brother, building a puzzle.

26

SOMEONE KNOCKED ON THE DOOR, STARTLING
Farzana from her meditation. That was probably for the best;
any longer and she might have fallen asleep in her armchair.
Again. Her neck was still sore from the last time. The gauzy
pastel curtains hanging on the window of her new bedroom
filtered the sunlight in a way that lulled her. How long had she
been meditating?

"What is it?" she asked as a second knock sounded.

"Araj is here." Enzi's voice conjured an image of his intol-
erant expression in her mind.

She stared at the door, bewildered. "Why is Araj here?"

"Ask him yourself," he retorted before his footsteps headed
down the hall.

Sighing, she got to her feet. She wore soft, shabby pajamas
but it wasn't like Araj had never seen her like this, so there was
no point in getting dressed. Her hair was a wild and untam-
able mess, so she left it that way before grabbing her cane and
leaving her room. No one stood in the hall, so she set off for
the family room.

Araj was pacing the length of the empty room when she
entered; when he saw her, his eyes lit up.

"Farzana!" He rushed over to give her a careful embrace. "Oh gods, I thought I had lost you again. Erasto said you had been 'misplaced' and I didn't know what to think."

"How did you find me?" she asked, pulling away from him with suspicion. If Araj could figure it out, what was stopping Erasto? Would he be there soon?

"I asked Ettares," he answered in a suspiciously meek voice.

"You asked her?"

"Well, I might have yelled at her to find you. And possibly said something she didn't want to hear. And then she told me you were safe, here." He had a contrite expression which didn't appease Farzana.

"You yelled at her?"

He raised an eyebrow. "You're on her side all of a sudden?"

"After she saved my life? After she saved Laraf? Yes, I'm on her side." Farzana barely stopped herself from glaring. It wasn't his fault he hadn't been the one to save her. It wasn't his fault that she had provoked her father's deadly ire. Even so, she couldn't help feeling derision toward him for going to Ettares and asking her to find them and even more so for showing up at the House of Amber. What if Erasto had spies following him? Were they truly safe?

He must have sensed her anger because he held up his hands to placate her. "Fine. I'm not here to argue. I came here for a reason."

"What reason?"

A wide grin spread across his face. "I know why Erasto is here, on Faerth."

Farzana's jaw dropped. All that questioning with the bright and Araj was the one who held the answer? "You've got to be kidding me."

"I'm not kidding."

"Well, tell me, tell me! Wait." She stopped and held up a finger. "We should call Ettares. She should know this too."

"What? Why? Who cares about her?"

Farzana shot him a glare. She still remembered the warning he had given her right before...right before he had assaulted her.

It stung, recalling it all, as well as knowing he hated the subject of her infatuation. "I care. And she's been helping me figure stuff out with Erasto, so she should know."

"Whatever," he said, rolling his eyes. He followed her to the mirror and slumped onto the couch facing it.

Farzana turned on the mirror and flipped through the contacts list to find Ettares. After she placed the call, the mirror beeped rhythmically, a waiting dial spinning in the center of the screen.

Ettares's face filled the mirror. "Farzana!" She beamed before noticing Araj; the smile transformed into a scowl. "What does he want?"

"We have some news for you. Or rather, Araj has some news," Farzana said, stepping to the side so Araj could talk.

He stood and cleared his throat, glancing between Farzana and Ettares before saying, "I know why Erasto is on Faerth."

Ettares gasped.

"I know, right?" Farzana said, excitement lifting her voice.

Araj rolled his eyes again even though he seemed pleased by their reaction. "I just got back from visiting my great uncle, who is currently on his deathbed. He's the head of the House of Sapphires if you didn't know, and he has chosen me to be his heir. So of course he wanted to entrust me with the family secret, which also happens to be why Erasto is here: Chaos Theory."

He spread his hands wide, a satisfied smirk on his face as if that explained everything. Ettares and Farzana exchanged a look of confusion.

"Okay...and what does that mean?" Farzana asked.

"In the days following the planetary split, when Faerth and Earth tore apart to become two separate planets, there was a convention. It was made up of some of the most brilliant minds on Faerth, and together, they sought to understand why the planets split. Instead, they figured out something else: Chaos Theory. The amount of chaos in the universe is finite, fixed. This means that if chaos goes up on one planet, it goes down on the other one."

"But there are five inhabited planets," Farzana pointed out. "So does it go down on the other four?"

Araj and Ettares blinked at her in silence.

"There are what now?" Araj asked, incredulous, at the same time Ettares said, "Five? But I thought…"

Farzana waved away their words. "The bright told me there are five worlds. I trust it."

"The bright? What on Faerth is a bright?" Araj looked from Farzana to Ettares as they both laughed. "Am I missing something? What's going on?"

Farzana took a deep breath; none of this was funny. "The important thing is that there are worlds other than Earth and Faerth, and they must be a part of chaos theory too. What does this mean, though?"

"Okay, but before all of this five worlds thing, I had a point. The records from the convention which detailed the secret Chaos Theory findings were stolen from the House of Sapphire a hundred and sixty years ago. That's when Erasto first went to Earth."

Farzana nodded. "When I was born."

"You're only a hundred and sixty?" Ettares's eyes were wide.

"Is that a problem?" Farzana asked defensively. She had no clue how old Ettares was. Even more importantly, Farzana didn't know if her youth bothered Ettares or not. She shook her head to clear those thoughts from her mind. Getting distracted by Ettares's approval was not going to help things.

Ettares gave her an unreadable look and shook her head.

"Anyway, this makes a lot of sense. Erasto is a leader on Earth, and he promised them peace and prosperity."

"Isn't Earth in the middle of a planet-wide war?" Ettares asked.

Farzana clicked her tongue. "That's it! The only way for Erasto to lessen the chaos on Earth is to raise the chaos somewhere else. Like here, on Faerth."

"It's a balance. See? I was right."

"And this is why he tried to invade Dradour," Farzana continued, ignoring Araj.

"He tried to what?!"

"He tried to teleport an army of wights into The Center," Ettares said as way of explanation.

Araj threw his arms in the air. "I don't have a clue what either of you are talking about."

"Well now we know why," Farzana said, collapsing onto the couch. She held her head in her hands. It was all too much; Erasto wouldn't stop until he created enough chaos on Faerth to fix his predicament on Earth. He had failed in his invasion attempt but that didn't mean he wouldn't try again.

Farzana snapped her head up with a start. "What happened when I damaged the teleportation unit that night? When the wights were teleporting in?"

Ettares looked uncomfortable as she answered. "Most likely, they were all killed. Or rather, lost, in some sort of space warp. They were in the middle of the journey, so once the link was cut, there was nowhere for them to go."

"I killed them," Farzana said bleakly.

"You did what you had to. You saved us, Farzana."

"I still don't even know what a wight is," Araj protested.

"Shut up, Araj."

"Fuck you, Ettares."

"Stop! What are we going to do? He lost his army, but what's to say he won't find another one?" Farzana was on the verge of tears, her voice shaking.

"We can destroy his interplanetary teleportation unit when he goes to Earth next! That will force him to go through official modes of transit, and I doubt they will let him through," Ettares said.

Farzana frowned. "Didn't I already destroy it? I broke the tank thing."

Araj sighed. "Is any of this supposed to make sense?"

"I'm not sure. He might have fixed it by now. It should be such a small thing for him to replace the fluid conduit. Did you damage anything else?" Ettares asked, ignoring Araj completely.

"I tried to break the control panels, but the teleportation pad only shut off after I broke the tank."

"So we find out if it's fixed or not. If it is, we wait for him to go off-world and then destroy it again."

"How do we know if it's fixed? How do we know if breaking it again will do anything? If he can fix it once, he can fix it again, and security will just get tighter, and one of us could get caught, and hurt, and—"

"Farzana!"

"What?!"

Araj gave her hand a gentle squeeze. When had he grabbed her hand? Why was it so hard to breathe?

"We have to try. What else can we do?" Araj's voice was quiet and subdued for once. He looked exhausted.

"Maybe instead of damaging anything, we can just try to find out when he leaves next. Once he leaves, we can..." Farzana trailed off. Her friends continued to look at her, waiting for the rest of her plan, but her mind blanked. What could they possibly do to fix this? What could three pixies realistically do to save an entire country—the entire planet, even? Farzana couldn't even save herself. A tear welled up in her eye.

It's hopeless.

Ettares cleared her throat. "Regardless of whether he's fixed it already, we know that he will try. That's his plan, right? Bring in an army. So maybe, instead of damaging it, we sabotage it. Switch the coordinates of the planets."

Araj scoffed. "And how are we going to do that? Do you know how to program interplanetary teleportation devices?"

"Actually, yes, I can. And I'm even willing to instruct you on how to do it."

"Fuck you. You do it!"

Farzana sighed again. "Let's think logically, okay? You live there, Araj. You can find out when he leaves."

"And then what?"

"And then you get in and reprogram it," Ettares said through gritted teeth.

"How will I get in?"

"Bribe a guard."

Araj shot Farzana a look before scrubbing a hand across

his face. "I might know a guard."

Farzana wasn't sure why he was acting like he wasn't close to Melara but it had to be because of Ettares. Whatever the reason, it didn't matter so long as he was able to complete the task.

"Once you're in, you can call me and I'll walk you through the process."

Araj burst out laughing. "Yeah, okay. So let me get this straight. I will be risking my neck bribing someone, breaking and entering, and attempting to reprogram the fucking solar system, all while you sit comfy in your home chatting with me on your pocket mirror?"

"As if I won't be stressing out the entire time knowing I have to rely on you to save all of Faerth." Ettares snorted.

"You—!"

Farzana elbowed him in the ribs before he could finish. "Yep, that's the plan! Glad we are all on the same page."

"Great," Araj wheezed, giving Ettares a forced smile. "No use still talking to you, then."

Ettares glared at him. "Whatever. Good luck." She glanced at Farzana, and for a moment, her lips softened into a slight smile. Then the mirror went blank and Farzana was left staring at her and Araj's reflections.

"I can do this," he said, turning to her with enthusiasm.

Farzana couldn't help laughing at the stark contrast between how he acted around Ettares versus just her. "I know you can."

"First thing tomorrow, I'll ask Melara if she knows his schedule. And I'm sure I'll be able to sweet talk her into letting me know how to open his door."

"Oh, that. I know how, but I'm sure he's changed the password by now."

"Oh." Araj deflated.

"But if you can find a hacker, we can pay them to hack the security. I'm sure there has to be someone who can do it."

"That sounds more like something Ettares would know about," Araj grumbled. "She has illicit contacts all over the country."

"Well, then I'll talk to her about the hacker, and you get his schedule from Melara. Deal?"

"Deal. I can't believe I'm actually working with Ettares."

Farzana gave him a gentle shove. "Hey, be nice. We're all friends now."

He snorted. "Yeah, sure."

"And thank you for coming to me with this. Chaos Theory was the missing puzzle piece we didn't even know we needed."

He brightened. "Happy to help."

"We are going to get rid of that tyrant for good."

A strange look flickered in his eyes. "We better." He pulled her into his arms for a hug and pressed a kiss to her temple. Farzana stiffened at the too-familiar feel of those lips, but he stepped back a moment later with a smile.

"Stay safe, Farzana."

"You too," she said, watching him walk away, his blue wings shimmering behind him.

27

FARZANA WOKE NATURALLY WITH AN AIR OF quiet excitement. It was the day of the Harvester Festival, the end of the year, and the day of giving thanks. She dressed leisurely, enjoying the feeling of soft, black stockings sliding up her legs. Next came a plain black shift dress, belted at the waist. Black clothing and makeup honored the androgynous god of death, so she sat at her mirror and painted on thin strokes of black face paint in a swirling design around her eyes and cheeks. Lines crossed her nose and dots trailed after her eyebrows. When she finished, she admired her reflection for a moment and reminisced on the past year.

So many things had happened in such a short period of time, to the point of being overwhelming. Her years usually passed in monotony, the vast majority of days blurring together with a few special days sticking out in her memory; since Erasto had arrived, it seemed like most days stood out on their own. Had a single day gone past that had felt normal? She couldn't think of one.

The year had started off with a chance at a promotion to upper management. When the day came for her promotion board in front of a panel of reviewers, Araj had asked her to cover for him at work, and she forgot to show up at her appointed time. She never told Araj about the missed opportunity because she felt it would be unfair to blame him; she had chosen to cover for him, and it had been her own fault for not better managing her time that day. She did still wonder, though, what would have happened if he had stayed at work. Or if she had told him 'no'.

And then of course, the royal murders happened. The riots, meeting Ettares, falling head over wings for her and… the betrayal. Even after hearing Ettares's explanation, thinking back to that moment in The Center when she found Ettares and Erasto talking had her feeling queasy.

Farzana hummed to distract herself from dark thoughts as she wove her hair into a loose braid around the crown of her head, the single fanciest thing she ever did with her hair—and only once a year. Tucking in a stray curl, she stood and admired her handiwork. Her cheeks had some color in them for once, and her eyes were bright from a restful night's sleep. She smiled at herself, flashing her pearly whites, and had to admit she looked attractive.

What would Ettares say if she saw her like this? Too swept up in wonder and excitement to chastise herself for the thought, she instead smiled at her reflection once more. Seeing Ettares yesterday, even just on the mirror, had done wonders for her mood the rest of the day. Was it ridiculous to attribute her uplifted moods recently to reconciling with Ettares? Was it prudent to be enthralled by her again? As much as she tried to act like she wasn't falling for the beautiful noble—*again*… Well. Maybe the new year would be kinder to them both.

Farzana grabbed her cane and headed downstairs toward the kitchen; she knew Enzi would be there, cooking up a storm. The stairs proved difficult as her leg couldn't bend very far in the cast, but she hopped her way down, trying not to think how on Faerth she would be able to get back up.

Enzi was indeed in the kitchen, his face done up in black makeup in an elaborate design of spirals and flower petals. He grinned when he saw her and waved. "You're up! Well, down. I was going to help you once I finished cooking."

"No need," she said, plopping into a stool out of his way. "I'll definitely need help getting back up, though. What are you making?"

Enzi gestured around the kitchen as he listed off his menu for the feast. "Giant roasted dragon, rosemary and thyme dressing, crispy pan-fried string beans, stuffed mushrooms, cheesy garlic potato casserole, and—your favorite—candied nuts."

Farzana's eyes lit up as she searched for the bowl, mouth watering when she saw it. "I better taste test these to make sure you got it right," she said with a sly grin.

He rolled his eyes but grabbed the dish and offered it to her. "Don't eat them all at once," he chided.

She popped a candied nut into her mouth; the explosion of sweetness and bitterness on her tongue had her sighing in pleasure. "So good! But maybe one more, just to check for consistent quality."

"You're awful," he said, turning back to the stove.

After sneaking two more nuts, she pushed the dish away and watched as Enzi bustled about the kitchen, stirring and chopping and tasting. He was a master chef, and Farzana was always in awe of his talent. She could barely boil water.

This was a nice break from her horrible life in The Center, but the thought of Erasto barging in at any moment kept a shiver of anxiety sliding down her spine even as she forced herself to smile. All of this could come crashing down at any second, upending her freedom, and who knew what he would do to her family who had so graciously housed her and kept her safe? She was a fugitive, after all.

Would she ever be at ease and truly happy? Or would he haunt her forever?

"Good morning! Happy Harvester Festival and happy end of year," Sitra said as she whisked into the kitchen, holding Laraf in her arms like a baby. Her eyes were adorned with black glitter, and black lipstick rimmed her mouth.

Farzana grinned at her mother. "Happy Harvester Festival!"

"Happy Harvester Festival," Enzi echoed, tossing some string beans into a sizzling pan.

Sitra rocked Laraf who looked like she was still asleep, though how anyone could sleep through the din Enzi created, Farzana had no clue. She marveled at the fact that Sitra could hold her up like that, too; Laraf was so small for her age but, even still, she had filled out since Farzana had found her, and she no longer looked more like a child than a young adult.

"Why didn't you leave her in bed?" Farzana asked.

"Poor baby had a nightmare and didn't sleep well last night," Sitra said, continuing to rock her. "I didn't want to leave her in there alone."

Farzana's smile collapsed. It was to be expected; though she couldn't know for sure what Laraf had endured before Farzana found her, there had to have been trauma. And the fact that Erasto had used imps to beat them…it had to haunt the poor thing. It made Farzana sick to think back on how battered her face had been that day when Erasto hurt her. And yet she had been so strong after, had only caved to fear when the imps arrived.

"I'm glad she was with you," Farzana said.

Sitra nodded. "It's like having my babies back again. You two are too big for me to hold but Laraf is still so little."

Farzana wasn't sure how much longer they could call her little, but she smiled at her mother before turning back to watch Enzi's choreographed dance. Finally, he finished.

"Done!" he said, holding his hands up in triumph. "Let's go relax."

"I've been relaxing," Farzana pointed out.

Enzi shot her an exasperated look. "Must be nice."

"Children," Sitra said, trying and failing to hide her mirth. "Let's go to the family room and relax with your grandparents."

With Enzi's help, Farzana made her way back up the stairs. Grandmother Lanis and Grandfather Oteza sat in the family room in matching reading chairs, each nose-deep in a book, though they glanced up when everyone walked in.

"Happy Harvester Festival!" Oteza said with a twinkle in

his eye and a wide smile. His dark hair was feathered with gray and his smile had a host of wrinkles, but he jumped up onto his feet and hustled over for hugs.

His arms were strong as he enveloped Farzana in an embrace, and he smelled of pine and soap. "How you doing, kiddo? You look better than when I last saw ya!" He held her at arm's length, looking her up and down.

Farzana couldn't help grinning back at him; the cheery tone of his voice was intoxicating. "I'm doing great, Grandfather."

He patted her arm. "Good, good. Now let's get you off your feet and into a comfy chair, eh?" Obediently, she followed him to a loveseat and sat down, nestling in the cushions. "You read?" he asked, heading over to the bookshelves that lined the back wall.

"I prefer adventure books," she said, twisting to watch him peruse their library.

"Here we go," he said, snagging one and walking back to her, a skip in his step.

She accepted the book and studied the cover; it had an illustration of a merfae fighting a water nymph pirate beneath the sea.

"That was one of my favorites when I was your age," he said, a fond smile on his lips as he no doubt reminisced on the memories associated with the book.

It was quite old; the pages were yellowed when she flipped it open, and the type font was worn in some places. But the scent... The scent of old books was something Farzana would never tire of.

"Thanks, Grandfather," she said, burying her face in the pages. She glanced over to see Laraf had woken up; she was chatting with Enzi and Sitra as they all resumed working on the puzzle from the other day. Farzana watched them interact for a moment, a warm, fuzzy feeling blooming in her chest. She couldn't remember the last time she had seen her whole family together in one place. The carefree air brought a tear to her eye.

She was happy. She was happy, safe, and free; so was her family. She knew then what she was most thankful for: she was thankful that the attempts on her life, orchestrated by both herself and Erasto, had failed.

Farzana was thankful to be alive.

The Harvester Festival feast was a jovial affair. Farzana couldn't remember the last time she had laughed so hard; Enzi's hilarious antics had everyone roaring as he regaled them with stories of his time working as a chef in The Center. Who knew the inner workings of the kitchens were filled with so many mishaps? Every time Farzana had visited the kitchens, it had felt like a carefully orchestrated dance but, evidently, a single misstep threw the entire thing into chaos.

When it was Laraf's turn to recount her last year of life, the room grew quiet. She stood and smiled, a dazzling display of fangs.

"This year was the best year of my life. I met so many new friends. I have a new family. I wasn't in a good place when Farzana found me; I was waiting for my mother, who never came back to get me. But I was scared to leave, so I waited. And Farzana came." She stopped to give a soft smile to Farzana before continuing. "I don't know what my life would be like if she hadn't found me, but she did, and I don't regret any of it. I'm so, so happy to be here."

Farzana sniffled, dabbing at her eyes with the edge of a napkin so as not to smear her makeup. Enzi reached over to grip her shoulder for comfort, his dark eyes kind. Grateful for the support, Farzana shot him a smile. It was times like these when she most appreciated her brother; he knew when she needed words and when she just needed silent support.

It was Farzana's turn after that, and she cleared her throat, looking around the room at her loved ones. Five expectant faces stared back at her, and she couldn't help it; she laughed.

"I'm not sure how I can top that," she admitted, and everyone joined her in laughter. "I've had a bit of a trying year. Everyone knows this. I've often felt like I was watching these things happening instead of experiencing them. It doesn't feel real. This all feels like a bad dream that I need to wake up from." She paused and took a shaky breath. It wasn't for worry about crying in front of her family that had her steadying herself, but rather the urgent need to get this out, to tell them how she felt, how much they meant. She needed to say it. There would be plenty of time for falling apart after. "I'm grateful for all of you. My family. You mean the world to me, and I'm not sure I would have been able to survive this year without your support. I want you to know that. I love you," she said, choking up.

Enzi stood and wrapped her in a hug. "And we love you," he whispered. Farzana wondered if he, like her, was thinking of her suicide attempt when he said that.

"I'm okay," she whispered back, and he nodded, pulling away. "Anyway, what a year! And here I am, safe and surrounded by loved ones. Here's to happy endings!"

"Happy endings!" The room drowned in the volume of the cheer.

Grandmother Lanis and Grandfather Oteza took turns interrupting each other during their stories, teasing as they went. Lanis's eyes crinkled in the corners as she laughed at a joke Oteza made, his face mischievous. She reached over and gently smacked his hand, and he looked around the room, feigning shock and hurt. Even after so many centuries together, their love stayed strong. It was something Farzana admired. She wanted what they had, and she couldn't help that her thoughts drifted to Ettares. What was she doing for the holiday? And then Lanis told a joke that had the whole family roaring.

Farzana sat back in her chair as she listened to the sounds of joviality, her heart full and her chest warm. She could get used to this.

28

A KNOCK WOKE FARZANA FROM DREAMS OF dancers, dressed all in midnight black, waltzing through her mind. Farzana sat up in bed, sleepily calling out, "Come in."

"I wanted to wish you a happy new year," Ettares said with a soft smile as she stood in the doorway.

Farzana pulled the covers up around her, hiding her worn tank top, blushing even as she grinned. "Happy new year! Let me get dressed real quick, and I'll meet you in the family room."

"Of course," Ettares said, ducking her head and shutting the door.

Farzana breathed a sigh of relief and reached for her cane. She was glad to see Ettares, though a little mortified that Enzi had shown her to her room without a warning. Dressing as quickly as possible by pulling on a comfy pair of black pants and a loose lavender shirt over her tank top, Farzana spent a minute wrestling her hair into a messy bun before leaving her room.

Ettares sat ramrod straight on the couch opposite Grandmother Lanis, who stared at her over the top of a book. Neither of them blinked. Enzi sat at the table with Laraf, snickering at the tension.

"Hey," Farzana said, noting how fast Ettares twisted in her seat to face her. "On second thought, maybe we can hang out in my room? Now that I'm dressed?"

Ettares nodded so hard that Farzana winced—her poor neck!—and shot up onto her feet, bowing her head toward Lanis before crossing the room in large strides to follow Farzana. "Oh, thank gods you rescued me," Ettares murmured as they walked down the hallway. "I wasn't sure how much longer I could keep up eye contact. Does she even blink?"

Farzana stifled her laughter. As matriarch, Grandmother Lanis could certainly be intimidating. As a grandmother, she was supportive, caring, and sometimes even funny. "She's not that scary," Farzana said.

"Maybe for you! I was sweating a rainstorm," Ettares said, ruffling her hair. At that, Farzana did laugh. "Anyway, I'm glad to see you."

Farzana gave her a smile and pushed open her bedroom door. "I'm glad to see you too!"

"How was your Harvester Festival?"

"Wonderful! How was yours?"

"Oh, I don't have any family to celebrate with," she said, looking self-conscious as she sat on the bedside chair. "Usually, I'm invited to the palace with the king and queen, but…well."

Farzana felt awful. How could she have forgotten that Ettares's father had been killed? Why hadn't she thought of how alone she would be? "I'm so sorry! I wish I had invited you over."

"Oh, no! Please don't feel bad. I had a great day," Ettares said with a too-wide smile that didn't quite reach her eyes.

"What about your mother?" Farzana realized she had never asked about Ettares's family before.

What a lousy friend I am.

"My mother died when I was young, still a child. I was raised by nannies."

"Oh…I'm sorry."

"No, I'm sorry! I'm making this all about me, but I came to see how you are. I noticed you still have a cast."

Farzana looked down at her leg, entombed in the wide pant legs which hid her cast. "How-"

"I saw it during our mirror call the other day," Ettares said, a crimson stain flushing her cheeks.

Farzana loved the way Ettares blushed, all rosy and beautiful. She could have looked at her for hours, but she tore her eyes away and nodded. "Um, yeah. I guess the healing sleep wasn't healing it properly, so I have to wait for it to heal on its own."

"How archaic."

"I know, right?"

Someone knocked on the door before it swung open, revealing Araj's smiling face. "Hey! ...Oh." His smile transformed into a frown. "I didn't know she would be here."

"Be nice to Ettares," Farzana chided.

An unfamiliar voice from behind Araj said, "So that's your name!"

Ettares and Farzana startled as Araj stepped to the side, revealing Melara. "What on Faerth?" Ettares leapt to her feet, hands curled into fists.

"Whoa, whoa, calm down," Araj said in a deprecating tone. "I invited her here."

The blood drained from Farzana's face. "Why? She works for Erasto!"

Melara held up her hands in a placating manner. "I come in peace. I'm here to help."

"Says who? You? Why should we believe you?" Ettares asked, not relaxing from what was—even to Farzana's untrained eye—clearly a precursor to a fighting stance.

"If you don't trust her, at least trust me. Come on, why would I put Farzana in danger?"

Farzana glared at Araj, sweat beading on her forehead. When did the room get so hot? "I can't believe you would do this without talking to me first."

"I wanted to surprise you! Melara knows when Erasto is leaving! It's tomorrow."

"So? You could have asked her for that information and then told us." Ettares threw her hands in the air. Farzana couldn't help noticing that Araj took a step back at the movement.

"Well, we were out already, and we were passing by, and I thought we would stop in to say Happy New Year," he said, squirming as though he was beginning to realize what he had done.

A scream built in Farzana's throat. How could he be so foolish?

"Seriously, I'm here to help. Araj told me you had a plan to stop Erasto."

"You told her that?" Farzana yelled, voice shaking. "For the love of all the gods, Araj! What is wrong with you!"

"Okay, fine, I can see this isn't going well," Araj said, taking another step back and grabbing Melara's hand. "We'll leave if we aren't wanted."

"Get. Out." Ettares growled low in her throat, taking a step toward them.

Araj flinched before puffing out his chest and glaring at her. "I'm leaving because Farzana is upset, not because you told me to."

"Yeah, like you would ever listen to me anyway. I know," Ettares snapped.

"Whatever. Bye, Farzana."

Farzana stayed silent, vibrating with fury. He gave her one last look before turning, still holding Melara's hand, and heading back down the hall with her in tow.

"Nice to meet you, Ettares!" Melara called.

Ettares walked to the door and shut it, resting her forehead on it as she seethed. "That...ass," she said, her husky voice low and dangerous.

Farzana covered her face with her hands, mortified. "I can't believe him." The words came in a whisper.

Ettares started pacing the room. "I'm a bit surprised, honestly. Araj has always been stubborn, but he's usually not reckless or irresponsible."

Farzana bit her lip. He had been plenty reckless and irresponsible in the past. At this point, she was struggling to find reasons to stay friends with him. It seemed every time she turned around, he hurt her again. Scrubbing her face with her hands, she let out her breath in a gust. "Well, what's done is done. Do you believe her?"

"What, that she's not going to turn you in?" Ettares turned to face Farzana, her mouth in a hard line. "No, I don't. You need to leave, now."

Farzana's eyes welled with tears. "Where can I go?"

"I would offer my place but who knows if Erasto will pay me another visit? Especially now that Melara saw me with you and knows my name. I could smuggle you out of the country though."

Farzana couldn't imagine a life without her family. Could she really up and leave them behind? Walk away and…and what? Be in exile forever? What if no one ever stopped Erasto? What if her leaving ended up being permanent? She wouldn't be able to handle that. Ettares watched expectantly as Farzana cleared her throat. "I…I don't think I can do that."

"Well, what will you do?"

Farzana burst into tears, sobs wracking her throat. Her happy life was shattering again, too fast for her to pick up the pieces. Safety, happiness, peace—it was all an illusion. When would it all end?

"Hey." Ettares knelt beside Farzana, grabbing her hand and squeezing it reassuringly. "I'm here for you. Whatever you need me to do, I'll do it."

Sniffling, Farzana looked down at her with watery eyes. The concern was so apparent on Ettares's face that she knew there was nothing she could ask that Ettares wouldn't do for her.

"Give me a day to say goodbye? And then I'll leave." Ettares didn't look convinced. "Promise."

Ettares nodded, though her frown remained. "I'll be back tomorrow." She stood, hovering over Farzana for a moment before stooping to press her lips to Farzana's crown of curls.

"See you tomorrow," Farzana murmured as Ettares left the room.

~ ☼ ~

Laraf's screams tore Farzana from her packing; her suitcase fell to the floor with a crash. She turned toward her bedroom door, intending to rush to Laraf's side, before fear gripped her spine and she fell to her knees, her heartbeat thundering through her head.

What was happening?

More screams and yells echoed throughout the house, and Farzana's breath fled, leaving her gasping for air. A dark haze intruded on her vision as the room spun around her. The dying sunlight of the afternoon sputtered through her window for a second before it vanished.

Oh gods, what is happening?!

Banging. Screams. Thundering footsteps. Shouts of anger, pain, and authority. Farzana looked around the room, frantic for somewhere to hide. It's not like she could run anywhere, and if the intruders were imps...

I'm going to die.

She choked on silent sobs and cowardice as she crawled with desperation toward her closet. The image of Laraf's battered and bloody face haunted her when she heard another scream. Her heart broke in pieces as she dove behind her clothes.

Forgive me.

The bedroom door slammed open right as she pulled the closet door shut. Someone barked, "Find her!"

Farzana covered her mouth with both hands, snot dribbling from her nose as she hardly dared to breathe. She could hear several faeries slamming around the small room. She wouldn't remain hidden for long.

"Here she is!" Someone grabbed her by the hair and yanked her out.

Farzana screamed, clawing at the hand holding her and writhing to get free. "Let me go!" She was flung to the floor and landed face-first onto a pair of shiny boots. Craning her neck, she looked straight up into a pair of infuriatingly familiar bright green eyes.

"Well, hello, sunshine," Melara said with a wink.

"What the f—"

Something slammed into the side of Farzana's head. A bright light burst behind her eyelids, and she crumpled into unconsciousness.

INTERLUDE

ERASTO WORKED TO DIRECT HIS FUMING AT-
titude inward. It would be less than ideal to allow anyone to see
the extent of how this had affected him. He hadn't prepared for
this occasion, because it should never have happened. Everything had been executed perfectly…and now this, this defiance.
Rebellion. Even—dare he say it?—betrayal.

Fortunately it had been easy to track down his disobedient
child. Her ability to so earnestly trust others had been her down-
fall once, and yet it seemed she was not quick to learn from
her mistakes. A flaw passed down from her delicate mother,
no doubt. Yes, fortunate for him indeed.

His meticulously and thoroughly laid out plans were as wayward as this child, full of dismaying tributaries of dysfunction.
One could blame chaos, of course. And in doing so, wouldn't
it be clear to any that this was ironically Erasto's own fault?
It would be amusing, perhaps, if it wasn't first and foremost
utterly infuriating.

When had he last strode through the halls of this despica-
ble House? The grand House of Amber; aristocratic enough
to be called such, and yet so lacking in every other aspect. Its
disappointing features had made it perfect for his plans of

233

assimilation, but the spawn had been an undeniable mistake. He shouldn't have been tempted by the flesh, the warmth. Those secret smiles, coaxed into existence solely for him. It should have been easy to manipulate Sitra for his ends while staying a safe distance away. And yet...

The redolent air of the House haunted him as he followed his guards to the library. The double doors stood open, awaiting his entrance, and he paused to ground himself. It wouldn't do to allow any of these slimy faeries to observe his hectic emotions. He was better than them, in every way. He knew this. They knew this. This was not the time to display anything to the contrary.

"Good morning, everyone." His voice drifted before him as he entered the room, his eyelids carefully lowered to the exact degree to convey boredom. As his glance landed on each faerie in turn, he drank in their fears, their panic, their embarrassingly bare emotions. Sitra, defeated and broken as she was, didn't even raise her face to meet his. Just as well. Her parents too, frail and old as dust itself, drooped against each other, as if they could gain strength from each other's presence alone.

Pitiful.

When his eyes alit on the young imp though, he saw the process of her temerity steel her spine. Her eyes bore into his with an intensity he would have loved to utilize. It seemed her spirit remained, perhaps even flourished within the company of this House. Astonishing, truly. These faeries had only ever flooded him with unease and disdain. His lips curved into a slow smile of their own accord, and he yearned to devour her vitality and leave her as a husk. But he was not here for her.

At last, he turned to his own flesh and blood. Melara, no doubt, had been the one to so expertly tie Farzana to the dining chair, those violet wings—his wings—pinned to her back. It looked painful. He hoped it was. Focusing on her, he glided forward in that easy movement which predators reserve for their prey.

"Farzana, you wound me. Have I not shown you every ounce of hospitality? Have you not wanted for nothing? And still, you run, despite knowing very well I am entitled to my claimed period of parental time. Tell me, is this fair?" He lowered himself to look at her face-to-face. Purple held purple, as he watched the conviction drain from her eyes. Finally, she looked away. He stood, assured in his victory.

"As I thought: a short-lived defiance. You may yet prove yourself to be a good child." On the last word he turned to Laraf, sauntering to her. "So here is what we will do, daughter. You, the little one"—Laraf twitched—"and I will head back to my High Management Center. We will pretend this mess never happened. It will be as it should; we will be as one happy family."

"No!"

The outburst cracked through the air around him and he stiffened. How dare she defy his word? He couldn't help the glare that shot to Farzana as he approached her yet again. "No?" he whispered, not trusting steadiness in his voice if he were to raise it. No matter; she shivered and licked her lips in fear as he had hoped.

"I mean, not the little one. She...she's a stupid baby, a nuisance. I'm t-tired of taking care of her. Please." Her face took on an expression of desperation. "Don't make her come with us."

Her attempt at assuaging him was feeble at best. After what she had done, she couldn't possibly believe that he would give her what she wanted simply for the sake of wide eyes and a tremble. Still, she hadn't argued against going back herself. Perhaps this small grace could secure a promise of good behavior from her. He had enough to manage without having to additionally keep his fickle offspring under the watchful eye of that Sapphire Aristo-fae. Another slip-up like this and the pixie would become of little use, and it was still too early in the game to waste subservient bodies.

"Indeed, she is an annoyance. Sniveling, whining. The little one can stay here for all I care."

Farzana breathed a sigh of recognizable relief.

"Will you come with me willingly, daughter?" He stretched his hand to her, a symbol of a peace they both knew was a mockery of their arrangement. Better that she was bound, so he would not have to guess whether she would have sought his touch and given her acceptance.

She nodded. "Of course, Father."

Erasto beamed at her, releasing the chokehold of his charm. He watched her face smooth out into relaxation in his presence, for the first time. Just like her mother, she proved to be so malleable. He needed to remember that she responded better to honey than pain, no matter how much fun inflicting pain on her entailed.

"I'm delighted to hear it. Melara, dear, untie my beloved daughter immediately."

"Yes, sir," Melara responded. She sashayed to Farzana, hips swishing and green wings fluttering behind herself provoca-tively. He should remind her to control herself in the presence of others, else she would find herself barred from his bed. Her prettiness and skillful wielding of pleasure wasn't enough to excuse her public indecency. After eliciting a hiss of pain from Farzana, Melara finished releasing her and came back to stand at his side, a smirk perched on her lips. Fine, then. He would discipline her later.

Erasto snapped his fingers, as much for her as for Farzana. "Come. I'm impatient to return home. The pixies in this House have always left me feeling ill." After a swift and sweeping ma-levolent glance around the room, he turned on his heel and left.

29

ALONE AND BACK IN HER ROOM AT THE CEN-
ter, Farzana lowered herself onto the bed and rocked back and
forth, hugging her knees to her chest. She couldn't believe she
was back in her gilded prison. Melara had betrayed them, and if
she had told Erasto her location, she definitely told him about
their plan or whichever part of it Araj had told her.

Araj!

Farzana shook with fury. He was the real betrayer, leading
the enemy to her and letting them drag her back. Everything
had been fine before he ruined it. Everything was a gods-
damned dream come true before he brought Melara over.

If he ever showed his face again, she would...

She sighed. What would she do exactly? What could she do
to the only person who had shown her kindness back when she
was still a lowly bastard, working her ass off at the Fae Resource
Manipulation and Distribution Center? The one who took her
under his wing and helped her apply for a lower management
position? The one who had taught her how to dance, held her
hands and guided her body to make art?

Despite everything, she did still love him. She should
have listened to Ettares and fled the country. Instead, she had

trusted Araj's attraction-fueled thinking and allowed herself to be captured again.

She had to stop blaming others for her own problems when it was all her fault. Why did she keep messing up? She was a veritable wreck of a pixie. She sprawled back on her bed and stared at the ceiling. Whining about her situation wouldn't change anything. She had to accept her fate. For the foreseeable future, that meant being stuck under Erasto's thumb, locked away in his tower.

Someone would eventually stop Erasto, but it wouldn't be Farzana. Hopefully the real hero came in to save them all— sooner rather than later.

Farzana settled back into her life at The Center with remarkable ease, as though her time away had simply been a dream. The difference, of course, was that she was back to being alone. Pangs of guilt struck her whenever she thought of little Laraf; Farzana hoped she was happier with the family than when she had been at The Center. At least she was safe and loved, free of Erasto's control. That was more important than Farzana's loneliness.

Farzana spent her days lazing in bed, watching random local channels on the mirror stream. The country was descending into chaos even without Erasto's invasion; his new capitalist plan meant hundreds of job layoffs at various Centers all across the country, not just in The City. Apparently, it was more cost efficient to hire imps for labor because, according to Erasto, they didn't have to be paid as much. He had implemented an 'imp wage' which was far below the normal wages set in place; companies all over were jumping at the chance to raise their profit margins.

Protestors marched in the streets as faeries demanded their jobs back. Violence against imps was at an all-time high as faeries blamed them for stealing their jobs. It seemed like every news channel had a story about an imp being attacked in broad daylight, and Farzana recoiled from the pictures they showed of the victims, some alive, some dead. Unable to handle it anymore, Farzana resorted to watching dance competitions, lamenting her own loss of graceful movements.

After a couple days alone in her room, a knock sounded on the outer door. Farzana shot up in bed to stare at the entrance. It wasn't yet lunchtime, so it wasn't someone delivering her meal. Could it be...? She didn't want to get her hopes up at the thought of seeing a friendly face. But a moment later, another knock sounded, this one tentative.

"Come in," she called, her voice rusty. The door creaked open, and a head poked through the crack.

"Hello?" Ettares called, looking around the empty sitting room before she spotted Farzana in the bedroom. Her icy eyes lit up, and she quickly stepped inside, shutting the door behind her. Her figure was obscured by a bulky coat, which also hid her wings. She rushed over to Farzana's side. "Oh gods! I'm so sorry, Farzana. Are you okay? Can I hug you?"

Farzana held her arms open wide in a silent invitation; Ettares gathered her into strong arms, held her tight. Farzana breathed in the scent of freesias and relaxed into the embrace, allowing some of the stress and anxiety of the past few days to melt away.

"I'm okay, just lonely," Farzana said after a bit, easing away.

"That's understandable! I went to the House of Amber the other day to pick you up and, of course, you were gone." Ettares ran a hand through her curls, making them stand on end. "I would have come here sooner, but I was working. And I..." She trailed off, looking distraught.

Farzana gave her a small smile. "I know you get busy. It's okay, really. How is my family? And how are you allowed to visit me when they know you helped me?"

"Your family is doing well. Erasto stuck by what he told you and hasn't harassed them at all. Laraf is having more nightmares, but I guess that's to be expected. As for me, I no longer have teleportation access here, but that doesn't stop me from just taking the trolleys here and walking in. None of the guards even noticed me."

"Should probably credit the coat for that," Farzana quipped.

Ettares huffed out half a laugh and sat on the bed beside her. "We need to start your training," she said, tracing a pattern on the blanket. Her fingers touched the faint stain of blood from where Farzana had fallen during the imp attack.

"Training?"

She nodded, looking Farzana in the eye. "I need to teach you self-defense. I'm not sure why I never did before, but now is as good a time to start as ever. You need it."

Farzana balked. "B-but my leg! I can't—I can't do anything."

Ettares jumped to her feet. "There is so much you can still do! You're not a fighter, but that doesn't mean you can't learn how to defend yourself. You're not an invalid, Farzana."

"I feel like one," Farzana muttered, and Ettares shot her an exasperated look.

"Use it or not but I'm going to teach you anyway," she said, gesturing for Farzana to stand. "Come on, let's start."

Farzana groaned but got to her feet anyway, feeling wobbly without her cane.

"Get in a fighting stance—whatever you think a fighting stance is."

Farzana bent her knees slightly, bringing her hands up to chest level and curling them into tight fists.

"Okay, good. Now, I'm going to give you some corrections, and I want you to focus on them so you can remember them."

With a gentle hand, she guided Farzana's arms higher, tucked her right elbow close to her body, and loosened her fists. Farzana's hands were at jaw level, which felt awkward as she worked to keep everything in the correct position.

"Why like this?" she asked, struggling to keep her arms tucked as well as up.

"The right elbow is protecting your liver. One hit to that and you could be incapacitated, though I doubt Erasto knows that. The hands should be up by your face to deflect any attacks aimed there; head injuries are disorienting, and you don't want that in a fight."

Farzana nodded, flexing her fingers and shifting her weight

back and forth. "Why can't I have fists?"

"Because the best deflection is an open palm, to smack away a fist or weapon coming at you. I'm teaching you self-defense, not how to attack. You don't need fists."

Farzana chose to ignore the mention of a weapon and instead looked down at her loosely curled fingers. "Ah. Makes sense. I don't think I could attack anyone anyway."

"You never know. One day, you might find a reason to attack someone. And on that day, you can use fists."

"Any punching pointers?" Farzana asked with a grin; she jabbed at the air in front of her.

"Punch like you mean it. Aim with your last two fingers and throw your arm like you're going to go straight through them."

"Gotcha." Farzana dropped her arms and relaxed, leaning against the bed for support. Standing without the use of her cane was exhausting.

"Okay, again," Ettares said after letting her rest a moment.

"Ugh," Farzana groaned before doing her best to get back in the same position. Elbow tucked, arms up, knees slightly bent…

"Hands," Ettares said, circling her.

Farzana looked down at her hands; they were clenched into fists again. Sighing, she loosened them.

"Good," Ettares said, coming to stand in front of Farzana. She had a crooked smile on her full lips, one fang shining in the light. "You look good."

"I know," Farzana said in a cocky tone, relaxing her stance.

Ettares chuckled. "I mean, yeah, in that sense too."

Oh.

Farzana blushed, heat spreading across her face as she looked away and down at the blankets on the bed. That was the wrong place to look; she was staring at the dried blood stain and remembering the last time she and Ettares had been in the room together. She hadn't been entirely lucid then.

"Hey," Farzana said, tracing the blood stain. "Thank you, for saving me—us. I don't think I could have survived another hit from that imp, and I know Laraf wouldn't have made it."

Ettares shrugged, looking uncomfortable. "I did the decent

thing, that's all. You don't need to thank me for it."

"Incapacitating an imp... How did you even do that?"

Ettares rubbed the back of her neck, not meeting Farzana's eye. "I...um, I cut her throat."

Farzana gulped, wide eyed. "You—what?"

Tears glistened in Ettares's eyes. "I had to save you, Farzana. I wouldn't have been able to live with myself if I hadn't. So yeah, I ran in here, and I slit both of their throats. Then I grabbed you and Laraf, and I ran to the teleportation room and took you home."

Farzana was speechless. Ettares had killed two imps, for her. How much blood was on her hands, really?

"You don't understand," she continued. "Seeing you there, seeing your face split open and your leg broken, and—and you were bleeding everywhere. Laraf was screaming...I couldn't leave you. I did the only thing I could think of."

"Do you carry knives with you everywhere?" Farzana asked in a whisper.

She nodded. "Of course."

Of course.

"Can I see?"

She hesitated before reaching in her jacket pockets and pulling out two curved bars of metal. With a flick of her wrists, blades sprang out of the handles, their warped edges shining.

Farzana felt sick.

"Okay, you can put them away now," she said in a small voice.

Ettares gave her a sad smile and flicked her wrists again; the blades vanished. Replacing the bars in her pockets, she said, "I don't go anywhere without them."

And that was the only reason Farzana was still alive. Ettares saved her; no matter how gruesome the outcome, Farzana was grateful. She would never be able to repay her.

"Thank you," Farzana said again, reaching for Ettares's hand.

Ettares fingers curled around hers, and her eyes shone as she looked at Farzana. "I would do it all over again for you."

"I hope you don't have to."

They sat in silence, their fingers intertwined, before Ettares cleared her throat and released her. The empty spaces between Farzana's fingers were a vice on her throat, strangling her until Ettares spoke.

"I'll try to visit you every day. And I'll teach you more self-defense."

Farzana's heart skipped a beat as she took a deep breath. "I'd like that."

"Good," she said with a grin. "See you tomorrow, Farzana."

"See you tomorrow, Ettares."

Farzana spent the morning lounging in bed, waiting for Ettares to show up and wondering what Araj was up to. When the afternoon sun slanted through her windows and neither of them had shown up, she decided to get up and go for a walk. Maybe she would run into one of them in the halls. If nothing else, she could go visit Enzi or Sitra and ask about Laraf. As much as Farzana knew that keeping her away from The Center was the right thing, living alone again after living with Laraf was proving to be an adjustment. She missed her little sister.

Farzana made her way with careful steps, leaning on her cane for support and watching her feet. As she rounded a corner, she noticed a pair of imp guards standing close together, whispering. At first, she wondered if they were there to keep an eye on her, and her heartbeat thundered with panic at the idea of being trapped in her room. She tried to retreat but ended up tripping on her cane, alerting the imps to her presence.

When they turned to her, their faces bore identical sneers; then they turned and left her alone in the hall.

A weird feeling sat in the pit of Farzana's stomach. What could they have been whispering about, hidden in a back hallway? At least they didn't seem to be there to guard her, which meant she was free to roam, right? Regardless, she now had an urge to run back to her room, where she felt safe.

She chuckled darkly to herself as she turned back around, though it felt more like a sob than laughter. Safety was a luxury she couldn't afford. She was safe so long as she obeyed...and so long as Erasto ignored her. She shivered, chilled to the bone.

Back in her room, Farzana drew a bath and floated on her back for a while, letting the heated water soothe her muscles and warm her to the core. When would Ettares show up? Cupping water in her hands, she let it drip down onto her body, the droplets sliding down her sides, tickling her as they went. If she closed her eyes, the water felt like a warm hug, like someone carrying her in the safety of their arms. She wrapped her own arms around herself.

Ettares said she would visit. And yet...

Farzana turned on the mirror and tried to call Ettares only to have a message pop up that read 'Could not complete call.' Frowning, she tried to call Araj and received the same message. After attempting to call the House of Amber and seeing the message a third time, she gave up. Of course Erasto had removed her only way of communicating with the outside world. Why was this coming as a surprise?

Farzana lay on her bed and resorted to flipping through channels. Channel after channel, random faerie after random faerie. She stopped on a scene of chaos: a riot taking place outside the palace gates. Why would anyone be protesting at the palace? Surely it was abandoned, since Erasto had set up headquarters in his Center?

The screams reverberated in her room, and she shut off the mirror, disturbed. Despite losing his wight army, Erasato's plan to instill chaos on Fearth seemed to be working well. The country would tear itself apart in the search for justice, though the fact that imps were being blamed wasn't fair, considering it was Erasto's policy that was stealing jobs. What would it take to sate his thirst for destruction? How long until Dradour fell into anarchy? And if it did, would Erasto finally leave them? Farzana couldn't imagine Erasto simply slinking away with his victory. There had to be something bigger than that in his mind. And gods only knew if anyone would be able to stop him before then.

Alone in the silence, she found herself nodding, eyes

drooping and vision blurring. It was getting late, and she hadn't napped all day. She was so…so tired…

"Hey."

Farzana jerked awake, eyes wide. Ettares stood at the end of the bed, looking at her.

"I let myself in. You really should keep your door locked."

Farzana blinked at her.

"And I'm sorry I'm so late. Do you still want to hang out?"

"Yes!" Farzana sat upright. "I do."

"You're sure? You're not too tired?"

"I'm wide awake," Farzana said with a smile. "Promise."

Ettares grinned, showing her crooked fangs. "Okay. What do you want to do?"

Farzana pondered that for a moment. What would make her happy? "I wish I could go for a walk, but like, a real walk. Outside."

"Why don't we?"

Farzana raised an eyebrow, scoffing. "Because Erasto would be furious."

"Look," she said, hooking a stray curl behind her ear, "you can stay here, locked up forever, or you can go outside and breathe some fresh air and take a damn walk. We'll take a guard with us."

The idea of going outside for the first time in who knew how long was overwhelming; it was a compulsion. "Let's do it," Farzana said with excitement.

"Great!" Ettares bounced over to the closet. "Do you have a coat?"

"I should."

Ettares helped her bundle up and then they left, took the lift to the ground floor, and walked up to the imp guards at the front entrance. Farzana's anxiety spiked as they approached the guards. What if they recognized Ettares? What if they called Erasto?

"Excuse me, we need an escort," Ettares said.

The imps stared at her with a bored expression before exchanging a glance. "Where are you going?" asked the masc-fae imp.

"We want to take a walk. Farzana needs the fresh air."

He grunted then motioned for the fem-fae imp to go with the two of them. Satisfied, Ettares linked her arm with Farzana's; together, they walked out the front doors.

Farzana stopped on the sidewalk and stared. The trees were bare of any leaves; the remnants of the dressage lay on the ground in colorful mounds and danced across the street in the breeze. She pulled in a breath of crisp air and shivered with delight. How could she have stayed inside for so many days? She had missed the remainder of autumn. Soon the frost would come, and it would truly be winter.

Hit with the urge to stare at the stars, she craned her neck to look up and was disappointed to see what little of the sky wasn't blocked by buildings was obscured by the glow of the streetlamps.

"I want to see the stars," Farzana murmured.

Ettares squeezed her hand. "I know just the place."

They walked for almost an hour, stopping several times so Farzana could rest her leg and catch her breath. The imp guard shadowed them the whole time, silent and part of the surrounding night. Ettares kept Farzana's spirits up by telling her it was just a bit farther, just a little bit farther.

"Here it is," she said at last, gesturing at the park before them.

Farzana was stunned. A little outcropping of trees whispered forest. A pond sat before them, and a multitude of tiny flowers dotted the tall grass, reaching for the sky with all their might. With no buildings anywhere nearby, the stars shone crystal clear across the dark blanket of night.

She knelt on the ground, feeling the grass between her fingers, exhausted but exhilarated. Why had she never gone to parks before? The City felt far away; she couldn't hear any sounds other than the murmur of water over stone and the rustle of naked tree boughs.

A waterhorse, freed from its trolley, emerged from the water and stood at the edge of the pond, watching them. Its ears pricked forward as they took a step closer, and with a gentle *whuff*, it wandered over.

Having never seen a freed waterhorse, Farzana was mesmerized. It was magnificent. The black hide was velvet beneath her fingers, and its coarse mane moved as though it was underwater. She gazed into its glowing red eyes. Was this how it tricked faeries into getting onto its back and following it into the depths, never to be seen again? Farzana wouldn't mind that. It sounded much more pleasant than being under Erasto's control.

"Hey," Ettares said, snapping her from her reverie. Her hands were tight on Farzana's, and only then did Farzana realize she had been in the process of mounting the waterhorse.

Shaken, she allowed Ettares to extricate her hands from the mane and pull her close. With a disappointed snort, the waterhorse turned and headed back to the pond, submerging itself and leaving no sign of its presence other than the rapidly fading ripples on the water's dark surface.

"I...tried to mount a waterhorse," Farzana said with a laugh of dismay. "Oh gods." She turned to look at the guard sheepishly only to see her with her back to them, staring back at The City.

"I wouldn't let you do that," Ettares said with a gentle smile as she released her hold on Farzana.

"Thank you. That's twice you've saved my life now."

A crimson stain worked its way up Ettares's neck and splashed across her face. "It's nothing, really," she said, her voice low and husky.

Farzana reached for her hand and gave it a squeeze. "Well, it means a lot to me."

"Did I ever tell you my favorite animal is the waterhorse?" Ettares said, changing the subject. "I even wanted to own one when I was a wee little fae babe."

Farzana stared at her, confused. "You wanted to own a waterhorse? Like, enslave it?"

"No! Gods no, nothing like that. I wanted a pet, that's all. I didn't know at the time that only water nymphs could tame them." She chuckled. "Imagine my heartbreak when I found out."

"Who told you?"

"One of my nannies. I told her I wished I could have been born a water nymph instead of a pixie noble."

"And what did she say?" Farzana asked, sitting down in the grass and kicking out her legs.

Ettares settled beside her, her posture impeccable. "She told me I was a spoiled brat who didn't deserve to be a noble anyway."

"Sounds like a mean nanny."

"She was actually my favorite! She was the only one who didn't treat me like a little prince."

"How refreshing," Farzana said dryly.

Farzana had never considered that a noble would want for anything; they were the richest of the rich, the top social caste right after purebloods. If Queen Tatiana hadn't eventually bore a child, they all would have been in line for the throne. How funny that the only thing Ettares had ever wanted that she couldn't have was a beautiful waterhorse.

They laid back on the grass, looking up at the stars. Ettares pointed out different constellations for her, naming famous pixie heroes, gods, and goddesses. Lulled by that soothing voice, Farzana tucked her head into Ettares's side and found herself falling asleep.

"Farzana," Ettares said, shaking her awake. "We have to go back."

"Why can't we stay?" she whined.

"Because if we are still gone when Erasto wakes up, he'll send guards to your grandparents' house to try and find you."

That thought had her groaning and sitting up. "Yeah, let's go."

Ettares handed Farzana her cane and helped her to her feet, and they set off on the trek back to The Center, their watchful guard close behind them.

The sky began to lighten as the dawn approached; stars disappeared one by one, replaced by red and orange threads of light. In silence, they made their way through The City as it slowly came to life around them.

30

ARAJ WAS PACING THE LENGTH OF THE SITTING room when Farzana and Ettares entered the suite; his eyes lit up with fury as soon as he saw Ettares. "What on Faerth were you doing?" he yelled, throwing his hands in the air. "How could you be so reckless and irresponsible?"

Farzana bristled with anger at his words, shutting the door behind her and leaning back against it. "Excuse me? You want to talk about reckless behavior now?"

"Where were you?" he asked, crossing his arms.

"None of your business," snapped Ettares. She shifted forward toward Araj and, in a panic, Farzana reached out and grabbed her arm. Ettares relaxed back on her heels and turned to face her, a wry smile on her lips. "I guess I should go…. Are you going to be okay?" Her eyes flickered between Farzana and Araj with obvious concern.

"I'll be fine," Farzana said with a forced smile. "Go."

"Yeah, run away. You're good at that," Araj called as Ettares left the room with her head held high.

"Gods, what is wrong with you?" Farzana asked, hobbling to the bed and sitting down. Her legs ached from the long walk, and her joints were tender from having to lean on the cane for support.

"What's wrong with me? What is wrong with *you?* I can't believe you. After everything that happened, you were going to put your family through even more misery?"

Farzana glared daggers at him, her vision blurring with tears at his insinuation. "What is that supposed to mean? I didn't do anything wrong."

"How could you go back to their house and put them in danger, put Laraf in danger? Enzi almost lost his job because of you."

"Because of me?" Farzana said with incredulity. "Araj, *you* are the reason I'm back here! You and your oh-so-precious Melara. You were the reckless one. You were the one who acted without thinking. Everything is *your* fault!" she screamed, finishing her tirade at the top of her lungs.

Gulping air, she worked to calm herself. A fight wasn't going to help either of them feel better. Though, if he hadn't goaded her into yelling at him with his horrible accusations, maybe she wouldn't be so angry. Her eyes stung with unshed tears as she tried to reconcile that Enzi's job had been threatened because of her. She felt awful.

"If you really feel like that, then why am I even here?" he asked quietly.

Farzana raked a hand through her curls, yanking on a tangle. "Because you care about me."

"I guess not, since I'm stupid and don't use my brain," he said, his voice low and nasty. His face twisted in disgust as he looked at her, and she shrank under the weight of his withering gaze.

Farzana wiped at her tears with shaking hands. "Araj, please. I'm tired, and I'm angry, but I don't want to fight."

He snorted. "Could have fooled me."

"I'm sorry. I'm—I wasn't thinking." A tremor crept into her voice as she worked to deescalate the situation like she had so many times with him in the past.

"Clearly. I just don't understand why you would go back to

the House of Amber and put everyone in danger. It's irresponsible. That's all I was saying."

Farzana bit her tongue before saying, "But I didn't go back. Ettares and I went for a walk to a park and then came back. We even had an imp guard the whole time."

He pursed his lips, looking taken aback. "Oh."

She hung her head, curls falling forward and hiding her face. "I don't have a good excuse but I am sorry for yelling at you."

"Sure."

Farzana looked up at him to see him with his back to her. "Hey, are we good?" she asked. He always accepted her apologies, just like she always accepted his.

"Sure," he repeated. "We're fine. I'll leave you so you can sleep." Without a backward glance, he left, slamming the door shut behind him.

~ ☼ ~

She waltzed around the room, flitting from Araj's arms to Enzi's. Enzi whirled her around, hand in hand, while Araj danced in place, waving his arms in the air. Farzana laughed, delighted with his dance, her cheeks flushed from the rush. She reached out to Araj and grasped his hand. It was wet.

Her hand came away covered in red and she gasped, staring at Araj's blood-stained hands. Blood flowed freely from a slice in his neck, coating the front of his shirt, his arms, his hands.

He grinned at her, fangs flashing in the light. "Dance with me, Farzana," he said.

Farzana screamed, pushing him away, but he wrapped his arms around her, pressing his sticky lips to her neck; it burned her flesh like a brand.

She glanced at Enzi, but in his place was Ettares, holding her hand out.

"What's wrong, my love?" Ettares asked. Farzana stifled another scream as a naked blade sprouted from the center of Ettares's chest, blood seeping into her floor length gown, spurting out and splattering Farzana's face.

"What is happening?" *Farzana sobbed, collapsing to the floor. Her throat began to close; she couldn't breathe.*

The light in the room grew dim, and her vision narrowed to the twin pools of blood that Ettares and Araj danced in. More blood than could possibly fit in their bodies poured out, covering the entire floor, flooding the room. The music slowed until the stillness between the notes stretched into infinity and the light extinguished fully.

Farzana drifted in silence on a sea of blood and darkness.

Hands grabbed her and shook her.

"Farzana! Wake up!"

She let out a breathless scream and opened her eyes to see Ettares standing over her, worry filling her wide, pale eyes.

"You're dreaming. It's okay. It's just a dream."

Farzana sat up, panting, and tried to orient herself. She was in bed, in her room, in The Center. She was safe. Ettares was safe. No one was bleeding.

"Oh, gods!" she cried, launching herself into Ettares's arms. "I thought you were dead." Ettares held Farzana in an awkward embrace as though she wasn't sure how tight she could hold her. When Farzana looked up, concern wrinkled her face. Farzana pulled away, leaning back against the bed, and cleared her throat. "Sorry," she whispered, shuffling her feet and staring at the ground.

Ettares reached out and tilted Farzana's chin up to meet her eyes; kindness lit up her face. "I'm sorry you dreamt that," she said in a soft voice. "But I'm perfectly fine."

Farzana nodded. "I'm glad you woke me. That was terrifying."

"Want to talk about it?"

She shuddered. "No. I don't want to even think about it."

"Okay." Ettares turned and headed to the sitting room before coming back, her hands behind her back and a smile on her face. "I got you something."

"Oh?" Farzana sat on the edge of the bed, excitement making her heart race. "What is it?"

With a flourish, she revealed her surprise: a dozen long-stemmed roses.

As the rich scent hit Farzana, she began to choke, and only then realized that the skin where Ettares had touched her before was burning. Looking down, her hands were bright red with a rash.

Farzana waved her away, trying to breathe even as her throat began to close. Gagging, she stumbled to the bathroom and shut the door behind her, then scrubbed at her skin vigorously with soap and hot water. Steam quickly filled the space, easing her breathing.

"Farzana! Are you okay?" Ettares's voice came through the door muffled.

"I'm allergic to roses," she croaked, finding her voice again now that the roses weren't in front of her.

"Oh, gods! Oh shit, I'm so sorry! I'll get rid of them." Her footsteps retreated.

Farzana gargled cold water, hoping to lessen the swelling in her mouth and throat, and felt marginally better. Unsure of when Ettares would be back, or if she would be, she decided she might as well get dressed in clean clothes. She had crawled into bed that morning still wearing the previous day's clothes, and at that point, she smelled more than a little funky.

Stripping off her clothes and carefully giving herself a quick sponge bath, she found a pair of comfy looking sweatpants and a tank top and pulled them on. Feeling refreshed, she peeked out the bathroom door to find an empty room, no Ettares or bouquet of roses in sight. Relieved, she crawled into bed and pulled the covers over her.

A knock sounded on the outer door, and she yelled, "Come in!"

Ettares popped her head in, looking contrite. "I'm so sorry," she gushed, wringing her hands as she stood at a distance. "I threw out the roses and washed my hands several times, but just to be safe, I won't touch you."

Farzana gave her a warm smile. "That's probably best."

"Are you okay?"

She nodded. "I'm fine. I guess I never thought of telling you about my allergy."

"I'm glad I know now—though what a way to find out!" Ettares laughed, shoving her hands in the pockets of her puffy coat. "Gods, that's awful of me."

Farzana joined in her laughter. "I'm fine! I promise. And now you know."

"Now I know." She sighed, looking around the room. "I wanted to bring you something to brighten this place up since I'll be gone for a couple days. And, you know, help you remember me until I get back."

As if I can forget you.

"Is everything okay?"

"Yes, everything's fine. I have a contract with an elven family to find their son, and it looks like he's out of the country. I'm guessing it will take me a few days to find him and bring him home. I didn't want you to worry when I didn't show tomorrow."

Farzana worked to keep her disappointment from showing. "Ah. Well…thank you for telling me."

"Of course! I should go," Ettares said, taking a step back. "I'm sorry for almost killing you. Please don't take that as an indication of how I feel about you."

Farzana snorted, trying not to giggle.

Ettares winked. "See you in a couple days."

"Stay safe." Farzana waved as she left. Ettares hesitated in the open doorway for a moment, her lips parting as if in surprise. Farzana watched a battle of expressions storm her face before a soft smile won out.

"You too," she said, barely audible. Then she was gone in the blink of an eye.

Something about Ettares's response had Farzana wrapping her arms around herself to suppress a shiver. Had Ettares taken on a potentially dangerous bounty contract? Even if she had, it's not as if Farzana had any right to protest against it. Ettares loved her job, and Farzana knew she could handle herself. Still, it had her feeling some sort of way…and she wasn't ready to dig down and figure out why. Best to keep a smile on her face and pretend everything was fine.

31

"LARAF'S DOING WONDERFULLY," SITRA SAID AS she whisked about the gallery, propping up cards and straightening paintings. "She's the little princess of the House, always waltzing around and singing the day away."

Farzana smiled at the thought of a happy Laraf. She deserved to be happy, though Farzana missed her presence. "Why hasn't she come to visit?"

Sitra pursed her lips, studying one of her merfae paintings. "Well, baby, she's a bit traumatized. Nightmares every night. She barely goes outside. She's terrified Erasto will attack her again. I've told her that won't happen but…"

Farzana winced. Of course Laraf was traumatized. There was no way of knowing if that one imp guard had in fact been Laraf's mother, and there was no point in asking. The imp was dead. And Laraf…Laraf was so small and innocent. Even after everything she had gone through in life, all the obvious abuse and neglect, she was so soft and precious. Farzana hated that she had allowed Laraf to endure more trauma.

Choking down her feelings, Farzana gave her mother what she hoped was a positive expression. "I'm glad she's doing well during the day. I hope…I hope the nightmares end soon."

"I hope so too," Sitra sighed. "I really hope so." She turned to Farzana with a discerning look and asked, "How are you handling things, now that Laraf isn't with you?"

Farzana bit her lip. "It's really lonely. But Ettares visits me most days."

"I'm glad. She seems like a wonderful friend."

"She is," Farzana said with a small smile. The smile died when she remembered she wouldn't see Ettares for a few days.

"Oh! I have something for you." Sitra rummaged in her purse and produced a pocket mirror. "You left this when—when you left," she stammered.

Taking it, Farzana worked to suppress a squeal of delight. Finally, a way to contact others. "Thank you! Erasto switched off the communication in my mirror. I would have called you before now."

Sitra patted Farzana's hand. "I know you would have, baby. Don't let him find it, okay?"

Farzana watched as her mother walked to the door beside the counter and keyed in a combination—5 7 2 9—to unlock it. "What do you keep in there?"

Sitra looked embarrassed. "It's more of a panic room than anything, but I keep food in there for when I want a snack."

Farzana mused over that. Her mother more than most needed solitary space for when she got overwhelmed, but wanting a panic room? That was a new development. She could only guess that the usefulness of her grandparents' panic room had brought this about.

"You hungry, baby?"

"What do you have?"

"Fruit bars and granola."

Neither sounded appetizing. "I'm actually a bit tired," Farzana said, hopping down from her perch behind the counter and fetching her cane.

Sitra came over for a hug, enveloping Farzana in her arms and swaying back and forth. "I love you, baby," she murmured. She smoothed back Farzana's curls and placed a kiss on her forehead. "You look a bit peaky. Make sure you eat something, okay? And get some rest."

"Love you too," Farzana said as she left the gallery.

Farzana meandered down the crowded walkway toward the lifts, watching her cane so she wouldn't trip. People tended to part around her due to her slow gait and the cane, which she was grateful for. Her luck ran out when someone stepped right in her path; before she could stop herself, Farzana ran into the faerie face-first. She stumbled back, groaning and trying not to fall.

"Just like a pixie to not watch where they're going," came a haughty voice. "I'm sick and tired of you lot lording over us like you're so much better."

Farzana's cheeks burned as she glanced up, meeting the gaze of an adolescent imp. "I'm a prisoner here, actually. I'm not lording over anyone."

The imp looked taken aback. "Oh you're...you're the daughter."

"Yeah, I am." Farzana struggled to keep her voice from trembling as she spoke. "I'm Erasto's daughter. I'm the last faerie who would think I'm better than you. And I was watching my cane because I keep tripping over it."

The imp's face softened. "Oh."

"I'm sorry I ran into you."

"Oh, gods, no worries," the imp said, running a hand through her long hair. "I mean, I should be apologizing to you. I heard what the guards did to you that day."

"Don't be silly," Farzana said, feeling self-conscious. Did everyone know about it? What a mortifying thought. "It wasn't your fault."

"Still, I feel awful. Hey, can I buy you a coffee? There's a neat little cafe that just opened up just down the way."

Farzana looked into the imp's dark eyes and saw chagrin as well as friendliness. They were nothing like the imp guards who had attacked her. Their eyes had held her terrified reflection and nothing else. They had been soldiers intent on following orders; she hadn't meant anything to them.

And there wasn't a reason for her to associate this imp with those imps. Besides, Farzana had nothing else to do that day. Coffee sounded lovely. Why not sit and chat with someone?

"I'd love that," she heard herself say.

"Great!" A broad smile revealed a gap between the imp's two front teeth. "Follow me!"

With an imp leading the way, even an adolescent one, the path before Farzana cleared easily. No one wanted to run into someone almost twice their size. Despite being taller and larger than Farzana, the imp was light-footed, nearly dancing as she walked ahead. Farzana wondered why she had never seen an imp in the dancing competitions. They would be great at doing the complicated lifts in certain routines, and they were so quick on their feet.

A tiny cafe nestled between two larger stores appeared in front of them as they rounded a corner, and Farzana's eyes lit up. It had strings of lights hanging from the ceiling as the only light source, giving the inside a cozy sort of glow. The imp walked over to an empty table and pulled out a chair for Farzana before taking a seat across from her.

"I'm Galesh, by the way," she said, twirling a lock of hair around her fingers. "I'm sorry, but I don't remember your name. I know I've heard it many times but I'm bad at names."

"It's Farzana."

"Right! Merry meet, Farzana."

Farzana's lips quirked up into a real smile. "Merry meet, Galesh."

"Do you come to the mall often? I mean, I know you live here, but I don't think I've seen you around. I'm here every day."

"No... I don't leave my room much."

Galesh nodded. "I don't blame you. It must be hard getting through the crowds with a cane. What happened to your leg?"

Farzana's smile froze. "I, uh, the guards..."

Galesh looked mortified. "Oh, gods! The attack, of course. Shit. I'm so sorry."

Farzana ducked her head, curls falling forward and shielding her face. "It's fine," she mumbled. She regretted accepting Galesh's offer. What a ridiculous thing to do, sitting down with a stranger. Especially one who only knew her only as the pixie who was beat up by Erasto's guards. What were they even supposed to talk about? What could steer them away from the subject of the attack? Why was it so hot?

"Y'all ready to order?"

She peeked up to see a handsome elf standing by their table with a mirror tablet in hand. Galesh beamed at him.

"I will have an iced cinnamon mocha, please."

"And for you, miss?" The words screeched through the air, bombarding Farzana with claws and teeth.

Farzana stumbled over her words, still feeling raw and anxious. "I'm not sure. I've never been here." She could vaguely understand that he was describing something to her, something with chocolate—*I like chocolate*—and then he was asking her something again and she still wasn't ready, still couldn't figure out which way was up and which way was drowning.

But he was waiting, they were both waiting for her.

Say something!

"That sounds good," Farzana whispered, head down and eyes shut. If she didn't look at either of them, maybe they would stop looking at her. Maybe she would disappear.

"...Okay, then. I'll have those drinks right out," he said, footsteps receding. One less set of eyes staring at her, watching her every clumsy move.

"Hey, are you okay?" Galesh actually sounded concerned.

Farzana worked to steady her breathing. Everything was fine. Nothing bad had even happened. "I'm fine."

"Do you want to leave? I won't be upset."

It was a moment of kindness and understanding she hadn't expected from a stranger. Swallowing a sob, Farzana nodded. "Please." She couldn't be sure the word even left her lips.

"Okay. What's your room number? I'll grab our drinks and bring yours up to you, okay?"

Numb, Farzana rattled off her suite number and lurched to her feet, knocking over her chair. Too mortified to right it, she fled toward the lifts without a backward glance. She was in her room, on her bed, the ceiling pressing down on her as every inch of her body trembled.

Breathe. In, 2, 3, 4. Out, 2, 3, 4, 5.

Once she was feeling marginally calmer, she sat up, wiping tears from her eyes. What was wrong with her? She needed to wash her face; heat pulsed from her cheeks, stealing her breath.

A timid knock on her door startled her into dropping her cane. It clattered to the floor as she stared at the door, not daring to breathe. Had she really given a stranger her room number? What had she been thinking?

Another knock was followed by a quiet, "Hello?"

Feeling ridiculous, Farzana snagged her cane and made her way to the door. Opening it revealed Galesh's smiling face.

"Okay it is you! I was worried I got the wrong door."

Farzana tried to smile. "Nope, this is mine."

"Well, here you go," Galesh said, holding out a steaming to-go cup. "He forgot to ask if you wanted it hot or iced so they made it hot. I hope that's okay."

"That's fine. Thank you, Galesh."

"Any time! I'm at that cafe for lunch almost every day, so if you're ever lonely, come find me, okay?"

Farzana nodded, not daring to speak.

"See ya!" With a jaunty wave, Galesh turned and headed back down the hall, nearly upending Araj.

"Excuse you," she said, glaring at him.

Araj rolled his eyes as he walked past her and made his way to Farzana. "Some faeries are rude as shit," he said under his breath. "Who was that, anyway? Are you okay?"

Farzana stepped back so he could walk in, careful not to spill her hot coffee on herself. "Someone I met today. I don't think she likes pixies much."

"Why was she here then?"

"She bought me a coffee." She raised the cup for him to see, and he scowled at it.

"I could have bought you coffee."

Farzana managed to not roll her eyes as she sat on the couch, placing her drink on the coffee table. For once, it was serving its true purpose.

Araj stood behind her and placed his hands on her shoulders, kneading her tense muscles. "You don't seem okay. What's wrong?"

"I was talking to my mother. She said Laraf is having nightmares every night."

"Are you blaming yourself?"

Farzana almost admitted she was until she remembered who had led Erasto back to them in the first place. Biting her tongue to keep from saying something scathing, she realized just in time that it wouldn't have mattered anyway; Laraf had been traumatized long before Araj had messed up.

"Yeah," she grumped. "You know I am."

His fingers smoothed and pushed, loosening muscles aching with stress. "Erasto is to blame, not you. Remember that. You didn't hurt her; you rescued her. You gave her a home, a new mother, friends. Erasto gave her pain."

Farzana sighed. "You're right, of course."

"Let's take your mind off of it."

Her spirits lifted for a moment at the thought of a distraction. "How?"

Araj gave her shoulders one final squeeze. "Let's go for a walk!"

A walk? When her limbs were already shaking? Her spirits fell back to their abysmal depth.

"I'm in a lot of pain. Maybe another time?"

His hands stiffened before he withdrew them from her.

Farzana twisted around and caught the stony expression on his face.

"I see how it is," he seethed.

Her brow wrinkled and she opened her mouth to speak, but he cut her off with a slash of his hand.

"You'll go on nighttime adventures with your precious Ettares, who betrayed you, by the way, but with me? Your best friend? You're too tired, or you're in pain. You have no time for me anymore."

Farzana's chest was hollow as his words hit her. "Ettares isn't the only one who betrayed me. Maybe you didn't mean to, but telling Melara about me, where I was, was just as much of a betrayal, Araj."

He scoffed. "This isn't about Melara. I'm not even seeing her anymore. This is about you and me. I shouldn't have to beg for your attention."

"That's not—"

"When was the last time you saw fit to spend any time with me? Me, your supposed best friend."

She opened and closed her mouth as though gasping for breath and remained speechless. What was there to say? It wasn't her fault she was in pain when he asked and had felt better the other night with Ettares.

"Whatever. Enjoy your time with little miss backstabber." He turned on his heel and left the room before she could come up with a retort, not even bothering to shut the door behind him.

Eyes burning, she went to shut it. A heavy blanket of silence descended, suffocating her as she made her way to bed. Why was her life a series of sob stories? Why couldn't she be happy?

She slumped onto the bed and lay there, staring up at the blurry ceiling. Somewhere above her, Erasto was up to gods knew what. Probably torturing another innocent soul to further his grand scheme of throwing Faerth into chaos. And yet she lay in bed, crying about how pitiful and hopeless it all was.

How pitiful and hopeless she was.

Anger blossomed in her heart. When had she become so damn helpless? Why couldn't she be fearless and strong, like Ettares? Or obstinate and reckless, like Araj? Instead, she was a scared, timid, and helpless little faerie who couldn't even walk properly let alone stand up for herself. She wanted to scream!

The sound tore through her throat before she could stop it, echoing through the suite: the screech of a dying soul. She let it fade away before screaming again.

And again.

And again.

She screamed until her throat was too ragged to even whimper. Until she could only lie there in agony.

32

FARZANA WASN'T SURE HOW LONG ETTARES
would be gone but that didn't stop her disappointment from
waxing as the day passed without any word. Araj hadn't returned
to visit and wasn't answering her calls. She had thought he
would have calmed down after sleeping it over but apparently
not.

Worrying at a hunk of bread with her fingers, she realized
her appetite had left her long before lunch had arrived. The
roasted chicken salad lay untouched, charred tomatoes and
ripe avocado laid out artfully across the plate, begging her to
taste them. She was still thin and weak from her hunger strike
as well as from multiple healing sleeps. She knew she needed
to eat, and yet...

Sighing, she glanced up and realized her coffee from the
previous day was still on the coffee table, untouched. Had it
gone bad? Groaning as she stood, she made her way to it and
brought it to her nose for a sniff. It smelled divine. Curiosity
piqued, she hazarded a sip.

Tart and sweet. Fruity and rich. The unmistakable tang
of raspberry married with thick chocolate and bitter coffee
was heaven in her mouth, lingering on her tongue even after

she swallowed it. Eagerly, she quaffed it down, hardly pausing to breathe. When she finished the last, delicious sip, she stopped to look at the cup in disappointment. She wasn't done tasting it.

Well, she knew where to find more. Slipping on her shoes and making sure she had her pocket mirror, she made her way back to the cafe.

Galesh was sitting at a table in the corner when Farzana walked in; she waved, a broad smile on her face. "Farzana! Come, sit!" Galesh jumped up and pulled out a chair for her.

Farzana accepted the invitation with a smile, feeling silly for her panic the day before. "Sorry about yesterday," she mumbled.

Galesh waved away the apology as she sat back down. "Please. It's all good. You thirsty?"

Nodding, Farzana looked around for a waiter. The same elf from before saw her looking and came over, tablet in hand.

"Welcome! Same as yesterday? Or something different?" he asked, eyes kind.

"Same, please."

"Ah, you liked it! It's a customer favorite for a reason."

Farzana couldn't help smiling as she remembered the flavors rippling over her tongue. "It was amazing," she said, knowing she wasn't doing it justice.

The elf nodded with a smile. "Coming right up."

"So? Tell me, who was that pixie coming to see you yesterday?" Galesh leaned forward on her elbows toward Farzana, her dark eyes alight with curiosity.

Farzana hesitated. "He's...a friend."

"Ah, I see." Galesh winked.

Heat spread over Farzana's cheeks as she realized what she had said. "No! Not like that. I'm a lesbian."

Galesh threw back her head with laughter. "Oh gods, the look on your face!" She wiped away tears of mirth and sobered. "I'm sorry. I shouldn't have assumed."

"No, it's okay. I think a lot of people assume that, but I've never liked him like that. As much as he wishes I did."

"Ugh. One of those."

Farzana frowned. "One of what?"

"Someone who thinks they're entitled to your feelings." Galesh scoffed. "He struck me as a shitbag when I first saw him. No offense."

Farzana wasn't sure what to make of that. "He's...a difficult friend. But he's been good to me." Her lips felt numb, phantom pressure bearing down on them. He was a good friend...right?

Galesh studied her for a moment. "Hey, it's okay. I won't say anything about him anymore. What do you want to talk about?"

Farzana gave her a small smile of gratitude. "Um..." She looked around the cafe for inspiration. "Why do you come here every day?"

"Ah, that's easy." Galesh leaned back in her chair, grinning. "The coffee! But it's mostly because I have to stay in the mall all day, and this is one of the few places I can sit and relax."

"Why are you here all day?"

She looked contrite for a moment. "My father works here as a guard. I haven't been able to enroll in tertiary school yet, so I tag along. It's more fun than staying in our hotel room all day."

"You live in a hotel?"

Galesh nodded, sipping her iced coffee. "There aren't many places here that want to rent to an imp family, so we stay in a hotel. My father makes good money, though. We get by."

Farzana shivered. She couldn't imagine being homeless. At least a hotel was better than the streets. An imp family on the streets, in the current social upheaval, would have been asking for trouble.

"Why did you come to Dradour then? I mean, didn't you like your old home?"

Galesh pursed her lips, staring at the ceiling. When she spoke, her voice was soft. "We've been hopping countries my whole life. Always looking for work, for a home, for something better. When Erasto put out the advert looking for imp guards and posted what he would pay, we had to jump at the opportunity."

Farzana nodded.

"Here you go, miss," the elf waiter said, handing her a steaming mug of coffee. "That will be one draden."

Farzana fished her mirror from her pocket and opened it, holding it up to the tablet. They both beeped and flashed green before she put the mirror away. She thanked the elf before he walked off.

Blowing on her coffee, Farzana chanced a tiny sip. The scalding liquid seared her tongue and she hissed, putting it down on the table.

Galesh chuckled and shook her drink, ice cubes clacking. "This is why I get iced."

Making a face, Farzana laughed as well. "I'll have to remember that for next time."

Galesh hummed to herself as she took the last drag of her drink. Pouting, she placed the cup on the table. "Well, there's my treat for the day." She cocked her head, looking at Farzana. "Do you come to the mall to shop?"

Shaking her head, Farzana said, "I only come here to visit my mother. She owns the art gallery."

"Sitra's Space? It's so beautiful in there. Your mother paints it all?"

"Yes! She's a great artist."

"I'll say! You must be proud."

Farzana beamed. "I am." Thinking of how well her mother was doing had her on the verge of tears.

Galesh looked at her with alarm. "You okay?"

Swiping at her eyes, Farzana nodded. "Yeah. I'm just emotional. I love my mother so much, but she's had a rough time in the past. And now she's doing so well!"

Galesh's expression softened. "I'm glad she's doing well."

Farzana hugged herself. "Me too."

Her whole family was doing well, Enzi as head cook, Sitra as gallerist and painter, Laraf healing and thriving. And then there was Farzana. Wallowing away in her room all day, pining for someone she wasn't even sure she really wanted, and squashed beneath her father's thumb. Her mood darkened, though she worked hard to keep the smile on her face.

Picking up her cooled coffee, she sipped it, reveling in the richness. At least here she had a yummy treat and some good company. For once, she wasn't hiding away. It felt…nice. Was this optimism? Despite her world being plagued by chaos?

33

MOTES OF SUNLIGHT SIFTED THROUGH THE
thick curtains, lending a modicum of sight in the otherwise
dark room. Farzana wasn't sure what had woken her, but she
hummed to herself as she slipped out of bed, using her cane
to get to the bathroom. Nightmares had plagued her in the
night, sweat plastering her top to her chest, but despite that she
felt oddly refreshed. Stripping down so she could take a bath,
she nearly missed the knock at the door. She was debating on
answering or not when Ettares's husky voice drifted through
the door.

"Farzana? I brought lunch."

Lunch already? Time had no meaning.

"Come in!" she yelled, deciding to sponge herself down
rather than take a full bath. Drying as quickly as possible, she
pulled a simple shift dress over her head.

She could hear Ettares moving around in the bedroom,
and her mood brightened as she pictured that crooked smile.
Humming under her breath, she twisted her curls up into a
messy bun before stepping out.

Ettares stood in the bedroom doorway holding a bouquet
of purple…roses?

"Wait!" She held up a hand at Farzana's panicked expression. "I learned my lesson. These are silk."

A shaky laugh escaped Farzana's lips. "Oh! Silk roses? That's...kind of perfect."

"That's what I was thinking!" Ettares grinned, clearly pleased with herself. "Your favorite color, plus they'll never wilt."

"How practical," Farzana said. She reached for them and stopped, looking around the room. She didn't own a vase. "Um..."

With a flourish, Ettares revealed a crystal vase from behind her back, the facets throwing a rainbow across the walls. "I figured you would need this as well."

Farzana squealed in delight. "You think of everything!"

A blush spread across Ettares's face as she held out the vase and roses. Farzana took them, plopping the roses in the vase and setting them on the nightstand. When she turned around, Ettares was holding a brown paper bag.

"I brought lunch too."

"Of course you did." Only then did the aroma of yeast and rosemary reach Farzana's nose, and her mouth watered as she realized what it was. "You brought bread from that place! Um, Twy's Cafe, right?"

Ettares perked up at her enthusiasm. "You remembered!"

Farzana snorted and settled into a velvet armchair, gesturing at the coffee table. "How could I forget? It was our first da—lunch together."

Ettares peeked at her from beneath lowered lashes as she plated the food but didn't say anything, for which Farzana was grateful. She knew what their first date had been—how could she forget such an incredible experience? But for some reason the cafe lunch had a special place in her heart. And apparently that meant forgetting that it hadn't actually been their first date.

"There we go," Ettares said, sitting back in her seat.

The table held a spread of breads, fruits, and various dips: jams, oil, and vinegar for the bread, plus melted chocolate and a dish of some kind of soft, white cream.

"You have to try this," Ettares said, grabbing a strawberry and dipping it into the mystery dish. "It's a whipped sweet cheese dip, and it's divine."

Farzana obediently opened her mouth for the offering; when she bit down, the juice flooding her mouth and the sweet and tart cheese on the tip of her tongue, she had to hold in a moan. Forget berries and cream—this was her new favorite fruit treat.

She covered her mouth as she continued chewing, languishing in it. "Oh gods, it's sinful."

Ettares chuckled, her delicate tongue flicking out to clean the ends of her fingers. "I wouldn't make you sin, Farzana."

Farzana bit back her next words and instead concentrated on savoring the food. Maybe she wanted to sin with her. Maybe she wanted... It had been so long since she had found out Ettares had worked for Erasto. Some days it felt like it never even happened, that they were still blissfully dating.

But she knew better. She had told Ettares they could be friends, and at the time, she meant it. There was no point holding out hope that Ettares still had feelings for her, though the silk roses might have been a sign. A sign she couldn't afford to read into; she wouldn't be able to handle the possibility of her feelings being unrequited.

"You're quiet today," Ettares said, tossing a berry into her mouth as she gazed at Farzana.

Farzana shrugged, not sure what to say. She usually spoke her mind, but there was no way she was bringing any of that up. "Is that blackberry bread?" she asked instead, pointing at the darker loaf.

Ettares nodded, swallowing before saying, "Blackberry and basil. They changed up the recipe, and I must say, it's even more amazing than before. Try it with olive oil."

Dipping a piece into the dish of iridescent oil, Farzana popped it into her mouth. The sweetness of the blackberry with the sharpness of the basil and richness of the oil was, indeed, amazing. Farzana closed her eyes in bliss and hummed.

"Mm, you're right. I love it." When she opened her eyes, she saw Ettares resting her chin in her hands, watching. Farzana blushed. "What?"

Ettares's lips parted a whisper before hesitating. She flushed and reached up to ruffle her hair, not meeting Farzana's gaze. "I like watching you enjoy things."

Farzana's heart thudded in her chest like galloping water-horses. There was no other way to take that, was there?

Be still, my heart.

She watched as Ettares selected a grape and dipped it into the sweet cheese spread before bringing it up to her full lips. Before her fangs could piece the tender flesh, Farzana looked away. The room swirled with heat, though she knew it wasn't entirely physical. She fanned herself, knowing that wouldn't help, and blew out a gust of air.

Getting through lunch was a silent, heavy affair as both pixies avoided getting caught looking at each other. Sneaking peeks between bites was exhilarating. As they cleaned up, their hands brushed; Farzana jerked away as though hit by lightning, immediately wishing she had grabbed her and held on tight. Her cheeks grew hotter. Farzana was sure she wouldn't survive the day.

"Oh, I brought this for you as well," Ettares said, pulling a small package from her pocket. "I hope you like it."

Farzana reached for it, curious and careful not to touch those slender fingers again. Pastel purple paper crinkled beneath her hands as she revealed a box of chocolates. These were handmade artisanal chocolates, something Farzana had never been able to afford.

"I can't take this!" she said, looking up at Ettares.

White lashes framed innocent eyes. "Whyever not?"

Farzana sputtered as she tried to figure out why this felt like a line was being crossed. She could accept flowers and lunch but not dessert? Shaking her head, she thrust the package back at Ettares.

With peals of laughter, Ettares pushed it back and whirled around to leave. Her hand closed on the doorknob even as it turned and someone else pushed it open, nearly upending her.

"Oof!" She stepped back, rubbing her cheek and scowling as Araj entered.

"Oh, joy," he said, sarcasm dripping from his lips. "Just who I wanted to see."

"Maybe you should knock first then," Ettares shot back.

"Or just avoid Farzana altogether since you're glued to her hip."

Farzana tangled her fingers in her hair, wanting to scream. Could they not fight for even one day? Pinching the bridge of her nose, she sighed. "For the love of the gods, why on Faerth can you two not just get along?"

"Get along?" Araj sounded incredulous. "I don't typically 'get along' with my exes, sorry."

Farzana jaw dropped as Ettares let out a low growl.

"We said we wouldn't bring that up," she said, her skin growing paler than Farzana had ever seen it.

"How long did you two date?" Farzana asked, her voice barely over a whisper.

"Too long!" snarled Araj. "And I ended it when—"

"No!"

"—she murdered someone."

Ettares let out a soft cry of anguish. "It was an accident! You know that! You said you would never tell anyone!" Her ice blue eyes shone bright, and her hands shook at her sides.

"I figured it was time Farzana learn who you really are: a murderer." Araj sneered at her, a sense of triumph apparent in his twisted features.

Farzana heard everything through a thick film, as though underwater.

Murderer.

That couldn't be. There had to be an explanation. Focusing instead on the fact that her two friends had dated each other, she felt anger bloom in her heart.

"You two decided it was okay to keep a secret from me? That you dated each other? What, I couldn't be trusted?"

Araj looked taken aback. "It's not like that. I was ashamed of dating her. I didn't want you to know."

Ettares dropped her head into her hands and let out what sounded suspiciously like a sob.

Farzana was floored. Ettares...crying? Not just that but openly weeping, and in front of Araj, of all faeries. Whatever had happened between them must have been horrific to elicit this response.

"I'll, uh, leave you to it then," Araj said, clearing his throat and beating a hasty retreat. He had never been able to handle tears.

After the door closed, leaving them alone, Farzana chanced a glance at Ettares. Her shoulders and wings trembled as quiet sobs wracked her body, and Farzana sighed. Making herself comfortable on the couch, she patted the cushion beside her.

"Come here."

Ettares peeked through long fingers and wet lashes, confusion on her face. "But...I should leave. I shouldn't be here."

Farzana worked to keep her voice as soothing as possible. "Talk to me."

After a moment of hesitation, Ettares crossed the room and sat on the edge of the couch as far from Farzana as possible, her body rigid as she held in her tears.

"What do you want to know?"

"Is it true? Did you m—kill someone?"

Ettares voice came in a whisper, and Farzana strained to hear her words. "I never meant to. I was given an assignment. Find this pixie and bring him home. He had gotten into some trouble with a gang, but his wife paid off the debt, and she just wanted him to come home. When I found him, he ran to the roof. I tried to tell him that he was safe. That I was s-sent by his wife. But he just leapt off..." Ettares looked at her then, red-rimmed crystal-clear eyes shining with unshed tears. "Farzana, it was a 20-story building. He didn't even try to use his wings."

Farzana gritted her teeth as she tried not to picture, not to remember, what that far of a drop did to a body.

"I jumped off after him and tried to catch him, but I wasn't fast enough. I...I couldn't save him. And he's dead because of me."

Farzana didn't know what to say. What could you say when someone thought a tragic accident was their fault?

"So, yeah, Araj is right. I am a murderer." Ettares stared her down, unflinching, unblinking.

Shaking her head, Farzana scoffed. "Araj is rarely right about anything, and he certainly isn't right this time."

A glimmer of hope appeared in Ettares's eyes.

"I don't blame you, Ettares. And I hope the wife doesn't either."

Ettares sniffed, wiping her nose with her sleeve. "She doesn't. None of his family does. Or at least, that's what they told me. When I brought them his body."

"See? How can you let others blame you when the ones closest to him don't even do that? Araj is an ass," Farzana said, moving closer to her. "And he's wrong. You're not a murderer."

"I killed those imps before, too."

Farzana waved her words away. "And I killed hundreds of wights. If that makes you a murderer, then I am one too. We both did what we had to, to save people."

Ettares's facade of composure wavered for a moment before she collapsed in Farzana's arms, weeping.

Farzana enveloped her and held her as close as she could, letting her grief pour out over a soul she never could have saved and instead mourned. She couldn't imagine the amount of hurt Ettares had been holding in for who knew how long, but Farzana was beginning to see a depth to her that she hadn't noticed before. This was someone who cared so deeply, she blamed herself for something she wasn't even responsible for. Someone who cared so much, she carried that pain with her everywhere, even though it wasn't her burden to bear.

Running her fingers through Ettares's curls and making gentle shushing noises helped her calm down, and soon—too soon—she pulled away, a watery smile on her perfect lips.

"Thank you, for everything. I never wanted you to know, but...I feel better now that you do."

Farzana returned the smile, holding her hand. "I'm glad I know. I'm glad I got to see a new side of you."

Her thumb rubbed a circle on Farzana's before she seemed to realize they were touching, and she pulled her hand back. "Ah, sorry."

Farzana's hand grasped at the empty air, longing for her warmth, but she clasped her hands in her lap instead. "You're feeling better?"

"Much." Ettares stood, her lithe frame unfolding and towering over Farzana. "I should go."

Farzana nodded again. "Will I see you tomorrow?"

She rubbed her jaw as she avoided Farzana's eyes. "I probably shouldn't. I need...some time, I think."

"Oh. Okay." Farzana could feel her stomach twisting into knots.

"I'll come see you the day after tomorrow, if that's fine?"

The knots loosened. "Of course."

"See you then," Ettares said, moving to the door. She stopped, her hand on the knob. "Thank you, Farzana. Seriously."

The door closed behind her, leaving Farzana alone with her thoughts. "You're welcome," she whispered, looking down at her empty hands.

34

A DAY WITHOUT ETTARES ENDED UP BEING A
day without Araj as well. Whether that was because he was
giving her space, or perhaps he wasn't sure if Ettares would be
there, Farzana couldn't say. She wasn't even sure if she wanted
to see him. But it made for a lonely day.

Late in the afternoon, Farzana got a craving for caffeine
and ventured out of her suite. Leaning heavily on her cane for
support, and with slow, steady steps, she made her way to the
lifts. After coffee, maybe she would peruse the mall. She was
in a shopping sort of mood.

Galesh wasn't in the cafe when she arrived, so Farzana ordered an iced raspberry mocha to go. Cup in hand, she made
her way through the mall, sipping on her drink.

A new store had opened—balloons and streamers in front
marking a grand opening—and she walked in, curious as to
what Stuffed Curios could mean as a store name. It turned out
to be full of stuffed animals and dolls. Farzana was delighted;
a whole store full of soft, warm, and fuzzy cuddle toys.

She browsed with leisure, touching a sequined merfae
here, petting a downy soft bear there. She spotted a life-sized
dragon, though why anyone would want one of those as a

companion, she had no clue.

And then she spotted it: a beautiful, shimmering water-horse. It's red glass eyes sparkled in the light, and its feathery mane swayed in a nonexistent breeze—or maybe a current? The sooty black coat was made of the finest velvet. She knew immediately that she had to buy it for Ettares and snatched it up without hesitation.

"Gift wrapped?" asked the pixie behind the counter as Farzana stared off into space.

"Sorry?"

He held up a roll of glittering gold foil wrapping paper. "Would you like it wrapped?"

A slow smile spread over her face. "Yes. Please." A real gift. Ettares would like that. It was time to pay her back for all the gifts she kept bringing.

Shiny parcel in tow, she made her way through the crowds and back to her suite, already exhausted from the short stint of walking. Once safe inside her room, she pulled the wrapped stuffie out of the big brown paper bag and placed it on her dresser. It was a lovely centerpiece, though she couldn't wait for Ettares to tear into it.

Feeling ravenous and remembering she hadn't bothered touching her lunch—a thick seafood stew and breadsticks—she rang Enzi and begged for some bread.

"Something sweet and savory," she said, twirling a curl around her finger as she spoke at the mirror.

"Sweet and savory?" He laughed. "What kind of fancy bread have you been eating?"

She rolled her eyes at him. "Blackberry and basil."

"Hm. Interesting. I'll see what I can do," he said, then ended the call.

Farzana gazed at her reflection as it appeared in the now blank pocket mirror and wondered when she had started looking so happy. Her dark circles were all but banished, her cheeks almost rosy. There was even a slight sparkle in her amethyst eyes.

Spreading her wings, she flopped onto her back on the bed, staring up at the ceiling. Unbidden, a thought crossed her mind:

she was overdue for a visit from Erasto. What was he up to? Why had his attention drifted from her? She wasn't complaining, but no news felt like bad news. And bad news... Well. She hoped whatever it was wouldn't be as bad as an invading wight army. She wouldn't be in the right place and right time again to stop a second attempt

~ ☼ ~

Farzana had barely finished checking her mirror messages— Enzi wanted her to know that Laraf would be visiting later, and they would be baking a cake—when a knock came at her door the next morning.

"Who is it?" she called, peeling the covers from her body and sliding out of bed.

"It's me," came a husky voice, soft through the door.

"Come in!" She ran a hand through her hair, yanking on a knot in the curls.

The door creaked open, and Ettares's tall frame glided in, a smile on her full lips and a twinkle in her eye. She stopped abruptly when she saw Farzana.

"Farzana! You're, um...not dressed."

Farzana looked down at the nightgown she had worn to bed. Soft lace edging cupped her breasts, and the hem hugged the top of her thighs; she at once felt scandalous. Her cheeks burned as she looked up at Ettares, who was bundled up in a thick coat, though the shimmering, silver pin-striped legs of her black pants were visible below it. The juxtaposition of overly dressed Ettares and scantily clad Farzana was painful.

"My apologies," Farzana stammered, looking at the floor. "Give me a minute."

Ettares turned to face the wall, cheeks stained red. "Of course."

Shutting herself in the bathroom, Farzana hobbled to the closet and flung it open. What to wear? She hadn't done laundry in weeks; all her simple dresses were dirty. Grabbing a cobalt blouse and a long, flowing black skirt, she dressed, fingers fumbling with buttons. Tucking the front of her shirt in, she opened the door to see Ettares fingering the tag on her gift.

She looked at Farzana, eyes bright. "This is for me?"

Farzana gave her a sheepish smile, pushing curls out of her face. "I figured it was time I got you something too."

"Can I open it?"

Feeling shy, Farzana walked over to it and picked it up, holding the gift in her hands. "Remember that night when you took me out to the park? I said I wanted to see the stars, and you took me on an adventure."

Ettares leaned her hip against the dresser, arms crossed. "An adventure? I remember you tried to mount a waterhorse."

Farzana grimaced. That wasn't what she wanted her to focus on. "Okay, yes, you saved me. But remember what you told me? That when you were a wee little one, you wanted—"

"A waterhorse. Yes of course." She chuckled.

Farzana held the package out to her and saw the question in her eyes as she took it. With gentle hands, she unwrapped the stuffie, holding it out in front of her. Ice blue eyes met red; an eternity passed. Farzana thought she saw her lip quiver, but she couldn't be sure. Finally, Ettares looked at her, eyes misty, and Farzana had enough time to wonder if she was going to cry before she was pulled into a crushing embrace.

A kiss landed on Farzana's cheek. She felt it sink into her skin, tugging a string through her body, before Ettares pulled away, a shaky smile on her lips.

"Oh gods, I'm so sorry. I shouldn't have."

Farzana reached up to press her fingertips to the kiss. She wanted to taste it. "It's okay."

"I'm…I'm overwhelmed. Farzana, this is the most beautiful, most thoughtful gift anyone has ever given me… Thank you."

Farzana tried not to look too pleased with herself as she saw the emotions bursting in Ettares's shining eyes. She knew she didn't have any right to tell Ettares that she loved her, but she hoped the gift got close to saying it for her.

Ettares reached a hand up to dab at a tear that hadn't yet fallen. Sniffling, she said, "I brought you something as well. I saw it, and I couldn't help myself."

"Oh?" Farzana made her way to the edge of the bed and sat down, her leg trembling.

"I hope you like it," she said, pulling a book from her jacket pocket. "I didn't get to wrap it all fancy, though. I hope you don't mind."

Farzana scoffed, pleased she had liked the wrapping job. "Like I care."

Ettares handed her the book, their fingers brushing, and Farzana looked at the cover to keep herself from thinking about why it felt like pure energy coursed through their touch.

Two women were on the cover, holding hands. One held a blitz in her free hand and she had it pointed at...a giant dragon?

"The bookseller said it's a fantasy adventure story about two humans hunting giant dragons," Ettares said, hooking her thumb into her pants pocket. "I figured you might like the idea of hunting dragons."

Farzana laughed. She did hate dragons with a passion. "They are so annoying! I wouldn't mind a couple being hunted."

"I should go; I don't want to keep you. And you should rest—you look shaky."

Farzana hated that she noticed. "I took a walk around the shops yesterday."

"Ah. Hence my gorgeous gift," Ettares said, holding it up to her cheek.

"Yes."

"I appreciate it, Farzana. I really do. I hope that was apparent." Her eyes twinkled with mirth.

Farzana chuckled, feeling her cheeks heat. "I kind of got that idea." She resisted the urge to touch the kiss again.

"Good!" Ettares flashed her fanged smile. "I'll be back later, okay?" She walked backwards toward the door, her eyes never leaving Farzana's. "Have a good day."

"You too." Farzana could barely breathe.

The door closed, leaving her alone, and she slid to the floor, trembling. Ettares had kissed her. Ettares *kissed* her! Biting her lip, Farzana reached up and touched her cheek. What she wouldn't give to have had Ettares's lips slip and land on hers. To feel their breath mingle. To tangle her hands in Ettares's hair, pull her closer. To lose herself, only to find herself.

Letting out a shaky breath, she stood to grab a blanket and drag it with her to one of the plush armchairs. Maybe reading would banish these wild, impossible thoughts. Wrapping herself in the blanket, she snuggled down to read her new book.

The first chapter hooked her into the adventure. A horde of dragons plagued the land, launching organized strikes at the human strongholds. The two humans were lesbian lovers intent on finding and hunting down a mythical dragon queen who supposedly controlled all the other dragons with her mind. If they killed her, the other dragons would lose their organization and flee the land.

Or so they hoped. It was a brutal story fraught with terror. In the end, they found the dragon queen and managed to slay her but not before she inflicted a mortal wound on one of the humans. Her lover held her as she died. It was only after she closed the book that Farzana realized her cheeks were streaked with tears.

Had Ettares known the ending? Was this supposed to mean something? Just as Farzana had hoped her gift would say 'I love you,' had Ettares hoped this gift spoke to the depths she would go to protect her? Was Ettares willing to do anything—even die—for her?

Farzana shook her head to clear that thought from her mind. The world was perilous indeed, but she refused to believe that Ettares would be put in mortal danger. If it came to a one-on-one fight, she knew Ettares would be able to beat Erasto. Her father was no match for the bounty hunter; if he had half the talent she had, he wouldn't feel the need to beat up helpless faeries. Assuaged by the fact that Erasto couldn't hurt Ettares, Farzana snuggled deeper into her blanket.

35

FARZANA BOLTED UPRIGHT IN HER SEAT AS the door slammed open, hitting the opposite wall hard enough to leave a dent. She hadn't realized she was on the cusp of sleep, slumped in the armchair and cradling the book in her arms. With bleary eyes she looked up into Erasto's outraged face.

Vaguely, she understood he was screaming at her, but her brain couldn't process the words. She wanted to ignore him and go to sleep, but she knew that wouldn't end well. Instead, she put on what she hoped was an appropriate mix of fear—easy—and submission—difficult—and kept her eyes trained on his shoes.

The words eventually started to make sense as she woke up fully.

"I provide everything for you! I give you everything you could ever want! And yet you still run off? Leaving The Center? Without my permission?"

She risked a glance up at him and regretted it as soon as he stopped his speech to suck in a deep breath, eyes murderous with rage, tightly clenched fist shaking at his side.

This won't be good.

"I'm sorry," Farzana whined, hoping this was what he wanted to hear. "I just wanted to see the stars."

"THE STARS!" His voice went up an octave, cracking. "You disobeyed me for a look at the stars? Unbelievable."

She hung her head and cowered.

"I clearly have not fully impressed upon you the amount of the respect I deserve. I see now that you need to be taught another lesson in obedience."

She braced herself for his fists, but the hit never came. When she looked up at him, a cold sneer twisted his lips.

"Perhaps I should find Laraf and deal your punishment to her. Maybe then you will listen."

Farzana's blood boiled; with a howl of outrage, she launched herself out of the chair. "Leave her alone!" she shrieked, slamming her fist into his jaw just like Ettares had taught her.

His head snapped back, and he wobbled on his feet; for a moment, Farzana hoped he would go down. Instead, he uttered a howl of his own before snatching her up and throwing her to the floor. She landed with a thud, the wind knocked from her, and she belatedly remembered that he was stronger than her.

Much stronger.

His screams started up again, incoherent in their volume, as he dropped to his knee beside her and began to pummel her with his fists.

Please not the leg. Please not the leg. Please not the leg...

As his beating rained down on her head, arms, and ribs, she could only be grateful that he seemed to have forgotten her weak point. She couldn't handle her leg breaking again.

Her head swam from the blows; her arms shook from trying to protect herself under his onslaught. At one point, he punched her bladder, and she forcefully relieved herself. The attack became bloody as her skin split from his knuckles. The sickening sound of his fists hitting her pulpy flesh left her reeling.

After an eternity, his blows slowed, his breathing heavy as he got to his feet. Through a haze of red, she watched him flick her blood from his fingers, straighten his jacket, and leave.

She laid in a pool of sweat, blood, and piss, too exhausted to move. The pain no longer came in waves; in fact, she had risen above it. It couldn't touch her where she floated.

Harvester, take me…

At peace, she closed her eyes.

"Farzana!"

Soft hands cradled her face and pulled at her eyelids. She gazed up into the ice blue of Ettares's concerned eyes for a moment before closing her own again.

"Farzana, wake up. Oh, gods. Come on, let's get you cleaned up."

I'm a disgusting mess.

"You're not disgusting."

After a quick and futile attempt to get away, Farzana gave up, letting Ettares carry her to the bathroom as she whimpered. She heard a bath being drawn and felt someone pull her soiled clothes from her bruised body. She couldn't have mustered the strength to open her eyes even if she had wanted to, but it was better not to see the disgust on Ettares's face at the sight of her filth.

Steam caressed her face as the water heated, and the smell of eucalyptus and lavender flooded her senses. Gently, so gently, she was lowered into the tub. A sponge patted her face; it was both heavenly and excruciating.

Farzana's lip was swollen and split; she knew her right eye would be black soon if not already. Her jaw felt bruised as well. But none of that compared to the pain in her right side.

When the sponge brushed her ribs, she let out a breathless scream. "Not…there," she gasped. "Hurts."

"I have to check for broken ribs. This will hurt; I'm sorry." Farzana braced herself but Ettares let out a low chuckle. "You need to relax, Farzana. It will hurt more if you tense up."

Taking a shallow breath and letting it out, Farzana forced herself to relax.

I'm floating. I'm floating away.

Feather touches on her ribs, swift and sweet, and then the hands retreated.

"Nothing is broken but it's bruised really badly, and you probably strained a couple ribs," she said, her husky voice tugging at Farzana's wayward attention.

Nothing broken. Good. Farzana couldn't handle more broken bones.

"Do you want a healer? A healing sleep would be good for you."

Farzana moved her head, the smallest shake.

Water sloshed against the side of the tub as Ettares lathered her curls with soap, massaging her scalp. Farzana moaned, though whether from pain or pleasure, she couldn't be sure. Maybe both.

She heard Ettares scoop up water and then felt it run down the back of her head, tickling her wings and spine.

Don't think about how you're naked in front of Ettares. Don't think about it. Don't think—

"I'm naked."

Ettares let out a loud laugh, startling Farzana into wrenching her side.

"Oh, gods, I'm sorry. Don't hurt yourself please. And don't worry about it. You needed help, and I'm here."

Farzana nodded. As Ettares smoothed her curls, Farzana grabbed her hand and pressed it to her cheek. Ettares relaxed her arm, letting Farzana hold her there for a long moment before pulling away.

Farzana heard a rustle as she stood. Then footsteps as she walked to the closet, and the sound of fabric cascading against itself.

Ettares came back, putting her hands under Farzana's arms and pulling her to her feet; a thick towel was wrapped around her shivering body. With the slightest pressure, Ettares began to dry her, patting her wings, sliding the towel down her arms and legs.

Farzana didn't have the energy to feel self-conscious. She barely had the energy to stay vertical.

Ettares led her back to the room. Farzana had just settled on the edge of the bed when a door opened, and her eyes flew open, expecting to see Erasto's glowering frame in her doorway.

Instead, it was Araj. Still glowering though.

His expression softened when he noticed the state of her face. "Farzana! What happened?" He must have noticed the towel and still dripping hair because at that point, he bristled at Ettares. "And what have *you* done?" he hissed.

"Erasto paid me a visit," Farzana said in halting words. She collapsed back against the pillows Ettares had fluffed for her. "He was in a mood."

Araj looked aghast. "He did this to you?"

Ettares snorted. "It's not like this was the first time."

"What are you talking about?"

"You haven't noticed?" Ettares tucked the blankets around Farzana, her back to Araj.

"What are you talking about? Why would he hurt her?"

"He hurts everyone, Araj! That's kind of his thing. He's good at it." Ettares rested her hip against the bed, arms folded over her chest. "I've been trying to teach her self-defense but I haven't gotten very far with it."

"I'll say," he huffed, still standing in the doorway. "She wouldn't look like this if she fought back."

"Excuse you," Farzana said, struggling to sit up in indignation. "I hit him first."

"What!" Ettares and Araj both whirled on her.

She shrugged, immediately regretting it as pain shot through her side. She sucked in a breath as stars flashed before her eyes. "Uh...h-he said he was going to find Laraf and beat her to teach me a lesson." She grimaced. "I figured I would either knock him out or make him mad enough that he hurt me instead and would forget about her." Exhausted, she laid back against the pillows.

Araj fumed, his hands balled into fists at his side. "I'll kill him."

Ettares scoffed. "Yeah, okay."

"I'm being serious! Someone has to actually do something—unlike you, Ettares," he spat. "So I'm going to kill him. Shouldn't be hard; he has his imp guards gathering everyone in the mall for some kind of announcement. He'll be alone."

Farzana couldn't believe what she was hearing. "Araj, don't—"

But he was already gone, door swinging shut behind him.

Ettares looked thoughtful.

"Don't tell me you're thinking of killing him too," Farzana said, gritting her teeth as a new wave of pain wracked her body.

"It would solve our immediate problems. It's an interesting thought. I doubt he could beat me," Ettares said.

"Stay with me," Farzana whimpered, grasping her by the sleeve.

Ettares smiled down at her, icy eyes soft. "Of course."

"Hold me?"

Without a word, Ettares stripped off her jacket and tossed it to the floor. She slid into the bed beneath the covers; Farzana felt the heat of her through the towel and wished the layers separating them were gone. Ettares's arms wrapped around her. For a moment, Farzana allowed herself to feel safe.

36

FARZANA LISTENED TO THE SOUND OF Ettares's breathing, a steady rhythm that coaxed her toward sleep. Before she could drift off, a clamor arose from beyond the front door. What started as a minor disturbance erupted into screams and a thundering of panicked faeries passing by.

Something slammed against the door; whatever—or rather whoever—let out a wail.

"What on Faerth?" Ettares sat up, crouching over Farzana protectively.

"Oh, gods," Farzana whimpered, pulling the covers up to her nose. "What's happening now?"

"I'll check it out." Ettares shifted her weight to get off the bed.

Panic engulfed Farzana at the thought of being alone. "Don't leave me!"

Ettares turned back with a wry smile. "You want me to take you with me?"

The door splintered open, a pair of imp guards hulking in the new opening. A dead pixie fell slumped over the threshold. Farzana let out a breathless shriek and Ettares leapt off the bed, drawing two daggers from wherever they had been hidden on her body. Landing on her feet, she spread her crimson wings wide in a threatening stance.

Unable to watch, Farzana cowered beneath the covers, eyes shut tight, straining to hear everything. A clang of metal on metal, the squelch of blade through flesh, and the thud of a body hitting the floor. The tang of blood scented the air even through the thick blanket and Farzana struggled not to vomit. Another clash of weapons and a sickening crunch before a second body fell, and the blankets were wrenched from Farzana's feeble grasp.

"We have to go," Ettares said, eyes wild. Blood dripped from her daggers, pooling on the floor, and behind her, Farzana glimpsed the lifeless bodies of the imps.

Farzana stared at her, unsure of how she was supposed to get up and leave in her current state, but Ettares hauled her out of bed, shoved her into a shirt and pair of pants, leaving bloody prints all over the clothing, and pulled her through the suite and out the broken door.

The hallway was littered with bodies—some still, some moving and moaning. Sanguine splatters on the walls looked like some macabre, abstract painting style. Farzana sucked in a breath and regretted it as the stench of feces, urine, and blood flooded her lungs. She gagged but, before she could heave, Ettares scooped her up into her arms and took off running.

"We have to take the lift. The public teleportation pad is under lock and key now, and it won't be safe to face the guards there. I don't have time to deal with them," Ettares said, her breathing hitching as she adjusted to her burden.

The lift came into view as well as the surrounding crowd of panicking faeries. Ettares elbowed her way through the mass, stride unhindered as they gave way before her. As the lift doors opened, she lunged through them and landed inside. Several other faeries attempted to enter but Ettares slammed her hand against the first floor rune, and the doors slid shut on their fear-filled faces.

Ettares kept her hand on the rune, securing a fast-track downstairs without any interruptions. What little color in her face drained away as the rune sapped energy from her unchecked. The arms holding Farzana developed a slight tremor, and Farzana shifted in her grasp, wishing she had her cane and could walk on her own while also knowing she would just hold Ettares back with her slowness.

The lift came to a stop, doors opening, and as Ettares stepped out, The Center plunged into absolute darkness. Farzana stifled a screech as Ettares stopped in her tracks. Screams of panic echoed around them as the few faeries who still lived lost their sight.

Farzana's heart rate sped up dangerously as she turned her head this way and that, useless eyes trying to find their position and a way out. Slowly, her eyes adjusted enough to notice a dim glow emanating from the direction of the main entrance. A faint flicker also came from the illuminated sign above the lift, the only other source of light on the first floor. Ettares took off running toward the exit, tripping over bodies in the darkness but somehow maintaining her balance. They were so close; Farzana could see the doors, see the motes of sunlight creeping through the tinted glass.

Without warning, Farzana was thrown from Ettares's arms; after flying through the air, she landed on something soft and wet. She tried not to think about what sort of liquid was now covering her as she lay there, dazed. Pain rippled through her side, and she gasped for air.

In the scant light, she looked up to see an imp squaring off with Ettares. His blade was three times the length of her curved daggers, which flashed through the air in graceful arcs. The imp swung his sword down hard; her blades met it, holding it above her head. Even from where Farzana lay, she could see Ettares's arms straining to hold the sword at bay; her swings were slowed, her feet faltering. Farzana couldn't bear to watch and couldn't even begin to imagine looking away.

In what felt like slow motion, the imp lunged at Ettares; with a neat side step, she brought her dagger up, slicing his throat. A torrent of blood sprayed out, coating her in crimson as the imp fell to her feet.

Even in the darkness, Farzana saw the victorious smile spread across Ettares's face as she turned to face her. Picking her way through the bodies, she reached her arms back to sheathe her daggers at the small of her back.

In the blink of an eye, a blade sprouted from Ettares's stomach, tip drenched in her blood; her daggers fell from limp fingers, clattering to the floor. In the stillness, Farzana heard the sucking sound as the attacker, a second imp, drew the sword from her body, heard Ettares gasp as she sank to her knees. The imp reached out, grasping one of her wings in a mammoth hand, and with a tremendous wrench, ripped it from her back.

Farzana couldn't stop the whimper that fled from her throat. The imp turned in her direction, vermillion wing still in hand, and cocked his head. Pressing a damp hand to her mouth, Farzana began to scoot backward toward the lift, back toward the darkness.

Away from Ettares's crumpled body.

After an eternity, she reached the lift, all the while watching the imp prowl over the bodies, searching for her. She pressed the call rune, forgetting the doors gave a chirping *ding* when they opened. She shrieked when she saw the imp's head snap up, eyes trained on her. The imp sprinted toward her as she scrambled inside the lift, slamming a fist against the rune for the shopping center.

The doors began to slide shut even as the imp reached a hand out to stop them. Farzana's heart skipped a beat as the imp barely missed the gap and tripped over something. The thud of the body against the closed doors reached Farzana's ears as she started to ascend.

The lift shuddered to a stop five floors up, having seemingly given up. It opened its maw to the darkness, exposing Farzana to whomever was near. Thankfully, no one seemed to be alive. What a dark thing for which to be thankful.

Farzana had to get up to the shopping levels; if she could

reach her mother's shop and access the panic room, she would be safe. It would likely be the only place in the entire Center where no one could hurt her.

She just had to reach it.

On stiff, wobbly legs, she made her way to the stairs. The spiral went up, into ebony, a mere ten steps visible from the meager light of the lift runes. She was surprised by the brightness of the runes; in daylight they barely glowed, but in otherwise total darkness, they shone like a beacon.

A beacon from which she must get far, far away.

So up she went, one step at a time. As she rounded the curve of the spiral staircase, she lost any light, and instead relied on her faltering feet and death grip of the banister to lead her onward.

At times, it looked like apparitions surrounded her. Little flickers of light bloomed out of the corner of her eyes, specters that were unable to be found when she turned her head. Soon, she reached a point where the glow from the next floor's lift runes could illuminate her surroundings with the barest of light.

She stood on the landing, breathing heavily from her ascension, and wondered whether the whole of The Center might hear her breath, so thunderous it was to her ears. When no one jumped out at her, she crossed the landing, tottering like a new babe, and made her way up the next flight of stairs.

After an eternity of climbing in sensory deprivation, she reached the shops. Her legs strained to hold her, muscles burning from the exertion. She could have sobbed when she realized she would no longer have the banister for help and would have to walk unaided from the stairs to the gallery.

Stifling her whimpers and tears, she made her way onward, toward safety, toward uncertainty; first, she had to cross the desolate no man's land littered with bodies and blood. Occasionally, a groan could be heard from a dying faerie intent on surviving, and Farzana wondered whether any of them would still be among the living when the healers eventually showed up.

If they ever came.

As Farzana moved past the lift, giving it a wide berth, the

doors slid open with a soft *ding*. Farzana flinched when she recognized the sweetest face she had ever seen, a face she had hoped was far from The Center. Laraf stood in the opening, uncertain, eyes wide and fear painted across her delicate features.

"H-hello?"

As her bell-like voice rang out in the stillness, Farzana heard it: the sound of someone running toward them. She whirled and saw an imp guard, a blitz in hand. He raised the weapon, finger on the trigger, and Farzana felt a peace come over her before she found a hidden store of explosive energy deep within herself. Unleashing that force, she leapt at the imp, saving her adopted baby sister the only thought on her mind.

With a shriek of rage that mingled with Laraf's scream of terror, Farzana raked her nails over his face, bowling him over with the ferocity of her attack. On the ground, she grappled with him. Her newfound energy dissipated quickly as she found herself fighting a bigger, stronger faerie. He rolled them over, his weight crushing her as he attempted to bash her head with his fist. Kicking him in the groin, Farzana managed to give herself a moment to disentangle herself, enough of an opportunity to crawl away.

Harvester, save me!

The god must have been listening because rather than being attacked by the imp's razor sharp claws or having her head blown off by the blitz, the imp instead chose to throw the weapon at Farzana, clipping her on the temple.

Stars swirled in her vision as she, as though in a dream, reached out and grasped the blitz in her hands. Falling onto her back, she looked up to see the imp pouncing at her, saw the gleam of his claws, the hatred in his eyes. She saw the end of the blitz, her finger on the trigger, the beam of light shooting out. There was red, red everywhere, bits of brain and bone showering down on her, and then an audible snap as the headless body of the imp slammed against her leg.

Dimly, distantly, she realized Laraf had fallen, fainted, and someone stood there cradling her, holding her in strong arms. Farzana recognized her mother's face then, saw the shock in her eyes as she took in the sight of her daughter covered in gore.

Sitting up, Farzana did the only thing she could think of: she laughed.

She was alive! She was covered in various viscera, but she'd survived! Who would have bet on that?

She laughed until a slap across the face snapped her out of her meltdown and brought her back to reality. Still holding tight to the blitz, which showed that it had two charges remaining, Farzana got to her feet and followed her mother meekly to the panic room.

37

SAFELY ENSCONCED IN THE STORAGE ROOM,
bolt locked, Farzana slumped to the floor; all strength had long
fled her limbs. Tremors wracked her hands and she fought to
keep her grip of the blitz. She wasn't going to part with her
only weapon, their only defense.

Sitra pulled out her pocket mirror and set it on the floor;
the glow from the display gave them all enough illumination to
see each other's fear stricken faces. Laraf slowly stirred, eyelids
fluttering as she came to.

"Why are you up here instead of with Enzi?" Farzana heard
herself ask as if from a distance.

Laraf met her eyes, sniffled, and wiped her nose. "I was
with Enzi. He was making me a chocolate cake, because the
chocolate here is better than at the House of Amber. We were
laughing, and then…" She stopped and let out a single sob.
"Then the guards started attacking everyone. And the lights
went out, and I ran." Her tiny body shook as Sitra wrapped
her in a hug.

"Where is he?" Farzana's voice came out rougher than she
intended but gods damn it, she had to know what happened
to her little brother.

Laraf's lower lip quivered, her eyes glossy and unfocused. "I don't know," she whispered in horror. Another sob. "I don't know!"

Sitra clapped a hand over Laraf's mouth as she started to wail, shooting a glare at Farzana. "Farzana, now is not the time."

"Forgive me for worrying about my brother," Farzana huffed. The shadows cast across the storage room shifted then, and she swallowed a scream.

No one else is here. We are safe. I am safe.

Blinking away the terror, she focused on her mother and saw her gazing back at her with a softness at odds with her withering stare only moments before.

"You are hurt. What happened?" Sitra asked, her voice low and gentle.

Farzana shrugged, uncomfortable with her pain being perceived. "Erasto paid me a visit earlier. He was...not happy. Ettares found me after and was patching me up when"—she gestured around vaguely—"all of this happened."

Sitra stiffened, her face tight. "Erasto hurt you?"

"He hurts everyone, Mother."

Sitra averted her gaze, petting Laraf's head as the little one continued to weep quietly into Sitra's clothes. Farzana shifted her weight as her leg began to cramp from sitting on the hard floor; sucking in a breath and gritting her teeth to keep from crying, she worked to relax the muscle. She remembered the sound her leg had made when the imp's body had fallen on it. Had the bone been rebroken?

"You must be stressed beyond belief," Sitra said finally, a quiver in her voice. "I'm not doing a good job taking care of you, am I?"

"I can take care of myself," Farzana said, her voice strained.

Sitra chuckled. "Yeah, I can see that."

A smile quirked Farzana's lips. "Sarcasm? From you, Mother? The world must indeed be ending."

They shared a smile. In that moment, it felt like they were just a mother and daughter bonding over something silly. Then Farzana remembered they were hiding in a locked closet, fearing for their lives.

They sat in silence then, listening, waiting. Hoping for a miracle.

Farzana must have checked the time on the mirror a dozen times before she heard it: the scuff of footsteps as someone entered the gallery. Whoever it was walked right up to the door and called in a low voice, "Healers. Does anyone need a healer?"

Farzana bolted upright and glanced at Sitra who had a panicked expression on her face.

"No," Sitra mouthed, shaking her head.

Gritting her teeth, Farzana got to her feet, pain shooting up her leg and side, and unlocked the door, blitz at the ready. Opening the door a crack, she saw the maroon robes of a healer worn by an elderly elf with kind eyes. They widened at the blitz but then the elf held her hands up in the air.

"It's okay. We are here to help." She turned and gestured behind her. "Survivors over here."

Lowering the blitz, Farzana opened the door wider. A group of other healers stood in the gallery, each of them holding a lantern. Several of them rushed over. A handful of plain-clothed faeries—survivors of the attack, perhaps—stood off to the side, no doubt tagging along with the healers for safety. A lone water nymph stood by the entrance, holding a blitz and staring out into the gloom.

Seeing Farzana struggling to pull the door open with only one arm, the elder elf healer helped her fully open the door, exposing Sitra and Laraf.

"Oh," she said, seeing Laraf's face, clearly taken aback by the sight of two pixies guarding an imp child.

"That's my sister," Farzana growled, worried she would do something to her.

Instead, the healer nodded and smiled. "Of course. You're lucky, you know. We haven't found many survivors. And to find a group... Very lucky."

Farzana collapsed as a strong wave of pain flooded her, spreading from her leg and engulfing her midsection. A healer rushed forward, catching her in his arms before she could hit the floor.

"Easy there," he said, lowering her down. "Where is the wound?"

"M-my leg," Farzana hissed, pointing.

His hands brushed over her calf over her pants and stopped as he felt the cast. "When did you break it?"

Time had no meaning. "A couple months ago?"

"And it is still broken? Did you use a healing sleep?" He withdrew his hands, folding them in his lap as he looked at her. His eyes were a gorgeous light brown.

"Um, yes. I did. And yes, I think so."

"What's your name?"

"Farzana."

A glimmer of recognition appeared in his eyes as he glanced behind her and saw her wings. "You're the daughter…and your mother is of House Amber?"

She nodded.

"Well, Farzana, you have a bone condition. It's quite rare, actually, but knowing your House medical history, specifically your Grandfather's, makes it clear to me. Unfortunately, your bone might never heal fully. You'll likely be disabled for the rest of your life. I assume you have a cane?"

Farzana's heart thundered in her chest, and she could have sworn several faeries looked back at her, wondering at the sound.

I won't be able to dance, ever again? I'm like this…forever?

"That can't be right. It's just taking longer to heal."

The expression on his face was one of pity and kindness. Farzana wanted to smack him. She was not in the mood to be pitied. Not when she knew he had to be wrong.

"Sure, some bones don't heal completely during the healing sleep. But all bones should heal within a couple weeks of a full healing sleep. If they don't, that's indicative of a genetic problem."

The room spun. Genetic problem?

"So, I was born like this?" She needed to lie down.

"Have you ever broken a bone before, Farzana?"

She shook her head and immediately regretted it when the room spun harder.

"Genetic problems like this often aren't found until a faerie breaks a bone and it fails to heal. It does run in families, and is more common in families with histories of blood sugar disorders." He must have seen something on her face then because he paused for a long moment. When she stayed silent, he sighed and continued, "There's a chance I'm wrong, of course. But I've seen this before, Farzana, and it's usually permanent."

Permanent.

"Oh," she said, not sure what else there was to say.

The absence of a strong, visceral reaction seemed problematic; after all, she was known for them. Hyperventilating at an inconvenience, sweating with anxiety. But this… She didn't have the energy to muster up a reaction. She was so tired.

The healer patted her shoulder, gave her a sad smile, and stood, leaving her alone on the floor with her thoughts. Abandoning her.

Like she had abandoned Ettares.

"Wait!" she whispered as loud as she dared. "Did you find a noble on the first floor? Her name is Ettares."

His eyes held questions, but he only shook his head. "I'm sorry. I didn't see her."

"I did," came a familiar voice.

Farzana looked up into Araj's stormy blue eyes. In his hands, he held a short sword—*where did he get a sword?*—crusted with dried blood. He practically vibrated with fury. The healers gave him cautious looks as he shifted on his feet.

"You saw her?" Farzana couldn't ask the next question.

"I don't know, Farzana. I saw some healers carry her out on a stretcher but…I don't know if she was alive."

She threw her head back and keened, her soul on the verge of being torn apart. She had been a coward to leave her. And now there was no way to know if she even lived.

Sitra reached out to embrace her, but Farzana pulled away. "I'm so sorry, baby," Sitra said.

"I left her," Farzana moaned, tears cascading down her cheeks. "She needed me, and I left her."

Araj shuffled his feet, looking uncomfortable. "Okay, good talk," he said, turning to leave.

"Where are you going?" Farzana asked, hiccuping through her sobs.

Araj pivoted to face her. "I said I would kill Erasto."

Farzana stared at him before struggling to her feet. "Now? Araj, the whole Center is a war zone. Hundreds of faeries are dead. He has to be holed up somewhere with the rest of the guards. It's not safe." She reached out to him, but he shoved her hand away.

"Someone has to do it, Farzana. We need this to end, now! Someone has to step up! Someone has to be a hero." He stopped, looking her up and down, his gaze lingering on her leg and again on her battered face. "And let's face it: it's certainly not going to be you."

Stung, she withdrew her hand and watched as he stormed off toward the lift. The light from the lanterns allowed her to watch as he jabbed at the lift call rune and waited.

No. I lost Ettares. I won't lose my best friend. Not like this.

"Araj, wait!" She tried to run after him only for her leg to give out, sending her crashing into her mother who steadied her.

"You can't go," Sitra said, holding her back.

"Let go. Let me go! I have to stop him!" Farzana flailed against her, hitting her arm with the blitz before finally being released.

Araj stepped into the open lift. He turned, faced Farzana, and watched as she fought against the healers to reach him. Then the lift doors shut, and he was gone.

38

"NO!" FARZANA SCREAMED, THE ECHOES OF her fear swirling in the darkness. She clawed at the arms around her in desperation until someone hissed and her bonds fell away.

Before anyone else could think to restrain her, she whirled around, holding the blitz up in trembling hands, aiming at the healers. She wasn't sure she could even use it again, but she knew she had to do everything in her power to stop Araj.

And that included being the bad guy.

She backed slowly toward the lift, agony cocooning her. Without taking her eyes from everyone, she pressed a hand to the call rune, grimacing as it sucked precious energy from her. Energy she needed.

Sitra's disappointed eyes held hers in a vice; Farzana's throat convulsed as she worked to keep tears at bay. "I'm sorry," she whispered, choking, hoping Sitra would understand. She longed to explain, to give a proper apology, but there was no time. Araj would die if she dallied.

The lift doors slid open behind her and she lunged inside, slamming a palm against the rune for Erasto's private floor, and watched as the betrayal on everyone's faces disappeared behind the closing doors.

Her leg wobbled and threatened to collapse again, but she strapped some mental backbone to it as she waited for the lift to reach her destination. When the doors opened onto a well-lit floor, she blinked back tears at the sudden brightness. After being in darkness so long, her vision blurred before it adjusted. Of course Erasto's floor hadn't lost power. Why was she surprised? He always thought of himself first.

She stepped out, cautious of an attack, and stopped in her tracks as she realized someone was still alive, and sitting on the floor in front of her. The faerie, an imp judging by the size, cradled the head of a dead imp, long hair obscuring their face. Sobs fell as a shaking hand stroked the bloodied face of a masc-fae guard. The imp must have finally realized the lift had opened and turned.

Farzana startled as she recognized Galesh, her lip quivering beneath her delicate tusks, dark eyes red from crying. Recognition dawned on her face, and for a moment, Farzana thought she would smile. Instead, she sobbed.

"Why?" Galesh asked, staring at Farzana.

Farzana cleared her throat, looking around for possible attackers before stepping closer. "Why what?"

Galesh sniffed, rubbing her nose with a bloody hand. "Why did this happen?"

"I don't know. I don't know what's going on. Faeries are fighting, dying... It's a massacre down there."

"We wanted respect... We wanted to be equals. We didn't want...this. This wasn't the plan."

Farzana gaped at her, mind whirring. "You staged a coup because you felt inferior? You did all of this on purpose?" She gestured wildly at the gore, the bodies.

"It wasn't a coup, or it wasn't supposed to be. It was going to be a show of force, of solidarity and unity. Don't fuck with us, sort of thing."

"Galesh, that's not what happened. I saw them, the other imps, the guards. They slaughtered innocent faeries."

Galesh looked down at the dead imp with an unmatched tenderness. "We weren't fighters. We never wanted violence."

She sighed, a lovely sound. "I wanted to be a painter."

"Like my mother," Farzana said quietly.

Galesh nodded. "I love her gallery. I wanted my paintings to be in there someday. But now…"

Shifting on her feet, Farzana felt a twinge through her leg from bearing her weight unaided for so long. "Why can't that still happen?"

Tracing the cheek of the dead imp, Galesh gave a sad smile. "Father is dead. Who will take care of me? Who will house me, clothe me, feed me?"

"You can live with me." Farzana held out her hand. "You don't have to be alone."

"You… all of this, you can fix it."

Farzana furrowed her brow, confused. "Me?"

A fervor lit up Galesh's eyes and a lopsided smile tugged at her lips. "You can help me! Erasto will stop this, will fix this, if we have you. He'll have to listen."

A shiver of fear raced down Farzana's spine as she took a step back. "That's not going to work. You don't know him. You don't know what he's done to me."

Galesh looked straight through Farzana as if she was no longer there. Like Galesh was stuck in a different time, a different place. "I can fix this," she whispered, dropping her father's body. Grunting, she heaved herself up onto her feet. "I can do it. It'll be okay. We'll be okay." Her gaze flitted back to her father, her expression softening.

"Galesh…"

She turned to Farzana, all semblance of recognition gone; in its place burned pure, unbridled hatred. "This is ALL because of YOU!" With a howl of rage, she launched herself at Farzana.

Self-preservation kicked in and Farzana's arms snapped up, raising the blitz to meet the imp. Her finger squeezed the trigger, and Galesh's head exploded in a shower, painting the floor red. Shaking, Farzana lowered the blitz, its handle warm in her hands. Only one full charge left. That would have to be for Erasto. No matter what might happen after, he had to die.

Unwilling to look at Galesh's headless body, Farzana kept her eyes trained in the distance as she carefully picked her way through the bodies and made her way to Erasto's quarters. The door to his hallway of chambers stood unlocked and ajar, and she pushed her way in as quietly as possible. The sounds of low conversation came from the far end, out of view in the teleportation room. She crept toward it, peeking around the corner. Three pixies stood in the center of the room: Araj, Erasto, and Melara.

Erasto paced the far wall as Melara held Araj's sword in her hand, gesturing at him, tip first. "On your knees, traitor."

Sinking to his knees, Araj knelt in a pool of blood flowing from the neck of a decapitated guard. Farzana could only assume this was the one kill Araj managed to make before being disarmed.

Erasto's voice raised enough for Farzana to hear his words clearly. "All I do for Earth, all I have sacrificed, all the work I've done here, and they want to leave me high and dry? They have sorely underestimated me."

"They need to be reminded of who is in charge, sir," Melara said, keeping her eyes on Araj.

"And you!" He spun to face Araj, stooping to scream in his face. "You think you can double-cross *me*? We had a deal! You keep my daughter in check, and you can have her once my battle on Earth is won. You said it would be easy. You have *failed* me! And now this?"

Farzana's heart froze. Araj...working for Erasto? Bile rose in her throat as she worked to control her stomach. Who else in her life was a traitor? First Ettares, now Araj? Was her loyalty so cheap and unquestionable that they knew they could take advantage of her?

"Now she's probably dead. And you! You will die as well. I don't pardon traitors." Erasto sneered down at Araj.

Glaring up in defiance, Araj said, "She's alive. And she's coming to kill you."

Fury lit Erasto's eyes, and with a slash of his hand against his throat, he motioned for Melara to finish him off.

"No!" Farzana yelled, stumbling into the room, blitz aimed at Melara.

"Oh please," she said, rolling her eyes. "What's a pathetic thing like you going to do? You're going to shoot me? Really?"

Farzana blinked back tears. "Shut up! Put down the sword! I'm w-warning you!"

Melara gave her a look of pity as she reached out, grabbed Araj by the hair, and jerked the sword against his neck. Blood gushed like a fountain as she smirked, dropping his body to the floor.

Through a haze of red, Farzana heard a scream—her own scream—as she pulled the trigger. She saw Melara's head erupt like a geyser and her body slump to join Araj's.

Farzana swung around to point the blitz at Erasto, who had turned a sickly pale. He held his hands in the air; veins bulged in his forehead as he worked to stay silent. Flecks of blood speckled his face, and he licked his lips.

A dull click echoed in the silence, and they both realized the blitz was empty of charges at the same time. Farzana met his eyes and watched as his mouth twisted into a cruel smile.

"Poor Farzana. Always fucking up everything. You can't even manage to kill your unarmed father."

Oh gods, what have I done?

She should have killed him instead of Melara. Now, nothing changed. He remained in control. He'd won. Her arms dropped to her sides in defeat, and she glanced down at Araj. His blue eyes were dark and a trickle of blood stained his lips.

Erasto chuckled. "You'll never do anything right. You'll never be anything but dead weight. But thank you, for killing Melara. I made her promises I'd rather not keep."

Farzana pressed her trembling lips together as hard as she could. Erasto knew he had won and seemed content to brag and pepper her with insults. So long as she stayed silent, maybe that's all he would do to her. She watched as he did a little skip toward the console of his teleportation device. Her hand holding the blitz shook as the strain of it all weighed on her. It was over. Everything she had done, everything she hadn't done—none of it mattered. She didn't matter.

She couldn't focus enough to hear the words tumbling from Erasto's mouth but she could hear the glee and excitement. Her little finger moved in slow circles on the handle of the blitz, a tiny stim to keep everything else perfectly in place. Energy hemorrhaged from her, little by little, and the longer she stood still, the harder it was to stay upright.

Finally, Erasto seemed to have finished his task of setting up his device. The machinery began to hum as he turned to her with a triumphant expression. He brushed invisible dirt from his clothing, straightened his tie, and ran a hand through his hair. Blood staining his face, he grinned. "How do I look?"

A headache bloomed in the corner of her mind—a runic headache. But why would—she glanced down at the handle of the blitz to see a small rune set in the handle, right on the edge of the path her little finger had been roaming. A rune that had been sapping her energy, bit by tiny bit. With a soft gasp, she glanced back up at Erasto and saw the smile fade from his thin lips as he realized what she had found.

Her teeth bared in a feral grin as she swung the blitz back up at him, her vision blurring and darkening. A surge of energy left her all at once as she activated the rune with her finger. His enraged face leaping at her was framed in a vignette as she squeezed the trigger one last time before she slumped to the floor.

Ringing.

Her ears were ringing.

Her eyes opened; everything spun around her, the floor and the ceiling and the walls and time all stitched into one long, loopy plane. Her mouth opened and she retched onto the eternity plane, onto herself, the smell clawing its way up her throat and attacking her sinuses and—*help me!*—she gagged, vomited, again and again, stars exploding in her eyes until she shut them, until nothing but bile and pain stuck in her throat.

And she found she could breathe.

As she focused on her lungs and the air rushing in and out of them, the ringing faded and the spinning slowed. She realized she could feel her arms at her sides, her hands touching the floor beneath her, her fingers wet and cold. She reached up and wiped at her mouth, clearing the vomit from her lips, and dared to open her eyes.

Erasto lay slumped against his precious teleportation device. His hands, stained scarlet, shook as they grappled with his intestines, pulling and pushing in a futile effort to keep them in place. Sweat dripped from his brow and he coughed; droplets of his blood reached for Farzana's face.

Crawling over to him, her pants soaking with his blood, she relished in the fear and panic in his eyes. Closer, closer... When she reached him, she pressed a bloody kiss to his temple, felt him tremble under her touch, a terrified animal caught in its death throes. Her lips drifted to the shell of his ear and with her breath ghosting over him, whispered the last words he would ever hear.

Erasto's eyes went wild in their sockets and with one final spasm, he was gone. Farzana waited a moment to be sure before crawling over to the wall and leaning back against it. From there, she had a vantage point of the whole room and could see each body. Her eyes lingered on Araj and his now cloudy eyes. She tried to feel sorrow, tried to summon the words to pray to the god of death to take care of him, and found she couldn't. No part of her felt that he was worth it, and a large part of her was glad he was dead. No more fights. No more being made to feel worthless. With Araj and Erasto both dead, she was finally free.

Farzana looked back at Araj. "Guess you weren't the hero after all," she said. Her words fell on dead ears, and she settled down to wait.

The healers found her there, surrounded by silent death.

39

SNOW FELL IN FAT, SLOW CLUMPS, LENDING A
sense of stillness and peace to the chilly affair. Araj lay in a
closed casket of simple pine, the bonfire for his cremation
arranged around him.

One by one, faeries stepped up to the podium and spoke of
his merits, of his strengths, his charm. Faeries whom Farzana
had never met, not once during their entire five decades of
friendship. Faeries who regarded her with a mix of admiration,
fear, and disdain.

Megami had declined the invitation, and Farzana couldn't
help wondering if it was because of the last time they had
spoken. Sitra had told her that was much too self-centered of
a thought, however, so Farzana dropped it, at least around her
mother; Enzi however wholeheartedly agreed with her.

Ettares sat beside her, resplendent in an elegant gown of
crushed black velvet. Her high neckline dripped with tiny seed
pearls, more of them woven into the webbed framing of her
chest. She outshone everyone in attendance by a long shot,
despite the slightly off shade of red of her prosthetic wing;
no amount of healing at The Center could repair that injury. Farzana had asked her why she even wore it, and Ettares

replied with a rueful smile that without its weight to balance her out, she couldn't walk straight. Farzana had chuckled and pointed out that she wasn't straight, at which point Ettares had smacked her.

When it was Farzana's turn to speak over Araj, she stood, grasping her cane—black for the occasion—and made her way to the stage set before the pyre. She had spent hours debating what to say; funereal customs dictated that they not speak ill of the dead, but what else was there to say? As his 'best friend' she wasn't able to refuse to speak. Everyone knew of their close friendship.

Looking at the small crowd—the only faeries left who cared about Araj, she did her best not to freeze up. Public speaking had never been her strong suit. Ettares met her gaze, nodding for her to go ahead, and Farzana took a deep, steadying breath.

Time to lie.

"Araj was my boss, I suppose, but more than that...he was my best friend."

And a traitor.

Farzana cleared her throat and focused on a spot in the distance. "He died trying to save me, to save us all. He knew the risks, and he went to face Erasto anyway. Alone. I wish he hadn't. Maybe together, we would have both made it out alive. But I wasn't fast enough to save him."

She stopped, working up tears, and let them drip down her cheeks. They were tears of anger, not grief, but that didn't matter. No one knew of the betrayal except Ettares. Farzana couldn't bear to tell anyone else.

"Sorry," she said, her voice cracking. "I just have so much I want to say to him. I didn't even get to say goodbye. We have such unpredictable lives. Don't wait until it's too late to say how you really feel."

Ducking her head, she made her way back to her seat to the sound of scattered applause. Sitting eased the pain in her leg, and she was grateful when Ettares reached over and squeezed her hand.

"You did amazing," she whispered. "I believed it."

"Thanks," Farzana murmured, keeping her face neutral.

Someone else took her spot at the podium and praised Araj, and so on, until it seemed like the proceeding would never end.

Finally, the pyre was lit. Ettares and Farzana stood before the crackling flames, holding hands and watching Araj burn. Farzana couldn't help feeling victorious. She had survived. She had defeated Erasto. She was freed of Araj's treacherous, ulterior motives. And Ettares stood at her side, a survivor, like her.

"I'm glad you came," Farzana said, admiring Ettares's profile. She would never tire of looking at her.

"Of course," Ettares said with a crooked smile. "I was close to him once. He was a good friend...until he wasn't."

"I know what you mean." Farzana sighed.

He had been a good friend at one point. Right? She shut her eyes tightly. She wanted to believe that. She wanted to believe he had cared about her, like she had cared about him. That he had loved her. Because if it was all fake, if he had been lying about all of it...

"Excuse me," came a gravelly voice from behind her.

Farzana and Ettares turned to see a stout elf with graying hair and a grim smile. He held a bunch of papers in his hands as he bowed.

"Might I speak with you for a moment, your nobleness?"

"Of course." Ettares released Farzana's hand. "I'll be right back," she whispered.

Ettares followed the elf a little ways off. They spoke in hushed tones Farzana couldn't make out no matter how hard she tried, passing papers back and forth before Ettares nodded. Raising her hand in farewell to the elf, she made her way back to Farzana's side.

"What was that about?" Farzana asked, reaching for her hand.

"That was an old family friend, the royal advisor to the crown. He fled the kingdom after the murders and managed to stay alive. He's working to rebuild a council to help find the new ruler."

"Oh?" Farzana's curiosity piqued. "Who is he aiming to crown?"

Ettares smiled, ice blue eyes crinkling in the corners. "Me."

Farzana's eyes widened as she realized how well connected Ettares was. Being considered for queen! "Wow," she breathed, turning to stare back at the flames. This was another step being placed between them, another reminder that Ettares was so far above her; she should be kissing her feet, not holding her hand.

Farzana's hand twitched, and Ettares squeezed their fingers together, her thumb tracing a circle on hers.

"What are you thinking?" Ettares asked.

Farzana shrugged, overwhelmed with sadness. "It doesn't matter. Do you want the job?"

Ettares pursed her lips. "I'm not sure. It would be an honor, of course. I could make real changes to this kingdom."

"What would you change?"

"I would subsidize businesses so lifts no longer use worker energy. Place teleportation pads around The City for commuter use. Break down the hierarchy of caste. Get rid of these horrible capitalist policies; they never should have taken root here anyway."

Snow drifted down between them as Farzana contemplated Ettares's words. It sounded like a dream come true. She had no doubt Ettares would make an amazing and progressive leader.

"You would do all that?"

"Of course!" Ettares looked down at Farzana through thick white lashes. "I want what is best for the faeries in this kingdom. All faeries."

Farzana's hopes lifted. "Does that mean—"

"I would make imps equal citizens and write laws prohibiting racist policies and persecution. I want this City to be a safe place for everyone. That includes Laraf."

Farzana's heart swelled with emotion. After the attack on The Center, it wasn't safe for Laraf to be seen in public. The public oppression of imps had reached an all-time high as Dradour citizens claimed the nomadic species wasn't welcome in their country. The only silver lining through it all was that Enzi, now out of his job, had unlimited time to dedicate to teaching Laraf how to cook. None of them could have predicted how much joy it would bring her but Enzi wasted no opportunity to point it out to all of them.

"I think you would make an amazing queen," Farzana said, her voice thick with emotion.

Ettares beamed at her, though her eyes held sadness. "I think so too. If I want it."

"You've thought about this a lot."

"I knew that if Erasto was ever…dealt with, the new ruler would most likely be a noble. I'm the second oldest of us half siblings. The oldest is a drunk who can't remember to lock her front door let alone figure out how to run a kingdom, so I always assumed it would be me."

Farzana nodded. "Makes sense."

They stood in silence, their bodies warmed by the flames of death. The snow had slowed to almost a mist, floating on gentle air currents.

"So, if you don't know if you want the job, what do you know you want?"

Ettares squeezed her hand but remained silent.

"Ettares?"

Her husky voice was soft, so soft Farzana had to strain to hear it.

"I want…you."

Farzana's mind trilled at those three words, her heart picking up the pace as she tried not to hyperventilate from excitement. She felt lightheaded. "Me?" she squeaked, not daring to look at Ettares.

Ettares let out a low laugh, facing her. "Of course, silly." She reached out and delicately traced the edge of Farzana's jaw with the tips of her fingers. "I want to make you happy. And selfishly, I want you to be happy with me."

Farzana's vision blurred as tears sprang to her eyes and she grabbed Ettares's hand, bringing it to her mouth. "I want that too."

A soft hush stretched between them as they gazed at each

other. Farzana remained hyperaware of Ettares's knuckle against her mouth. A creeping blush grew over Ettares's face before she cleared her throat and asked, "May I kiss you?"

Farzana flung herself into Ettares's arms in answer, mouth pressed against hers. The cold condensation on their lips had Farzana shivering; Ettares pulled her closer. Farzana could have stayed that way forever, but she began to pull away for decency—though not before giving into a sudden carnal desire and flicking her tongue out to taste Ettares.

With a groan, Ettares latched back onto Farzana's mouth, their tongues dancing together. It wasn't until someone loudly cleared their throat beside them that they sprung apart, a brazen blush across Ettares's face.

"Tathi!" Farzana grinned at her old friend.

"You two," Tathi said, shaking her head with a stern look. Her eyes twinkled however, and Farzana reached out for a hug.

"I told you that you'd be okay," Tathi whispered in her ear.

"You were right," Farzana agreed.

"Come on," Tathi said, pulling away. "Let's pay our respects to the dead." She gestured to the line of faeries tossing flowers onto the pyre.

"Of course," Ettares said, offering Farzana her arm.

Farzana accepted, and together they made their way to the basket of flowers. She picked out a violet, a tiny sprig of a flower, and Ettares grabbed a dahlia, dark as arterial blood.

Farzana pressed a kiss to her flower before throwing it to the flames. "Harvester hold you. May your rest be sweet."

Ettares repeated the words and tossed her flower into the fire.

Their respects paid, they bid farewell to Tathi—though not before promising to meet up for lunch soon—and made their way toward a bench at the end of the park. Ettares swiped the thin layer of snow away and helped Farzana sit comfortably before settling beside her.

"So, this is happening then," Farzana said, avoiding Ettares eyes lest she throw herself back into her arms. Her ear tips burned at the thought of that kiss.

She could hear the smile in Ettares's voice when she said, "I suppose it is. And this is what you want?"

"Absolutely. What about you and the crown? That's important to you."

Ettares hummed her agreement but said nothing more.

"You should take it."

"You'll be happy with me still if I accept it?"

"I wouldn't dare keep you from your dream of bettering this kingdom," Farzana said softly. "But how can a low-level aristo-fae bastard court the queen?"

Ettares snorted. "You're not a bastard, Farzana. And I'll court whomever I please. I'll make sure that's understood before I accept." She reached for Farzana's hand and waited for her to meet her eyes. "Farzana, I want you at my side. No matter what. And don't forget: you're the hero of Dradour. You deserve to be part of the ruling body."

"I would rule?" Farzana looked away, feeling faint.

"You would be my ruling partner. Not able to enact laws on your own, but you would influence me, and everyone would know that."

"Ah." Farzana couldn't wrap her head around that. "I guess that makes sense."

"You still want this?"

With all of my heart.

Taking a deep breath, Farzana looked up into those crystal blue eyes. "Yes."

Ettares flashed her a crooked smile as she pulled her pocket mirror out of her velvet clutch and dialed a number. "Yes, Utis? I have some conditions to go over with you, but I would like to accept." There was a murmuring of conversation on the other end and then Ettares said, "Of course. See you then." Flipping the mirror shut, she turned back to Farzana. "We have a meeting tomorrow…and they want to coronate me next week!"

Farzana couldn't stop herself from leaning in for another kiss. In spite of everything, they had made it. The kingdom would be a better place with Ettares as queen, and she would be by her side every step of the way.

Pulling away for breath, she took in the sight of Ettares's flushed cheeks and ice blue eyes, a face she hoped to cherish for the rest of her life. Farzana brought Ettares's hand to her lips.

"Long live the queen."

GLOSSARY

SPECIES OF FAERIES

Pixies
Winged humanoids with long, pointed ears, fangs, and sharp nails. Able to fly though this is frowned upon in certain kingdoms/countries. The indigenous species of the kingdom of Dradour. Social caste is dependent on wing color which is determined by bloodline/distance from purebloods in the genetic pool.

Elves
Wingless humanoids with small, pointed ears. Enhanced sense of balance and rhythm. Known for being excellent dancers, thieves, and assassins. Indigenous species of the kingdom of Ostrana. In pixie-dominant kingdoms, they are sometimes considered second rate citizens due to their assumed criminal nature.

Sirens
Wingless humanoids with small, pointed ears, fangs, and a spine with outwardly-spiked vertebrae. Can enchant people with their voice, singing or talking, though talking is usually a strong suggestion rather than a command. Persecuted in certain kingdoms due to their powers. Were enslaved as a species for thousands of years and only recently are seen as citizens.

Imps
Large hulking humanoids, like small giants with comparably smaller heads in proportion to their bodies, tiny pointed ears, tusks, and large razor sharp claws. Usually seen in manual labor jobs or hired as guards. Seen as the lowest citizens in Cities and are often nomadic.

Water nymphs
Hairless amphibious humanoids who can breathe underwater using gills in their necks. Skin is various shades of blue, green,

and purple. Webbed hands and feet with sharp nails on their fingers. Have 1-3 fins running down their back which can be flattened under clothing but also look kind of like wings. Ears have spines with webbing on them so they can move their ears to hear better underwater. Can bond with waterhorses and therefore run the trolley systems in Cities.

Merfolk
Singular: Merfae. Hairless half-humanoids with long tails. Long, tactile tendrils on their heads act as lures when hunting fish. Webbed hands and ears, fangs and claws. Speak using sign language. One large fin runs from the base of their neck to the base of their torso. Including their tail, which is three times the length of their upper body, they are the size of an average elf, which makes them very petite. They are considered dangerous in groups as they can work together to overturn small boats and can deliver a paralyzing bite but are seen as harmless creatures of luck to those onboard ships. Merfolk are considered to be the reincarnated souls of those who died at sea. They do not have the capability to reproduce and do not have a concept of gender.

Sprites
Tiny, winged humanoids about one third of the size of an elf/pixie/siren. They generally stay in their own colonies which are considered off limits to other faeries due to their poisonous bite. As such, not much is known about them, though many faeries speculate they feed off the blood of other faeries.

PIXIE CASTE SYSTEM

Purebloods:
The original indigenous family of the area. Each pixie kingdom has a pureblood family which are usually the rulers of the kingdom. The purebloods of Dradour are umber skinned with blood red wings and black hair with a streak of white at the forehead; King Oberon, Queen Tatiana, and their son were the only faeries left of the original Dradourian pureblood family. Purebloods are able to deliver a venomous bite with their fangs, which are elongated compared to other pixie castes. Purebloods have a hard time producing other pureblood children which aren't miscarried or stillbirths. They have an extended life span and can live for almost ten thousand years. They reach adulthood roughly around 100 years of age, which is average for most faerie species.

Nobles:
Half-pureblood. These are children of a pureblood and either a non-pureblood pixie, a pixie not indigenous to the area, or a faerie of a different species. Due to a genetic quirk, Dradourian nobles all have albinism. Nobles inherit their wing color from their pureblood parent. They are seen as royalty though they are all bastard children of the king or queen. If the rulers are unable to produce an heir before they die, the nobles are next in line for the throne.

Aristo-fae:
These are the descendants of nobles. Over time, different wing colors emerged as nobles and children of nobles mated with pixies from other areas of Faerth. All aristo-fae have bright, jewel-toned wings. In the kingdom of Dradour, each aristo-fae House is named after a different gem or precious metal that correlates to the dominant color of their wings. Higher level aristo-fae Houses have lighter colored wings, whereas lower-level Houses, which are seen as being furthest from pure-

bloods, have darker colored wings. If all nobles were to die, the higher-level aristo-fae Houses would form a committee to choose one of their own to be ruler. This caste is generally upper working class, though some lower-level Houses might be middle to lower working class.

Common-fae:
These pixies are so many generations removed from purebloods that their wings are muted and dark. Most of their wings are a dark brown, black, or dark gray. These pixies do not have any call to royalty and will never be a candidate for ruling the kingdom. Pixies in this caste are middle to lower working class and form the general population of most pixie-dominant kingdoms as well as a large percentage of the immigrant population in elven kingdoms.

RELIGIONS

Pixie Pantheon:
- **AJAKIN, THE KING OF THE GODS:** the god of strength, war and peace, and justice. Call on him for protection in your endeavors.
- **MAJAKIM, THE QUEEN OF THE GODS:** the god of love, nurturing, home and hearth, buildings and structure. Call on her for blessings in the House.
- **ARDER, THE READER:** god of literature and arts. He is a god of education, learning, and hard work. Call on him for aid in memory.
- **TALEAHA, THE HEALER:** god of healing. God of childbirth and pregnancy, of gender transformation and sexuality. Call on her for fertility aid.
- **THE HARVESTER, DEATH:** (agender) god of journeys and the unknown. Of winter and the harvest, of abundance and famine. The god of economics and resource manipulation. They cradle you in death and give you sweet rest.

Elven Pantheon:
- **DEATH** is the god of friendships, of journeys, of the unknown. Death greets everyone like an old friend.
- **FATHER** is the god of building, of structure, of outer strength. He is the roof over your head; he is your shelter.
- **MOTHER** is the god of love, of peace, of inner strength. She is the hearth in your home, the blanket of dreams.

Water Nymph/Merfae Pantheon:
- **THE SEA:** She is a goddess of chaos and destruction. She is the goddess of passion, trust, and emotional strength. She brings all to rest in the depths of her bosom and cradles them as her children.

- **THE MOON:** She is the goddess of time and change, of direction and purpose. She is the goddess of thieves and lovers. Her changing light shows both her reliability and her fickle nature as she vacillates between illuminating the soul and blanketing her followers in darkness.

Siren Pantheon:
Any mention of siren religion was eradicated when sirens were first enslaved. Since then, many sirens have chosen to worship the gods of the elves, pixies, or water nymphs, with many also forgoing religion at all.

Imp Pantheon:
The imps are largely a nonreligious species, preferring to believe in hard work, the luck of chance, and the reward of effort. No gods answered when they called, so they quit calling to them. As such, imp religious texts do not exist, or if they do, no one knows where to find them.

Acknowledgments

When I was in high school, I had a dream. I don't mean an aspiration—I was much too depressed to imagine a life where I could make and meet goals of my own volition—I mean while I was asleep. In my dream, I was running after a man who I somehow knew was my best friend. I knew he was in love with me. I knew I had hurt him. And, as I watched him get into an elevator and speed upward toward what I knew would be his death, I knew that I needed to try and save him. Back then, I wasn't out as trans. I didn't even know that such a word existed. Despite that, I knew I wasn't the girl everyone told me I was, the girl I was supposed to be. I was a failure and disappointment in many ways, to myself and those around me. When I woke up, the dream was still so vivid in my mind. All day at school I couldn't stop thinking about it. What did it mean? Why did it feel so real? My chest hurt whenever I thought of how hard I had been running to try and save this "friend" that I had never met. I hadn't even seen his face. I had that same dream again and again over the next couple months, and finally I decided to write it down. After I wrote it down, I realized this wasn't the beginning of a story; it was the end.

I was very into fanfiction, both reading and writing, during my middle school and high school years. But this story, initially titled *A Faerytale*, was the first story I ever wrote that was entirely original. Entirely mine. I worked on it for a couple years, with a burning desire to one day publish this as a book. I was going to be an author. I was going to touch people's lives, inject stories into their minds, and influence their dreams. But, one day, while trying to update my laptop to Windows 10 (holy shit this was a long time ago), my harddrive was wiped. Just like that, my dream was gone. Everything I had ever written, including a dozen poems, half a dozen half-baked novels, and countless fanfics, were gone. Vanished into the ether. And with them went my hopes and desires of being an author. I gave up on writing entirely. I stopped talking about it. I stopped reading. I stopped caring about my future, and ended up getting into some very bad relationships and indulging in horribly self-destructive behaviors.

In 2018 my sibling sent me an email. Specifically, they forwarded it to me. It was an email that I had actually sent them almost a decade before, with a partial draft of my lost story, *A Faerytale*. I can't even begin to explain how I felt being reunited with such an important part of myself, something that I thought I had lost forever. Maybe some of you understand what that feels like. What I can say is that once I received this precious, invaluable gift, things changed. I read through the entire thing with a fervor. I cringed at some of the adolescent writing, and I laughed at the sarcasm and jokes. But most of all, I felt hope, and love. And when I finished reading through it, I made an outline for a total rewrite. I wasn't the same person as the one who wrote that story, so it only made sense for me to rewrite it as the person I had become.

Once upon a time, I had full confidence in my writing skills. I loved writing. It was like breathing. But after forgoing writing for 8 years, I was daunted. My sibling told me about this organization called NaNoWriMo that they had been using for years, so I decided to check it out. I had my outline, and it was late October, so I was ready. I was going to knock out 50k words and make a novel. What actually happened, though, was I wrote 12k and fizzled out. I panicked. I was trying so hard to make this story perfect that I couldn't see where I was going or how to get where I wanted. All I saw were flaws. So

I gave up on NaNoWriMo (kind of like how they gave up on respecting their volunteers, but I digress) and instead decided to just write when I felt the urge.

In spring of 2019, I finished draft 2 of *A Faerytale*. It was 30k words. Imagine my horror when I sat back and checked the word count only to see this tiny, baby of a story before me. I needed more. More words, more plot, more finesse. In November of 2019, I once again began a total rewrite of my story, and I finished the month with a 60k word story. I was thrilled; my story was finally at the bare minimum word count for a book. It wasn't perfect, though. It wasn't quite the right story. See, as time went on, as I was writing this story, I kept changing. I kept growing as a person, and finding new things about myself and my identity. Draft 3 of *A Faerytale* was great, but it wasn't ready. So, in November of 2020, I once again began a complete rewrite of the now-titled *Farzana's Spite*, and finished it off at 82k words. And she was done. She was finally ready to have someone other than me read her.

Now here comes the part where I thank everyone, starting with my amazing editor: Charlie Knight. Charlie, you're more than just my editor, more than just my best friend. You are a part of my heart and, because of the love and care you put into this book, you're a part of Farzana as well. I couldn't have made it this far without you, both in life and as an author.

Thank you to the writing community that I met on Twitter. I had so much fun and found such a fount of strength, courage, and joy from you all. For the first time, I had friends who were authors, poets. Friends who shared a passion with me: creating brand new worlds and characters out of nothing but our imaginations. I regret that Twitter has declined to the point that I have lost touch with so many of you as you left to find a healthier place to exist.

Before writing Twitter was writing Tumblr (for me at least). Many of the writing friends I made there are still with me to this day, and even the ones I no longer talk to remain a part of me. Reem, Maia, Flynn, Mo, Lyss, and Misha, I will be forever grateful for the love and support you gave me. And Joy, I hope you know how much I cherish you. I can't wait to see where life takes you next.

Thank you to Lost Boys Press for accepting and publishing my first short story, *Color Unknown* (fun fact: this story is also set on Faerth). You fired me up with courage and belief in myself as an author. Special thanks specifically to Ashley Hutchison and Chad Ryan; y'all started something great, and I'm so excited to see what y'all do next.

To my amazing girlfriend: you inspire me every damn day. You are so badass, passionate, hilarious, supportive, loving, steadfast—I could go on and on but I've got a time crunch to get this book released. You deserve the world. I hope not a day goes by without something bringing you happiness. And to Artemis, Mister, and Hobbes, I'm sending you so many kisses and boops. Thank you for being so freaking cute and adorable and cheering me up on the bad days.

Thank you to my spouse for listening to me infodump at all hours of the day and night about the creepy characters, horrific plots, and fucked up events that I dream up in my head and pour out onto paper. Even without being a fan of dark fantasy and surreal horror, you've always supported me and my writing and been my biggest cheerleader. Life is brighter, happier, and funnier with you at my side. And since you've said that once I finally publish this book you'll read it, here's hoping this story doesn't traumatize you too badly!

Last but not least, the biggest thanks goes to my sibling, Adik Graves. Without you, this book literally wouldn't exist. Without you, I wouldn't have started writing again. I wouldn't have had my first short story published before I turned 30. I wouldn't have found the amazing writers, authors, artists, poets, and friends that I have now. I don't know what my life would be like if you hadn't gifted me with my recovered story and been with me for every step of my writing journey. I don't even know who I would be as a person if not for you. You are the best alpha reader, brainstorming buddy, and publishing partner I could ever ask for. You're so freaking cool, and I love you so much.

Okay I lied; my last thanks goes to you, my readers. Thank you for taking a chance on this book. Thank you for keeping Farzana company. And thank you for visiting Faerth. I hope you enjoyed your stay.

About the Author

Felix Graves is a queer, trans, disabled, neurodivergent, AAPI author and artist. Most of his writing involves queer romance and faerie-inspired creatures. His debut novel, Farzana's Spite (2024), is the first story in the Faerth anthology series. He prides himself on writing stories with a starkly honest own voice commentary on mental illness, disability, and queerness, in an effort to bring awareness and representation to marginalized populations that feel unseen and unheard. He currently lives in the U.S. with his husband, their two kids, a ferociously adorable pitbull, and possibly a ghost or two. When not writing, he can be found rapidly alternating between projects in a desperate attempt to stock up on dopamine.

content warnings

Farzana's Spite is a dark fantasy and as such contains scenes and topics that may cause distress for certain readers. A non-exhaustive list includes:

- depictions of symptoms of depression, anxiety, and panic disorders, including thoughts of despair, suicidal ideation, panic attacks, nightmares, disordered eating, self-harm, and intrusive thoughts
- depictions of emotional, mental, and physical abuse, including gaslighting and other manipulation
- on-page suicide attempt
- on-page sexual assault (one brief scene with a non-consensual kiss and groping)
- depictions of fantasy species-based racism
- depictions of violence and gore
- casual use of ableist terms by two characters (not MC)
- multiple deaths, murders, and one infanticide
- on-page fatphobia from one character (not MC)
- depictions of permanently disabling events
- depictions and implications of parent-child neglect and abuse